T0283354

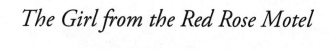

The Girl from the Red Rose Motel

Also by Susan Beckham Zurenda

Bells for Eli

The Girl from the Red Rose Motel

A NOVEL

Susan Beckham Zurenda

MERCER UNIVERSITY PRESS
Macon, Georgia

MUP/ H1039

27 26 25 24 23   5 4 3 2 1

Books published by Mercer University Press are printed on acid-free paper that
meets the requirements of the American National Standard for Information
Sciences—Permanence of Paper for Printed Library Materials.

Printed and bound the United States.

This book is set in Adobe Garamond Pro.

Cover/jacket design by Burt&Burt.

ISBN (print)   978-0-88146-901-1
ISBN (eBook)   978-088146-905-9

Cataloging-in-Publication Data is available from the Library of Congress

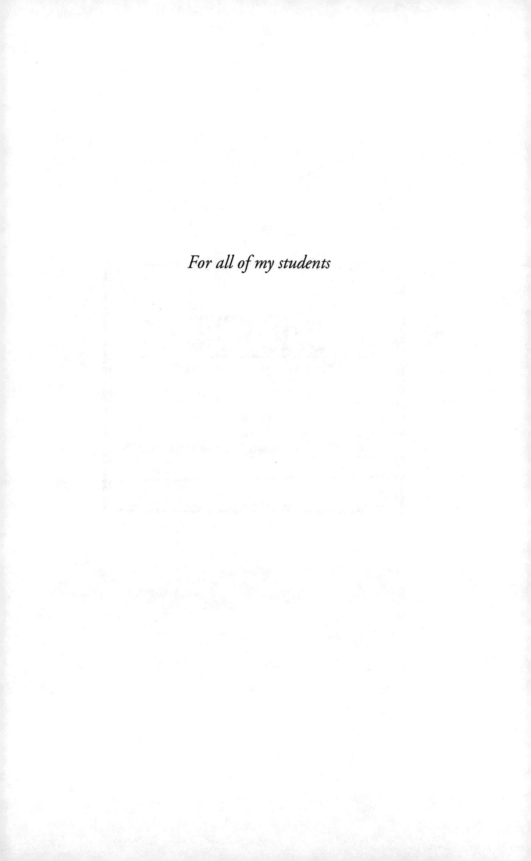

For all of my students

MERCER UNIVERSITY PRESS

Endowed by

TOM WATSON BROWN
and
THE WATSON-BROWN FOUNDATION, INC.

"…come what sorrow can,
It cannot countervail the exchange of joy…"

William Shakespeare, *Romeo and Juliet*, Act 2, Scene 6

RAMSEY HIGH SCHOOL 2012

Chapter 1

Hazel Smalls

Wear her wrinkled JROTC uniform soiled with pizza sauce rimming the right cuff of her jacket over her stained shirt—the result of a pepperoni slice dropped onto her chest during last Friday's school lunch—or wear regular clothes. Either way Hazel would be in trouble. JROTC students were required to wear their uniforms, clean and pressed, every Friday. The jacket needed to be dry-cleaned, and her mother had no money for dry-cleaning this week. Hazel had tried to tackle the blouse herself, but though she vigorously scrubbed it in the bathroom sink, an egg-shaped grease spot remained, spread across her boob. No way could she wear the upper part of her uniform.

Trying to look inconspicuous, she wore a dark green sweater that nearly matched the pants. But when she walked into JROTC class third period, Sergeant Riel called her out before she even reached her desk. "Cadet Corporal Smalls, what are you wearing?" he asked in that ramrod tone to make any of them cringe. "You do know it's Friday?"

"Yes sir," she said, her voice coming out like a mouse squeak.

"Speak up, Corporal Smalls," he directed.

She licked her lips, a nervous habit since childhood. "Yes sir, I know," she tried again.

"Then where's your uniform?"

"I'm sorry. I forgot." She yearned for the tube of Chapstick in her purse.

"It doesn't look like you forgot. You're wearing your trousers," he countered. She looked at the floor, concentrated on a long heel scratch etched across the tile. "Go on to your seat. I'll set you up on Monday so you won't forget when next Friday comes around."

She felt her classmates' eyes on her, assessing, as she pulled off her backpack and slid into her seat. They all knew what he meant. Detention hall after school, but how was it her fault if she couldn't get her uniform cleaned? That didn't make her delinquent.

Detention hall didn't let out until 5:00 pm, and she wouldn't have a ride. Her father would be home but couldn't pick her up because her mother drove the car to work second shift as a nursing aid at Elysian Fields Home for Seniors. No school bus transported students after normal hours.

As she suspected, when she failed to report for her punishment on Monday, her sentence automatically turned into a day of in-school suspension on Wednesday. Because it wasn't the first time she'd skipped detention and landed in ISS.

All kinds of kids got detention hall for one reason or another, but ISS was different. It had a specific population of idiots and smartmouths. Plus, you had to sit still the whole day with mostly nothing to do—it took maybe an hour or two to complete the classwork teachers sent. She hated that silent dungeon of a room, its desks covered with graffiti, the only sounds coming from the wet smacking of the fat baseball coach chewing his gum and the ancient wall clock's annoying click as each minute passed by.

Silently, she cursed for dropping pizza on herself, and she cursed Sergeant Riel, too. Of course, JROTC meant strict discipline, but he was meaner than hell. He enjoyed embarrassing cadets. The reason she had joined up again this year—if she could stick it out—was maybe she could get a scholarship to a college that would get her out of here.

Chapter 2

Sterling Lovell

Sterling Lovell and his buddies started second semester referring to their AP Literature teacher as a female Ichabod Crane, and since they were top of the heap in the twelfth grade at Ramsey High, the image caught on. Sterling knew the comparison wasn't accurate. Ms. Wilmore was tall and skinny like Ichabod, but "willowy" was closer. Even aging into her fifties, she was attractive with large green eyes and a wide, full smile. And not the least bit timid like the small-headed Ichabod. All well and good as far as Sterling was concerned. Her confidence gave the boys a greater challenge.

High school was nearly done. Seniors could slide. And luck of the draw had landed four of his seven cohorts in Ms. Wilmore's fifth period. He knew she'd taught at the local community college until this fall, but to them she was a rookie with plenty to learn about kids headed for top universities. Like Mr. Curtis's student teacher in AP Calculus his buddies Richard and Kipling had crushed last week. They didn't set out to make the poor guy completely break down, but you couldn't help it if you knew more than he did.

Sterling and his group had ruled ever since joining forces in middle school. He suspected the guidance department tried to keep them separated because teachers had complained about having them in class together. Rarely now were more than two of the "Crazy Eights" assigned to the same class. And it wasn't fair. Just because they liked to play off each other and challenge a teacher's position during discussion, they were singled out.

But in this case, uptight Mr. Oliver, head of guidance—personally supervising Sterling's applications to Brown, Yale, and Stanford, though Sterling thought he'd prefer to stay in the South, somewhere like Duke or Vanderbilt—either had no choice or hadn't noticed four of them thrown together.

Ms. Wilmore's first assignment of the semester was *Trifles,* a literary, one-act whodunit, a relic from the early twentieth century. True, it was a persuasive and nuanced read, but the playwright's feminist bias so blatant, even the most clueless would get it. As Ms. Wilmore passionately examined clues the female characters collected to establish a motive for Mrs. Wright sitting in jail for murdering her husband, how could Sterling and his friends resist jerking their teacher's chain? They loved this kind of fun, especially when a teacher was really into it.

"How can we be so sure Mrs. Wright is the killer?" He forced his face serious.

Ms. Wilmore swiveled toward Sterling. "What do you mean?" she said, calm and forthright, but maybe not for long. "Could you show us any indication to the contrary? And raise your hand to be called on before you speak?"

"Certainly," Sterling said, raising his hand and lowering it again. He produced a red herring, claiming Mrs. Wright was too much of a mouse to kill her husband. His pals made grunting noises of approval, following his lead.

"A dead canary, really?" Kipp interrupted their teacher. She gave him the evil eye and tried to get going again. Sterling covered his mouth to keep from laughing out loud at Kipp's absurdity because, of course, the canary was the climactic clue.

"The canary was the only living creature that provided Minnie Wright comfort," Ms. Wilmore countered, her expression still calm, but Sterling could feel her heat rising. Game on.

"I'm just saying, I got to agree that's a stretch," he broke in. "What do those farm women checking out the Wrights' house know about criminal investigation?"

"The whole point," his teacher started, "the women understand more than the sheriff who ignores—"

"Dadgum," Rich interrupted, practically hollering, "if birds of a feather don't flock together when it comes to the women." Alex jumped up, ran over to Rich, gave him a high five for his stupid comment.

"Shut up, why don't all of you? Don't you ever get tired of pulling this crap?" Bonnie Henderson, sitting in front of him, turned around and hissed into Sterling's face. "Some of us would like to learn."

He wiped his eyes to make her think she'd sprayed him with spit. "Tell it, sister," he said, grinning at the girl who would surely be their valedictorian.

"Grow up," Bonnie said and turned back around.

Behind her, Sterling chuckled because everyone heard Bonnie's declaration, and it put Ms. Wilmore over the edge. She slammed her book shut with a solid thwack.

In truth, he was a little stunned by this victory—Ms. Wilmore was a sharp and resilient teacher—when she announced, "I cannot continue. Some of you are determined to undermine the literature. You may do as you wish. I apologize to those who came to class today to think and learn." She left her book on the podium, retreated to her desk, and turned to her computer. Sterling couldn't resist one more step. He walked to the stand and opened his teacher's book. He cleared his throat. He began to teach the play.

***

When their twelfth grade principal Mr. Jenkins, one of four vice principals at Ramsey, called him, along with Kipp, Alex, and Rich, to his office at the end of the day, Sterling couldn't fathom why. Until Mr. Jenkins showed them Ms. Wilmore's "writeup" accusing them of "effrontery," a situation, she claimed, making it impossible for her to teach.

"What?" Sterling threw up his hands. "We were having an academic discussion. It's not our fault if she can't see other points of view."

"Not buying it," Mr. Jenkins said. "Not for a minute. Your gooses are cooked."

"What are we looking at?" Kipp asked, sounding stupidly sheepish, folding his hands at his waist. Alex gave Kipp a shove at this affectation and Rich rolled his eyes.

"If a teacher can't teach because of student disruption, it's grounds for out-of-school suspension. But Ms. Wilmore asked for in-school suspension instead."

"What the…?" Alex started, but Mr. Jenkins gave him a killer stare, and he stopped.

"Just send us home," Rich muttered.

"Your teacher wants you all in school, not at home raiding the fridge and watching Netflix, and I concur. In this case, less is more." Mr. Jenkins all but snickered.

"Sir," Sterling said, "with all due respect, we were building a case regarding a piece of literature that didn't agree with Ms. Wilmore's view. Shouldn't we be free to think?"

"Certainly, when it's for the right reasons," their grade principal said, fingering his ridiculous horseshoe mustache. "But that's not the case. I'll check on you fellows tomorrow at first bell."

"My parents taught me to challenge authority," Sterling said, trying another approach, using his most polite voice.

"That's right," Alex added. Rich and Kipp nodded.

"That's dandy, but you crossed way over the line," Mr. Jenkins said. "End of discussion. Report to Room 252 tomorrow."

Sterling was dumbfounded. He'd never been sentenced to any kind of school punishment, much less ISS. It was crazy to sit bored all day in a classroom with a bunch of losers. The only positive was maybe his parents wouldn't know. Even if he was certain they'd have agreed with his defense.

***

Sterling and his pals were spaced far apart in ISS so they couldn't shoot the shit. He sat near the door in row one. When he'd signed in, the facilitator, a fat assistant baseball coach, handed him a load of busywork compiled from all his classes. Such crap. He finished it all in a couple of hours. Too bad they'd taken his phone. He could have played Quarrel or Junk Jack when the coach wasn't looking.

Now, Sterling had nothing to do, so his eyes roamed Room 252. The room held a subtle but definitely foul odor. He concluded it came partly from unwashed hair and flesh along with stale cigarette smoke sealed in clothing. His view grazed across this bleak bunch. The guys wore t-shirts with inane slogans like "Blink if You Want Me" and "Bustin' Ours to Kick Yours." But in spite of the cold weather outside, many of the girls wore tops barely reaching the required coverage. He could get used to this look.

His gaze stopped on a girl beside him in row two. Her tank top was tight, pressing across a pair he could tell were exquisite. She was exotically beautiful with dark, deep eyes and golden skin. And gorgeous, full lips. He'd never seen this girl in the halls, much less in his classes, populated mostly by WASPs like himself.

Ramsey's demographics didn't follow the traditional bell curve. If he thought of a shape, it would be like the letter U with rich kids at one end, underprivileged kids at the other, and a small middle population. He kept his sight fixed on this forbidden girl from the other leg of the U.

At the same time he thought about his girlfriend Courtney. He'd considered himself the luckiest guy on earth when this good-looking girl began flirting with him in tenth grade. They'd been together since.

His parents called it going steady. They'd loved Courtney immediately because, hell, she checked all the squares. Beautiful. Father respected in the community. Conventional values. Plenty of money.

God, his parents. Not that Sterling didn't know to appreciate his advantages, but sometimes, like right now, it felt like he was stuffed into a too-small box with the flaps folded tight across the top, suffocating him. It was probably at least part of the reason he went overboard in Ms. Wilmore's class and ended up here in ISS. For stimulation. For fresh air. Everything was so mapped out. What to do, who to be with, where to go.

He considered the girl sitting across from him again. No way was she affected like most of the girls he knew. She was real. He could tell just by watching her work diligently on an assignment, head bent over in concentration, shoulders pulled in, creating—by the way—one incredibly deep cleavage.

His sister Livie was real, too. She'd ripped that box open, forsaking their parents' standards to live an authentic life with her partner Elodie after college. She would tell him to follow his gut right now.

He continued to stare at the stunning girl across from him. Finally, she noticed and looked shyly his way. He felt his groin tightening.

"I'm Sterling Lovell," he whispered. "Who are you?"

"Hazel Smalls," she whispered back. They weren't supposed to talk in ISS, but Sterling had observed if the prisoners kept it low, the coach didn't bother with them.

"Hazel, are you kidding? Who is named Hazel?" The girl looked hurt, and he wanted to kick himself for trying to act cool. He attempted to recover. "It's just old-fashioned, is all. It's nice, really," he said.

"My mother named me for her foster mother," Hazel responded. Sterling raised his eyebrows, and she continued. "My mother moved in with foster parents when she was thirteen. When they moved to Florida, she got a job and lived on her own."

"When was that?" Sterling asked.

"I think she was seventeen."

"Whew," Sterling answered.

Hazel squinted at him.

"I mean your mother must be amazing, Hazel," he said.

"My family calls me Zell," she said, and he knew it was because he'd made a deal out of her name.

"Nice. So, Zell...what're you in for?" She didn't answer. Instead, her face stiffened. He offered, "I got written up for busting a teacher's lecture," and chuckled.

"What does that mean?" she asked. The drawn muscles around her mouth relaxed a little.

"It just means my buddies and I had some ideas our teacher didn't like about this play we were studying. Sucks, man." She nodded slightly. "So," he questioned again, "what did you do, or more like, what do they say you did?"

Again, she ignored him. It was like he'd never spoken. "It can't be that bad," he urged. He reached over and touched her arm. He gave her a sincere look. She pulled her arm back.

Sterling jerked his own hand back like a bee had stung it when she turned her head away. He glanced down at the completed classwork on his desk, pretended to be engaged. Minutes passed before he tried again. "Hey, Zell," he whispered, "didn't mean to get in your space. Whatever it is, it's us against the establishment, right?" She cut her eyes toward him. Sterling lifted his hands, open palmed in a plea.

"I didn't wear my uniform to ROTC class like we're required to on Fridays," she said so suddenly he knew she'd spoken in spite of herself.

It took him a moment to grasp the absurdity. "That's beyond stupid. You got ISS for that? I've seen that sergeant in the halls. He looks like an uptight ass. Why would you want to be in ROTC anyway?" Sterling couldn't imagine anything worse. The fat-ass coach looked briefly toward them, and Sterling made a choking motion to his throat to show he would quiet down.

"I got detention hall, but I didn't go," she said, lowering her head. "So they gave me ISS."

"I don't blame you for blowing off detention. Drop ROTC," Sterling suggested. It never occurred to him then that she might have no transportation home at 5:00 pm when the buses were long gone.

"I want to get an ROTC scholarship, go into the service, to get out of here," she said. He started to ask why she didn't plan to go to college instead of getting stuck in the Army, but caught himself. Maybe no one in her family had gone to college. And if they had any money, college wasn't likely something to spend it on. He wasn't ignorant. He could picture how the other half lived.

"So why not wear your uniform?" he responded instead.

"It was dirty," she said.

"You forgot to have it cleaned?"

She shrugged her nearly bare amber shoulders. The gesture seemed to say it couldn't be helped, though Sterling could not imagine the big deal of taking the damn uniform to the cleaners. "I'm sorry you're in here for such a dumb reason," he said. All of a sudden, he didn't just have the hots for Hazel. He felt so bad for this beautiful girl. He wanted to take her in his arms and hold her. It was crazy how he wanted to know Hazel.

"You want to go to a movie and pizza tomorrow night?" he asked abruptly. Courtney passed through his mind.

"No, I don't think so," she said. She looked down, wrapping her arms around her middle. She reminded him of a hunched, scared rabbit.

"I promise I don't bite," he said. He held up his hands in a surrender motion.

She smiled a little. "It's not that."

"Then what? You have a boyfriend?"

"No," she said.

9

"I'll pick you up tomorrow night. Where do you live?"

"No," she said and turned to the papers on her desk. When the bell finally rang, she darted out, again reminding Sterling of a skittish rabbit. He followed her at a distance to the bus exit, where he lost her in a pack of students clamoring to leave. But Sterling wasn't giving up. There was something more than a challenge here. Something about this girl grabbed him from the inside out.

***

He went by his grade-level office the next day on the pretense of telling Mr. Jenkins he was sorry about being a disturbance in English class. His tactic worked. After his spiel, he asked his grade principal to look up what period and teacher Hazel Smalls had for English (a sure bet since all students took it), and Mr. Jenkins, though he glanced a moment at Sterling, went right to his computer.

Hazel had first period English with Ms. Wilmore. It might be a sign. Ms. W taught all the twelfth grade AP classes, and it turned out a general level of juniors filled out her schedule. Bus students typically arrived early, so he'd surely have time to catch Hazel before school. Some kids waited in the lobby for first bell, but they could also wait in their first period classroom. He had a hunch Hazel didn't socialize in the lobby.

Students weren't supposed to hang out without passes in the halls before the school day started, so he hid behind a storage door down the hall a little ways from the classroom. Soon enough, he saw Hazel strolling quietly up the hall.

He stepped out, and she stopped, startled. Her hand flew across her chest, clutching at her blouse. "Hello, Zell," he called. "It's Friday! Come on," he said, striding toward her. "I told you I don't bite." He smiled broadly. "Really. Why don't I pick you up tonight? 6:00?" And although she shook her head, she rewarded him with a wistful expression.

It was a glimmer and he seized it. He picked up her free hand, the skin tight over the delicate bones. She submitted to his touch. "Okay, we're doing this. What's your address?"

"I could meet you in the lobby of the downtown library. I got some work to do there."

Sterling thought it an odd request, but he was willing to do things on her terms. "Sure thing," he replied.

***

After he took her for pizza at Marelli's, she said to drop her back at the public library. But he wasn't leaving her alone in the cold dark. She wore a too-thin jacket in the January weather as it was, and he'd been taught manners, dammit. Plus, the library was in the Southside, a bad part of town.

She wouldn't give in. She insisted she was meeting a girlfriend who'd invited her to spend the night. She'd wait in the library lobby. It wasn't even a good lie.

It was obvious she didn't want him to know where she lived, and he told her so. "What? Is your family hiding a serial killer who carries a double-edged stiletto knife at his waist?" he asked. She looked abashed, her hands pressing over her nose and mouth. He let up. He'd only meant to tease her.

Still, he was frustrated as he sped off. Not until a few minutes later did he realize he could have simply remained in the parking lot to see where she went. But she might have seen him and no need to upset her after she'd already looked like a scared rabbit again after his murderer joke. He was sorry about that. She didn't know him well enough yet. Better to savor the evening—her incredible lips, wet, pillowy, and warm when she allowed him to kiss her, his tongue roaming her mouth, filling it, while they embraced in his car in Marelli's parking lot.

Oh what a night, Sterling thought driving home, reassured by the rhythmic thrumming of his Audi TTS—a hand-me-down from his father, seven years old but a damn cool car. Forget the girls he was supposed to impress. God, how he dreaded the pompous spring debutante ball, where—to his parents' delight—his services as an escort for his girlfriend Courtney had been enlisted.

This girl he'd met in ISS was beautiful and mysterious. She was also delightfully forbidden, far from the socialites expected in his future. He rolled the vision of Hazel, Zell as he thought of her now, around in his head. She had him on fire, but he would go easy because she was shy. Forget his parents would have twin strokes even to imagine he might invite a girl from the other side of the tracks on a date. Where did she live, he wondered again.

Chapter 3

Angela Wilmore

After twenty-plus years of teaching English, Angela Wilmore believed she'd encountered every student scenario possible. She'd been wrong. In her new position teaching AP English at Ramsey High, it wasn't a week into the school year before a cell of brilliant and miscreant boys began to present themselves. Their mission quickly became clear: to prove their dominance continually and to obliterate whatever teacher happened to think he or she was in charge of a classroom.

There had been a particularly disturbing day back in late October when Angela walked into the teachers' lounge between classes to use the bathroom and saw a young student teacher—fresh from his pedagogy at the nearby university—weeping. The young man, Greg something or other, was assigned to Martin Mathis, a popular and seasoned instructor.

Greg was funny and engaging—he seemed a promising future teacher—but there he was sitting bent over in the lounge, his head cupped in his hands and his legs splayed awkwardly at the table where Angela typically ate her twenty-six-minute lunch with a flock of other fast-eating teachers chirping between mouthfuls about the highs and lows of their day. She might not have noticed, hurrying to her classroom before the bell, except Greg's strong exhale when she exited the ladies' room caused her to look his way.

"Greg, is everything okay?" she asked.

He'd looked up, flattening his hands on the faded floral tablecloth. She saw the wet shine on his eyes.

"You're not okay. Wait just a sec. Let me run down the hall and ask Judson to listen out for my kids. He has planning this period. He won't mind. Just wait."

"No, no," Greg responded. "I'm just on a break. Mr. Mathis has tenth grade Honors this period and I haven't started with them yet."

"Nonsense," Angela replied. "I'll be right back."

She dashed to the end of the hall, ducked her head in Judson's room, asked for ten minutes. Wry as always, he said, "You owe me," rubbing his thumb against his forefinger for effect. She waved at him behind her head. If you could call it teaching, Judson taught some of the most challenging students in eleventh grade English—all reading far below grade level—and no one, absolutely no one but Judson Moore could motivate them.

When she returned to the lounge, Greg was sitting up straight. His eyes had dried. "Sorry," he muttered. "You didn't need to come back."

"Bad class?"

He shrugged. "I guess this is why they make you practice teach. To find out if you're cut out for this job. I think not."

"Not?" Angela felt the ugly dent forming between her eyebrows, the one her father always warned would become permanent if she didn't stop squeezing up her eyes that way when she was anxious.

"I know my stuff, but I can't always manage the students," he said.

"Oh, students, yes, you mean those hormonal creatures we see five times a day, five days a week until we can't think straight." Angela pressed her hand onto her waist, her elbow jutting out sharply.

"It's these guys; they won't let up.

"Let me guess," Angela offered. "Do any of these guys have names like Walker, Bennett, Kipling, Richard?"

Greg nodded.

"And what about Sterling, Alex, Lucas, and Jake?"

Greg nodded again.

"I know them well," she said. "Who's in your class?"

"Walker, Sterling, and Lucas."

"Enough said," Angela informed him. "You've been hit by members of the 'Hateful Eightful.' That's what I call them. Mr. Mathis should have warned you. They have a gang mentality."

Greg looked at her quizzically, his own brow creasing. "Listen," Angela said in her calmest teacher voice, "these boys...I deal with them, too. All of us do. They are smart; they are cocky; and they are out to prove themselves to everyone. You're not alone. Don't take it personally."

Greg described their interruptions as he attempted to discuss how to develop emotions in characters for their writing assignment in Martin Mathis's creative writing class. She pictured the scene as he described Walker faking tears, Lucas snarling, and Sterling cheering with delight. "It's not the first time they've cut up," he confessed. "This time, I just quit. I didn't know what else to do."

"It won't be the last time. I know it's hard. But don't let them get to you. If you show weakness, they get stronger."

Greg smiled weakly. "So what do I do?"

"They want to see you crack, so you ignore them and keep going because we're not allowed to take them into the hall and beat their behinds." Greg laughed and wiped his nose. She patted him on the shoulder, feigning composure, but Angela went back to her classroom furious on Greg's behalf.

***

Now, only a couple of weeks into second semester, after that shameless performance by members of the "Hateful Eightful" during discussion of the play *Trifles,* she had been the one to quit teaching the class.

Angela had skipped lunch with her colleagues, walking instead from D-wing to the twelfth grade vice principal's office on B-wing while her chicken salad sandwich and sliced avocado remained in the refrigerator.

She was acquainted with Vice Principal Early Jenkins, of course, a stocky, sturdy middle-aged man. She had occasionally written up a student for an infraction of some sort, usually in her general English class, but she'd never had reason to go to his office until now. Early's administrative assistant, a tired-looking woman who appeared loose in her skin, greeted Angela perfunctorily and pointed an index finger toward the vice principal's private space.

Early stood and gestured for her to sit. She dropped onto the closer of two black vinyl chairs, each spilling white foam down a cracked center. "What can I do for you?" He sat back at his desk. Angela wondered how many hundreds of times he had uttered the same question.

"I've got some boys causing trouble to the point I couldn't teach my fifth period AP class today," she said and explained.

Early Jenkins rubbed his right palm along his upper jaw and up to his ear. Then twisted his moustache. "Who are these boys?" he asked.

"Sterling Lovell, Richard Evers, Kipling Robinson, and Alex Myers. They're half of a larger group, not counting the wannabes, who have given me trouble since I started teaching this year."

"Ah," Early responded. "No surprise there."

Angela thought his tone an odd combination of reserve and enthusiasm. "Not surprised?" she asked.

"No," he said. "I know who they are. Mostly, teachers overlook their antics."

Angela had stared incredulously. "Today was not antics," she said, fingering the feathery tail of her light brown hair pluming out of its twist in the plastic comb at the back of her head. "I cannot be the first teacher to turn these boys in," she added.

"Yep, you are. And I, for one, thank you. I can give them three days of out-of-school suspension since they prevented you from teaching class."

Angela said she didn't want them at home playing video games all day while their parents were at work. That would be a reward. She wanted them in in-school suspension.

Early Jenkins stood and stroked his chin. "'Bout time," he said, his right eye twitching briefly, surely a wink.

***

Word of the boys' fate raced through their crowd the next day. As early as second period, Angela overheard a pair of cheerleaders talking, their tone smug, when they entered class. She'd created a scandal among the upper echelon of Ramsey students. It was hard not to laugh out loud.

At the end of the school day, packing her bag with essays to grade, Angela looked up at the sound of a knock on her classroom door. Eyes squinted into crescent moons beneath tortoiseshell frames below wiry gray brows, peering at her through the narrow glass slit in the door.

She had never formally met Carlisle Clark, the venerable AP Calculus instructor and probably the oldest teacher at Ramsey, but she knew who he was. She jumped up and walked quickly to open the door.

16

"Ms. Wilmore," he started.

"Angela," she said. "Please. Hello."

"Angela, thank you," he said, shaking her hand at the threshold. "You've done something that should have been done long ago."

Of course, she knew what he meant. She nodded. His hand gently let go.

"Come in, please." She gestured into her classroom.

"No, no, I won't stay. I just stopped by to say thanks. That gang has been out of control since they entered this building. Hellions."

"I'm told they've misbehaved since middle school," she said.

Carlisle Clark stood barely inside the door. "That I don't know, but they have wreaked havoc here."

She wanted to ask the obvious. Why were these boys in the second semester of their senior year before someone stepped up, and why her, the new kid in town?

But she knew the answer. Even if their almighty egos ruled them much of the time and they could make life hell for their teachers and their classmates, the boys were, after all, brilliant. She knew their standardized scores. Most were headed to top-tier universities. They were destined to make Ramsey—an ordinary high school in an ordinary, mid-sized South Carolina town—proud. Plus, there was the matter of their parents, well to do and leaders in the community. No one wanted to be the teacher to come down on these sons. Until Angela Wilmore.

She didn't have the history many of her colleagues shared in this comfortable, insular community. Before moving into her little 1930s bungalow in Ramsey's historic district in the early fall, she'd lived on the "other" side of the city, the newcomers' side, for almost twenty years. She and Randal had built their home in Hallow Hills because it was convenient: ten minutes from Bonds Cross Community College where she'd taught and closer still for Randal, manager of a large printing company near the interstate. But after her husband died from a brain aneurysm at age fifty—she woke to find him unresponsive beside her in bed one February morning—she couldn't stay in the house they'd built together. She couldn't bear it.

Nor could she stay at the college, because she needed more income. She learned the public school system would pay her $10,000 more per year than the community college. It didn't make sense, but that's the way it was. It took two years to talk herself into it—nearly tapping into her and Randal's savings—before she applied at the only high school in the county where she'd heard teachers were treated with autonomy.

The twelfth grade AP English teacher had resigned unexpectedly in the summer, and the principal, Finley Copeland, needed a teacher experienced in college-level instruction quickly. Angela fit the bill. Having taught Intro to Literature at the college all those years, the course comparable to twelfth grade AP literature, she was hired. It didn't matter that she wasn't AP certified. She could teach for a year on a waiver and gain certification online the next summer at Clemson University.

Second semester, and Angela was still adjusting. She missed the community college where she had close friends and ample office hours and flexibility. At Ramsey, she lived from bell to bell with little time between to breathe. Yes, she'd made new friends, English teachers on her hall mostly, but talking to coworkers was perpetually rushed. It was all about the bells. Less than a half hour at lunch, five minutes between classes standing outside her classroom door, and what brief time teachers conversed after students let out at 3:00 pm. That was about it.

Yet she wouldn't go back, even if the salaries were equal. She loved her students at Ramsey High. She relished their vigor. Fresh and full of life and questions and the future.

"I'll be going," Carlisle said. "Just wanted to thank you and put in my two cents."

"Oh, goodness," Angela stammered. "Forgive me. I wandered off for a moment."

Carlisle smiled and glanced toward her leather satchel laid sideways on her desk, essays partially stuffed inside. "As of today, you have officially changed a game plan. I'm quite sure of it. Thank you again." He touched two fingers to his brow and backed through the doorway. "I'll see you about."

"I hope so. Thank you for supporting me," Angela said.

Chapter 4

Hazel Smalls

ISS was full of derelicts and losers she recognized—typical—except for this guy sitting across on the next row from her near the door. He was way out of place, wearing like an ironed checked shirt and khaki pants. It got her attention, and she watched him give stupid looks to three other misfits just like him seated in other corners of the room. The four of them made faces back and forth like they'd landed on Mars or something. She'd like to know how rich boys from another planet ended up here.

And just like that her wish came true. The boy near her started up a conversation, saying his name was Sterling. She thought at first he was kidding. Because who names their kid Sterling like a piece of silver or something. He dissed her own name as old-fashioned, when she hadn't chosen it for God's sake. She felt ashamed and told him her family called her Zell. Then the slow way he said he didn't have a nickname made her think Sterling really was his name.

He told her he got ISS for stopping a teacher's lesson, and though she didn't know why—because she didn't tell her business to anyone, much less a rich boy—when he asked, she told him.

She was stunned when like out of nowhere, he asked her on a date. Hazel had never been on a real date, much less with some high and mighty boy from another world. The thought terrified her. Yet she couldn't help but imagine it. Sterling probably had a car and money to hang out in cool places. He was good-looking, too—eyes dark brown as the chocolate of a Hershey bar under heavy black lashes any girl would envy. Though he looked nothing like a girl, not with that strong, square chin. He must be very popular at Ramsey High with those movie-star looks. Likely, he had a beautiful, blonde girlfriend who lived in a mansion on a hill, too.

He asked her out for a movie and pizza. Crazy for even thinking it, for wanting to say yes, for feeling the tingle inch up her back, she wasn't that dumb. She told him no and scuttled quickly from sight at the end of the day in ISS. But that night, in bed with her little sister Chloe's body pressed against hers, her father and mother keeping her awake with their snoring in the bed beside them, she kept thinking about Sterling. Was he for real? Or only making fun of her? The more she tried not to think about him, the more he wouldn't get out of her head.

Getting ready for school the next morning, impulsively, she pulled on her favorite jeans. Not too short or frayed at the hem or that used-up faded blue from hundreds of wearings. They were deep indigo, nearly new—the tags still attached when she bought them at Goodwill with money from cleaning motel rooms. Over the jeans she wore a soft green blouse that had been her mother's.

Maybe it was her good clothes giving her confidence because when Sterling jumped out like a vision in front of her in the hall that morning, she surprised herself. Her fist nervously grabbed up the material of her blouse, but she didn't run.

"Where did you come from?" she asked, knowing, dammit, her voice was squeaking.

"Hiding behind the door of the storage closet." He grinned.

Hazel blinked at him, twisted her blouse.

"I won't bite," Sterling said.

She made herself look up at him, and he smiled. It made her smile, too. Then, she glanced down, tugged the puffed-up fabric back over the waist of her jeans.

"Zell," he said. She looked up. He took her hand. His keen expression made her say yes.

***

They didn't go to a movie, but they did go to a place called Marelli's for pizza. She'd thought they'd go to Tiffanys, where all the kids went. She'd been there once herself, last fall after her friend Rhona Williams talked her into going to a Ramsey High football game. Rhona wanted to watch Malcolm Cureton play. His position was wide receiver, and she was crazy for him. Hazel cared nothing about football, but she went for Rhona's sake.

They pooled their money afterward—Hazel had $10 left from cleaning rooms and Rhona had a $10 bill from her grandmother—and walked to Tiffanys. It was full of Ramsey High kids. They had enough to split a deluxe large pizza. And when you ordered a large, the soft drinks came free. Even if they didn't talk to anyone besides the waitress and themselves, they'd liked being there.

"Why you call it Tiffanys?" The skinny waitress looked funny at Rhona for asking. "Somebody named Tiffany own it?"

The waitress pointed at the ceiling. "Tiffany lamps, get it?" she said, crossing arms no bigger around than a mop stick. The girls had looked up at the multicolored shades of stained glass covering light bulbs. Rhona shrugged like she knew what Tiffany meant.

"They ain't real," the waitress said. "It's Tiffany style."

Later, Hazel looked it up on a library computer. "You won't believe it, but if it's an authentic Tiffany lamp, it costs thousands of dollars," she reported to Rhona.

"Get out of here," Rhona said, shaking her head like Hazel had made it all up, and the subject dropped.

Hazel's shame of living cramped up in a motel room for more than two years with her parents and her sister Chloe kept her secretive. She didn't seek out friends. But Rhona was safe because she lived at the motel, too, with her grandmother Lolly. Rhona had been there nearly forever she told Hazel when they met at the icemaker in the breezeway not long after Hazel arrived. The machine was old and slow, dropping one cube every once in a while. Now the machine didn't work at all, and no one had come to fix it. It sat there rusting. If they wanted ice, they bought a bag at the Mini Mart and kept it in a cooler.

Rhona's parents left her with Lolly when she was very young and never came back. Rhona didn't know where they were and didn't want to know. Wouldn't speak to them if they happened to come back looking for her, she told Hazel. They were sons of bitches for ditching her.

Lolly kept a picture of her son Kelvin and Rhona's mother Inetta on the dresser, but Rhona said she didn't think about her parents. Lolly was her family. At night, Rhona sometimes massaged the muscles in Lolly's lame leg so it wouldn't throb so bad. It was the leg, though, that gave Lolly social security payments, cash money every month. Still, it hadn't been enough to support two of them plus Lolly's apartment, so eventually they got evicted. They moved to the motel and had been there ever since.

Now Hazel sat across from Sterling—wearing her favorite skirt that hit at her knees—at an Italian restaurant she'd never heard of on the outskirts of town. She'd gotten over not being at Tiffanys because Marelli's was amazing. The tables had white cloths. Soft music played in the background. A real candle burned in a glass tube on the table.

"What you think, Zell?" Sterling asked after they sat.

"It's beautiful," she answered, keeping her voice low because other than the music, that was all she could hear.

"This place has been here since my parents were young," he said. "Old man Marelli thinks it's stupid that people our age in America can't order wine, so he looks the other way. The drinking age in Italy is sixteen, and that's good enough for him. You like wine, Zell?"

Hazel and Rhona bought Arbor Mist at the Mini Mart when they had the money and wanted a buzz. Usually the strawberry or pear variety, but sometimes pineapple, which Hazel liked but Rhona didn't. "I think so," she answered.

"You think so? What does that mean?" Sterling flipped his hand. "How about I order us a nice bottle of Chianti and you tell me what you think."

Hazel nodded. Like magic, Mr. Marelli—a stout silver-haired man wearing a white jacket with double buttons down the front—appeared at their table. "So nice to see you, Sterling," he said.

"Glad to see you, sir." They shook hands.

"And who is the lovely young woman tonight?"

"This is Zell. It's her first time here."

"Ah, then it should be special." Mr. Marelli reached over to touch Hazel's hand. "Tonight I make gemelli and shrimp with garlic and feta. Very good."

"We're up for a pizza night," Sterling said.

"Young people, they love the pizza," Mr. Marelli said, shaking his head. "Very well."

"We would like a nice bottle of wine, a Chianti?"

"Of course," Mr. Marelli said. "You want I should choose?"

"Sure thing," Sterling said.

Minutes later a young woman brought a bottle of red wine bound halfway up in its own straw basket to the table. She poured a tiny bit in Sterling's glass and he took a sip. He nodded, and the waitress, a white lace apron tied around her waist, poured wine into Hazel's long-stemmed glass. Then she poured the same amount for Sterling. Hazel wondered why the waitress hadn't finished filling Sterling's glass before switching over to hers.

If there were such a thing as dry liquid, that's what this wine felt like going down Hazel's throat. She struggled to keep from coughing and drank the first glass very slowly. It tasted like sour cherries sprinkled with pepper. The second glass she drank more normal as the taste grew more agreeable.

Sterling began to ask questions, questions she didn't want to answer. Why did he want to know anyway? But he kept smiling, looking at her, telling her not to look down so that he could see her face, pouring her more wine. So she told him she had a sister Chloe in fifth grade who never shut up. She said her mother worked at a nursing home and her father drove an LTL dry van trailer (not now because he'd temporary lost his license, but she didn't tell that part).

What was a dry van, Sterling wanted to know. And what was LTL? She explained it was a big box truck like you saw all the time on the interstate. Dry meant there was no temperature control so you couldn't haul meat and stuff like that. And LTL meant less than a truckload.

Where did her father drive and why wasn't his truck full?

Hazel wanted to ask why he cared so much about what her father did, but she didn't. She said her father—Burl—drove all over the state of South Carolina to distribution centers, plants, and places like that.

Sterling tilted his head at an angle like he didn't get it, so she kept going. "Like the truck might really be full, but it means there're a lot of different orders on a LTL truck at the same time. Maybe you dropped off bathroom tile at one place and furniture at another, tires at another. You do pick-ups, too." Finally, Sterling nodded like he understood.

The most delicious-looking pizza Hazel had ever seen—smelling of onions, sausage, and things she couldn't name—arrived on the table be-tween them. Sterling had asked if she wanted him to order his favorite, and knowing nothing about some of the unusual toppings on the menu, she quickly agreed. He picked up the wine bottle and Hazel saw it was empty. He handed it to the waitress and said he'd like to order a second.

She looked unsure and said, "Let me see."

Within a minute, Mr. Marelli arrived. He clasped Sterling's shoul-der with a large hand. "So you like the Chianti. Is good, isn't it?" he said. "I tell you what, maybe not another bottle, but I send two glasses on the house for you and the lovely young lady to accompany your piz-za. You must walk a straight line to your car," he said and patted Ster-ling's shoulder as he released his grasp.

Sterling thanked Mr. Marelli, though Hazel could see in his expres-sion what he really wanted was another bottle.

"My old man is a real estate investor and manager," he volunteered, picking up a slice of steaming pizza.

"I don't know what that means," she said, seeing it was her turn not to understand but glad he was talking about his father instead of hers. She picked up a piece of pizza, set it on her plate, cut a bite with her fork because she didn't want it to flop around. She thought briefly of the pepperoni stain on her blouse that sent her to ISS.

"He buys up places and rents them mostly. Some he manages him-self and some he has other people manage."

"Like what kind of places?"

"Apartment complexes, rental houses, commercial property, too, like motels and shopping centers."

At the word "motels," a bite of pizza clenched going down Hazel's throat. She began to cough. She covered her mouth with her red-checked napkin.

"You ok?" Sterling asked. She nodded and pointed at her cheek to show she couldn't speak with her mouth full.

***

Hazel watched transfixed as Sterling paid the check at the table with a credit card. What guy her age had his own credit card? Was he flexing with his parents' card or was it his? Whatever, with only three dollars in her purse, she couldn't offer to help pay.

She startled and nearly fell when Sterling came behind her, pulling out her chair when she was already halfway up. "Oh gosh, sorry," he said, grabbing her by the arm. It took her a second to realize the gesture was meant to be polite.

He looped her arm through his as they walked into the parking lot. He opened the passenger door for Hazel to climb in. This must be the way Cinderella felt at the ball, she thought, watching this very handsome boy walk in front of his very fancy car to the driver's side.

"What you think?" he asked, leaning toward her in the car.

"Mmmm, it was really good, thank you," she said, thinking he meant their dinner and wine. Her stomach was full and her head was swimming a bit in a way that felt very good.

"You're amazing," he said, leaning farther until his face was close to hers. She smelled the spicy Chianti. He picked up hair that lay across her shoulder, tucked it behind her ear. She felt his other hand slide behind her head. Almost like a reflex, Hazel opened her lips. A small sigh erupted.

The first sensation of his mouth was taste, not just the wine or pizza but something sweet that she wanted to swallow. His tongue touched hers, and she touched his back. For a long time they kissed, until her head was all the way dizzy. When he released her, she felt astonished.

"Guess I'd better get you home," he said, and she was amazed in a different way. She expected him to want much more, especially after all the money he spent. Maybe Sterling truly was a prince. Only she couldn't run to a coach made from a pumpkin guided by mice turned coachmen to take her away at the stroke of midnight. No, she had to ride in the prince's sports car for him to take her somewhere. She could never let him see where she lived, so she said she was meeting a girlfriend back at the library to go for a sleepover. She hadn't had a sleepover with a friend since elementary school.

Sterling saw the library was closed and gave her a hard time about it being too cold to leave her outside, but finally he drove off, and she began walking home to the Red Rose Motel, the beat-up place downtown where she lived, not far from the library. Far from the land of make-believe.

Chapter 5

Sterling Lovell

Sterling waited outside Ms. Wilmore's classroom door for Zell most mornings. When his buddies asked why he wasn't showing up in the courtyard before school, he claimed he was working extra time with the tennis coach, a safe bet with the season approaching, since no one else in his crowd was on the team and the courts were a ten-minute stroll from campus.

As for Courtney, thank God she played violin in the orchestra because it required early practice before school that continued through first period. He'd never been so glad her parents refused to let her drop out when she begged last year.

He hadn't been able to hide for long from Ms. Wilmore, though. One of the first mornings, she walked out of her classroom toward the teachers' lounge and saw him, half concealed behind the storage door. "Sterling, you need to see me?" she'd asked. He stepped out, shook his head, announced forthrightly he was waiting for Zell.

Ever since the shellacking she'd dealt him and his crew, he'd been a model student, along with the others, especially considering their senioritis. In his other classes, too, because rumor had it other teachers came to her door to thank Ms. Wilmore personally. He'd misjudged the depth of his English teacher's chutzpah and would rather play dutiful student than see ISS ever again, even if that hellhole had introduced him to Zell. Actually, he thought Ms. W—his new nickname for her—liked him now. And he had to admit she was a teacher who could keep his interest.

He tried to see Zell during the day as well. He knew her schedule and could sometimes catch her briefly in the hall between periods, alone. After school, though, was impossible, not because of Courtney, who usually had one extracurricular activity or another, but because Zell dashed for the bus. Over and over, he offered to take her home, but she refused. On Friday evenings—Courtney demanded his Saturdays—he picked up Zell at the library. He knew something wasn't right, but he didn't want to rock the boat. He took her somewhere away from the crowd, admittedly so no one could tell Courtney, to eat. She always seemed hungry, and he liked her appetite. Afterward, they parked at Kinsmen Lake not far from his parents' Georgian brick home in Stockton Estates.

***

Sterling's father woke him in the still dark the last Saturday of January to accompany him to the Red Rose Motel to check on frozen water pipes. Rudie Jones, his father's manager, had come down with flu and wasn't going anywhere. It wasn't the first time lately his father had bugged him to go to one of his properties. Sterling put his pillow over his head, tried to beg off. He had no desire to freeze his butt off on a morning cold as a witch's tit at a dump like the Red Rose. But Hugh Lovell wouldn't relent. Misery loved company. No breakfast, no nothing. Just ten minutes to brush his teeth, pull on flannel-lined pants and a sweatshirt, and find his heavy jacket stuffed in the back of his closet.

Walking into the motel office, Sterling's father extended his hand, causing the dude behind the counter to stand abruptly, his stool teetering. The guy wore a buttoned-up parka because it wasn't much warmer in here than outside. Sterling hadn't been in this office in a long time. It had been forgettable then. Now it was abysmal. He looked at the cracked linoleum counter, glanced across the room. Inside the dirty beige walls was nothing but a pair of grungy, tweed-upholstered chairs in a corner and a rack with a few pamphlets by the door. Leaflets for tourist attractions? No tourists here, no way, not in this dump that smelled like sweaty gym socks. What a joke.

"Sterling." His father's voice made him turn. "Meet Malik. He takes care of things here." Sterling nodded. He wanted to be anywhere else on this frigid Saturday morning.

"Brought my son along to see the lay of the land," his father continued.

"Ah, I see," Malik answered, nodding hello to Sterling. "No water in the faucets and the toilet in any room. It's frozen."

"Let's see the pipes," Hugh Lovell said, brisk. Malik walked from behind the counter, motioned them through the smudged glass doors and along the sidewalk until they were behind the motel. They looked at the exposed pipes. "No wonder. No insulation. Doesn't usually get this cold, but they ought to have insulation. Rudie should have seen to this. But right now, got to keep 'em from bursting. Let's get things thawed quick before we have an explosion," his father announced. Ever in charge, his old man, Sterling thought, shaking his head at nothing.

"You got somebody in maintenance who can get some hair dryers out here?" His father sounded irritated, thinking, Sterling supposed, that Rudie had no business being sick.

"Sure, yes," Malik responded. "I will get hair dryers now."

"God knows it's cold. Must be breaking a record." His father stomped from foot to foot, hands thrust in his pockets against the icy air. "And let's get some insulation tape on these pipes when they're thawed."

Malik nodded enthusiastically.

While his father waited and Malik ran off to retrieve drop cords and hair dryers, Sterling wandered off. Nothing he could do to expedite the process. He walked around the Red Rose Motel in a stiff lope, hands in his jacket pockets, wishing for gloves. The place was a relic of concrete block and metal railings built decades before. If it once evoked the idea of romance with its name, that day was long gone. He passed by the open door of a room and looked inside.

Orange and black geometric wallpaper from another era covered the walls. Seeing no one, he stepped inside. Someone or something had peeled the paper back to bare wall on one side of the bed. Bad trip, Sterling thought. The dark, no-color carpet, alive, sucked at his feet. Towels hung on the racks in the bathroom, so he figured the room had been cleaned, in spite of the wide yellow stripe ringing the tub midway up.

No one in his right mind would stay overnight in this crummy place, he thought, even as he knew people actually lived here, day after day, week after week. Sterling walked back outside, shuddered. He wandered back to the office because what was the point of freezing his ass off to watch people blow hairdryers on frozen pipes. The office might not

28

be warm enough for comfort, but it was a hell of a lot better than outside. He would sit and wait.

Approaching the door, he saw the arm of a slim figure inside rubbing a cloth up and down the clouded glass. He didn't want to startle the cleaning lady who wasn't looking out, her head turned down and covered in a furry black hoodie, so he knocked. She spooked anyway, stepping back. Sterling opened the door. "Sorry, didn't mean to scare…," he said and stopped, as the person under the hood looked up at him. For a moment they stared at each other.

"Go," she mumbled, backing away.

"Zell, what? It's you. What are you…," Sterling exclaimed. He reached out to touch the sleeve of her jacket. She jerked her arm away.

"Let me by," she pleaded.

"Hey, Zell, it's okay. You work here?"

She nodded yes and then no. Like the scared rabbit when they first met. But worse. She sprang from one foot to the other, frantic.

"Zell, it's okay. You work at my old man's motel? I'm here same as you. Working. Or I'm supposed to be. Helping thaw frozen pipes, but I left so now I'll probably be in trouble with my dad. What the hell." Sterling reached out again and this time made contact with Zell's arm.

She looked at his hand on her sleeve. "Please go," she said, so quiet he could hardly hear her.

"Why?" Sterling asked. "It's cold as a witch's 'you know what,' and I don't want to freeze," he said and grinned.

Zell shook his hand from her arm. "It's not…with me…," she started and stopped.

"What's not?" he began but she hurried around him, nearly tumbling out the glass doors. He followed, calling her. She didn't turn back. He sprinted, trying to catch up along the sidewalk. But she got away like her life depended on it. Yards ahead, she turned a right angle and ducked into a corridor. Panting, he stopped then, knowing. She lived here. Otherwise, she wouldn't have run like that.

No wonder she didn't want to tell him. This awful place. No home at all, this piece of shit, part of his old man's empire. Zell wasn't so much shy, he realized, as she was ashamed. An image of Courtney flashed across his mind. Cool, calm, stunning in one of her expensive brightly patterned—Lilly something or other—dresses all the girls wore. A dress like that might pay half a month's rent in this place. What did Zell think of him? He couldn't put words to his thoughts.

She had seemed uncomplicated, not like the girls in his world with their cat and mouse games. She was beautiful, natural, and he wanted her. Easy enough. But now, seeing her bundled up against the cold in a too-big, furry-hooded sweatshirt, her mortification when she saw him, knew his father owned this joint, made his chest tighten. It did something to him, something he never felt before. Way more than her body and face, it was the sensation of her.

Bent over, catching his breath, almost lightheaded from his dash and the image of Zell, vulnerable, he saw himself in middle school again. The Halloween carnival approached. His seventh grade Sunday school class was in charge of the annual haunted house in the fellowship hall at St. Luke's Episcopal. His classmates made him a laughingstock, said he looked like Fred Flintstone with Dumbo ears. Franklin Johns, an asshole to this day, said Sterling didn't need makeup to scare the elementary-age children walking through the dark maze behind the stage curtains. Kids hooted at Franklin's remark. The sound rang now in Sterling's ears.

Their good-looking youth leader had walked from the other side of the room at the commotion. Keeping his mouth covered to contain his laughter, Franklin said they were discussing how Sterling should be the creature to scare the little kids that year.

Miss Sims glowered at Franklin; her attention caused the kids to stare harder at Sterling. He'd looked away, over his shoulder. She turned to Ronnie Rentz, the tallest boy in their group, and asked if he'd dress up as the monster and wear a mask to scare children. He agreed and everyone went back to the task of decorating. But the damage was done. Sterling, a fat boy with an underbite and elephant ears, had again been humiliated.

He was assigned to supervise little kids bobbing for apples that year, but he didn't go to the carnival. He couldn't bear it. By the next Halloween, though, things were different. Braces, surgery during the Christmas holidays to pin back his ears, and fat camp in Melbourne, Florida, during the summer changed everything. Camp had the biggest effect. It wasn't just health and fitness and meal control. It was how they taught you to think, to believe in yourself. But Zell, what chance had been given to her? She was beautiful all over, but she had nothing, living in this place. Suddenly, his bowels tightened, and he dashed quickly back to the office for the toilet, hoping the pipes were working now.

Sterling was sitting in one of the broken-down corner chairs when Malik led his father back into the office. "Could have used your help. Where the hell did you go?" His father jerked his thumb toward him.

"Here," Sterling responded, pointing to his chair. "Looked like you had enough hands for hair dryers and mine were freezing."

"Yeah, well, all right," his father said. "We thawed out those suckers. Done. We got a guy on the way to insulate the pipes. Too damn cold for Ramsey." He stamped his feet and rubbed his hands together, turned to his shift manager. "Okay, Malik, we're good," he pronounced.

"Fine, sir," he answered.

"We'll be on our way." His father gave Malik a mock salute. Sterling rose from the low, lumpy chair.

"Seat getting warm?" his father asked on the ride home, his new BMW X5 purring in the cold.

"Sure, yeah, fine," Sterling said.

"What's eating you? Pissed 'cause I got you up early? You need to know about operations. It'll all be yours one day. Plus whatever else you want to do." Sterling shook his head.

They rode in silence for a few minutes. Stopped at the light on the corner of Main and Gibson, his father looked over, poked an index finger into Sterling's thigh. "What gives?" he asked.

"Why do you own that place?" Sterling asked back.

"What do you mean why? What do you think? I own real estate all over. It feeds our family."

"How do you sleep at night, knowing those poor people are stuck living at the Red Rose Motel?" Sterling stared forward, not looking at his father.

"Jesus, son, you got a lot to learn. It's a hell of a lot better than being on the street." The light turned green, and the BMW roared forward. Sterling continued to stare straight ahead.

Chapter 6

Angela Wilmore

She knew she wasn't supposed to be, but she couldn't help it. Angela was intrigued by the relationship she saw emerging between sweet Hazel Smalls and Sterling Lovell, one of the smartest boys she taught—polite ever since his punishment but ever self-assured of his status. How had he met a poor, young woman in Angela's general studies English class? And what drew them—because he went with Courtney Powell, one of the most popular girls at Ramsey. These two were a coveted couple. In the old days of her own youth, Sterling and Courtney would surely have been crowned king and queen in the senior superlatives.

Angela had lived on the fringes during high school with no superlatives to her name. She made good grades and had a few close friends. She attended events—like junior-senior or homecoming, say, with a date—but she wasn't anyone special. Thank God the days of choosing the "best" students in a hundred social categories were long gone. It was painful to be a teenager and feel excluded.

Where would these students' paths have crossed? Sterling's classes were all top tier, full of other kids like himself, while Hazel—she was almost certain—was in all general classes, including Angela's English section. It wasn't that Hazel wasn't smart enough. She certainly was. But she was disadvantaged, a condition that could cause inattention, defensiveness, even unexplained anger, though she'd never seen Hazel bristle. Kids like Hazel often had no one at home who either could or would encourage them to reach their potential. It dawned on her suddenly that Sterling must have met Hazel in ISS. But what was she doing there?

Hazel possessed verve that most young people in her circumstances lacked. Angela thought of her as having "umph," though how such metamorphosis happened, Angela did not know.

She didn't intend to intrude, but when Sterling walked Hazel to class one morning before the bell—Angela long ignoring the school rules—then dashed off to who knew where, a student council meeting or maybe to meet Courtney, she couldn't help herself. She stepped over a line she maybe ought not to cross. She called Hazel to her desk.

"Yes ma'am?" The girl advanced, timid, because teachers didn't normally call students to their desks without something being wrong.

"Oh, goodness, Hazel, there's nothing amiss," Angela said. "I just want to ask you a question."

Hazel stood at attention, saying nothing.

"It's not my business, but...I see...you and Sterling Lovell have become friends?"

Hazel shrugged.

"How did the two of you meet?"

Hazel shrugged again.

Angela cleared her throat. "Forgive my nosiness. I am just a bit surprised you and Sterling have made each other's acquaintance."

"We met in ISS," Hazel said abruptly, scowling. Angela straightened in her seat, her notion confirmed. She twisted her necklace and set her gaze hard on Hazel.

The girl stepped back.

"It's okay. I'm the one who asked," Angela said.

"I know, pretty stupid, right?" Hazel said, her manner shifting, contrite. "I don't know why Sterling wants to hang around with me."

"Because you're a lovely young woman," Angela countered. "I only wondered how you met." She flushed, knowing she'd upset Hazel and that none of this was any of her business.

Hazel's gaze was penetrating. It took Angela aback knowing her student was searching for an explanation, too.

She stood and walked around her desk, put her hand on Hazel's shoulder. "I'm not a bit surprised Sterling is taken with you. Keep your head up, young lady. He's lucky to have met you."

"I didn't do anything wrong, not really, to get in ISS," Hazel said. "I mean, I did, because I didn't wear my ROTC uniform like I'm supposed to. I told Sergeant Riel I forgot, but I didn't, and he knew it—I didn't want to wear a dirty uniform."

"Oh, Hazel," Angela said. She didn't know Sergeant Riel, but she felt an impulse to kick him in his shins or worse. Dense fool. She squeezed Hazel's shoulder, and the girl gave her a grateful look. Angela's heart tightened.

The bell rang to start school. Hazel scuttled from beneath Angela's touch, headed back to her desk, their moment together as though it never happened, except for one thing. As she walked away, Hazel said quietly, "Some people call me Zell."

Angela smiled, rolled her shoulders back, and took her station at the door to welcome the class that started her bipolar day. Kids who needed all the help she could give followed by four classes of AP students, most of whom had the world by the tail.

***

After working with her first period students on how to develop a body paragraph (had no one ever taught these kids anything about writing an essay?), followed by discussion of Faulkner's story "Barn Burning" with the AP's during second and third periods, Angela flopped into her desk chair, stretched her neck back, and rubbed her temples. She loved her job, but teaching teenagers took all the energy her fifty-three years could muster. Fourth period was her oasis. Planning period. No issues, no disturbances. She would run to the office and make copies of a timed writing practice to give students the next day in preparation for the free-response question on the AP exam, then spend the last part of her hour studying the two stories she'd assigned for later in the week.

For five precious minutes she closed her eyes, then forced herself into action, starting with her email. There was something from the principal, and it wasn't a group email. Damn, she thought. He probably wasn't writing to recommend her for teacher of the year. Sure enough, far from it.

> Hello Ms. Wilmore,
> When you have a moment, could you drop by my office to discuss a student matter? I've got a pair of parents complaining about the content of a story you taught in your AP Lit course. I'm sorry to bother you with this, but they want a meeting.

"Damn, indeed," she said out loud. Why couldn't these anonymous parents contact her directly instead of going over her head, treating her as though she weren't in charge of her own decisions about the literature she taught?

One of the benefits of being the AP Literature teacher at Ramsey was developing her own curriculum geared toward the exam her students would take at the end of the school year in hopes of gaining credit for the Introduction to Literature course in college. She'd taught the course at the community college for more than twenty years, and so far, no one in the high school administration had asked to examine any of her lessons.

Angela ditched her plan for the copy machine and walked to the principal's office. Mrs. Bagley, his assistant, wasn't at her desk, and Finley Copeland's door was partway open. She coughed to get his attention, and he looked up from his computer.

"Ms. Wilmore, come in. Thank you for responding to my email."

"Angela," she said. Other than the interview to be hired for her job, she'd not had a face-to-face meeting with her principal—a man she guessed in his late forties, handsome in an athletic, chiseled kind of way.

"Thank you," he said. "Like I said in my note, I'm sorry to call you in, but this father is breathing down my neck. I thought if you could explain your rationale for teaching whatever it is he's so hot about, it might calm him down. I tried to explain that teachers make their own curriculum decisions based on state guidelines. But he insisted."

"He didn't want to call me directly?"

"Apparently, he wants a meeting with you *and* me."

"Your message mentioned parents plural," Angela said.

"Yes, well, he said 'he and his wife' were outraged, but I never talked to her. I'm sure she will be with him. Sit, please." He motioned Angela to a dark leather armchair, much different from the ragged thing on rollers in Early Jenkins's office. She supposed he had people to impress while Early had only to listen to teachers' troubles and discipline students.

"May I ask the names of these parents, Mr. Copeland?" Angela said, tipping forward in the chair toward his wide desk.

"Finley, please," he said. Angela nodded. "Donovan and Genny

Powell; their daughter is Courtney."

Briefly, Angela's breath caught, for the irony startled her. She'd thought about Courtney this morning when she was talking to Zell because she was Sterling Lovell's popular girlfriend. Long blonde hair, translucent blue eyes. A student who, while not particularly inquisitive in class or an innovative writer, dutifully did her work. Her grades were good enough. Quickly, Angela recovered, saying, "Courtney has never said anything to me about finding any of the literature we've discussed offensive. She is a good student. Why would she go to her parents instead of consulting me? Or maybe her parents are in the habit of reading her assignments?"

Finley Copeland shrugged. "You never know what they're thinking," he said. "Her father's a preacher. Could you meet after school tomorrow?"

"Yes," Angela responded. "Did he tell you the piece of literature that's troubling them?"

"Here, I wrote it down." He scrambled through loose papers on his desk, found what he was looking for. "A story titled 'Happy Endings' by a woman named Margaret Atwood. Doesn't sound like anything too troubling to me."

But Angela had an idea what she might be up against.

***

Angela preferred loose shift dresses, but she wore a tailored skirt and white crepe blouse tucked in for the meeting with Donovan and Genny Powell.

Finley rose when she walked into his office. He introduced Angela to the couple before she sat in a straight chair, the one she'd been in yesterday and its mate occupied by the parents. Sitting side by side, a thick man with his elbows out—coat cuffs rising over the forearms of his starched shirt—and a thin, mousy woman in a solid black pantsuit posed stiffly beside her husband. They acknowledged Angela with twin nods.

"Happy to meet you both," Angela said crisply.

"Yes, so we're here to discuss…," Finley began.

"Lewd literature," Donovan Powell finished the sentence. Angela bristled. Her principal cleared his throat.

"I beg your pardon," Angela responded. Finley cleared his throat again.

"This story you taught—it's full of disgusting language and indecency. I want it removed from the curriculum. And I want to make sure no other so-called literature like this is presented to my daughter or other young people." Donovan Powell pulled his elbows in tight to his sides.

So much for this parent's diplomacy, Angela thought. She looked at her principal. Shouldn't he be defending her? But he appeared to have swallowed a live mouse and was trying to force it down his gullet.

Blood pumped hot beneath Angela's cheeks as she looked directly at Donovan Powell and said, "The literature in this class is college level. It's meant for mature students. If Courtney is uncomfortable with the premise of the story, she should have talked to me. I chose it because it is an excellent model of the conventions of storytelling for the beginning of our unit on the short story." Angela strained to keep her tone smooth and even, not to sink to his level.

"I don't know about any conventions other than this story encourages wicked behavior." At the word "wicked," Genny Powell placed her hand on her husband's arm. Angela wasn't sure whether the woman meant to encourage or dampen her husband's momentum. Well, she's alive at any rate, she thought.

Angela looked again toward Finley Copeland for support, but none was forthcoming. He sat bug-eyed, like the mouse he'd swallowed had not gone down at all but had caught in a balled-up wad in his throat.

"This Margaret Atwood, she's been published in *Playboy* magazine," Donovan Powell pronounced.

"As have many distinguished authors," Angela said.

Donovan Powell pulled a sheet from his pocket and unfolded it. He had done his homework. He rattled off some of the most influential writers of the twentieth century who were published in *Playboy*: Joyce Carol Oates, John Updike, John Irving, Stephen King, the list went on. Even Shel Silverstein, the children's author of *The Giving Tree*. Angela would have bet her life Courtney had read this book.

At the least, she was confused by Mr. Powell's argument. Wasn't the man undercutting his claim? It made her wonder, with brief glee, whether he might actually be a longtime closet subscriber. If he wanted to condemn Margaret Atwood because she'd been published in *Playboy*, wasn't naming numerous famous American authors—including a famous children's author—an endorsement of the publication's literary reputation?

She made an attempt to point out this fact to the fuming father. Was his purpose to denounce all of these acclaimed American writers? But either he didn't get it or wouldn't listen. He simply repeated his declaration, louder, that Margaret Atwood had been published in a "dirty magazine."

How could she counter an argument that made no sense, especially to a man who interrupted her? Finley finally spoke. "If I might say a word, sir," and the man immediately shut up. He would listen to her male principal. "Ms. Wilmore is an experienced teacher with an excellent reputation. She has a great deal of knowledge in her discipline, and I trust her to make appropriate choices." Finley cleared his throat again.

Donovan Powell glowered.

"The anthology I use is approved by the state of South Carolina for teaching AP Literature." In spite of her efforts at diplomacy, Angela's tone was getting testy.

"Yes," Finley dittoed. "Of course, Ms. Wilmore is teaching approved literature for this advanced class."

"Then the state of South Carolina needs to change this so-called approved textbook," Mr. Powell said. His wife nodded affirmatively, but she didn't speak.

"I'm afraid that's something that's out of our hands," Finley said.

"Well, what's not out of your hands is requiring Ms. Wilmore to choose writing from this textbook that does not warp young people. How could a story with a passage containing the 'F' word possibly be constructive?"

Angela well knew the section of the story he referred to. Her initial suspicions were confirmed. It wasn't the word *fuck* disturbing Donovan Powell in that section so much as the author's caustic tone toward the female character Mary's desperation to please her boyfriend John: *"He*

comes to her apartment twice a week and she cooks him dinner, you'll notice
that he doesn't even consider her worth the price of a dinner out, and after
he's eaten dinner he fucks her and after that he falls asleep, while she does the
dishes so he won't think she's untidy...."

"Courtney was too embarrassed to speak to Ms. Wilmore, and we
want assurance our daughter won't be exposed to this kind of language
again," Donovan Powell continued.

It was clear. This was not about the language in the story. It was
about Courtney's father not wanting his daughter reading literature in
which a male character was ridiculed for controlling his girlfriend. It was
hard to believe this guy was for real in the twenty-first century. Yet here
he was in the flesh, hefty and overbearing. The term "male chauvinist
pig" came to Angela, a phrase they'd used to describe such men when
she was young in the late sixties.

Finley looked at her. "Could we assure the Powells there will be no
more literature of this nature?" he asked. Though he sounded desperate,
she stiffened at his suggestion of censorship. She thought if she had a
flaming dart, she would throw it at Mr. Powell's smug, beefy face. And
she wasn't like that. She'd been a teacher for nearly three decades, and
part of her job was maintaining calm. But it was also to expose her students to the human experience through literature, and this story happened to satirize an experience of an unequal sexual and romantic playing field in John and Mary's relationship.

"There is a way to come to an understanding among us," Finley
said. "Ms. Wilmore, could you offer Courtney an alternative assignment
if she isn't comfortable with a particular selection?"

Angela stared at him. She'd given students separate lessons in the
past, sent them to the library to work independently for various reasons.
She wondered, though, if this father would now find fault with numerous assignments. And if she made concessions for Courtney, others
would likely follow. Because if she knew students, she knew some would
jump at the chance to do their own thing out of class.

"As the minister at Grace Church, I am sensitive of others' welfare,
including my daughter's. We don't want her or anyone separated from
the group and singled out," Donovan Powell said, glancing at his wife
for confirmation. The poor woman was good at nodding her head. "I

would never endorse anything that might ridicule young people," he added.

Minister at Grace Church. Angela put her palm to her forehead, almost in relief. She wished she'd known from the start. It was a church well known for its fundamentalist principles, which would include a woman obeying her husband in every circumstance.

"An option is for Courtney to transfer to Honors Level English, which is still an excellent choice for a college-bound student. The text is different because it's not a college course," Angela offered.

"That's a good option," Finley agreed, reaching his hand up to scratch into the crown of his thick head of brown, curly hair.

"It's not a good option. Our daughter tested into AP English, and that's where she'll stay." Reverend Powell grabbed the fly of his pants and scratched. Angela turned her head away, hoping the act was unconscious.

"We appreciate your position," Finley said, standing. Angela could see a slight wet sheen on her principal's temples. "Ms. Wilmore and I will meet and get back to you."

"Very well," Reverend Powell said and rose. He took his wife's hand, and she stood. "We look forward to hearing from you soon."

***

"I'm sorry," Finley said, sitting again after he had ushered the Powells through his office door.

"I have never endured a grilling like that," Angela said.

"I'm sorry," Finley repeated. "I don't know anything about literature. I was a PE teacher before getting into administration."

Angela wanted to feel sorry for him, to allow his purported ignorance to excuse him, but she couldn't. A principal was supposed to protect and guard his faculty in front of parents and students. Defend your people and sort through the right and the wrong in private. And she wasn't even the tiniest bit in the wrong.

"We got blindsided," he said.

"Yes, we did," she answered, her voice drained.

"Can you give Courtney a different assignment if it comes down to it in the future? If there's something else he doesn't like?" Her principal laced his fingers.

"If that's what you tell me to do, but if we start coddling one student, it could lead to more." Angela watched Finley's thumbs twirling.

"I know you're right. But this guy, in charge of that big church out on the interstate with the flashing sign out front. He might preach about this." He looked bug-eyed again, like the mouse had climbed out of his stomach back into his throat.

Was this why he hadn't told her the man was the preacher at that ginormous church? He was afraid of what he might do?

Now Angela did feel sorry for her principal who'd begun fingering strands of his curly hair. She didn't want either of them to be the subject of a fire and brimstone sermon. "If I need to prepare some separate lessons, I will," she said. "I'd rather do that than be told what I can and can't teach by one narrow-minded parent. But you heard him. He doesn't want her to go to the library for independent learning."

"I'll work it out. You're doing your job. You're teaching from an approved textbook. I'll handle it."

"I don't want to see that man again," Angela said, feeling, in spite of herself, like a defenseless little girl instead of a grown woman.

"It was a difficult meeting. If I had known…. Could I just ask that if you have a choice between several pieces of literature that would accomplish the same goal, you choose the one least likely to stir up this guy?"

"That's censorship, isn't it?"

"A compromise? I'm saying if you have a choice between equal selections that would meet your objective." Her principal's hand was now grasping at his ear.

"It is censorship, but okay. I'll agree if I never meet with that man again?"

"Not on my watch, Ms. Wilmore…Angela," Finley Copeland said.

She stood and he stood also. His hand dropped from his ear and clasped his other hand. "Thank you," he said.

"You're welcome," she said and hurried away.

Chapter 7

Hazel Smalls

That cold Saturday, Hazel had run as fast as she could along the sidewalk, then ducked into a covered passageway among the motel rooms, deliberately dashing down the wrong direction to throw off Sterling. When she could no longer see him behind her, she turned and bolted to Room 103, her family's home.

Her father sat in his grubby, green velour recliner—patches of fabric missing from the arms, the headrest stained from his oiled hair. It was his throne, and the rest of them had better not sit there if he was home. He looked up when she banged the door open.

"Whoa, Zell," he said, looking up from the television. "What you doing back this soon? You not through cleaning, are you? Where's your mother?"

"I don't know. Still at the nursing home, I guess. They must not have let her go on time," Hazel said, heaving, bending double. "I'm done."

"Why you breathing so hard? Ghost follow you back?"

She stared at her father and his surroundings. It was still morning, and a Pabst can lay on its side near his feet, the red and white Playmate cooler beside it. Her father had been out of work for nearly a year with the trucking company after he lost his commercial driving license when he was stopped for weaving on the interstate in the middle of the night. Drunk. It took all they'd saved toward a deposit on an apartment to bail him out.

Before the Red Rose, her family lived in one side of a two-bedroom brick duplex on North Park Drive overlooking the neighborhood lake where she and her sister Chloe walked at dusk, observing turtles lined shell to shell on fallen oak limbs floating on the water, wood ducks gliding across the lake's expanse. Before her father quit working with his brother. A distant memory.

"Something like that," she answered. Her father grunted and went back to the screen.

Hazel would feel better if she washed her face. In the bathroom, her ten-year-old sister sat on the toilet lid, reading, away from their father's grunts and groans. Chloe glanced up and leaned forward, holding her library book aloft. Hazel looked at the title: *Because of Winn-Dixie*. She had read this book at around Chloe's age. Mainly, it had made Hazel sad that she couldn't have a dog, too.

"Hey, Zell," Chloe said. "What you doing back so soon? Mama's not even home yet."

"I finished early. I guess she's still working," Hazel said. Her mother should be home by now from her night shift as a CNA at the nursing home. But she was glad her mother wasn't home because Hazel's heart was frog hopping all over inside her chest. The last thing she needed was more questions.

"Oh, she's gonna be some kind of tired," Chloe said and leaned back against the tank of the toilet, feet dangling toward the linoleum floor, to resume reading.

Hazel turned on the cold faucet. She splashed water onto her face, rubbed the chilly spray into her temples. She looked up into the mirror and shrank. Because what she saw was not her own self but an imagined reflection of what Sterling saw, her shocked expression. Holding her head in her hands, she sank to the floor. Was it seconds or minutes when she heard her sister call: "Zell, are you ok? The water's running." Hazel didn't move. Above her, Chloe turned off the faucet.

Hazel walked back into the main room and opened her book bag. She had a lot of homework. She would start with reading the chapters for history class because she liked history, and it would distract her. She pulled out the heavy volume and sat at the small table that doubled as both their eating place and workspace. But she couldn't concentrate with the noise of the television and her father talking to the screen. Not to mention the neighbor in the next room—a man who heard voices that weren't there—stomping loud and banging something, somewhere. Her thoughts returned to Sterling.

Some crazy, unknown part of her wanted to believe he might really like her. But how could that be? His father owned this dump and probably others like it. People like Sterling and his family cared only about their own kind and about getting richer off of people like her family. Still, after the meal and wine he bought her at Marelli's, he hadn't acted like she owed him. He'd only kissed her in the parking lot, nothing more, and the kissing had made her dizzy. She'd wanted to talk to him this morning, but she was too ashamed.

She returned to the bathroom. She sat on the edge of the tub, watched her sister reading. "At least it's quieter in here," Zell said. Chloe looked up, nodded, and went back to her book. Zell wished she could tune out distraction as easily as her sister.

"Zell," her mother's voice came toward the bathroom, concerned. "Burl says you're home early." Leave it to her jobless father to rat her out.

Her mother appeared at the bathroom door, her lips strained into a pink-brown strip, her dark eyes clouded—eyes their father once described on a happy day as onyx jewels. She pushed back the red rag tied around her head. A few crinkled curls sprang out.

"You're tired, Mama. You need to go to bed," Hazel observed.

"I'm okay," her mother said. "A first shifter called in sick. I had to stay until they found a sub."

The television roared beyond them with sounds like chainsaws chewing wood. It was really tigers snarling at one another on a Saturday morning wildlife program her father liked. Hazel knew her mother would get in bed and somehow sleep through this commotion.

"Did you finish the office and the rooms you were assigned?" her mother asked now. More tiger noise, deep and growling. Hazel cupped her hands over her ears. Her mother pulled Hazel's arms back to her sides. "Answer me."

"I finished the office," Hazel said.

"What about the guest rooms?"

Chloe looked up from her book, suddenly interested.

"No."

"What happened?" her mother asked.

"Nothing," Hazel replied, her heart leapfrogging again.

"It's not nothing if you didn't finish the work."

44

"I'll go back this afternoon," Hazel said. "I didn't feel good. I'll tell Malik."

Her mother sighed and looked toward Chloe. "What you doing, little girl? Reading? I need you to start me a piece of cheese toast browning."

"Okay, Mama." Chloe left her book beside the toilet and darted from the room.

Once her sister was gone, Hazel's mother bore down. "What you doing not finishing your work, Zell? We can't afford laziness." She pulled the rag from her head. Wiry curls popped out. She slapped at her hair.

"I'm sorry. I got cold."

"Cold? You got a coat. Jesus, I hope Mr. Rudie doesn't know."

"He's not here today. He's out sick."

"Well, thank the good Lord he's not here," her mother said. "Go on back and finish whatever wasn't finished by somebody else."

Reluctantly, Hazel nodded, put on her coat, pulled the fuzzy hood over her head, and left.

***

Returning from cleaning—the worst of it, like always, the grimy bathrooms; she'd nearly retched over a toilet seat ringed with puke that resembled lumpy pink lemonade—she heard her parents through the door.

"Leave me be, bitch," Hazel's father shouted when she was still several yards away.

"I'm gonna leave you be when we 'bout done with staying in this little bitty hell hole," her mother answered. "You getting your license back this week. You call Stan at Grayson and see what he's got for you."

"They're a bunch of asswipes. They ain't got my back."

"They don't got to have your back. They just have to give you a route," her mother said.

"I'll deal with it. Leave me alone," her father said as Hazel opened the motel door, unlocked, and entered.

"Zell knows what I'm talking about." Her mother pointed at her, as though Hazel had been present the whole time. "We got to have some stability."

Hazel passed by her parents, eyeball to eyeball on each other, and continued into the bathroom to look for Chloe. She would grab her sister and go somewhere, away from the never-ending argument over her father's lack of work. He could have done a lot of things this year, but he didn't. One man came to their motel room to offer her father work with a tree removal service. Burl said he wasn't risking his life in a damn cherry picker.

"Where's my sister?" Hazel asked, returning from the bathroom.

"She's gone over to Fawn's room, if you want to know," her mother answered. Fawn and Chloe were friends who rode the bus together to the middle school. Hazel was thankful her sister was out of earshot.

"Never mind you should have been working something all this year, when all you did is feel sorry for yourself about getting a DUI that was nobody's fault but yours. But that's water gone under the bridge. So now you can drive again. Your year is up." Her mother's tone was edging up.

"I'm not crawling back," Burl Smalls growled.

"Daddy, it's not crawling. They couldn't keep you when you couldn't drive," Hazel interjected.

"Horseshit. People ignore it all the time, but those asswipes let me go. And you stay out of it, Zell. It's not your business."

"Why isn't it her business, Burl?" Her mother shoved a hand onto her husband's shoulder. "She's got a right to get out of this sorry place same as us."

"Leave it, Etta." Burl flicked his wife's hand away and raised his own above his pale face, cheeks red with anger.

"Daddy, stop," Hazel wailed.

"Get the hell out," he yelled. "I told you this ain't your concern."

"You're a lazy piece of drunk shit," Etta responded. Burl slapped his hand across the side of her face.

Her mother jumped back and Hazel jumped with her. She put an arm around her mother's waist. Her mother bent over, massaging her cheek.

"She's tired, Daddy. She works six days a week." Hazel spoke in spite of herself. Her voice quivered.

"I told you, Zell," her father snarled, not unlike the tigers' sounds a few minutes before.

Then, suddenly, her mother collapsed onto the floor.

Hazel went down beside her mother, put a hand to her wrist.

"Her pulse is slow," Hazel said in a few moments. "Call someone."

Her father stood bewildered, as though his wife had copped out on the fight.

"Jesus," Hazel exhaled, rising, dashing to the motel phone on the table between the beds, dialing 911.

Her mother spent the remainder of the day and the night at the hospital, diagnosed with psychogenic blackout, which meant, as far as Hazel could determine, fainting because of stress.

In the afternoon, with his wife woozy and nauseated in the hospital, Hazel's father called his old boss at Grayson trucking.

Chapter 8

Sterling Lovell

After school without his phone—confiscated during calculus when Courtney texted and it chimed because he'd, dammit, forgotten to silence it—Sterling drove to Fantastic Franks because he'd seen that much in her text before Mr. Clark demanded his "device." Stupid word. God forbid, if your phone made a sound, a teacher could (and usually would) impound it.

First offense, with Sterling now, meant the teacher took your phone to the principal's office for a parent to retrieve. Second offense, your phone was not returned at all. Period. Third offense was three days of suspension. It was ridiculous.

Fantastic Franks, the hotdog joint near school where they all hung out, was a cool place. But today, needless to say, Sterling was pissed when he arrived. Courtney perched on a swivel seat at the counter holding court with two other Ramsey superstars—her besties she called them—on either side.

He was nearly on them before Courtney noticed and said loud enough for everyone at the counter and a few nearby tables to hear, "Sters, why didn't you text back? I was worried!"

"You don't look too worried," he griped, nodding to Courtney's cohorts, Jill Goforth and Madison Hardley.

"Good God, Sterling," Jill said, "what's up with you?"

He didn't answer.

"Guess we should scoot," Madison said, rising from her stool.

"No need to leave," Sterling said. "I was summoned and here I am." He grinned like the Joker. Grabbing up her drink, Jill scurried up behind Madison. Sterling watched them retreat to a table across the room. He sat heavily on Jill's seat, warm from her prominent cheerleader cheeks.

"Sterling," Courtney drawled his name. "What's wrong with you? You were rude to Jill and Madison."

"My guess is they'll get over it," he answered. "I forgot to put my damn phone on silent, and now it's sitting in Ms. Bagley's desk drawer because you texted."

"Oops, sorry," Courtney said, but Sterling could see her quelling a giggle.

"It isn't funny. Now the parents have to go get it. They'll probably ground me."

"Don't be dramatic. No, they won't. You just have to come up with something to tell them." Courtney fluffed her blonde bangs down over her eyebrows and peeked out at him.

Sterling shook his head. "Such as?"

"Such as it wasn't your phone that dinged. It was someone else's, but you didn't want to rat, so you took the fall." Sterling shook his head again. Courtney was the queen of avoiding trouble.

"Duh, I was caught red-handed." He slid forward on the slick purple vinyl.

"Easy enough. You say you thought it was your phone because you heard the ding nearby, so you pulled it out of your pocket, even though you were sure you put it on silent."

Sterling slapped a hand to his forehead. "How do you come up with this stuff so fast?"

"With a father like mine, you got to stay on your toes." She brushed her bangs back now, bending close into his face, so that Sterling saw the gleam in her eyes, that stunning sapphire blue.

Courtney's father was a sanctimonious prick. Big man preacher of his megachurch, always acting like he was God in charge of the world, especially when it came to his family.

"Speaking of…that's why I texted you to meet me. I had a run-in with the parents yesterday. It got ugly." She sat up straight on her stool.

"Oh," Sterling exclaimed. "Now there's something new."

"Stop being sarcastic, Sters. You can't totally blame me about your phone." She swiveled to and fro, her motion uncharacteristically nervous.

"Okay, okay." He grabbed the edge of her stool to stop her turning.

It was making him dizzy. "What happened with your parents?"

"Mother was messing in my room. Why she looked in the storage space I don't know. I mean, I've done nothing. She found an ashtray with some cigarette butts. Madison was at my house all upset about nearly failing a big test in AP European History, and we smoked a few to chill out. I forgot to flush the evidence."

Sterling detested cigarettes and thought it was just as well that Courtney had been caught. "Well?" he asked.

"*Well,* Mother came unglued and told Daddy as soon as he got home, and they lit into me. I thought about saying the cigarettes were Madison's, but after finding the ashtray, Mother plowed through my drawers. She had the pack of Marlboros in her hand, so I was like caught." Courtney crossed her arms.

"You're grounded?" Sterling asked.

"No," she said. "At least I think I fixed it. What's that term in logical fallacy for throwing someone off the track? Oh, red herring. I created a red herring."

"What the heck are you talking about?"

"I'm talking about getting the parents off my back with a more pressing issue," Courtney said. "I used that story we just studied in English. Remember? I think it's called 'Happy Endings.' It was the first thing that occurred to me. Something to set my father on fire. And it worked."

"That's a story about paying attention to what we have before the end of life comes," Sterling said.

"Au contraire," she admonished him. "That's what you see, but the dad sees bad language and a woman in control."

"And what does any of this have to do with you smoking?"

"They forgot all about the cigarettes after I told them I was troubled by the story's immorality. If they do come back to the cigarettes, I'll get off a lot easier. Daddy called the school pronto to meet with Ms. Wilmore. Then he started looking up stuff about the author so he could tell Ms. Wilmore a thing or two about what she couldn't teach to 'impressionable young minds.'"

"Are you kidding me? Tell me you didn't involve Ms. Wilmore in order to save your own ass." Sterling spun around on his counter stool, ending full circle eye to eye with his girlfriend. "Why would you do some crap like that?"

"Duh, earth to Sterling. Aren't we talking about the teacher who put you in ISS?" Courtney straightened her short, pleated skirt, letting it crest above her crossed knees.

He considered his English teacher, a woman he'd failed to stump. A woman who now had his respect. "We deserved it," he said.

"Whoa, what the...?" Courtney put her palm on Sterling's forehead. "Do you have a fever or what?"

"Cut it out, Courtney. There isn't any 'what.' She's smart. She's got her act together. We'll all frigging be ready for that AP exam and you know it." Sterling stood suddenly, and the stool squealed.

"Calm down, Sters, really. It's not a big deal. I'm sure Ms. Wilmore can handle herself. If a meeting with Daddy for him to pontificate about the evils of literature gets him off my back, she'll be none the worse for it."

Heat flushed his neck. "When is this meeting?"

"I don't know. Today maybe." Courtney sighed. "Gosh, let it go. I thought this was about me going through trauma. And here you are upset for Ms. Wilmore."

"You're so damn selfish, you know that?" Sterling turned, not waiting for her response, and walked out of Fantastic Franks without so much as ordering a Coca-Cola.

***

Driving back to the school to call his mother to meet him and retrieve his phone—dreading her condemnation—Sterling felt a little sorry about walking out on Courtney that way. He knew he was lucky to have her. He'd always be amazed how she came after him in tenth grade after class elections, how he'd landed her. A hundred guys at Ramsey would like to be in his shoes.

His parents had pushed him to run for class president until he caved. He won in a landslide. Mainly because his primary competition was an overbearing redhead appropriately named Ginger Bolden, whose tendency to tell everyone exactly what she thought of anything and everything had been going on since elementary school.

He didn't dwell on whether he'd have won if he'd had real opposition because for whatever reason, his win impressed Courtney. She began flirting with him in math class. Soon enough they were dating and had been together ever since. His parents were thrilled and gave him the Audi to, as his dad said, have "his own wheels for dates." His allowance went up, too. Nice, because money from his summer lifeguard job at the country club didn't last much past the season.

His parents had also offered Lavinia perks to encourage her to embrace their upwardly mobile lifestyle, but Livie—his name since childhood for his older sister—rebelled 180 degrees into a life their parents detested. Livie attended Emory University, an approved school, but she majored in sociology, the tuition costing "squads of money for a no-count major," their father was fond of saying, to become a low-paid social worker in Atlanta. After Emory, not only was his sister uninterested in a socially beneficial marriage, she professed she was lesbian.

Eschewing all social obligations, plus choosing to be a social worker when she had "brains galore"—another of Hugh Lovell's phrases—made Livie persona non grata. The parents cut themselves off from her, and Sterling was left holding the bag to fulfill their hopes and dreams. He felt constant pressure to atone for his parents' disappointment in their daughter. He rarely saw Livie, though they emailed frequently. She was free and on her own, full of life like her name.

He pulled into a parking spot near the school office and cut the engine. Even if she deserved him walking out, Sterling did feel for Courtney. If he had it tough to live up to his parents' grand expectations, she had it tougher as a preacher's kid, especially being the only child of Donovan Powell, who thought nothing of humiliating anyone whose beliefs did not agree with his, and was especially hard on his wife and daughter. Sterling understood the fear of ridicule. The sting of being the fat boy with protruding ears, the butt of countless jokes. It punctured your soul.

He'd overcome those low days, thanks in large part to his parents' investments to improve his physical and mental condition. And Beatrice, who'd worked for his parents since he had memory. Her love was unconditional.

Over time, he developed a bravado that served him well. He never let down his guard. He'd made the varsity tennis team last year, finally an athlete who could earn a letter. Not a star, but he put his all into every match, and Coach Elmore was always in his court—good pun, he chuckled to himself. And his girlfriend, well, was simply one of the most popular and blondely beautiful girls in the school. What more could he ask for?

Still, every morning when he stepped onto the bathroom scale, if the number rose above 160 on his six-foot frame, he skipped breakfast, lunch, or whatever it took to bring his weight back down. Last thing before he left each morning, he looked in the bathroom mirror, comb poised to arrange his dark, straight hair over his ears.

Sterling stepped out of his car. The wind had picked up, and he was suddenly cold. He zipped his parka to his chin, fast-stepping it into the front building. Turning left toward the office, he nearly collided with Courtney's mother, who was looking down. Sterling jerked back as Donovan Powell took his wife's elbow.

"Goodness, what on earth are you doing in here after school, Sterling?" Reverend Powell said sternly.

Sterling looked at Courtney's father, at his round, smug face, the fuzzy eyebrows cocked upward. Then he glanced at Mrs. Powell, looking up now, her expression curious.

"I have an appointment with Ms. Bagley. A little technology issue," Sterling said.

"Technology issue?" Reverend Powell frowned.

"You got it, sir, and what about you two? What brings you to the main office?" Sterling locked eyes straight with the preacher's.

Donovan Powell cleared his throat, tightened his grip on his wife's arm. Her blue eyes—the same incredible blue as her daughter's—tensed. Sterling saw her discomfort. "Making sure your curriculum is in order," he finally said.

"When did you become a curriculum advisor?" Sterling couldn't help the sarcasm. It felt good.

Chapter 9

Angela Wilmore

Angela's principal allowed youth leaders and ministers into the school during lunch periods to sit with the students. She thought it absurd. Where did you draw the line in deciding who could and could not be an influence from the outside?

What she'd learned during her own lunchtime in the teacher's lounge early in the school year was Finley Copeland actually hated the practice, but his predecessor, who'd left her post for a career in real estate, had started it and he was stuck. If he banned these religious leaders from the cafeteria, he looked like an ogre. But allowing the situation was risky, her department head Watson Stiller—chewing earnestly on a bite of pear—had declared. It violated the separation of church and state, and the principal was playing with fire.

Angela didn't know how a person became an approved cafeteria visitor. Frankly, she didn't pay it much attention. In spite of Watson's warning that September day, when he'd pounded the table for emphasis, she thought if the school allowed adult volunteers to hang out with teenagers on their lunch break, so be it. Not a controversy she wanted to get involved in.

Fifth period, longer than the others, incorporated three lunch breaks to accommodate Ramsey's 1600 students. Angela's class had the middle break, the worst of the schedule. Her students met for half a class, ate, then returned for the second half. Even being the smartest kids, and seniors, they were still teenagers, and it could be difficult to rein them back in after thirty minutes of freedom.

When the bell ending middle lunch rang the first Wednesday in February, Angela—as required—stood at her door waiting for her students' return, chatting with her colleagues: Dianne Steward, who taught eleventh grade Honors English next door, and Judson Moore, a young teacher who taught tenth grade general English across the hall.

Angela marveled at Judson. He taught a rough collection of students—most of them socially and economically disadvantaged—who generally wanted to be anywhere but school. Teaching teenagers was challenge enough, but teaching those most in need was a super challenge. She knew, from her own first period class of similar students. Judson had a gift.

Sometimes he entertained Angela and Dianne between classes with stories of his students. That particular day was about Fiona. She'd turned in her essay surprisingly on time and was looking forward to a reward from the grab bag, as Judson often gave out treats for completed assignments. When Fiona pulled out a box of Milk Duds, he told her to choose M&M's instead. Because God only knew, he told them, leaning casually against the doorframe of his room, how her family had been able to afford those braces, and he wasn't going to be responsible for a broken wire because of some chewy Milk Duds.

His directive hadn't gone well. Uninterested in M&M's, Fiona thudded on heavy legs—Judson pulled away from his door to demonstrate her rigid walk down the aisle to her seat, all the while declaring him a cheat while the other students hooted. "I don't want yo M&M's 'cause they nasty, and you is childish," he mimicked her words. "You can't make this stuff up," he added, his face ironically straight.

Angela and Dianne shook with laughter—thank God for this friend who never took any situation too seriously, even on a bad day. Angela glanced up the hall, anticipating the usual laggards darting in before the tardy bell, and saw Donovan Powell approaching.

Her laughter stopped mid-breath. She froze. "Good afternoon, Ms. Wilmore." Donovan Powell stood inches from her face. "I'm coming from lunch with the kids. Thought I'd drop in to observe the second half of your class." Fifth period was his daughter's class.

"You need permission from the front office to sit in on class, Reverend Powell," Angela spluttered. Her knees locked, a tendency when she was startled or anxious. Then, immediately, she felt anger that this man would affront her again.

"Oh, of course. I have permission," he pronounced, pointing just below the collar of his dress shirt to his visitor's badge.

The second bell rang. Dianne cut her eyes toward Angela as she closed her door, then peeked out briefly through the narrow pane of rectangular glass, an exaggerated peephole in all their doors. Judson didn't move. Angela glanced into her own classroom to see her students waiting.

"This *is* Courtney's class, isn't it?" he asked, smiling. "I'll sit in the back. I won't be a bother."

"You can't without permission," she repeated. This overbearing man was not going to railroad her.

"Nonsense," he admonished her. "I'm on the approved list to be on campus with the young people." He pointed again to his badge.

"Only during lunch," Judson broke in, taking two steps forward. Donovan Powell jerked around toward him. "Judson Moore," he said and extended his hand.

"Young man," Donovan said, his tone patronizing, grasping Judson's hand. "I appreciate your watchfulness, but I assure you it's fine."

Judson's students had started a ruckus inside his classroom. He leaned in the doorway and yelled to them to calm down. The roar subsided slightly. He turned back into the hall holding his hallmark yardstick, a tool for blithely prodding students into class when they lingered loud outside his door.

Donovan Powell took a step toward Angela's door. How was she going to stop him without physically shoving the man back? She stiffened in place.

"Whoa," Judson said, also stepping forward toward Angela's door, extending the wooden yardstick in front of Donovan like a gate.

"Sounds like your students need your attention," Donovan said, pushing aside the long ruler.

"Mr. Copeland is planning to discuss Courtney's options with you again, Reverend Powell," Angela said. She glanced from one man to the other. Both were inches from her doorway. Neither budged. She drew in breath.

"This has nothing to do with administration," Donovan said. "I am simply here to observe my daughter's class."

"No sir," Angela answered, willing her voice firm. Judson's students sounded like a pack of hyenas chattering and shrieking. Judson walked back to his door, waved his wooden stick, told his class to pipe down or else.

Sterling and Rich appeared at Angela's door, scouts, obviously wondering. She shooed them to their seats and pulled her door to, leaving only a crack. She planted her feet apart at the entrance. Her heart was racing. Reverend Powell walked around her right side as though he might slip behind her into the room. Her fingers tightened into her palms.

Judson had quickly returned to the hall, staying behind the preacher's back. He waved his hand to get Angela's attention. He pointed his index finger to her left in a punching motion. She saw what he meant. Every classroom had an emergency button behind the teacher's desk. She should push hers. Since she'd been at Ramsey, as far as she knew, no one had ever pressed a red button. During orientation, she'd heard someone say, "Who knew if they were even operable anymore because no one ever used them."

"Yo there," Judson exclaimed, catching Donovan's attention, giving Angela time to duck inside her classroom. Her students fell unnaturally quiet. She was glad, at least, to see Sterling and Rich back in their seats.

"Soon," she announced in what she hoped was a nonchalant manner. "Gather in your study groups and discuss your responses to Polonius's decision to spy on Hamlet in Act II." They started shuffling and corralling their desks, and she turned to the wall behind her desk chair, hoping they were paying attention to each other and not her. Her hand hovered briefly before she hit the button.

When she stepped back out, pulling the door to again, she gasped. With two hands, Judson held on to Donovan's cowboy-wide belt from the back. The sight had barely registered when the preacher twisted around and swung hard, hitting Judson in the face. Reflexively, her colleague grunted and let go.

***

The three adults in the hall observed one another. Donovan Powell irate. Judson dazed. Angela a speechless statue trying not to wobble.

Some of Judson's students stood piled in the doorway of his classroom. They had witnessed the attack.

"He hit you first, Mr. Moore. You don't take that junk. You fight back," one called out. "Teachers ain't got an expulsion rule for fighting, like us, Mr. Moore."

"You get that punk," another bellowed.

Judson, his hand covering the right side of his face, yelled at them to sit down.

Maybe it wasn't much more than a minute, though it seemed an eternity, before the school security guard came running toward them with Early Jenkins on his heels. Thank God for a red button was Angela's first thought as she exhaled breath she hadn't known she was holding. She watched Judson rub his cheek where a rosy welt was forming. Then glanced toward Donovan Powell tucking in his shirt.

"Reverend Powell," Early said upon arrival. Apparently, everyone knew the man. "What's going on? How can I help you?"

"Oh Early, thank goodness. I wanted to observe Courtney's class today since I was already here for lunch, and Ms. Wilmore here isn't allowing me in. It's become a comedy of the absurd," he said, his manner suddenly cavalier.

"Yo, Mr. Jenkins," said a kid on his knees, literally looking out between Judson's legs, as Judson swatted at him to back up. Early looked toward the voice. "That dude done hit Mr. Moore in the face. We seen it happen."

Early looked at Judson, who pointed at his cheek and glanced back toward Donovan Powell. Aubrey Tidwell, their dumpy, lovable security guard, put his hand over his side where his gun was parked.

"Sir, I think we'd best go to the office and sort this out and let Ms. Wilmore and Mr. Moore teach their classes," Aubrey proclaimed. His feet separated as he twisted assuredly back and forth from his waist.

"Nonsense. Early, tell this gentleman, please, that I'm a welcome guest in the school." The preacher smiled, one side of his lip rising higher than the other.

Early cleared his throat before he spoke. "Well, now, I got to agree here with Officer Tidwell. You can come on back if Mr. Copeland approves."

Donovan Powell sneered, his earlier tone of appeal gone. He was a man accustomed to having his way. Aubrey tightened one hand against his holster, stepped forward, and held on to Donovan's forearm with his other hand. Donovan shook his arm as though extricating a fly. Aubrey tightened his grip. Before today, Angela would never have imagined this gentle man on the offensive.

Her students had become a loud discordant symphony behind her. They'd been alone too long. She stuck her head inside to issue a warning and collided head to head with Sterling, who was back, apparently by himself this time. "Yaow, sorry," he said, rubbing his forehead. "You okay, Ms. W?"

"I'm okay but you're not okay. Go back to your seat, Sterling. What business do you have out of your seat?"

"We were just checking to see if you need anything?" He maneuvered around her to peer out at the scene. "Hey, what's Reverend Powell doing out there?"

"This isn't your concern, Sterling," she said forcefully. "You can't help. We're fine. I'll be in shortly. Go back to your study group." She shut her door all the way, but it was too late. He had seen all there was to see and would make a report: four adults, three of whom didn't belong—his girlfriend's father, Vice Principal Early Jenkins, and their school security officer. Judson had left to save his class from implosion.

"We can call the office from here. I'm sure Finley will give his okay," Donovan was saying, his face composed again, flat and blank as the bottom of a collection plate. He reached in his trousers pocket for his phone.

"Like I said, sir," Aubrey's hand still on Donovan's arm, "we'll sort it out in the office."

Donovan huffed, but his calm demeanor remained.

Angela realized it had become very quiet inside her classroom. She opened the door to see a band of students bunched along the periphery. They tried to scatter, but not before she identified all of them, including Courtney Powell, who did not retreat to her desk as the others did.

"My father is out here," she said, pushing her way out the door. There was nothing Angela could do, short of elbowing her student back inside.

"What are you doing here?" Courtney asked her father, her voice rising, becoming frantic as she took note of her vice principal and the school's security guard.

"Get back in class," her father ordered.

"What's Officer Tidwell doing here?" she asked instead.

"A misunderstanding about visiting rights. Now get back inside." He pulled up tall and attempted to cross his arms, impeded by Aubrey's grasp.

"Why are you holding on to my father?" Courtney pointed at the security officer. Her brow furrowed, drawing a line across her beautiful face.

Aubrey let go of Donovan Powell's arm. For his daughter's sake, Angela thought.

"Young lady, do what your father suggests. Get back in your class, and wait on your teacher," he said gently.

"I'm not going anywhere," Courtney said, her demanding tone startling all of them. "Not until someone tells me what this is."

"Now…Courtney," Mr. Jenkins said slowly. "There's nothing for you…"

"I'm staying right here with Daddy," she said. She laced her fingers at her waist between her stylish skirt and crisp, white blouse. If she was nervous, she didn't show it.

Aubrey and Early looked at one another. "Let's get on to the office with this," Early said.

"If Daddy goes, I go, too." Courtney moved her hands to her hips and thrust one leg forward.

Angela looked to Early.

"Reverend Powell." He gestured the man forward.

"No," Courtney screamed loud enough for every class in the vicinity to hear. "My daddy is a leader in our town. If he wants to come into our class, he can."

"Let's go, Courtney," Angela said authoritatively, though inwardly she felt close to collapse.

The girl glared at her with fierce determination. "I'm staying with my father," she said. She stamped her foot the way a preschooler, not yet accountable, might do.

Angela turned on her heels and went into her classroom, closing the door firmly behind her. She had twenty minutes left to get into Act II of *Hamlet*. To consider, along with Hamlet's anguish over his hesitancy, Polonius's self-absorbed decision to use his own daughter to gain information about Hamlet.

60

Chapter 10

Hazel Smalls

Rhona was waiting outside the door at sixth period study hall. Her mouth opened like a bird's about to warble when she saw Hazel coming up the hall.

"Hey Rhona, wha's up? Watch out, or something will fly in there," Hazel said and grinned. It was the only time they saw each other during the day and Hazel looked forward to it.

"Girl, you shoulda seen what I seen from English class last period."

"Yeah?" Hazel glided past Rhona toward her assigned seat.

"I don't have time to tell it all before the bell," she said, trailing Hazel's heels. "Let's see can we get some library passes, so I can tell you all what you won't believe. And you got to pay attention."

"Got it." Hazel looked curiously at her excited friend.

"Tell Mr. Bodyguard that we're working on a research project together in US History. He likes you better."

Hazel rolled her eyes. "No, he doesn't. You better raise your hand, too." Mr. Bodyguard was a middle-aged Spanish teacher whose real name was Mr. Monty. He manned their study hall like the old troll under the bridge in *The Three Billy Goats Gruff.* Nobody better speak a word after the bell, and nobody went anywhere unless you produced a teacher pass to somewhere important. If a kid sounded desperate, Mr. Monty would sometimes, grudgingly, allow a pass to the bathroom. There was one exception: if a girl uttered the phrase "female trouble," he scratched out his name on a pass as fast as the ink could spread on paper.

As always, after roll call, Mr. Monty asked for a show of hands of those wanting a pass to the library. There was a limit of six and who got to go was Mr. Monty's whim. Hazel and Rhona lifted their arms, along with a dozen others. Hazel played air trumpet with her fingers, a little trick for getting noticed. Sure enough, Mr. Bodyguard pointed to her, and she used her sweetest voice to say she and Rhona needed to look up information on the Spanish flu pandemic for a history project. He flicked his hand dismissively, meaning they could both go.

Rhona darted her eyes at Hazel as if to say, how had she come up with that crazy topic. But Hazel didn't think it was a crazy topic. She wondered why Mrs. Clyburn didn't even mention the disease when they'd studied World War I in US History a couple of weeks ago.

A textbook photo of nurses wearing masks, tending to sick people on cots, had caught Hazel's attention. The caption said fifty million people around the world died of the Spanish flu. That was a lot more people than soldiers who died in the war. Reading about poor people living close together and dying in city slums made her grateful she wasn't living then.

"You don't like my topic?" Hazel asked as they exited study hall.

"No. It's morbid." Rhona stuck out her tongue. Hazel shrugged in response.

"You should be in the smart classes the way you're always studying all this stuff," Rhona continued. "Anyway, I got something more for you to worry about than people who died a long time ago." Hazel stared.

"Come on, I'll tell you while we walk." They moved slowly to give Rhona time to tell her story because Mrs. Perry in the library was a control freak like Mr. Monty. No talking in that wrinkled-up, flat scarecrow's jurisdiction, though if you could snag a study carrel, you could sometimes pull two chairs in close and whisper without being caught.

"There was a fight between Mr. Moore and a parent in the hall last period," Rhona started.

"Girl, that's trash. Teachers and parents don't fistfight," Hazel countered. She reached down to retie one of her Nike sneakers, nearly new and her exact size. Normally, most of her cleaning money went to help with rent, especially after her daddy got fired. But at Christmas, her mama said to keep her money and buy what she wanted. In addition to the Nikes from Goodwill, she'd bought a bunch of novels for a dollar each that her father complained crowded up the motel room. Her splurge had been a small butterfly tattoo—it hadn't hurt that bad—on her ankle.

"Well, there *was* today," Rhona said. "Quit messing with your shoe

62

and let me tell it." Hazel looked up. "A bunch of boys were packed into the doorway to watch, but I squeezed in at the end and saw this moon-faced dude reach around behind himself and hit Mr. Moore across his face." Hazel straightened and raised her eyebrows.

"I'm not making it up. I swear. I think it was 'cause Mr. Moore was trying to help Ms. Wilmore. I didn't see the beginning, like I told you, but afterward the boys talked about this guy who was all about himself demanding to sit in Ms. Wilmore's class, and she said no because he had to have permission from Mr. Copeland. The SOB wouldn't take no for an answer."

"Who is he?" Hazel asked.

"This is the main part you got to know because it involves that boy you like."

Hazel stopped stone still. "You mean Sterling?" She grabbed Rhona's arm.

"We can't get caught dawdling," Rhona said, removing Hazel's hand. "Put it in slow mo and keep walking."

"Tell me," Hazel said, her feet barely moving.

"I'm trying to. So here comes Officer Tidwell and Mr. Jenkins up the hall asking questions, and the man says he has permission to go into Ms. Wilmore's room, but Officer Tidwell ain't hearing it. Says they're going to the office. When all of a sudden, out into the hall, here comes that cheerleader who is Sterling's girlfriend."

"Courtney?"

"Uh, yeah, that's his girlfriend, right?" Rhona said sarcastically. "I told you not to mess with that boy. You'd better stay clear," she warned.

Hazel stopped again, and Rhona took hold of her wrist. "Come on. I'm almost finished," she said, pulling Hazel along.

"She hollered out her daddy was a pillar or something like that. Anyway, what she meant was he could do what he wanted. She pranced off to the office behind him in a big scene."

"What's it got to do with me?" Hazel asked feebly, because she knew what Rhona would say. They were nearing the double glass doors of the library.

"These are rich people, Zell. Whatever they want, they get. You keep messing with Sterling and that girl finds out, she will chew you up and spit you out."

"I think Sterling likes me," Hazel said.

"Well, he can like you all he wants in secret, but you think he's going to protect you against that bitch? Reality check, Zell. Not gonna happen."

They checked into the library and wound around bookshelves to the back where Rhona set her books in a carrel. She gestured to Hazel to do the same and pulled up a second chair.

But Hazel shook her head. She didn't want to hear anymore. She wanted her heart to stop fluttering rapid fire. She wanted to sit by herself and think. Rhona raised her shoulders in a "what the hell" motion. Hazel ignored her and walked back to the common area to sit in one of the cushioned chairs supposed to make the library look inviting.

Funny how if you didn't know a person you never noticed him, but once you did you saw him all the time. She wasn't a fool. She saw Sterling walking with his girlfriend when he didn't see her. So why had he chased her around the motel?

His popular, beautiful girlfriend had every opportunity in the world, and Hazel had next to none. What did he want? Still, she couldn't stop reliving the night at Marelli's, especially in the parking lot. It was likely Hazel's inexperience—staying away from boys because she knew where that got you—that made the night with Sterling feel perfect.

Rhona appeared suddenly, plopping into a cushiony chair across from her, a copy of *Essence* magazine flopping into her lap. "You mad at me?" she mouthed.

"Why would I be mad at you?" Hazel mimed back.

"'Cause you took off after I told you," she whispered, holding the magazine beside her face.

"I don't want to talk about it. Nothing else you can say."

"I thought you should know."

"Shhh," came Mrs. Perry's hiss from the front desk. Rhona started flipping pages. Hazel rose to get a magazine from the rack. They sat, magazines in front of their faces, until the time came to return to study hall five minutes before the bell.

"Hey, I'm just the messenger who's got your back," Rhona said outside the library doors, taking a running air jump, twisting around to land in front of Hazel.

"Look," Hazel said, pointing down the hall.

They gaped at the couple turning the corner, maybe fifty feet ahead: Courtney Powell and a moon-faced man with a thick head of very black hair, just like Rhona described.

"I told you," Rhona said.

Chapter 11

Sterling Lovell

Sterling was in awe of Ms. Wilmore's composure. She returned from the fiasco in the hall acting like it was a normal class day. Even with everyone twitching in their seats, dying for an explanation, she started into the second scene of *Hamlet*, Act II.

Sterling liked the short stories they'd studied the first few weeks of the semester, but the next couple of months would be longer works—especially important for the final essay prompt on the AP exam, Ms. Wilmore said, because it required analysis of an aspect of a novel or a play. Sterling was surprised how he'd gotten into *Hamlet*, but right now it was hard to concentrate.

He kept seeing Courtney flounce into the hall, leading lady in her own play, all to stay on her father's good side. He understood it was hard for her to be this man's daughter, to have every moment of her life scrutinized by his narrow standards. Sterling felt for her. But she knew her father was wrong. Of course she did. Yet she had callously undermined Ms. Wilmore.

Okay, so Courtney would say he wasn't any better. Not with the prank the guys pulled to overtake class discussion that day. And she'd be right. But he wouldn't do it again. And it wasn't just the humiliation of ISS. After all, something really good had come from it. He'd met Hazel. No, it was something about Ms. Wilmore. She didn't just know her stuff. She knew students, and she stuck to her beliefs. Hell, she was fearless.

"Sterling, are you there?" Ms. Wilmore asked. "You've been staring at the ceiling for quite some time." Yeah, she'd just called him out, dammit. But her tone wasn't pissed. It was concerned.

"Sorry," he said.

"How about you read Hamlet's soliloquy at the end of this scene?

Then we'll discuss it."

"Okay, right. Sure."

"We'll wait on you to find the place." She tapped her fingers lightly on her lectern.

"Gotcha, thanks," he responded, flipping to the end of the scene. "Sorry," he said again.

He'd done his reading homework and knew the speech. The hero's torment over his continued inability to avenge his father's death.

Sterling read with intensity, the poor prince down on himself for his lack of resolve. He was feeling Hamlet. Midway, though, he caught on the lines, "Am I a coward? / Who calls me villain? breaks my pate across?" and broke his stride. Ms. Wilmore cleared her throat, prompting him forward. He picked up, his voice more buoyant as Hamlet's mood lifted in the final lines of the soliloquy, the young prince confidently declaring he would uncover "the conscience of the king."

"Thank you, Sterling. I do believe you could have a future in performance," his teacher said.

"Don't you know it. We'll be seeing our man Sterling on Broadway," Kipp sang out. The class laughed.

"That will do, Kipling," Ms. Wilmore said.

Sterling looked up from his anthology, his head swimmy. Not from dramatic exertion. He felt what Hamlet felt. Not just acting but for real. He wasn't being true. Part of his anger toward Courtney was wanting to see Hazel. Admit it. He couldn't get that girl who lived at the Red Rose Motel out of his head.

***

At the end of the day, Sterling made a dash for Courtney's seventh period class to catch her before she left. He didn't have a plan, but he had to say something after what happened today. He arrived at her AP Psych class out of breath.

"Hey buddy, looking for your girl?" Benny asked, sauntering out, saluting to someone behind him as he exited. Bennett Bolin was a member of the pack, but he and Sterling didn't have a single class together this semester. Mr. Oliver had outdone himself keeping their crowd separated, except for putting four of them in Ms. Wilmore's fifth period.

"Yeah, guess I missed her," Sterling said, heaving.

"Nope, she was never here in the first place."

"She didn't come to class?"

"Not today. You break a record running the hall?"

Sterling gave Benny a look. "What?" Benny threw up his hands and laughed. "You worried she's cutting out on you?" He could be a jerk when he wanted to.

"Obviously word hasn't reached you. You should keep your damn ears open," Sterling shot back. He was taking out his frustration on Benny, which was stupid.

"Cool down. I was just messing with you. What word?"

"Courtney's old man tried to sit in on our class fifth period. Ms. Wilmore wouldn't let him in."

"That English teacher has balls."

"It got ugly. He smacked Mr. Moore in the face."

"Back up. You said Ms. Wilmore," Bennett interrupted.

"Mr. Moore was trying to help her keep Reverend Powell out of her classroom. It ended up with Jenkins and Officer Tidwell *escorting* him to the office. But before that, Courtney came out into the hall and created a big spectacle. She went with them to the office."

"Whoa," Bennett remarked. "I'm guessing Courtney left school early with the Reverend?"

"I guess," Sterling said. He felt deflated. He'd been ready to confront her before he cooled off. Now, it would be harder. Instead of reacting in the moment, the easy way, he'd have to think it through. And he didn't know what that meant.

***

Courtney got to him first. Her text arrived as he was climbing into his Audi to leave school. "Need to talk. Now."

"Where?" he texted back.

"Anywhere but my house. It's hell here." Sterling felt himself softening toward Courtney, thinking of her father's anger.

"Fantastic Franks?" he asked.

"No, alone. I'll meet you at Wylie Park in about ten minutes."

The public park—mostly kids' playground equipment and a couple of basketball hoops, some ancient shuffleboard courts—was around the corner from school, so Sterling arrived first. On a cold day like this, the park was mostly empty. He hoisted himself into a swing and pumped, feet pointed to the sky, considering the day's drama, when he saw Courtney's silver Camry pull onto the gravel parking lot. He dragged his feet in the soft dirt beneath the swing. He jumped out but walked slowly as she approached.

She reached out her arms and hugged him, resting her head on his chest. He hugged her back, but his body felt stiff. He was sure she could feel it, even through layers of coats, because she pulled away and looked at him funny. He pointed at a picnic table close by. He sat across from her.

"My father is a monster," she said. "I can't take it."

"I know, and I'm sorry. So why do you defend him?" He rubbed his hands together against the cold.

"Duh, to survive. I'm defending me," she said.

"You're doing it at the expense of innocent people," Sterling said. His heart suddenly pumped up high in his throat, like he'd run a 100-yard dash. Like he felt when he took it out on Benny. "Your father put Ms. Wilmore through hell, and then you come running out to hold his hand."

"I didn't come here for you to feel sorry for Ms. Wilmore," Courtney shrieked. "What am I supposed to do? He's my freakin' father." Her voice went up an octave.

"Freakin' is right. He was freaking out, and you supported his show. The world doesn't revolve around you, Courtney. Your parents have absurd expectations, but that's about it, isn't it? Okay. So my parents are demanding too, if differently. But you—both of us—have everything else." He was all of a sudden thinking about Hazel, who was basically homeless.

"How can you say that after what I went through today?" The nostrils of her perfect, pert nose flared.

"Your father embarrassed you. Hell, I'm embarrassed for you. But it doesn't excuse the scene you made. It's selfish, Courtney." He took a breath, leaned back into air from his straight position on the picnic bench, waiting, hoping he'd gotten through.

He remembered when Grace Church was a small building vacated by a dry cleaning business. Then, the membership hired Reverend Powell, and the congregation grew faster than kudzu. The new building was a flamboyant structure out on the interstate, its large marquee flashing platitudes. To become a member you had to agree to tithe.

His family attended the old Episcopal church where it would be vulgar for their rector to demand church members pledge a certain amount. Didn't matter. Donations freely given could be tainted, too. His own father was a prime example. Hugh Lovell was a stellar member of St. Luke's, their church, but he was a slum lord, too; his contributions came in part from the misfortune of others. It dawned on Sterling: both their fathers were double-dealers.

"You're a frigging hypocrite. You know that?" Courtney's shrill observation jerked him back to the moment. "I came here to confide in you. For comfort. And what do you do? You tell me *I'm* selfish when you and your friends have been terrorizing teachers since we were kids?"

"This isn't about me right now," he said, realizing he hadn't gotten through to her at all. She was too upset about herself.

"Oh, hell, yes, it is. You're so righteous. I pale in comparison to what you've done."

"True," he agreed, solemn. "True."

"And while we're onto true, I'd like to know about the trailer trash you walk around in the halls with."

A lump of air caught between Sterling's ribs. The pain was like a lit match searing his chest.

"Well?" she asked. She stared at him, her eyes blue crystal, nearly see-through. "Madison saw you with her before first period one day last week when she went in early to make up a French test."

His chest hurt. He took several deep breaths in an attempt to release the pressure. "You mean Zell?" He tried to make his voice sound flat.

"I don't know her name, Sterling. I only know that Madison told me she saw you in the hall with a hick girl she recognized from gym class. Tell me this is part of a Key Club project."

"Zell isn't a part of any project," he said.

"Then what?" Courtney pushed up the sleeves of her expensive jacket. He stared at the cream-colored material bunching into pillowy bubbles at her elbows, at her patrician beauty.

"I met her in ISS. She's a nice girl who has a really tough life." He was relieved to have it out.

"ISS? Are you kidding me? Why would you walk the halls with some girl you met in ISS?"

"I feel for her," Sterling sputtered.

"You *feel* for her? What does that mean?" Courtney howled. A couple of young mothers who'd arrived with their bundled-up kids—taking turns on the sliding board—looked toward them.

"I'm not sure what it means," he said.

"You're not sure?" Courtney demanded. The mothers looked their way again.

"I don't know her very well, but I know she's super smart and deserves a chance." His voice was more even now, his breath miraculously slowing.

"Since when did you become a savior?"

"You can call it what you want, Courtney. She's a lovely person with a hard life."

"A lovely person with a hard life. Oh goodness, me." Courtney cocked her head. She placed her snow-white hands—the right one adorned with the opal ring he had given her for Christmas—on the rough wood of the picnic table.

"It's hard to…," Sterling started.

Courtney's face crumpled. But if he thought she was about to cry, he was wrong. The sharp in her voice could shred the browned winter grass blades at their feet. "You know what, Sters? I have an idea. Enjoy your destitute girl. I'll solve my problems without you."

"Courtney, come on."

"Courtney, nothing," she stopped him. "I needed you. But turns out you aren't the person I thought I knew." She removed his opal ring with the little diamond twinkling in the middle and laid it on the peeling red paint of the picnic table. She stood. He stood, too.

"Wait. Let's talk," he said as she walked away, her full hips rolling beneath her tight jeans. "Come back." But even as he spoke to her re-treating figure, he wasn't sure he wanted her to come back.

"The talking is over," she called over her shoulder, resolute, as she walked away. Though Sterling was sure her voice trembled.

He sat again at the picnic table. He lowered his face into his cold hands. They'd been together for so long, and then all this…how was he supposed to…? He stopped his thoughts and stood. He picked up the ring, jammed it in his pocket, and left.

Chapter 12

Angela Wilmore

After fifth period left, Angela put her head on her desk and breathed deeply. Thankfully, with Judson's assistance, school security, and administration, Donovan Powell had been prevented from entering her classroom. And she had managed—she hoped—to conduct class efficiently. But she was mentally and physically exhausted from the effort.

In five minutes, she was due in sixth period senior study hall, a privilege for those with a GPA above 3.0, in a repurposed two-level room jumbled with donated sofas and lumpy upholstered chairs, along with a ping-pong table and six desks housing aged desktop computers downstairs. Overlooking this area was a space outfitted with a desk and computer for the supervising teacher.

Senior study hall was the easiest duty on campus. Angela's only requirement was to take roll at the beginning of class, which she did by leaning over the railing and calling down to the teeming bodies below, then return five minutes before the bell to take roll again to make sure all were accounted for.

In between, she ran campus errands or caught up on her work at the desk upstairs. She rarely ventured into the midst of these seniors lounging, playing games, and occasionally studying, but she could often overhear myriad student conversations. The acoustics of the open space caused sound to travel easily upward.

She had barely opened her textbook to prepare study questions for Act III of *Hamlet* when bits and pieces of her previous class hour came floating up. She leaned toward the rail and strained to hear voices distinctly.

"Ms. Wilmore didn't take any crap." She caught a high-pitched female voice. Was that Bonnie Henderson from fifth period? It surely sounded like her. Angela peeked over the rail to see if she could tell, but she couldn't. She sat back out of sight and continued listening.

"Wonder what Mr. Copeland did?" came another.

"Hope he told Reverend Powell to take a hike." A heavy male voice. She knew it all too well. It had to be Alex.

"Cut him a break. He just wanted to know what's going on." Another male. She was tempted to lean over again—determine who the challenger was—but didn't. If the students saw her, they would stop.

"Sure, he's a preacher," came a distinct response. Another dissenter.

"More like a pretender." Alex again, she thought.

Were all the voices students from her fifth period? Maybe. Because there were several more besides Alex and Bonnie in this senior study hall. But word traveled fast in the halls at Ramsey High, and likely a lot of kids already knew some version of the story by now.

Angela tried to force herself into *Hamlet*, Polonius's lines as he arranges to eavesdrop on a conversation between Hamlet and Ophelia. Later, Polonius will meet his end by listening secretly to the conversation between Hamlet and Gertrude. Okay. This wasn't working. She was not like sneaky Polonius. Stop listening to the students' gossip, she told herself. Write out your study questions, and be done. But she couldn't concentrate. She was too restless.

What she needed to do, she decided, was thank Finley Copeland for keeping Donovan Powell out of her classroom today. She closed her book, picked up her purse, and headed for the office.

"Is he available?" Angela asked gingerly—Beverly Bagley could be moody—as she pushed through the little swinging door beside the office counter into the administrative assistant's area.

"Yeah, he's in there. Go ahead." She pointed behind her toward the principal's office. "Some parents just left. Look to see if he's on the phone before you knock." Ms. Bagley didn't look up. She was filing a thumbnail with a slim emery board. She was having a good day.

"Thank you," Angela said and proceeded around the corner where she peeked through the small rectangle of glass above the doorknob, same as in all the classroom doors. Finley appeared to be staring into space. She knocked.

"Yes?" he called.

"It's Angela Wilmore. May I come in?"

"Yes, oh yes, Ms. Wilmore—Angela—you are on my mind." He stood when she entered.

"Please, sit," he said, and when she did, he sat also. They looked at each other.

"It's my senior study hall period, so I had some time," Angela started. "I wanted to tell you how much I appreciate what…"

"It was a bad predicament," Finley said, then stopped. "Sorry, didn't mean to interrupt."

"It was pretty awful," Angela agreed. She smoothed her hands along her skirt, crossed her legs at the ankles. "I've never been attacked like that. But then I've mostly been in the college classroom where, by law, parents aren't even allowed access to students' grades."

"Right," Finley said. "What happened today hasn't happened in my career as an administrator either. Between you and me, Reverend Powell seemed unhinged. He was hell-bent to sit in your classroom."

"Thank you for keeping him out," Angela said.

"It wouldn't surprise me for him to sic a lawyer on the school."

"Oh, no, I hope not," Angela sat up straighter, put a hand to her forehead.

"I shouldn't have said that. Please, excuse me." Finley leaned forward over his desk. "Don't worry. He won't have a leg to stand on. The rules for classroom visits are clearly outlined in the student/parent handbook by our district's attorney."

Angela was a tough-skinned teacher. Why did she suddenly feel her nose burning and her eyes getting full? She glanced down and rubbed her index fingers along the bridge of her nose. Finley stood and walked around his desk toward her. He put his hand on her shoulder. She jumped a bit.

"Would you like for me to get a sub for your last class today?"

"No, no, I'm fine," she said. She looked up into Finley's kind face. He removed his hand. He cleared his throat.

"As I told you before," he said, "you won't be meeting with Donovan Powell or his wife again."

"Back to my reason for coming unannounced," Angela said, rolling her shoulders back. She took a deep breath. "Thank you, again, for standing up for me today. Before I came to teach in high school this fall,

I heard horror stories of how public school administrators kowtow to parents and students."

"Not in this school. By God, not under my watch. I won't let you be railroaded," he erupted. Angela sat up straighter. She obviously wasn't the only one in a state. In that moment she felt a deeply human response for this man she knew only as a composed administrator. His fury calmed her. They were aligned in response to a Ramsey student's errant father.

Quickly, Finley's tone softened and his professionalism returned. "I'm glad you came by, Angela. From all that I see, you are an excellent English teacher. It is my job to have your back so that you can educate your students. Certainly, I listen to parent grievances and to students, but teachers are the lifeblood of education, innocent until proven guilty. And you are in no way guilty."

"I'm fortunate to have your support," Angela responded, matching his calm tone.

"I'm fortunate to have you on my staff," Finley said. He folded his arms across his chest, but too tautly, contradicting his composure and inadvertently trapping his necktie so that it pulled tight at his neck. Instinctively, Angela reached over and loosened the material—navy blue with pale red dots—from his grasp.

"Don't want you to choke," she said and smiled. Finley released his arms.

"Would you...," Finley started and stopped. Angela watched his right thumb slide nervously back and forth across the fingers of his left hand. "I could use a drink. Would you maybe want to meet at Junie's Bar and Grill later? Talk it out?"

Angela blinked in astonishment. She had not socialized with any man since Randal's death, going on three years. She'd had no inclination. But more than that; it was who the man was, her principal. What little she knew of Finley's personal life came from the grapevine. He was divorced. His wife had run off last year with a young man in his thirties. Finley and his former wife shared custody of their son, Scott—a middle schooler. Finley couldn't be older than mid-forties himself, and she was fifty-three.

"I...um...do you think?" she started, suddenly realizing she would very much like to relax over a glass of wine at Junie's, but not knowing what she should actually do. Would being off campus with her principal be against school policy?

"We've both been through hell today, but perhaps it's best not?" he interrupted her, stammering.

"No....I—," Angela began again. "I'd like to, I mean, if it's all okay."

"I see nothing wrong with two educators having a conversation in a public space to discuss a difficult situation," he said calmly, though Angela noted both his hands were jammed into his pants pockets, one of them jingling change.

***

Angela considered her impulsive decision as she pulled out of the teachers' parking lot in her Beetle. She'd bought the car new in the fall, impractical, of course, but she loved it. Yesterday, she'd put a fresh daisy from the grocery in the vase attached to the dash. A bright touch on a cold day. Once a child of the sixties, always a child of the sixties, she thought and accelerated. No point in second-guessing.

She didn't see Finley when she arrived, so she wandered to a table near the back, ordered a glass of the house Chardonnay. She'd never been of the mindset that wintertime meant you had to drink red.

She was halfway reading a review on her phone of *The Marriage Plot*, a novel Dianne had recommended, when a shadow glanced across her screen. She looked up to see Finley, without his tie, his white dress shirtsleeves rolled up.

"Had a call," he said, shaking his head. "The district office, so I had to take it. Sorry. Another discussion with Dr. Hoffman in curriculum about Common Core Standards. It's making everyone crazy."

"It is," Angela agreed, recalling the recent English Department meeting where everyone complained about Common Core's emphasis on informational texts over poetry and fiction. "The standards seem too much about rote skill instead of analysis and imagination, at least in the English curriculum," she said.

"May I quote you on that?" Finley asked.

"Sure, but whatever the state decides we have to do, right? Until the next thing comes along?" She was a newbie at the business of state standards, but she was learning fast from frustrated fellow English teachers.

"Right. Accept and carry on. Still, it doesn't hurt to speak out." Finley huffed and sat. "What are you drinking?"

"I ordered a glass of wine, but it hasn't arrived," Angela said, pointing to the empty tabletop.

"I'll run up to the bar, order a beer and check on your wine."

"Thank you," she called as Finley sped off.

He arrived back quickly, a glass of beer in one hand and her wine in the other. "It's all good."

"It's all good? You sound like the kids." She laughed.

"It rubs off on you." Finley set the glass of wine, fogged with chill, in front of her.

"Here's to surviving a difficult day." He raised his beer. Angela clinked her glass against his. Then she took a long sip. The wine was very cold, the way she liked it.

***

After two Bud Lights for Finley and two pours of Chardonnay for Angela, they agreed the day's fiasco was as much in control as could be.

"I'm looking forward to the weekend to rest," she said, spooning cheddar Goldfish into her hand from the bowl the waitress delivered. She was feeling mellow.

"You deserve the respite," he said.

"Tell me how you got to Ramsey," she said suddenly. Finley raised his eyebrows and drank.

Angela asked again.

"Okay, second string tight end at Clemson. Football coach and PE teacher at Sutton High, a small, rural high school in the county."

"Then what?" Angela persisted because he stopped talking.

"Went back to school while I was teaching and coaching. The wife's idea. MEd in Education Leadership at the University of South Carolina." The degree required lots of time and trips to Columbia for two years and hadn't done him many favors in his personal life, he said. He didn't elaborate.

"Oh," she exclaimed. She was definitely feeling uninhibited. Preposterously thinking of ordering another glass.

Finley gave her a bemused grin. "You aren't *that* new on campus. Come on now. You hear the scuttlebutt."

Angela nodded. "True confession: I know you're divorced."

"I was busting my butt, making a living as an assistant principal at Ramsey, the last to know my marriage was shot," Finley said, setting his glass on the table. "And that's all we need to say."

"I'm sorry," Angela said, meaning sorry for him and sorry she'd asked.

"Don't be," he responded. "Hey, your glass is empty. Hold on. We need to raise a toast."

"We already did."

"We need another," he called back, already halfway to the bar.

"Just a spritzer this time. I have to drive." Angela followed the athletic, inverted triangle of his back. It wasn't just the wine. She was very much enjoying the company of Finley Copeland.

Chapter 13

Hazel Smalls

On Friday night, Hazel sat cross-legged on the double bed where she and Chloe slept, reading a novel Ms. Wilmore had assigned—*Where the Heart Is,* about a pregnant girl named Novalee Nation who secretly takes up residence in a Walmart in Oklahoma after her boyfriend dumps her with no money in the parking lot and takes off. On the surface, the plot sounded bizarre, but Hazel could see it happening.

Chloe, propped back on pillows on the other bed, watched a fantasy film about fairies creating magic to make human lives happy and amazing. Hazel thought her sister would be much better off absorbed in a realistic story like the one she was reading. A story that could teach her things. But Chloe was content—not always the case with her ten-year-old sister—so Hazel was grateful.

Their mother was working her shift at Fields Home, and their father, after so many months, had finally gone back out on the road midweek. He was driving LTL—less than truckload—routes, meaning he probably had a dozen or more drops before he reloaded, dropped again, and came home. He would probably be exhausted and mean when he returned in several days. But for now, all was calm. Maybe, with her father working again, they'd soon move back to an apartment.

After Chloe's movie ended, Hazel looked over to see her sister had fallen asleep. She rolled onto her knees on the too-soft mattress and stepped onto the floor. She leaned over to the other bed, pulled her sister down into the covers, and smoothed her hair. She turned off the lamp and the television and padded to the bathroom, tossing her jeans and sweatshirt into the basket beside the toilet. Naked, she pulled her Disney World t-shirt—softened from many wearings before she bought it—from the hook behind the door.

Hazel lay in bed beside her sister breathing peacefully. Sleep did not come. Instead, the image of Courtney Powell and her stiff father walking down the hall at Ramsey played a loop in her head until the scene Rhona described took over. Reverend Powell fighting with Ms. Wilmore, and his daughter, Sterling's girlfriend, making a show of herself. She tried to dismiss the images by taking deep breaths and concentrating on a dark stain on the ceiling. It didn't work.

Her mind wandered onto what little she knew of Reverend Powell. Everyone in town, rich or poor, knew of his church, a huge, sprawling place out on the interstate, the steeple at night surrounded in bands of light that glowed yellow like a hovering UFO. It was a sight to behold. Reverend Powell must be very rich, and she hadn't known rich people, especially preachers, could make fools of themselves and get in trouble.

She heard her mama open the outside door. Hazel glanced over at the alarm clock: nearly 1:00 am. "You can turn on the light. I'm awake, and Chloe is dead out," she called.

Hazel saw her mama move in the shadows, taking off her coat, unwrapping her red head scarf, bending down to untie her shoes.

"Are you tired?" Hazel asked. Chloe turned over suddenly, her body twisting sideways and bumping Hazel to the edge of the bed.

"Not too bad. Shh." Her mother pointed at Chloe and put a finger to her lips.

A few minutes later, Etta was breathing softly in the other bed, her dark brown arms twined together. Hazel looked at the alarm clock for the last time around 2:00 am.

***

"Wake up, Zell, wake up." Chloe was shaking her shoulders. "It's snowing. Really. Look out the window."

Hazel felt her teeth rattling. She reached out to block her sister's arms. "Okay, okay, give me a minute, girl," she sputtered.

"It's piling up on the cars," Chloe squealed. "You and Mama need to get up and see," she shrieked again.

"What time is it?" Hazel asked, sitting up in bed.

"It's already eight o'clock, look"—Chloe turned the clock toward her—"but you don't know it because there's dark gray clouds outside.

Full of snow! Falling everywhere!" Chloe stood at the edge of the bed, springing up and down on the balls of her feet.

Hazel groaned from lack of sleep, though the idea of snow was beginning to energize her, too. "Come on, come on," Chloe urged.

"Let me pee," Hazel told her sister.

"Hurry up." Chloe danced in circles while Hazel limped, her legs not quite awake, to the bathroom.

When she returned, Hazel glanced over at their mother still asleep, or at least pretending to be.

Hazel pulled up the curtains and peered out. The cracked pavement of the parking lot with its beat-up cars and broken fencing was gone. There were no crumpled cigarette packs or empty potato chip bags covering the browned grass. Everything, everywhere, was covered in a spotless, white mantle.

Hazel sucked in her breath. "What did I tell you," Chloe exclaimed.

"It's so beautiful," Hazel said and turned toward her sister. "It hasn't snowed like this since I was little. It used to snow like this in Ramsey, 'cause we're near the mountains. But not for a long time."

"Let's go outside," Chloe said, tugging on her sister's arm.

"Sure, okay." But what would they do for boots? The snow looked at least six inches deep, maybe more. How had it fallen so fast? Hazel recalled a particular snow when she was ten like Chloe was now. They'd lived in an apartment, and kids were everywhere in the street playing. The girls built snow forts and lobbed snowballs over the top at the boys on the block. Hazel hadn't owned a sled, but she'd slid down their hilly street over and over on a pizza pan. It snowed for a week. The grownups built bonfires every night at the top of the hill.

Chloe opened the door. A blast of icy air poured in. "Whoo," she said. "It's super cold."

"Let's eat first," Hazel suggested, walking back from the window to the little area they called a kitchen. It consisted of a microwave, a tiny fridge, and a shelf her father nailed up. She pulled the box of Frosted Flakes and two bowls from the shelf and opened the fridge for milk. From the narrow drawer below the microwave that housed both silverware and her mother's underwear, she retrieved two spoons.

Chloe stuffed in mouthfuls of wet cereal. "Slow down, or you'll be sick," Hazel warned.

Minutes later, what with Chloe's commotion of rummaging in the dresser drawers for gloves and a hat, their mother had fully roused. "What in the world, little girl? You're a whirling dervish," she said and yawned.

"What is whirling dervo?" Chloe chirped.

"It's like you're a spinning top." Etta sat up, put her hands to her temples.

"It's snowing. We're going outside to play," Chloe yelped.

"I gathered as much," Etta exclaimed.

"We need boots," Hazel said.

"Are there still some Ziploc bags on the shelf?"

Hazel nodded.

"Put them on your feet and tighten them with a rubber band."

"Yay," Chloe squealed. Hazel cringed at the thought of bags on her feet.

Outside, though, she forgot her embarrassment when she turned her face to the sky to feel the tingling fat flakes touch her cheeks and forehead. Chloe darted about. It seemed every kid at the motel had come out to play. Hazel spotted Rhona approaching, toting a cookie sheet. "It works. Watch," Rhona said. She plunked her butt onto the pan and took off spinning down a little crest into the nearby parking lot.

"Let me try. Let me," Chloe called, her bagged feet awkwardly clomping into the snow as she attempted to chase Rhona around the parking lot.

"Okay, little sister, here you go," Rhona said, turning over her cookie sheet. They watched as Chloe spun herself around and around, her legs aloft.

The snow was beautiful and fun, but after a while Hazel's feet were frigid. Plastic bags did little to insulate cloth athletic shoes, even with two pairs of socks. Rhona, on the other hand, wore real boots with fleece lining from her grandmother Lolly's trunk.

"I gotta go in; my feet are freezing," Hazel announced, rubbing her hands around her ankles. "Chloe," she called, "you need to warm up," but her sister had disappeared into some other warren on the property.

"Go on, I'll watch out for her," Rhona said.

***

"My feet are ice blocks," Chloe said when she finally returned, nearly an hour after Hazel came in. "And my fingers are frozen together."

"Here," Etta said, pulling off Chloe's thin gloves. "Run your hands under hot water."

"I need warmer clothes," Chloe whined.

"Don't we all," their mother answered. "Let's fix somethin' warm for lunch." She walked to the shelf and retrieved two cans of chicken noodle soup, popped the tops, and poured the contents into a plastic bowl to heat in the microwave.

The snow kept falling. Sitting at the folding card table, swallowing the steaming soup, they watched the noon weather report: a depth of ten inches and piling higher. The temperature was predicted to fall into the low twenties that night, and the snow would continue.

"No school on Monday," Chloe slurped as she spoke.

"Probably not," their mother considered as they watched the local weatherman—bundled in a heavy plaid overcoat and fur-lined hat with earflaps—report from the square in the middle of town. "It snowed like this every winter when I was a girl."

"Did you have a sled and go down hills?" Chloe asked.

"My grandfather built us a sled long enough to hold four people. We rubbed paraffin on the runners to make it go fast," Etta said.

"Where is it now? The sled?"

"Gone," their mother said, her voice dark and wistful.

A sharp knocking, four quick repetitions, sounded at the door. Etta looked quizzically at her daughters. Hazel stood and approached the door.

"Yes?" Hazel called, thinking it was probably Rhona, but they never opened the door without knowing who was there.

"Hey, yeah, Hazel, it's me, Sterling. It's cold out here; may I come in?" he cried out. Hazel stiffened.

"Who is Sterling? Do you know him?" Etta asked, setting her spoon into her bowl.

"He's a boy I go to school with," Hazel answered.

"Then let him in. Does he live here? Don't let him freeze," her mother said, forceful.

Startled by her mother's vehemence, Hazel opened the door without thinking.

"Well, hi there," Sterling said from the other side, stamping snow from his boots.

"I…don't…," Hazel started.

"I apologize for turning up this way. I tried to call, but your telephone isn't working. I got your room number at the desk." Sterling stepped inside, pulling off a stocking cap. It and he looked very warm, in spite of his exclamation about the cold.

"A rat or a squirrel chewed through the line," Chloe announced. "They supposed to fix it."

"Hush," Hazel said, glaring at her sister.

"Ah, that explains it," Sterling said, removing his fleece-lined gloves and shoving them into his coat pockets. "Are you…?"

"I'm Chloe," Chloe said from the table. "Who are you?"

"I'm Sterling Lovell. I go to school with your sister. We're friends." Chloe raised her eyebrows into high arcs.

Hazel felt her face burning hot.

"I couldn't resist coming by, what with all this great snow," Sterling declared. "Maybe you'd like to go sledding, Zell?"

"I can't do that," she answered, involuntarily looking down at her feet.

"Why?"

"Scaredy-cat, scaredy-cat," Chloe taunted.

"Hush," Hazel hissed at her sister.

"Chloe, get busy with something," Etta said, rising. "Zell ain't scared of sledding."

Hazel looked at her mother in amazement. Had she forgotten there were no boots?

"Nice to meet you, Mrs. Smalls," Sterling said, extending his hand to her mother. In her shock Hazel had forgotten to introduce her.

"It's nice to meet you, too," Etta said, formal-like, then turned to Hazel. "Go on out and have a good time."

"Bundle up. Let's go," Sterling said.

Hazel looked again at her socked feet. She didn't speak. Her mother had disappeared into the closet at the back of the room. Mostly it held jackets and shoes and cardboard boxes full of junk.

"Have you been out yet?" Sterling asked, drumming his fingers on his chest. She felt sorry for him because he felt nervous. But it was his fault for coming here.

"Look what I found," Etta announced, ducking her head back out of the closet. She held up a pair of short, plastic see-through boots.

"What are those?" Hazel asked, forgetting for a split second that Sterling was in the room and could see what she saw, too.

"These are galoshes," her mother said.

"Ga la who?"

"They fit over your shoes to keep them dry. Here, try them on." Etta dangled the boots. Hazel thought she would die of embarrassment.

"I can't go with you," Hazel said to Sterling. "I'm not…"

"Of course you can. Put these on. They're one of a kind." He reached over and accepted the galoshes from Hazel's mother. The brittle, yellowed plastic crunched in his hands. "Cinderella's glass slippers," he announced.

Hazel sucked in her breath. She shook her head.

"Come on," he pressed.

Hazel pulled on her sneakers. "I'll be okay wearing these," she said.

"Nope, your feet will get wet." Sterling held out the left boot. Mortified, she grabbed it.

"Push your shoe into it," her mother said. Hazel scowled at her but thrust her shoe inside the plastic boot. "What'd I tell you? Pull that little strap around the button to make it tight."

"Now for the other." Sterling held out the right boot, just like he was Prince Charming or something.

"Where you going?" Etta asked, because of course her mother could tell he didn't stay around here. "You come in a car? It's not safe to drive."

"No worries, Mrs. Smalls. I'm in my father's all-wheel-drive truck. It's made for snow."

"Well, okay. I sure can't drive to work in all this, not on my bald tires, but if Elysian Fields sends someone to fetch me, I'll have to go,"

Etta said. "So you be home before 4:00 for Chloe," she told Hazel.

"I'll have her back in time," Sterling promised.

Hazel marveled at this handsome, confident boy, smiling now as he pulled his wool cap back down over his head. Even if she'd had the right clothes—instead of only a black fleece parka with a furry-lined hood and orange-striped gloves that looked like they belonged to a clown, not to mention the antique galoshes—she'd wasn't at all sure she should go. She was being swept along like the snow piling up against the door.

Sterling opened the passenger side of the enormous truck, and Hazel stepped one foot up. Her plastic boot slipped on the running board. "Whoa, there you go," he said, helping hoist her onto the seat.

"Headed to the country club," he said, climbing into the driver's side. "The golf course has the best hills around. And no cars."

"Will there be other people?" Hazel's right hand gripped the door handle.

"Of course. Hello to Zell, buckle up so we can get going."

Her hand didn't move. "You have a girlfriend," she murmured.

"Courtney and I are done."

"Oh," she sputtered.

"Seatbelt?"

"Okay," she answered and pulled the strap across.

***

Sterling drove behind the big front building with tall white columns into a parking spot that faced the golf course. From a distance it looked like heaped-up mounds of vanilla ice cream. She could see little specks on the hills. But it wasn't candy sprinkles on ice cream. It was people sledding, people she didn't know.

"We got this," Sterling hollered, jumping from the truck. Hazel heard the clang of the tailgate opening and shutting.

"Come on, Zell, what you waiting for?" he yelled. His face pressed up to the passenger window, a wooden sled with red runners hooked under one arm.

Slowly, Hazel opened the door and climbed down from the cab. The galoshes crunched snow as she landed. Sterling looped his free arm through hers. They walked toward the dots of people growing bigger with every step.

"Yo, Benny boy, I see you under that toboggan hat. How's the snow?" Sterling called as they approached the crowd.

"Good as it can get," the boy answered. He was tall and thin, even under a puffy jacket. His enormous dark round eyes, poking out from a brown knitted cap that covered his nose and mouth, looked slowly from her face to the horrid galoshes.

"Hey, here, Benny, this is Zell Smalls, my new friend."

"Hel—lo." He winked at Sterling. "I'm Bennett Bolin and pleased to meet you."

"See," Sterling whispered in her ear. "My friends are your friends."

A boy named Kipp walked up. Followed by another named Rich, huffing from climbing to the top of the hill where they stood. She recognized them both from the day in ISS when she met Sterling.

"Let's get going," Sterling announced. "Stand right here, Zell. I'll be back for you in a couple of minutes. One run with the guys." The four boys lined up their sleds at the top of the hill, fell onto their stomachs and shoved off. Hazel stood alone, watching the blur of bodies fly downhill, cruise along the flat white surface at the bottom and finally slide to a stop, almost simultaneously.

Hazel's breath plumed out before her, a silvery cloud caught among the falling flakes. Cold air filled her lungs. It astonished her—all of this—as she watched Sterling pull his sled up the hill where she stood.

"Fantastic," he exclaimed, arriving beside her. "Ready to go?"

Timidly, she nodded.

"All right, you sit in front the first run, and I'll sit behind to guide the sled with my feet. All you have to do is enjoy the flight."

Hazel climbed onto the sled. He jumped on behind and grabbed her around the waist.

"Ready, set, let her rip," he called, balancing his feet on either side of the steering bar, and they were gone. Sledding straight, fast, then curving to slow them a little, but hitting the bottom hard. Sterling hopped off, pushed at her back, then jumped on, so that they sped down another long hill. They stopped finally among a small stand of pine trees where the ground held less snow.

Sterling stood and turned the sled around. "How was it?"

"Wonderful," she said. "I'd forgotten."

"Forgotten?"

"How much fun it is to sled."

"Well, hang on, and I'll pull you back to the top so we can go down again."

"No," she protested. "I'll walk."

"Gentleman's choice; stay put." He held her shoulders when she tried to rise.

Hazel felt like a misfit princess in a winter wonderland.

When they finally returned to their starting point, Sterling bent over and held his knees, out of breath. He tried not to show it, but heavy billows of frozen vapor gave him away. "Guess I'm not Superman," he said.

"I think you are," Hazel said. Sterling grinned.

She was trying not to shiver, but the cold had seeped beneath her flimsy layers. She clamped her teeth to keep them from chattering. Still she shook. Sterling put his arm around her shoulders and pulled her to him. She welcomed his warmth.

"Looky who I see," a female voice exclaimed. "It's Sters and his rescue project."

Sterling dropped his arm and turned to the voice behind him. Hazel didn't turn. She went rigid.

"You got this," Sterling said close to her ear. His hand tightened back around Hazel's shoulder. "Don't let her get to you. It's not about you. It's me she wants to annihilate." Hazel forced herself to turn toward the voice.

"Goodness, Sterling, if you're going to rescue this girl, you need to get her some proper clothes. She must be freezing in that thin parka," Courtney tutted and adjusted her puffer jacket—bright fuchsia—across her torso.

The two other girls giggled.

"Mind your own business, Courtney," Sterling responded, his voice steady.

"Excuse us. Sure thing. Go on about your mission. We came to sled," Courtney said, twisting toward her friends. "But we'd love to know where you bought those darling, see-through boots, Zell. Oh no, wait. We're out of luck, I think. You can only find them on display in the Smithsonian."

The girls walked away, laughing, each pulling a shiny wooden sled.

"Ignore their idiocy," Sterling commanded.

"Damn right," said Bennett, who'd arrived back at the top of the hill during the confrontation. "Girls can be such bitches. Pardon me, Zell. Didn't mean you."

"Screw it, we're here to have fun," Sterling said. "Let's go down horizontal this time. Lie on top of me, Zell. Bend your knees for more momentum."

But all Hazel could think about as they zoomed down was her yellowed galoshes sticking up skyward for all the world to see.

Chapter 14

Sterling Lovell

Zell had been a good sport, but he knew she wanted out of there fast after Courtney showed up to insult her. So he took her quick down the hill, but she'd gone cold. Sterling knew Zell was probably freezing without heavier clothes, but more so because of Courtney's words. Rescue project. Man, it pissed him off. It took him back, too, where he didn't want to go.

Roly Poly—he'd not thought of that name in a very long time, until now at the country club with Zell. Memories of snow days and humiliation seemed a contradiction, only it wasn't. During a big snow back in grade school, the boys on his street made great fun of his size. Let's make Sterling into a big snowball by rolling him down the hill. He'll be Roly Poly. He's already got a good start. Bundled up, they all looked roly poly, but he was the fat kid, and they singled him out.

It wasn't Zell's fault she didn't have warm, expensive snow clothes. He'd figure out how to deal with Courtney. He wasn't surprised at her behavior. Used to having what she wanted, to being in charge, seeing him with Zell this afternoon threw her for a loop. Especially after their conversation last night. She wasn't letting go easy. Or maybe she only didn't have plans for the weekend and was bored. For so long, he'd thought himself incredibly lucky to call this gorgeous, smart, popular girl his girlfriend. But from the moment in the park when she walked away, he felt a yoke had been unhitched.

Courtney called wanting to talk about the debutante ball, of all things. An excuse, most likely. Who was going to escort her now if they were broken up? It wasn't until spring, he told her. There were plenty of guys who'd be itching to escort her.

She started soft-talking him then. She missed him—sexually, she emphasized and sighed. He hadn't felt the heat in his groin she was aiming for. Not really.

He made his voice pleasant and said it was the right decision, at least for now. It would be good for both of them.

His tone didn't work. Not at all.

The softness in her voice changed in an instant to fury. She accused him of purposefully humiliating her. "Being with that girl isn't funny. No way you're interested in that trash," she pronounced. "I don't know what this game is, whether you think I've done something to upset you and you're getting back at me, but it isn't cute."

"Listen to yourself," he'd said. "You don't even know this person, and you're judging her." It was hard to keep from lashing out. He made himself stay calm because losing control was exactly what Courtney wanted. She loved drama. "It has nothing to do with upsetting you," he continued. "I met Zell in ISS. By chance, we've become friends. I have no intention of changing that."

"Go ahead and ruin your reputation then," Courtney barked. "Go ahead. When you miss your real life, it might have passed you by." She hung up before he could respond. And that was fine by him. Nothing he could say would assuage her.

He wasn't going to dwell on Courtney. He turned his attention to Zell, sitting beside him in the truck. She'd pulled off the galoshes and her athletic shoes to rub her socked feet. He switched on the floor vent full blast and she spread her feet under the warm flow. "Are you warming up?"

"Feels good," she said, leaning back. "It's really cold out there." Her anxious look had disappeared. Instead, she was concentrating on her feet, rubbing them together frog-style.

"Truck thermostat says it's twenty-seven degrees," Sterling remarked.

"No wonder my feet were frozen," she answered. He glanced over at her again. An almost smile played at the corners of her very full lips.

"Listen," Sterling said, "I'm sorry about Courtney. It's not about you. She's mad at me because of our breakup, and you caught the flak because you were with me."

"Maybe she's right," Hazel said. Her gaze turned down.

"What do you mean? Right? What are you talking about?"

"I mean you're a rich boy who probably lives in a mansion somewhere, and I live with my family in a motel."

Unwittingly, Sterling's foot hit the brake. The truck spun off the icy road onto a shoulder of dense snow, and they both jerked back. He turned the truck back into the lane. Zell hugged her knees to her chest. "I didn't mean to do that, but Lord have mercy, Zell. Look over here for a minute. Does where we live make either of us less human?"

"Why do you meet me in the hall before school? Why did you take me to a restaurant and kiss me? Why did you want to go sledding with me?" she asked, finally turning toward him. The ease of the moment before had left her face. She wore a flat, serious expression.

"I like you," he said. "At least that's the way I feel." He checked his phone. "Hey, it's only 3:00. We have another hour. How about we get something hot at Starbucks, if they're open." She shook her head.

"Come on," he urged. This time she nodded forward, barely. He clicked on the radio, set to an oldies rock station. The opening lyrics of "Free Fallin'" by Tom Petty were playing. Could a song be more fitting, Sterling thought.

***

One customer sat in Starbucks—an artsy-type guy with three studs in one ear, typing frantically on his laptop. A cup beside him. A lone barista was working.

"I'm sweating," Sterling exclaimed as he removed his coat and parked it on the back of his chair.

"Not me," Zell said.

"Give it time and a stomach of hot chocolate," he said and headed to the counter to pick up their cups.

They sipped quietly. Normally, Sterling felt ill at ease with silence in the presence of others. He liked to keep things going, but he didn't feel that way at this moment. He felt content watching Zell. A wet chocolate moustache coated her upper lip.

Her world was rough, no question, and her tough manner showed it, yet she possessed a kind of innocence he didn't know how to define. Sterling reached across the narrow table and dabbed her lip with his napkin. Zell blinked, then put her hand over her mouth. He chuckled. She removed her hand and swatted him. His heart squeezed with an overwhelming need to protect this lovely, unpretentious girl.

"What time is it?" Zell asked.

Sterling looked at his phone. "Pushing 3:45. Time to go," he said, "in case your mom goes to work."

"Yeah, quick," Zell said, scrambling up. Sterling grabbed his coat, waving to the barista, who looked like she would give a week's salary for the place to close.

"I can hang out awhile if you want, with you and Chloe," Sterling said when they slid on the slick snow into a parking spot at the Red Rose Motel.

"Nothing to do here but watch TV," she said.

"Doesn't matter to me," he responded. She shrugged her shoulders.

But when Zell opened the door, she stepped back and held out her arms to keep him behind her.

"It's not a good time," she turned and said. "Maybe you could come back another day?"

Sterling wasn't one for backing away from anything. Plus, what could it possibly be? She'd seemed fine with his coming in. His curiosity was piqued.

"I'm already here," he said. "Come on."

"No," she said. Her voice was firm, but he didn't listen. Instead, he moved around her and walked in. He wasn't a member of the Crazy Eights for nothing.

A large, rust-bearded man reclined in the one upholstered chair in the room. His skin was pale, white as the snow. He was watching a wrestling match on television with a Pabst Blue Ribbon in one hand, the other resting on the arm of the chair. Mrs. Smalls and Chloe were nowhere to be seen.

"Who's this?" the man called, setting the beer on the floor before he stood, wobbling slightly.

"What are you doing home, Daddy?" Zell asked.

"Too much snow. Boss wants his trucks off the road."

"Oh," she answered.

"Who's this?" her father asked again.

"This is my friend, Sterling," Zell said, her voice quiet.

"Well now, glad to meet you," Mr. Smalls said. "Zell ain't said nothing about a boyfriend. I'm Burl. So call me Burl. You like wrestling?" His voice was too loud.

"He's not a boyfriend," Zell stammered.

"Okay, so he's a boy and he's a friend. What's the difference?"

Sterling held out his hand. The big man grabbed Sterling's in a hard, meaty shake, his hand crusty dry.

"You like a beer?" Burl asked.

"Sure, certainly sir," Sterling answered. Burl opened a Playmate cooler beside the chair. He tossed a Pabst to Sterling, who caught it midair. He popped the top and parked on the edge of the nearest bed.

"Where's Chloe? Has Mama gone to work?" Zell asked.

"Naw, the car can't drive in this stuff, and no one available to come get her. She's gone to get us some early dinner. Chloe's with her. I haven't ate since a truck stop in North Georgia this morning. I'm starving." Burl plopped back into his chair.

"I could heat you up some soup," Zell said.

"I need a helluva lot more than soup," her father growled. "I told you, I'm starving."

Sterling wondered where Zell's mother and Chloe could have gone on foot, but he didn't ask. He sat on the bed, drinking his beer. Zell paced around the room like she was looking for something she'd lost. No one talked except Burl.

"Look at that baby face. Good on his feet. Look at him. Looka there. The underdog is in control." Sterling glanced toward the screen. He knew little about wrestling holds. "See there, he's got a gas tank. He ain't giving up," Burl said. Sterling watched. The guy on top held on while the ref pounded the mat, counting.

"This bout is done, son." Burl Smalls jumped up from his chair, cheered, and plopped back down. Beer sloshed from his can.

"Cheers," Sterling said.

"You said that right."

The door opened wide, bringing in a strong gust of frozen air. "Shut the damn door before we all freeze to death," Burl called to his wife and daughter. "Where's dinner?"

"Albany's is closed," Mrs. Smalls said. She shrugged.

Zell's father rose again, tottered as he secured his footing.

"I told you I'm starved," he said, coming toward his wife, stopping in front of her. He shoved her shoulder. Sterling moved farther down the bed, his calves bumping the side. He looked over at Zell standing by the microwave. Her eyes looked suddenly scared.

"I can't help it they're closed. It's snowing. I can heat you up a frozen dinner. Zell, what we got in that little freezer?"

"I don't want no damn frozen dinner, Etta. What about McDonald's? It ain't that far. They bound to be open."

"You could get off your butt and walk out yourself to McDonald's," she answered. "Can you be nice? There's company." She pointed at Sterling.

"Be nice, there's company," he mocked her. "Company likes to eat, too."

"I have a truck. I can run to McDonald's right now if you'd like," Sterling offered.

Mr. Smalls didn't so much as glance at him. His head kind of rolled from side to side, close to Mrs. Smalls' face. Sterling realized the man was totally sloshed. It hadn't been so noticeable when he was in the chair. He shoved his wife, harder this time.

"Dad, no," Zell commanded. Briefly, he looked toward his daughter. She looked down.

"Let up, Burl." His wife's tone was steely.

"Don't provoke him, Mama, please," Zell begged. "Not with…"

Sterling watched Chloe bound from her stance into the bathroom before he heard the smack. He turned back to see Zell's mother holding a hand to her cheek. With her other hand she raked nails across her husband's arm.

It was impulse, not conscious bravery that made Sterling step forward and attempt to push Zell's father away.

"Don't," he heard Zell scream before two heavy hands thrust him backward. No match for the large drunk man's strength, Sterling lost his balance. His head hit hard on the concrete floor, covered with only a thin layer of worn carpet. He twisted onto his side, unaware now of the battle above him. He knew only the throbbing in his skull.

Arms reached under him. He opened his eyes. It was Zell. He rose with her help and found the world spinning. Something felt wet behind his ear—he touched blood trickling from his head. He saw Zell open the door, heard her voice shaking as she spoke. "He isn't always like this. He hasn't worked in a long time. He's frustrated not to be working because of the snow." Sterling staggered out, realizing once he hit the cold he'd left his coat.

In the truck, he pulled paper napkins from the glove compartment and stuck them onto the blood dripping down his neck. He shook his head, trying to clear his vision. There was a ringing in his ears. It took a moment to realize it was his phone, left on the seat beside him. He glanced at the number, saw it was his mother—no doubt checking to make sure he hadn't slid off into a ditch or calling him home, back to the world he knew. Far from Zell. He looked toward Room 103. He let the phone keep ringing until it stopped.

Chapter 15

Angela Wilmore

The only people who loved snow days in the South more than students were their teachers. They might have to make up the days at the end of the year, but it was worth it. There was something palliative about sheltering at home in the snow. Nowhere you needed to go—or could go for that matter—no obligations to meet, the real world momentarily gone. Even if Angela was by herself now making the snow ice cream she and Randal once enjoyed together.

It had been five days, and Ramsey was still frozen in. If they stayed out of school much longer, the governor would forgive the days, Angela thought hopefully, because it would be too many to tack onto the calendar. It had snowed on and off, with a mixture of sleet, every day since Saturday. At last measurement, there was a fourteen-inch layer on her deck. She wasn't complaining.

Once they reopened, merchants in Ramsey would likely hold big sales to recoup what they could after so many days of unsold merchandise. Angela loved a good bargain, a trait built into her blood from her frugal parents. When she and her sister were growing up, there was stability and money enough, but never more than enough. Her mother taught adult education, and her father taught history in middle school. "Cheap is ugly and it doesn't last. But to have quality, you have to wait for it to go on sale," was her mother's mantra.

"If you need a lot of money, don't become a teacher," her daddy advised when she told her parents during her sophomore year in college she wanted to be an English teacher. "You better love it because you won't ever make what you're worth. Plus English teachers have all those papers to grade. Think about it carefully," he urged.

Now, single and on her own, trying to hold on to her house with teacher pay…her father was so right. If she were paid outside of class for every essay she graded, she'd have ample money left over. She hated grading essays. Mainly because she felt guilty when she had to give a bad grade—her AP students thought anything below a B was horrendous—like it was her fault. Still, there was never anything else she wanted to do. As a child, she had seated dolls, a stuffed bear, and her little sister Joanie in the living room in front of her Mickey Mouse blackboard to teach.

Enough reminiscing, she thought, as she sat at her kitchen table eating tuna straight from the can, opened with a rusty metal crank she found in the junk drawer. Her power had gone out early afternoon after the temperature dropped midday just enough to make fat, wet flakes that collected heavily in the trees. Evergreen tips spiking beneath loaded white limbs were a beautiful sight, but they destroyed power lines.

Her landline was out, too, but she still had some power left on her cell phone. She called the automated report from Duke Energy and learned branches had fallen on a transformer one street over. It could be twelve or more hours before electricity was restored. She'd be fine. She had a gas stove, fireplace, and water heater. But she needed to get some essentials before dark descended. She made another call to the hardware store, and finding it open, she bundled up, happy for the fleece-lined boots she'd bought for nearly nothing at the end of the season last year. Dressed all in black, wool overcoat and wide-brimmed fedora, she felt like a 1940s film noir character as she set out along the sidewalk.

She looked up into white-shouldered pine trees along the way to Wilson Ace Hardware, located, along with a scattering of other small stores, less than a mile from her house. Probably the other businesses—she had Dolly's Deli in mind—would be closed. She would have loved a hot bowl of soup. During the span when she trekked along the edge of the road without a sidewalk, only one vehicle—a jeep—crawled by, its wipers unable to keep up with the falling snow.

At Wilson Ace, she removed her damp fedora and left it, more white now than black, on a bench under an awning. She bought the very last kerosene lantern in the store—talk about luck—a quart of fuel, and one of the last packs of D-cell batteries for her flashlight. She also picked up some expensive bath salts from the gift shop section. Why not? It was a time for relaxing.

She arrived home near dusk to her cold, dark house that felt perfectly peaceful. Angela poured kerosene into the lantern, and with the flick of a match, a welcoming glow lit the room. Enough light to read by.

She used her flashlight to rummage for tapers in a top drawer of the sideboard, a piece from her Grandmother Wilmore's family since before the Civil War. She retrieved an armful, along with an assortment of candleholders—crystal, silver, and brass—from the large middle compartment.

Angela spaced the candles around the den, bedroom, and bathroom, a cluster of four on the back ledge of the tub. She returned to the kitchen and poured a generous glass of Cabernet, carrying it and the lantern into the bathroom. She was ready for a deep, hot bath.

***

She soaked in the delicious aroma of lavender, occasionally draining bathwater when it got too cool and refilling with water steaming from the tap. Her mind felt clear and quiet—until knocking—insistent and rapid—began at the kitchen door. Angela jolted and stood, flinging bathwater onto the floor. Without drying off, she stepped into her fleece robe draped over the vanity stool. She quickly knotted her damp hair—when was she going to have it cut shorter to suit her age—into a clasp, grabbed the flashlight and hurried toward the door. It was too dark outside to see anyone through the peephole. "Who's there?" she called.

"It's Finley," came the answer.

Angela zipped her robe to her chin and opened the door to see her tall principal wearing a beige trench coat with the collar turned up like 007, a plastic grocery bag slung over his arm. "What are you…? How did you get here?" she stammered, shining the flashlight into his face.

"My truck is a four-wheel drive Tundra, so not impossible," he said, raising his free hand to shield his eyes from the glare of the flashlight. "Sorry for surprising you. I tried to call, but you didn't answer. I got a little worried."

"Goodness, well, I'm fine," Angela said. "I'm keeping the phone off to save the power."

"I see," he said, stomping from foot to foot. "Glad to see you're okay. May I?"

"Yes, oh, excuse me. Come inside."

"Certainly," he said, undoing the belt of his coat, slipping his arms out of the sleeves. She folded the long garment over a kitchen chair.

For a moment they stood awkwardly until she said, "It's cold in here. Let's go into the den where it's better."

Finley followed. "Wow, it's almost warm in here," he exclaimed when they crossed into the den.

"Unvented gas fireplace. It does a good job of warming the room."

"I'll say," he said. "It's freezing at my place. And dark. Nice light here." He removed the plastic bag from his arm and held it out. "Figured you couldn't get to the grocery store in that impractical Volkswagen."

"Once a hippie..." She shrugged. "Plus, my gas mileage beats yours." She threw him a genial smirk.

"Are you hungry?"

"Actually, I'm starving," Angela said.

"Okay, then."

"Excuse me for a minute? I'm a little chilly in this wet robe. I was actually taking a bath when you knocked."

"Oh, sorry," Finley said. "Oh, sorry," he repeated. "Of course."

Angela returned wearing an oversized gray sweatshirt and jeans. Finley had arranged the contents of his grocery bag on the coffee table.

"A cold picnic here," he explained from his seat on the sofa. "Found your dishes." He tipped his shoulders forward.

"Looks scrumptious." Angela surveyed the spread of sliced avocado, salami, and hard cheese beside a loaf of French bread. "I love avocado. How many men would purchase an avocado?"

"Uh, that would be a sexist comment, Ms. Wilmore," Finley said, tapping his finger emphatically on the table. "I have learned a thing or two about nutrition along the way."

"I'm teasing," she said. She could feel herself smiling too big.

"I have a bottle of Cabernet, but I couldn't find your wine opener," Finley said, pointing to the bottle beside the food. "I know you like Chardonnay, but I thought under the chilly circumstances, Cabernet?"

"Well, what do you know? I already have an open bottle of Cab.

Let me get it." Angela jumped up with the flashlight.

"Is this great minds think alike?" Finley called.

She returned with the bottle and one glass. He looked at her questioningly. "I was having a glass in the tub. I'll get it."

Finley said something as she walked out to the bathroom, but his voice was low, and she didn't catch his words.

***

Between glasses of Cabernet, they devoured everything but a few slices of bread.

"Mellow, full, and in the company of a beautiful, smart woman on a secluded snowy evening. What could be better," Finley mused. They were leaned back on her old leather sofa, their feet toasting—Angela's bare and Finley's in white athletic socks—before a ballet of yellow-blue flames.

Angela wasn't entirely sober, but perhaps more so than her principal when she asked, "What are we doing here together in my house? Sitting on my furniture? I work for you."

"The way I see it, you conduct your classroom, and if you need me, I'm here to support you," Finley answered, turning his head from the fire toward her.

"You know that isn't true. You're my boss."

"You're a professional," he said. He pushed his shoulders deeper into the cushions.

"Seriously," she said.

"I told you. I couldn't get you on the phone, and it worried me." He reached over and touched her hand.

"But why did you try to call me in the first place?" Angela looked down at Finley's hand now covering hers.

"I don't know how to answer that," he said, rubbing his thumb along her knuckles. "Can we chalk it up to chemistry?"

"I don't think that's supposed to be appropriate." Angela looked up.

"If I'm the boss, don't I get to decide?" Finley smiled sideways at her, his hand now a tight grip.

"I don't know," Angela said.

He exhaled and let go suddenly of her hand. "We're allowed to be human."

"Are we?"

"We are." Finley leaned toward her. She felt his breath on her cheek. His warm lips touched hers. Impulsively, Angela kissed him back, clasping her arms around him like a schoolgirl. She nuzzled her face into Finley's warm neck, breathed in his clean soap smell. Through the picture window, the night sky glowed with snowflakes falling as big as cotton balls.

Finley stroked a finger around the curve of her ear. Angela shivered. "I...don't...I...," she started. He lifted her face and kissed her again. It had been so long. The feeling of comfort, trust, pleasure. Finley put his arms under hers. It felt like she'd walked onto the set of an old-fashioned movie when he lifted her.

"Wait," she whispered. "Are we?"

"I am if you are," he said.

"We've got to...candles...so there won't be a fire," she said. Finley lowered her back to the sofa.

She watched him move around the room blowing out the tapers. Then he walked to the kitchen to extinguish the candles there.

"All out," he said, returning in the near dark. "What about the fireplace?"

"The switch is beside the hearth."

"Done." The fireplace went dark.

Using the flashlight, they walked through the bathroom. Angela released the drain from her tub of lavender water. She blew out the tapers behind the tub. Two candles lit the bedroom, on either side of the bed. "It's going to get mighty cold," she predicted.

"I don't think so," Finley said.

Chapter 16

Hazel Smalls

The skies cleared and the temperature rose on Thursday afternoon. They returned to school on Friday—a week since the snow began—on a two-hour delay to let the black ice melt enough so the school buses wouldn't slide everywhere. Hazel had been so excited by the snow, but it had turned out bad because of her father.

Starting Tuesday, Fields Home had sent a driver to pick up her mama. She and Chloe were left in the evenings with only their father watching TV, drinking one beer after another, making demands.

The first night, Hazel made him a peanut butter sandwich, and he threw it back at her, ranting he wanted a cheeseburger. She told him McDonald's was closed. She handed him back the sandwich and he grunted, eating it and asking for another. Soon enough, he dropped over in his chair, out cold from the cooler of beer he'd emptied. Everywhere else might be closed, but the Mini Mart was open with an endless supply of Pabst Blue Ribbon.

Chloe pulled the thin comforter off the bed and draped it over their father. Hazel nodded at her sister. Hazel didn't hate her father, but she feared him. He wasn't the father of her childhood, when they lived in the duplex. Then, he had laughed and talked and hugged them often. Hazel remembered her parents touching each other affectionately. But after her daddy and his brother Huck fell out, Burl Smalls changed.

The brothers started their own trucking company when she was in second grade. Before that, her father was an independent cab driver, mostly taking people to and from the regional airport while her mother cleaned houses.

"Smalls Brothers Deliver," they called their trucking business, shortened to "SBD." Burl got licensed to drive the semi, and Huck found business by going online to the free load boards showing freight to transport.

While it lasted—almost eight years—the brothers made good money, enough to support both families, enough for Etta to drop houses so that she cleaned only a couple of days a week to supplement her husband's income. Uncle Huck wanted to grow the company, buy a second truck, hire a second driver. Hazel's parents were excited. But all of a sudden Uncle Huck didn't want Burl to be an equal partner. He wanted his brother to be an employee. Because Huck owned the semi, he held the cards, and that was it.

After all the sweat and labor he'd put into building SBD, Burl said he wasn't going to be cheated out of his share and quit. Hazel hadn't seen Uncle Huck and his family since.

Her father went into a downward spiral. Etta tried to get him to look for work, but he refused. Said he'd work when he was good and ready. Instead of a beer or two in the evenings, he began drinking at a different pace, starting after breakfast. When her mother told him to cut back, he yelled at her to mind her own business. She persisted, and Hazel saw her father hit her mother across the face. After that, her mama shut up and picked her battles carefully.

They couldn't pay the bills. Etta got her CNA certificate and went to work at Elysian Fields, but it wasn't enough. They were evicted and ended up in the Red Rose Motel.

After a few months, her daddy finally went back to work driving loads at Grayson Trucking. It was just a matter of time until they built up the reserves to make a deposit on an apartment to move out of this cramped room that smelled always like mold. Where they had no space or privacy and no kitchen to cook a real meal. Where the toilet leaked every time someone flushed. Except the move didn't happen because her father drank on the road and got a DUI.

But now he had his license back. They were starting over. Hazel believed her father's foul mood this week was his frustration of the snow. He was stuck inside when he wanted to be working.

Yesterday, before it mostly melted, Hazel had ventured outside into the beautiful vista, but her heart wasn't in it. All she could think about was her humiliation. How Sterling would never come near her again. At least Chloe was happy in the softening snow, ideal for building snow people. Her sister and some other children created a lopsided father wearing a striped toboggan and pine cone buttons down his front, a squatty mother, long kerchief around her head and apron tied around her ample middle, plus three snow children.

Hazel had stepped over to Rhona and her grandmother Lolly's room. It always smelled good there, like cinnamon toast. It was comfortable, too, with a soft couch and chair, a coffee table with trinkets from Lolly's past. It was a place where Hazel felt safe.

Still, sitting on the sofa beside Rhona, she couldn't bring herself to tell her friend about her parents' fight when Sterling was there. What could Rhona do anyway? Feel sorry for her, that was about it. Or maybe tell Hazel again that she shouldn't set any thoughts on Sterling. He was a boy on the hill, and she was a girl from the Red Rose Motel.

She was glad when the 6:00 evening news on Thursday announced classes would resume on a two-hour delay the next morning. She could get back to the routine of school and out of the motel, away from the noise of the television and her father's mood.

Hazel missed her English teacher. She didn't know exactly how to explain it, but Ms. Wilmore was, well, almost like a friend. She spoke her mind; she'd send a jerk out of class to grade level for discipline in a minute, but she was caring, too. Before class, she was always asking Hazel how she was getting along. If there was anything on her mind. Probably, Hazel reckoned, because she arrived on the earliest bus and Ms. Wilmore knew what that meant. And if she didn't, all she had to do was look up Hazel's address. Plus, Hazel knew from experience: guidance counselors informed teachers about students who lived in cars and motels.

Hazel wished she could talk to Ms. Wilmore about Sterling. She couldn't tell her mother, who might ask what craziness was Hazel thinking, setting her thoughts on a rich boy like Sterling. But Ms. Wilmore knew Sterling. She wouldn't judge. She had a feeling Ms. Wilmore really cared. Hazel wouldn't be the only student who confided in a teacher.

***

Hazel's bus arrived thirty minutes before the bell. A big sign in the atri-

106

um announced they'd meet all of first period. Other classes would be cut short by fifteen minutes each to make up for starting late. Ms. Wilmore hadn't yet arrived when Hazel walked into first period.

"Goodness, what a mess," her teacher announced a couple of minutes later, clomping into the room. She wore black boots and a heavy black coat. "I was nervous about firing up my little car, so I waited a little longer to leave home. Like five more minutes of sun would make a difference, right?" She laughed. "Anyway, I didn't slide into another car or hit a fence. Hey, did you have a good snow week, sweetheart?"

Hazel nodded.

"We haven't had snow like this in I don't know when," Ms. Wilmore continued.

Hazel nodded again.

"I'm thinking we won't have a full house today, with some snow still around, and it being Friday, you think?"

Hazel shrugged.

"Good Lord," Ms. Wilmore said after she removed her coat. "They could have at least gotten the furnace fired up. It's freezing in here." She sighed.

Hazel was cold, too, even though her hoodie was tied tight around her chin, and she wore both a t-shirt and sweatshirt underneath.

"No worries," Ms. Wilmore said, walking to the cabinet at the back of the room. Hazel turned around and watched her teacher rummaging in a ceiling-tall cabinet. "Ta-da! Here it is. Whoo, this thing is dusty. Hope it works," she said as she held out a small space heater.

"I'll clean it with some wet paper towels from the bathroom," Hazel said, rising from her seat.

"Good enough," Ms. Wilmore said.

When she returned, her teacher had already plugged in the heater. Hazel wiped the layer of dust from the top and sides.

"Thank you much," Ms. Wilmore said.

Hazel smiled and walked to her seat. She shoved her book bag under her desk.

"You seem awfully quiet. Everything okay?" her teacher asked. She had set the heater on her desk facing out to the classroom and was rubbing her hands in front of it.

Hazel said nothing.

"The snow was fun, sweetie? Especially with no schoolwork?"

"It was beautiful," Hazel said, sitting at her desk.

"Did you get out?"

"Yes," Hazel responded. Then, on impulse, "I went sledding on the golf course at the country club."

"Oh, well, then. That must have been quite a ride. There're some fine hills over there."

"It was pretty cool," Hazel said.

"Good for you," her teacher smiled. "You went with Sterling Lovell, maybe?"

How did Ms. Wilmore know? But then, how would she not know? She'd seen Hazel with Sterling a lot of mornings at school. She knew Hazel would never be at the country club on her own.

"Yes," Hazel replied. "It was fun. Until some girls came."

"Some girls?"

"Sterling's girlfriend, and her friends. Only she's not his girlfriend now."

"You mean Courtney Powell?"

Hazel nodded. "I didn't cause her and Sterling to…" Hazel looked down.

"Oh, Zell, of course you didn't. Don't you take it personally. I think those two have been an item for a long time, and now they have to figure out—"

"She hates me," Hazel said suddenly. "She said I'm Sterling's rescue project."

"Oh, sweetie." Ms. Wilmore walked over to her desk and squatted beside her. "Please believe this isn't about you." She reached down and hugged Hazel's shoulders. Hazel leaned toward her.

"I don't know what to do," Hazel, her voice breaking.

"Let's talk," Ms. Wilmore said, releasing Hazel and rocking back on her heels. Her teacher's kind voice encouraged her.

"I think Sterling liked me," she said. "But he doesn't now." Unwittingly, her eyes had begun to water. "He came to our room. I live at the Red Rose Motel." She glanced down again. Ms. Wilmore patted her shoulder. Hazel kept going. "My father was…was angry at my mother.

108

Sterling tried to push my father back and got shoved onto the floor. He hit his head. It was…he will never want to see me now."

"Honey, why do you think that? You're a beautiful, smart girl. He'd be a fool not to like you."

Hazel looked up anxiously.

"Sterling wouldn't have sought you out if he didn't enjoy your company. He can be a handful, but I'm pretty sure he's got a true heart."

Hazel continued to look at Ms. Wilmore without speaking, willing the tears seeping out to stop.

"Do you want me to say anything?" she asked.

"No, oh no, please no." Hazel shook her head hard. Snot oozed from her nose. She wiped the back of her hand across her face. She was suddenly so embarrassed.

"I'm sorry. I didn't mean to upset you more. I just don't want you blaming yourself for anything."

"He didn't come to see me again during the snow," Hazel said.

"Did he call?"

"I don't have a phone."

"Let's give Sterling some credit, then."

Ms. Wilmore was about to say something else, but a couple of kids walked in, Gerard Barnes and Stokes Thomas. They were such clowns. They drove everybody crazy.

"Hey there, fellas," Ms. Wilmore called. "Your bus made it."

"Yeah, but it was nearly empty. Nobody's coming to school today," Gerard said. "So no lesson, right? I brought a deck of cards."

"I don't know about that." Ms. Wilmore put her hand on her hip and turned to Hazel. "Was your bus full?"

"No, not nearly," she said. But then, her bus never had more than twenty-five people.

"Okay, well, we'll see how many show up before I make a decision about Plan B."

"Where'd you get that heat, Ms. Wilmore?" Stokes asked. He'd walked up to the little heater and hogged it, standing with his big stomach in front of the blower.

"Had it forever. Comes in handy on a day like today. Long as we don't blow a circuit," Ms. Wilmore said. "Share the wealth, kiddo," she told Stokes. Slowly, he moved over.

Hazel glanced at the wall clock. Still fifteen minutes until the first bell. Even if most kids didn't show, she'd still rather be here than at the motel. She'd rather be anywhere else.

The four of them turned toward a light rapping at the door. Hazel's stomach knotted when she heard his voice.

"Yo, Ms. W, how was your snow vacation?" Sterling called from the door.

"Hello, Sterling. It was quite peaceful. And yours?"

"Can't complain. Hey, can I come in? Excuse me, *may* I?"

"You know you're supposed to go to your own first period," Ms. Wilmore admonished him, but Hazel could hear in her tone she wasn't going to make him leave.

"I know, I know, but there's hardly anyone around," he said, looking inside the classroom, one eye squinched closed.

"Alright, come on in until first bell," she relented.

"You're the best, Ms. W, and you know it." He pounced through the doorway.

Stokes and Gerard parked themselves in desks near the heater, and Gerard pulled out his deck of cards. Ms. Wilmore sat behind her desk and turned on her computer.

Sterling stood alone at the front of the room, his shoulders jiving up and down in his jacket. It looked like nerves, except why would he even come here? Unless maybe to tell her in person, so she'd be sure to understand, that he wouldn't be seeing her again.

She looked down into her lap. Watched her fingers lace and unlace while she waited.

"Hey, Zell." He came close to her desk. "Can I talk to you?" Hazel continued to look down. "Come on, Zell, at least acknowledge me."

"You don't need to come here to tell me what I already know," she glanced up and whispered.

"What are you talking about? What do you already know?" he whispered back.

"My family. Who I am."

"Alright, truth, I wasn't crazy about coming back over uninvited.

But I couldn't call you, you know?"

Hazel lowered her shoulders.

A girl named Molly who lived at the Girl's Home, a temporary place for girls who'd been abused or neglected, wandered into class. Ms. Wilmore greeted her.

"Listen, it's nearly time for the bell," Sterling said, "and there are only four of you here. Ms. W isn't going to have a real lesson for four students, right? Let's skip out."

"I can't. I'm already here," Hazel said.

"Hang on."

"No, don't," Hazel said, but Sterling was already sprinting toward Ms. Wilmore's desk. Hesitantly, Hazel followed him.

"You don't take roll until the last bell, right?" he was saying.

"Sterling, you're asking a lot here," Ms. Wilmore said back.

"No, think about it. There's hardly anyone here." He pointed behind him. "You won't have enough to have the regular lesson in my class either; I already know a bunch of kids are going mudding in the snow-melt and…"

"Sterling," Ms. Wilmore said, her voice sharp.

"How about this? You haven't taken roll. Zell disappears. It's not your problem if you haven't taken roll, right?"

Ms. Wilmore put her palms up to her temples. "You're going to be the death of me, Sterling Lovell," she said.

"Yeah, but you love me," he said with a grin. "No harm, no foul. Consider us absent along with most of the student body. We can't get caught for cutting if the day hasn't started."

Ms. Wilmore threw up her hands.

"Vamoose, Zell," Sterling instructed. "Later, Ms. W," he called. Hazel looked at her teacher, who smiled and nodded. Dazed, she retrieved her book bag and followed Sterling through the door.

***

"Truck's engine's still warm," Sterling announced when they were both inside the cab and he cranked the motor. "Hey, where do we go?"

Hazel looked at him dumbfounded. She'd never cut school, at least not with a teacher's knowledge. On top of that, she hadn't expected to see Sterling again, and here she was sitting beside him in his father's big truck.

"Zell?"

"I don't know. I don't know why you want to see me anymore. Not after…my parents…and you got hurt."

"I was okay. Why wouldn't I want to see you? Is it your fault? Hell, I wanted to help, but I was helpless. I'm the one who feels bad."

Hazel twisted a piece of wavy black hair around her index finger.

"Look, I haven't been where you are, and I can only see the surface of how tough it is, but I've been other places. Can we leave it at that?"

Hazel looked in confusion at the flush-faced boy sitting next to her. Where had he been? What was he talking about?

"We can't sit here in the truck all day. I'm burning fuel. Where do you want to go?" Hazel had absolutely no idea where to go. She felt suddenly light-headed and lowered her head to her lap.

"Whoa, Zell, you okay? Too much heat? Turning it off. Untie your hood," Sterling said. She heard the automatic window lower on her side of the truck.

She waved her hand up in his direction. "A little dizzy. I'm okay."

"Are you sure? What do you need?"

"Nothing. I'll be okay in a minute," she said. "It happens." She got woozy sometimes when she felt stressed. Most recently when Sterling tried to get in between her parents and overpower her father. She'd collapsed onto the bed after he left. She didn't want to think about it. A wave of nausea rose in her stomach.

She coughed in an attempt to hide the gag that sounded from her throat. Quit it, she told herself, even as another wave of nausea hit her.

"I'm on the way to the Zip Mart around the corner for a ginger ale. My mother says it's good for dizzy."

By the time Sterling returned to the truck, Hazel had applied Chapstick from her purse. Her nerves were recovering.

"Sorry," she said as he handed her the cold bottle. She took a long, slow drink. "Whew, that's good."

"Whew, you said it; you had me worried there."

"Sorry," she said again. "I think it's nerves." She took another sip, felt the burn up her nose.

"About what?" he asked.

"About why you want to cut school to be with me?"

"Are you kidding? Okay, let's start over. We met. I thought you were gorgeous and interesting. And now, you're quadruple that."

"But my family…"

"You're not your parents. You haven't met my family. Jesus, they're not perfect. Except for Beatrice. I think of her as family, and she's amazing."

Hazel looked at him quizzically. "Who is Beatrice?"

"A lady I love who's worked at my house since I was a baby. Hey, I have an idea," Sterling suddenly announced. "My old man's hunting property. It's about thirty minutes from here down Highway 421, near Crossover Creek. It has a little cabin. It's quiet. You game?"

Hazel laughed.

"I did it. Got you with the pun. Seriously, you want to?"

Hazel nodded, buckled up, and leaned back.

***

A sharp-peaked roof—the snow mostly melted off—came slowly into view as they drove up the long dirt road. Getting closer, Hazel marveled at the dark red shutters and small front porch with odd-shaped chairs.

"It looks like the Three Bears' cottage where Goldilocks made a mess," she exclaimed.

"Been reading storybooks lately?" Sterling mused. He twisted his mouth to the side and winked.

Hazel kicked her foot out at him.

"Hey," he said. "What'd I do?"

"You're mocking me."

"No way," he said.

Hazel jumped out of the truck, running to sit in one of the chairs that looked like it was made of sticks you picked up off the ground. The sun shone in a turquoise sky. The day had warmed tremendously. How did it go from freezing cold to this so quickly? She pulled her hoodie over her head and laid it over the banister.

"I take it you like this little place," Sterling said, approaching.

"I love it," she said.

"Feels good out here," he agreed, taking off his own jacket, slinging it over the banister next to hers.

She peered out toward the small pond in front of the cabin. "Ducks," she said. "Look."

They watched the pair slide into the pond. "That's gotta be some cold water. How do they stand it?" she wondered aloud.

"They like the cold water. They're mallards. The male is the good-looking one with the dark green head."

"Why does he get to be the pretty one?"

"Hey, what can I say? Men dress to impress."

"You're crazy," Hazel said.

"Wanna walk around?" Sterling asked, standing. Eagerly, Hazel stepped beside him.

"Are fish in there?" she asked, leaning over the perimeter of the pond, attempting to peer underneath the opaque brown water.

"Yep. Dad stocks it."

"What does that mean?"

"Means we buy fish to put in there from the Carolina Fish Hatchery."

"What kind?"

"The eatin' kind. Catfish and bream mostly."

"I eat fish sticks," she said.

"That ain't fish. Sometime we'll go fishing, right here, and I'll cook 'em for you."

They turned past the pond to a fenced pasture behind the cabin. Two matching creatures, the likes of which Hazel had never seen, in books or otherwise, walked up to the fence and stared at her. She jumped back. Sterling put his hand between her shoulder blades and pushed her forward.

"Say hello to Jake and Lizzie."

"What are they?"

Sterling looked at her funny. Hazel shrank into herself. The look on his face told her that obviously, any normal person would know what these animals were.

"They're alpacas," he said. "Dad thought about farming them, but turns out what you get for the raw fiber about equals the cost of care. So, after these two, he didn't buy any more. They get sheared in the early summer, and he sells the fleece, but they're pets more than anything."

"They're so cute," Hazel said, inching out her hand toward the fence. The brown one stepped up and nuzzled her fingers. The lighter one stood a little ways behind and studied her. "Did they get cold in the snow? Who takes care of them?"

"Are you kidding? Look at their coats. They're made for snow, and they have shelter over there." He pointed to a shed enclosed on three sides.

"But who feeds them when you're not here?"

"They eat grass dead or alive. Look around." Sterling swooped out his arm. "They're fine. Dad has a caretaker."

It all looked like a fairytale to Hazel.

"I'm hungry," Sterling announced, "but no food or drink out here."

Hazel had been far too enthralled to think about hunger and thirst.

"Listen, there's a Zaxby's just up the road. Shouldn't take much more than fifteen minutes roundtrip. You want to stay here and wander around?"

"Yes," Hazel said. She looked toward the tree line.

"Salad or sandwich?"

"Sandwich, thank you."

"Oh, wait. I almost forgot. I've got something for you. Hang loose. It's in the truck. Let's head back."

"What is it?"

"Guess," he said as they walked back toward the cabin. Hazel huffed.

"Something to keep us informed," he said. Hazel crinkled her forehead.

"Think hard," he encouraged her.

"This isn't fair," she declared.

"If you hadn't seen me for a couple of days and wondered what I was up to, what would you like to do?"

"Forget about you," she said.

"Wrong, wrong answer. No forgetting about me." Sterling shook

115

his head and sighed. He took Hazel's hand.

"I give up," she said, exasperated.

"Never give up," he said as they reached the truck. He opened the back door and retrieved a plastic bag lying on the floor. "Open it."

"Oh," Hazel exhaled, seeing the image of a cellphone on the front of the box.

"This is so we can talk whenever we want. I nearly went crazy worrying this week."

"But I...I can't pay for the service," Hazel said. "I wish..."

"This is a prepaid phone," Sterling interrupted. "Walmart special. I renew it every thirty days. All you got to do is talk on it."

"Oh," Hazel said again.

"Good enough?" he asked.

"Grayson Trucking gave Daddy a phone, but he's the only one who uses it."

"Well, now, sweetheart, you have your own communication. Please use it to talk to me."

Hazel opened the box and removed the phone. "Show me how?" she asked.

"Done," Sterling said.

***

After Sterling unlocked the cabin—if she wanted to go inside—and pulled away, Hazel walked into the woods beyond the pond. But she didn't go far because the ground was soft mud from the melting snow. She looked down at her good sneakers caked up the sides with brown muck. "Oh, how stupid," she said to the trees. She picked up a stick to scrape off the goo, not realizing it had briars. A thick thorn stuck deep into her right palm. She tossed the stick aside and examined her hand. The damn thorn had gone all the way in. "This hurts," she said aloud.

She was sitting in her muddy shoes on the porch, holding her puffed palm upright when Sterling returned.

"I got a splinter," she said when he neared the porch, carrying a large Zaxby's bag in one hand and a box holding two large drinks in the other.

"How'd you do that?" he asked, setting the food on the first step and jumping over the second to land on the porch.

"Walked into the woods. It was muddy. I was stupid. I tried to scrape my shoes." Hazel held out her hand like an offering.

"Okay, this is Boy Scouts 101. Let me get tweezers and alcohol," he said, walking inside the cabin where she hadn't yet ventured.

Returning, he squatted beside her chair and examined the splinter. "Too far embedded for tweezers. Can't catch a hold. I got to find a needle."

"That will hurt."

"It might, but you don't want it to stay in there and fester."

"Were you really a Boy Scout?"

"I didn't earn the First Aid merit badge for nothing. Made it to Star rank before I quit."

"Are you sure you can?" Hazel asked, pulling her palm into a fist.

"Sweet girl, I just told you," Sterling said, then darted back inside the cabin. He returned holding a small penknife, not a needle.

"No way," Hazel said. "You're not cutting my hand."

"I couldn't find a needle. I'll be gentle." He bent down on his knees in front of her. He opened the blade and poured alcohol over it. "Let me hold your hand." Hazel shook her head. "Don't be a baby, now. It will feel a lot better when it's out." His voice was like a doctor's, coaxing. Slowly, Hazel unfolded her palm.

"Easy, now," Sterling said as he touched the tip of the blade to the pad of her palm. Hazel jerked. "Don't move. If you move, I might really cut you."

Hazel squeezed her eyes shut. She felt a tiny pricking. Then she felt the blade dig deeper. "Ouch," she squealed.

"Almost there, hold on," Sterling commanded. "Got it. Looka here."

Hazel opened her eyes to see a quarter-inch-long pointed sliver between Sterling's thumb and index finger.

"That's that," he said and flicked the splinter over the porch railing. Then he poured alcohol over her palm without asking.

"Yow, that mess burns," she squealed again.

"Poor baby, I think you're going to make it." He held up her palm and kissed it.

"You always make fun of me."

"You make it irresistible," he said. "But you're the real irresistible." Still holding her hurt hand, he leaned his head into her lap. He looked up at her. "A kiss for my hard work?"

And before she could answer, he'd pulled himself up and was kissing her, deeply. She put her arms around his neck, holding her injured hand aloft.

"Want to go inside?" he asked. Something was burning in her gut, traveling down toward the private parts of her that made her want to keep kissing Sterling. Something that would have made her follow him anywhere.

She left her muddy shoes at the door, and crossed with Sterling into a den with big armchairs covered in blue jean material. She stopped to examine an animal head hanging above the mantel of a stone fireplace. The creature's widespread horns sprouted above and between its oval-shaped ears. Hazel thought it must be the head of a deer, though she'd never seen a deer up close.

"Not here," he whispered and guided her to a bedroom with a brass bed covered in a star-patterned quilt. Sterling turned Hazel toward him and kissed her again. His tongue slid along the roof of her mouth. She moved her tongue to meet his.

"Okay?" he asked, pulling away. "You tell me." She nodded.

He pulled down the quilt. Hazel climbed into the sheets, soft white like the snow.

For several minutes Sterling held her. His hands began to travel beneath her shirts, onto the bare skin of her back. Impulsively, Hazel sat up and pulled both sweatshirt and t-shirt over her head.

He reached up and unclasped her bra. "Oh my God. Look at you," he said.

Hazel pulled the sheet above her chest. Her bold act moments before now embarrassed her. No boy had ever seen her bare breasts.

"What's wrong?"

She did not respond.

"Zell?"

She burrowed herself under the sheet and quilt. Even as her insides throbbed with a yearning to cling to Sterling, she whispered, "I don't know."

"You say the word and we'll stop." But he misunderstood. He thought she didn't want to be with him.

"I mean I don't know what to think...," she started. No one had ever told her how to be with a boy. What she knew was boys got girls pregnant, so she steered clear of them.

He looked at her curiously. "You're not supposed to think at a time like this." They lay face to face under the covers. He held her tight.

Tentatively, she reached around and placed her hands under his shirt, ran her fingers up his bare back, as he had done to her. Sterling sat and removed his shirt. He leaned back and pulled off his pants, tossing both to the floor. He lay on his back on top of the quilt.

Hazel looked at Sterling's almost naked body. At his muscled shoulders. Briefly, she had an urge to curl a wisp of the sparse hair on his chest around her finger, but she didn't because she saw in that moment—below his flat stomach—a pointed hump beneath his briefs. Though she knew what it was, the sight astonished her.

He saw her looking and turned on his side to face her. "It's what you do to me," he said. He reached an arm toward her and pulled the quilt from around her chest. "Oh, yeah," he said. He laid his face between her breasts. Her insides softened below her stomach.

A small sawing sound erupted as Sterling unzipped her jeans. Then the tug of the jeans over and down her hips. Hazel closed her eyes. She felt like she was floating on the pond outside, water lapping over her bare legs, sunshine baking her in warmth.

"You're on birth control, right?" His voice tickled inside her ear. His body lay on top of hers.

"No," she said.

"What?" he said and moved quickly off of her.

She said, very quiet, "I don't...I...where I come from you don't or you get pregnant."

"So why not take birth control pills?"

She curled up into herself. The edge in his voice unsettled her.

"It's okay. I didn't mean to...," Sterling began. "I'm sorry. Unknot yourself, please." He pushed his hand between her stomach and thighs,

119

until he was touching the soft flesh of her belly. "I shouldn't have assumed."

"When it's time for sex, be ready for a baby," she whispered.

Sterling sat up. "What are you talking about?"

"You don't have sex till you're ready to have a baby. That's the way it is," she said.

"No, not so," Sterling said.

For a long moment, neither of them spoke.

"Okay, damn, this is really awkward, but if you're okay to—you know—stay here a few minutes until I get back, I'll go to the convenience store up the road, to buy—you know—take care of birth control," he said.

"Oh," she said. She pressed her lips together.

"Baby, I could try to…you know, to do something else, but it's not as safe."

Hazel looked at him, bewildered. "What?"

"You know, um, pull out before…never mind. Not a good idea. It won't take but a few minutes, I promise. Okay?" He leaned over and kissed her, his tongue tracing the inside of her upper lip. Zell inhaled deeply.

"I don't want you to leave." Her voice was wobbly.

"I've got to go so I can get back quick," Sterling said as he pulled on his clothes. "Don't move," he instructed and was gone.

***

Hazel heard fast steps walking through the cabin toward the bedroom. She was sitting up in bed, the quilt cocooned around her.

"I'm back. Warm you up in two secs," Sterling said, sitting on the edge of the bed, removing his shoes, sliding over to her.

"I hope I didn't seem like a jerk. I was just surprised is all," he said as he pulled off his shirt and jeans again and tossed them onto the floor. He lifted Hazel's hair and placed it behind her shoulders.

"I shouldn't let it get so long," she said, feeling suddenly self-conscious about her thick, frizzy hair. Because she felt awkward all over again.

"No way," he said. "I love your hair. It's crazy sexy." He snuggled up beside her and tugged at the quilt. "Make room for me? Start over?"

Tentatively, she touched her hands to his shoulders.

"Girl, where have you been all my life," he murmured, putting his hands in her hair, massaging her scalp. She began to relax. She wanted time to stop.

"Hold on," he whispered. He stood and walked to the bedroom windows, closing the blinds. He turned off the bedside lamp.

"We're gonna take this easy," he said as he rolled her cotton panties down her hips. She lifted her legs, and he slipped them all the way off. Sterling removed his underwear and slid his body up hers. Her legs spread naturally into a V-shape outside his. He grasped her ankle and kissed her butterfly tattoo.

***

"Hey, beautiful," he said. Except for the sound of their slow, deep breathing, they'd been quiet for some time, her body spooned into his.

She was still back there, still feeling Sterling inside her. She hardly understood it, but she understood how it made her feel. When she was a little girl, she'd helped her mother make bread many times. Enjoyed the sensation of kneading the risen dough in her hands, folding and stretching the spongy material. The rhythm was like that.

"You okay?" Sterling spoke again, sitting up partway. "I didn't hurt you, did I?"

"No," she answered, her mind struggling to return to the present moment. "I was startled at first."

"What does that mean?"

"I don't know," she said, rising onto her elbows. There was enough light from the bathroom that she noticed the faint, pink-red blot outside her knees on the white sheet. She pointed to it.

"That's nothing," he said. His arm tightened around her. "It's a normal thing that happens when you lose your virginity, right? I don't know much about the, you know, biology of it. But as long as you're okay, that's all that matters."

"Someone will see it," she said.

"No, we'll strip the bed and remake it. There're clean sets in the dresser drawer. I'll take our sheets home and wash them, bring them back. No one will know."

Hazel lay back and sighed.

"You're my forever girl," he said.

Later, famished, Hazel paid no attention to the Coke gone watery, the chicken sandwich now cold and soggy, or the fries clumped together. Everything tasted good.

Chapter 17

Sterling Lovell

Sterling was in love. At least he believed it must be so. He thought he'd loved Courtney; he'd told her so many times. Even when she drove him crazy, he remembered how lucky he was. Unlike him, she'd always been popular. People said they were perfectly matched. If there were still such a thing as high school prom king and queen—like his parents in the dark ages at Ramsey—he and Courtney would surely have been the royal couple. Bound for success; a tight circle of friends. And Lord knows, Courtney had known how to work him sexually.

But this feeling for Zell was way different. Like he would literally do anything, if he were capable, for her. Yes, he felt sorry for her living in that rundown slum, and guilty, too, because her family's rent put food on his table. His need to take care of her was real, and part of it, but not near everything. It went far deeper. After making love at the cabin, he felt…he didn't know how to express it, like she'd crawled up inside him. It sounded melodramatic, but he didn't know any other way to put it. So what if her world was different? He simply wanted to be with her.

On Sunday night, Sterling called the phone he gave Zell to talk about meeting at school on Monday. She didn't answer. Minutes later, she called back, saying she hadn't told her parents about the phone and was keeping it on silent. She was calling outside from the Red Rose parking lot.

"What's wrong with them knowing you have a phone?" he asked. "Tell 'em it's a gift from me."

"Nuh-uh, I don't want them in my business," Zell said. "A gift like that would make them think I…my mother expects me…"

"Okay, I don't have to get it. But tomorrow, I'm teaching you how to text because texting doesn't make any noise. Anything could happen to you out in that parking lot by yourself at night."

"Okay," she said. "But at school, you know, it's—"

"Listen, starting tomorrow, we're together, get it? At least we are if that's what you want. All this time, we've had the same lunch block, and I've had to look at you from afar. We're going to hang out."

"Okay," she said again, but he could hear the tremor in her voice. It might take time, but it would work. She'd get comfortable. Get to know his friends. He'd meet hers, too, starting with the girl she sat with every day at lunch. It was all good.

***

"You girls look splendid with that pink nail polish," Sterling said to Zell and Rhona at Thursday lunch. Zell had been tense this morning about a math test, so he was keeping it light. She'd let him go over some of the algebra problems before school. She'd be fine, even if she didn't think so.

"Thanks, dude," Rhona answered, poking her fork into a gob of spaghetti. "Most guys don't notice."

He winked at both girls. "Hey, I've even noticed Ms. Wilmore has started painting her fingernails. What's up with that? Is it because spring's coming?" He unwrapped his turkey sandwich from his lunch bag.

"Season's got nothing to do with looking good," Rhona said.

"Yeah, Ms. Wilmore's got it going on," Zell chimed in. She looked at Rhona's plate of spaghetti. "That doesn't look too good."

"It'll do. Try it," Rhona said. Zell took a tentative bite from her own plate.

"I can share this sandwich," Sterling offered.

"It's fine," Zell said, chewing and smiling. That smile melted him.

Sterling felt the interlopers' presence before he saw them standing beside the table: Courtney, Madison, and Jill.

"Well, hey there, guys," Courtney cooed. "Sterling, how *are* you these days? Introduce us to your new friends."

Sterling flinched at the patronizing tone. But he responded cheerfully. "This is Zell Smalls and Rhona Williams. We were just talking about spring coming. It's been a cold-ass winter." Why was he talking to Courtney at all?

"I'm sure what you're ready for is tennis season," Jill said. She cocked her head flirtatiously to the side.

"As a matter of fact, I am," Sterling said. "Definitely." He cleared his throat.

"Well, we'll be off," Courtney said. "Just wanted to say hi. Nice to meet you, Rhona and Zell. It's always fun to meet new kinds of people."

"Yeah, same here, always good to meet *new* kinds of people," Rhona said, giving it back. Dammit to hell, Sterling thought. All they wanted was to put Zell on the spot. Well, too bad. Didn't happen. She might not have said anything, but she didn't look down either. She held her own. He looked across the table and winked. Zell picked up her glass of tea and smiled again at him. She'll get there, he nodded to himself.

Courtney flounced off with a little wave. The others followed like ducklings, taking their seats at a nearby table.

"Girlfriend, don't you take that garbage off them bitches," Rhona said after Courtney and company were out of earshot. "You just as good, no, you better than them. You say something back."

"They got nothing on you, Zell," Sterling agreed. "But you were also fine not talking. Ignoring them is as good as anything. What they want is an opening."

"High five," Zell said. She reached out her arm, and the three of them slapped palms.

A few minutes later, Madison walked back by their table. She stumbled beside Zell's chair, kicking over her large shoulder bag. Sterling had noticed Zell never zipped her bag. He guessed she thought she had nothing worth stealing.

"Oh, excuse me," Madison said. "I'm sorry. I'm in a hurry to get to the bathroom."

The contents of the bag spread onto the floor. As Zell bent over to retrieve things—tissues, pen, a wallet Sterling suspected was mostly empty, a partial roll of cherry Life Savers—Courtney screamed loud enough for the entire cafeteria, "Oh my God, a knife. Look over there, under that table." She pointed in their direction. "Look!"

The entire lunchroom fell silent.

Sterling tumbled out of his seat and onto his knees. Under the table he saw a long knife near Zell's chair.

Two male teachers monitoring the lunchroom arrived one right after the other. One was Judson Moore.

"What's going on over here?" Mr. Moore asked Rhona, probably because she was his student.

"I don't know, Mr. Moore, but somebody threw a blade under our table. I ain't gonna pick it up. Get me in trouble."

Sterling knew the other teacher only by sight, thought he might teach chemistry to tenth graders.

"You guys got a knife over here?" the teacher asked. He was tall and heavily muscled under his tight shirtsleeves. They put teachers like Mr. Moore and this guy in the cafeteria for their duty period because they could stop a fight in a heartbeat.

"We don't have a knife, but yes, there's a knife under our table," Sterling responded. The teacher frowned at him.

Zell's bag still lay on its side, some of the contents still strewn on the floor.

"Is this your purse?" Mr. Moore asked.

Zell nodded. "But it ain't my knife. I don't own a knife. I swear." Zell stood, leaving her bag on the floor.

"Let's see if we can figure this out," Mr. Moore said. "None of you has a knife on you, but there's a bad-looking blade on the floor."

"Is that your purse spilled out, young lady?" the other teacher asked Zell.

"Yes sir, but it didn't have a knife in it," she said quietly.

In a side glance, Sterling saw Courtney and her friends huddled together, whispering. Their piqued expressions gave them away. He knew right then they were responsible. Somehow, one of them—probably Madison with her bathroom excuse— had dropped the knife either into Zell's handbag or under the table when they came by. It was all Courtney's plan.

He'd always known she was petulant. And since their breakup, he'd learned she had a great capacity for jealousy, but he hadn't known she was evil. He wondered if Courtney would have sabotaged someone like Jeannie Phillips if she'd been hanging with him. No way. Courtney despised Jeannie, her nemesis on the cheerleader squad, but no. Jeannie was her equal, and she wouldn't attack someone who could bite her back.

"Under the circumstances, you'll have to go to the office." The teacher's command brought him back.

"Sir, I'd like to introduce myself. I'm Sterling Lovell," Sterling said, momentarily distracting this teacher from his mission.

"I'm Mr. Barnhill," the teacher said stiffly.

"You teach chemistry?" Sterling asked.

"I do," he said. "Listen, none of this is my call, but I have to take this young lady to the principal's office."

"I'll accompany her," Sterling suggested.

"Me, too," Rhona said, "'cause that knife don't belong to any of us, especially Zell."

"Hey, thanks guys," Mr. Moore spoke up. "But we can handle it." He picked up the knife and handed it to his colleague.

Mr. Moore remained as Mr. Barnhill escorted Zell from the cafeteria. She looked back, and Sterling could see she was crying. Hell, he could see she was trembling. Of course, she was. Getting caught at school with a knife, or any other potentially deadly weapon, meant automatic expulsion, no negotiation, no nothing.

"Mr. Moore, you don't know Zell, so I'm telling you, she didn't have that knife on her. She's the sweetest person you'll ever meet," Rhona said.

"I don't doubt what you say, Rhona, but rules are rules. There was a knife on the floor and her purse was open. The administration will sort it out."

"It's a setup," Sterling said.

Mr. Moore cocked his eyebrows. "You're Ms. Wilmore's student, aren't you?"

"Yes sir, I am, and I appreciate what you did when Reverend Powell made that bad scene."

Mr. Moore straightened up like he was glad for Sterling's compliment but maybe thought a student shouldn't be commenting on that event.

"Zell is Ms. Wilmore's student, too," Sterling added. "Not in my class but first period. She knows Zell real well. She'll vouch for her."

127

The bell rang and the lunchroom, still mostly stunned and talking low, rumbled into action. Chairs scraped and students scrambled to their feet. Sterling trotted up behind Courtney before she could escape. "Hold on," he commanded, grabbing her arm.

"Let go of me, Sterling. Are you trying to make me late to class? Girls, wait on me," she called to Madison and Jill, who were scurrying forward.

"I know you planted that knife, and you won't get away with it. You absolutely will not," he said.

"You'd better not be threatening me, Sterling Lovell." Jill and Madison had walked back to flank Courtney like foot soldiers.

"You girls are culpable too; don't forget it," Sterling warned. "Zell gets in trouble, you'll all go down."

"You really are a fool, aren't you?" Jill blew air through her pursed lips. "You need a scapegoat because your motel girlfriend isn't the angel you thought?"

"Get over it," Courtney said. "I, for one, am not going to be late getting back to Ms. Wilmore's class. See ya."

For a moment, Sterling watched the girls parade off in unison, their backs stiff with confidence of their place in the world. Girls who'd been his friends. Girls of countless good times. He sprinted off to class.

Chapter 18

Angela Wilmore

Sterling rushed into class seconds before the tardy bell, stopping at Angela's desk to say he had to talk to her about something urgent.

"Is someone in immediate danger?" she asked, alarm rising in her voice.

"No, Ms. Wilmore, not that. It's something personal."

"If it's not a physical emergency, it'll have to wait until class ends." She hated teaching a class with middle lunch period. Something always got stirred up before they returned to class. "Go on to your seat, and we'll talk after," she assured him as the bell rang. Sterling went to his seat, but she could see he was nervous. His fingers drummed on the desk, reminding her of Mexican Jumping Beans her father once bought her at the 7-Eleven when she was a girl. The larvae inside the beans made them jittery jump in her palm. Just like the tips of Sterling's fingers were doing now.

The movement momentarily distracted her from discussing Tom's opening speech in *The Glass Menagerie*. Sterling was definitely in a fix. She noticed other kids looking at him, especially his buddy Kipp, who sat behind Sterling and had a view of his hopping fingers.

"I'm gonna need a pass in order to tell you everything," Sterling said after the bell rang and the other students exited.

"This better be good," she warned.

"That's the thing; it's not good," he said. "Zell is in terrible trouble." He talked about a knife under a table in the cafeteria near Hazel, her open pocketbook spilling. Angela stopped him when he said he knew Courtney, Jill, and Madison were responsible.

"I wouldn't be jumping to conclusions," Angela warned him. "That's an enormous accusation you're making."

"They did it; it's not an accusation," he insisted. "They made a show of coming to our table and stood around for a couple of minutes. One of them had to drop the knife then and push it under the table near Zell. A few minutes later, Madison bumped into Zell's chair and knocked over her bag on the way to the bathroom. It all fits."

"I understand the theory," she said, "but the first thing is the knife itself, and Hazel."

"That's what I'm saying. You got to help her, Ms. Wilmore. She can't get expelled for something she didn't do."

"I'll look into it," she promised. "But for now, you need to calm down. There's nothing you can do at the moment. I'm writing you a pass. Where to?"

***

After calling roll in senior study hall, Angela headed to Finley's office. Mrs. Bagley, busy at her computer, barely looked up and motioned her around the corner. She found Finley behind his desk with his head in his hands.

"The student I've told you about, Hazel, who lives in the motel. The one I've become so fond of...," she began from the doorway.

"I've just sent her home," he stopped her. "How did you know?"

"Sterling Lovell," she said. "Unlikely as it might seem, he and Hazel have become quite close. He comes every day to see her in my first period class before school starts."

"He's supposed to go to his own first period if he doesn't stay outside before the bell, isn't he?" Finley scowled.

"Yes, sorry. I bent the rules. It hasn't caused a problem, and they, well, I enjoy seeing them together."

Finley flicked his hand. "That's the least of my problems. I don't really care, as long as you take responsibility."

Angela nodded, relieved he wasn't angry. "What are you going to do?" she asked, sitting across from his desk without being invited.

"Sit," he said, after she had already planted herself.

"What *can* I do?" he asked. "I don't have choices here. Possession of a weapon means automatic expulsion."

"You can't," Angela pleaded. "I don't believe for a second Hazel

130

would carry a knife to school."

"It doesn't matter what you believe. Do you have a crystal ball?"

"No, but Sterling has a theory," she said quietly. Finley's testy tone discomfited her.

"Sterling Lovell? The kingpin of classroom disruption?"

"Yes."

"Well?" He leaned forward.

"I don't want to accuse young people who might be innocent, but he thinks some girls planted the knife. Maybe it would be best if you call him in?"

"I'll call him in, but you tell me about it first." Choosing her approach carefully, she did.

***

In the days following, Hazel suspended at home until a final decision, Finley told Angela the girls' parents had been summoned with their daughters for questioning in front of a special session of the school board. He wouldn't say much more, and she didn't ask, intuiting it was in Hazel's best interest not to.

Until out of nowhere—sitting on her sofa after a takeout pizza during what she thought was a calm weeknight evening—Finley yelled, "This damn thing is causing the worst stink of my career. Three sets of upstanding citizens with daughters immersed in the life of this school. And a girl who lives in the Red Rose Motel with a knife in her pocketbook. What would you think?"

Angela knew he wasn't yelling at her, exactly, but at the circumstances. Still, it felt personal because he knew her fondness for Hazel. His tone stung. It seemed he wanted to take the easy road, get it over with, placate the people with influence. What was the expulsion of a motel kid, more or less? A girl with no one of any consequence in the outside world to come to her defense?

"I thought you weren't afraid to stand up to better-than-thou people. After that scene Reverend Powell made in the hall with students watching?" she countered. Finley stared at her. Part of her regretted the outburst. He was struggling. She recalled the awful meeting with Courtney's parents, Reverend Powell criticizing her academic integrity, and how Finley defended her, protected her afterward by saying she never had to meet with that man again.

Still she couldn't help her feelings and her belief that Sterling's theory was correct, even if she had no evidence herself. She couldn't bear to see an innocent girl without means have any chance for the future ripped out from under her.

She turned to the man she'd begun to care about deeply and told him to leave. Finley looked at her, then got to his feet, saying as he walked out the door, "Maybe you're right about this principal-teacher relationship of ours. We can't seem to separate ourselves from the schoolhouse over this matter, can we? One of us is trying to stay open, and the other has already made up her mind." Later, she would see his jacket hanging in the coat closet and hug it to her chest.

Finley stopped calling. And why wouldn't he? She'd asked him to leave. She could return his jacket, an excuse to talk to him, but she didn't feel comfortable going to his office now. She missed him, but she was still angry. He didn't know Hazel.

Hazel wouldn't carry a knife. Not that kind girl. Unless it was self-defense against someone she feared at school. But Angela believed Hazel would have told her if she was afraid. Rather, it seemed Finley was unwilling to try to save Hazel from expulsion. He was right about her, though: she couldn't keep school and personal matters separate. Nor, as far as she was concerned, should she.

Days later, Sterling said Mr. Copeland had asked him to appear at a second school board meeting to tell what he witnessed. Hazel and Rhona, along with Hazel's mother and Rhona's grandmother, would also be present. Hazel would have an opportunity to tell her side, and Sterling would stand with her, he said.

Angela had mistakenly thought...well, what had she thought? Oh God, was she so rattled and predisposed as to think the other side wouldn't be called in? As quickly as she'd condemned Finley, she now felt ashamed. She'd sent him home without fully considering. She was the closed-minded person.

At least there was Sterling's courage to lift her. This young man who'd given her and a lot of other teachers pluperfect hell had now chosen to defend a vulnerable, disadvantaged friend. Likely he'd had the capacity for empathy all along, but it perhaps took meeting Hazel for him to find it.

***

The morning after the second school board meeting, Sterling entered Angela's classroom before school, boiling over. "I got big news, Ms. W," he said, huffing and puffing.

"Is it about Hazel?" she exclaimed.

"Yes, about their decision."

"Can you tell me about it, or does everything have to stay within the bounds of the meeting?"

"Doesn't matter whether I can tell you or not. I am."

"Sterling," she warned.

"Nobody specifically told me not to," he said.

"Okay, then."

He pulled a student desk up close to hers and began. He had told the board members the backstory of his breakup with Courtney and about her jealousy of Hazel. He told of the three girls stopping by their lunch table to talk for no apparent reason, *except* to plant a knife. He told of Madison kicking over Hazel's purse. Angela sat amazed—her hand propped on her chin—at Sterling's bravery. Revealing this information would likely cut him off from the elite circle he'd surely been a part of all his life. Not to mention his parents.

"And now, drum roll, Ms. W. You ready?" He leaned forward and beat his palms on her desk.

"Ready." Angela pulled her hand from beneath her chin and sat straight.

"Zell isn't going to be expelled. They decided the evidence is circumstantial. What with the girls' interruption, they can't prove Hazel was carrying the knife."

"Oh, Sterling," Angela said, exhaling loudly and jumping up from behind her desk. "I can't believe it. Stand up and let me give you a hug." She moved toward him. They clasped one another, quick and awkward, but a hug nonetheless. It must be his testimony that did it. Regardless of the cost to himself, he'd been willing to stick his neck out for what he believed was right.

"You're quite something," Angela said, stepping back to look at the young man who'd not long ago usurped her class.

"You got that right, Ms. W, and don't forget it," he said, nodding.

"No, I mean it, Sterling. I…" But she could see she was making him uncomfortable and stopped.

"Zell will be back on Monday. She got ten days of suspension, and it's nearly up."

Angela looked forward to welcoming her student back. It was a happy ending for Hazel. But maybe not for her. Would Finley accept her apology? He'd done the right thing, had always planned to, and she doubted him. He'd gone out on a limb in trusting a self-proclaimed, smart-aleck troublemaker. Finley gave Sterling the benefit of the doubt, and it made all the difference.

As her mother would have put it, Angela had a lot of crow to eat. She hoped Finley was a bigger person than she had been.

Chapter 19

Hazel Smalls

Walking with Sterling into the dark parking lot after the school board meeting, her mother several paces ahead, Hazel stopped, astonished. Had Sterling just whispered he loved her? She turned toward him. He put his arm around her shoulders and squeezed tight. Before, she would never have believed it, but only minutes before, he'd turned against Courtney and the other girls—all of them his friends—for her. To save her from being expelled.

Those important people sitting straight like a line of wooden clothespins behind that long table—Mr. Copeland called them trustees—would never have trusted her and Rhona's words over those rich girls. She knew by the stern, vacant looks on their faces. But when Sterling told what really happened, they paid attention, mouths creased and brows crinkling, because he was one of them.

Sterling convinced those nine men and women. Maybe not completely, but enough they couldn't prove the knife was Hazel's. The school board didn't punish the girls who set her up, except to warn they'd better be careful about making claims without evidence. But Hazel wasn't worrying about Courtney and her friends as long as she could stay in school and not have a mark on her permanent record.

Hazel leaned into Sterling's shoulder. "I love you, too," she whispered back.

"That's my girl," he said and swooped her up to his chest, kissing her quick before setting her back down.

Etta heard the commotion and turned around. She shook her head. "You are some innocent fools," she said. And then she smiled.

They arrived at her mama's old Honda Accord. Sterling walked around to open the driver's door for Etta. He'd started humming a song Hazel heard all over the radio, "Let Me Love You" by Ne-Yo. Still humming, he walked Hazel around the car and opened the passenger door for her. "You know those lyrics?" he asked.

"Sure, like who doesn't," she said, sitting inside the car. His hands reached out and grasped hers.

"*Girl, let me love you. Don't be afraid, girl let me help.*" He squeezed her hands before letting go.

He was still humming as he walked away and she pulled the car door shut.

***

The day she returned, Ms. Wilmore and Sterling and everybody else who'd already gotten there were waiting with those little birthday party blowouts you bought at Dollar General. They blew loud when she walked into class, paper horns unfurling like brightly colored tongues. "Welcome back, Hazel," Ms. Wilmore said, a bright yellow one dangling from her mouth.

Hazel smiled nervously and headed for her desk.

"Girl, you better look here," Sterling hollered. "This is a day to celebrate." He ran over and raised her arm. "Here's to Zell!" he exclaimed.

She jerked her arm back and whispered loud at him. "I ain't done anything."

"Are you kidding? Of course you have. You've proved yourself."

"You're the one did that."

"Au contraire, my dear." He stepped back. "One can only make a solid defense if the one wrongly accused is, in reality, worthy and true."

"That's about enough, Sterling," Ms. Wilmore called out. "Hazel needs to settle in. And you need to get on to class. It's only a few minutes till the bell. Shoo." Reluctantly, Sterling backed out of the door, waving happily as he went.

"We're all glad you're back," Ms. Wilmore said, glancing at Sterling's retreat and back to her. "Whew, that boy can make me crazy, so much drama, but I do appreciate him taking your lessons to you. Did you complete them?"

"Yes ma'am," Hazel responded. She opened her backpack and began to rummage inside.

"Good, I'll check them over. If I see anything you need to catch up on, I'll give you a pass to see me during your study period when I have senior study hall."

Students straggling in last minute looked around in bewilderment at the horns scattered about.

"What we got here?" Stokes asked as he and Gerard pounded their loud feet into class. "A party and I wasn't invited?"

"You didn't make it in time," Ms. Wilmore explained. "Here"—she opened her desk drawer and handed Stokes a red and white party horn—"give Hazel a toot to welcome her return." Stokes blew out a peppermint-striped ribbon.

Hazel had never been so happy to be at school. She went through the day turning in work to all her teachers, reconnecting. How stupid she'd been to think rich girls with pretty clothes were special. They looked better; they had nice manners and everything they could want, but she knew now they were no different from any other people if they were desperate. If you got in the way, same as anybody else, they might stomp on you.

Like the bald, skinny man at the Red Rose Motel she saw steal a needle from another man under the stairs, kick him to the ground, and shove the needle into his own arm. Or the fistfight between two winos— one breaking a bottle across the other's back—in the parking lot. Or a screaming match between two prostitutes, dressed like twins in tall black boots with skirts at the tops of their thighs, over whose turn it was to do the trick waiting inside a motel room.

***

Sterling ran up alongside Hazel as she walked through B-wing to the bus ramp. How did he get there so fast when his last class let out two halls away? Like he did with Ms. Wilmore to let him in her class before school, he must have sweet-talked his last period teacher to let him out before the bell.

She didn't need to ride the bus, he said. He would take her to the motel after they stopped by Fantastic Franks to celebrate again.

Hazel felt like the luckiest girl on earth, no matter if her mama thought she might be playing with fire. Her mama said she'd best stay away from Sterling before more trouble happened and Hazel was expelled for sure. Even though she was crazy about Sterling, her mama feared it would lead to no good. Her mama was wrong. Sterling loved her.

***

Her mother's car was still parked in the lot when Sterling dropped Hazel at the motel. They'd stayed only a few minutes at Fantastic Franks—guzzling Cokes fast—because she had to be home by 4:00 to tend to Chloe when her mother left for work and her father was on the road.

The school bus was pulling out of the motel parking lot as Hazel walked toward Room 103. Rhona and four other passengers ambled toward their own motel rooms. Hazel caught up with her friend. "Mama's still here," she said, pointing at their old car, bald on top where a wide streak of gray paint had peeled away.

Hazel pulled her phone from her bag and looked at the time to double check. A few minutes after 4:00. Her mama should be gone. Was she sick? Or Chloe?

"You reckon everything okay? Want me to come in with you?" Rhona asked.

"No," Hazel told her friend. "If I need you, I know where you are."

"Alright, girl. Glad you back at school today. I sure been missing you."

"Same," said Hazel. They punched each other's knuckles.

Before Hazel knocked—as she always did, too lazy to dig out her key—Chloe opened the door. Her sister had been watching for her out the window.

"You okay?" Hazel asked, trying to sound calm, though her heart had gone suddenly queasy because Chloe was hugging herself.

Chloe fell into Hazel's arms. "Whoa, sweetie, what?" Hazel said, holding on to her sister's shaking body.

"Daddy's dead," Chloe gulped and grabbed onto Hazel, squeezing her like a vise.

Hazel peeled her sister from her chest, grasped her wrists. "What are

138

you talking about? Where's Mama?" Chloe pointed to the bed where Etta lay, face up.

"Mama, what's wrong?" Hazel implored her mother. "Why aren't you at work?"

Etta turned on her side away from Hazel. Chloe still stood near the door.

"Mama, what is it?" she demanded. "You're scaring us." Hazel was yelling. Their mama turned her face back toward the ceiling. Chloe tiptoed up to the bed.

"It's okay, Mama," Hazel said then, her voice softening. "Tell me what happened. Chloe and I are here with you." Hazel pulled her sister close.

Slowly, Etta turned her body toward them. "He's gone," she mouthed. Her dark eyes had a hollow gaze like the look of the damned.

"What are you talking about?" Hazel shrieked, her momentary composure lost.

"Burl's been killed on the interstate below Columbia," Etta said. She wiped her hand across her eyes. "Passing a van with six people and swerved in too quick. The truck jackknifed when it hit the van, rolled upside down onto the shoulder. That's what the police said. He's dead." She shuddered and pulled her knees into a fetal position. "The parents in the front seat of that van are dead, too." Etta turned her head into the pillow and mumbled, "The four children in the back been taken to the hospital. Who've they got now to take care of them?"

"Oh, Mama," Hazel wailed. She leaned down and embraced her mother.

"I knew he shouldn't drive," Etta said, rocking back and forth in Hazel's arms. "We'll find out directly he was drunk."

"No, Mama," Hazel cried.

"What else?" Etta said. "He wouldn't drive fool like that if he was sober."

"Maybe he fell asleep," Hazel said.

Etta shook her head.

***

Burl had been transported alive from the scene but died on the way to Providence Hospital in Columbia. Etta wanted her husband out of the morgue. She was out of her mind. What could she do, she shouted, with no money to call a funeral home?

Hazel didn't know why she wasn't crying. She felt numb. Later, she would wonder what force propelled her to leave her mama and Chloe in the motel room, walk to the library, and log on to a computer. She understood the whole time that her father was dead, but she couldn't feel anything. She could only act. She had to figure what to do because her mother was overwhelmed. And when Hazel mentioned calling Uncle Huck, her mother shut down.

Sitting in a cubicle, she read about Indigent Care Services in Cassover County. She filled out a form online and sent it to the Wainwright Funeral Home, listed as a place that would assist families with no money for a burial.

She hardly remembered the walk home, her mind on autopilot. Back in their motel room, she told her mama and Chloe they would wait for the funeral home to call her cell phone. She called Elysian Fields to say there'd been a death in the family and Etta couldn't come to work that day. She promised the supervisor her mama would call the next day to explain.

She heated Campbell's vegetable soup and toasted slices of bread for supper. The three of them sat—mostly silent—at the card table in their room. Hazel ate a piece of toast and Chloe managed a few spoonfuls of soup. Etta ate nothing.

"I got to go to bed," her mama said as Hazel cleared the table.

"Of course you do, Mama; you need to rest."

"I wish I had something to make me sleep."

"I think we got some Tylenol in the drawer. It won't make you sleep, but maybe it would make you feel better?"

Etta nodded, and Hazel fetched the bottle and a cup of water, putting two capsules into her mother's palm.

Hazel turned out the overhead light and the floor lamp near the door, leaving on only the small lamp between the two beds. She handed Chloe one of the soup bowls while she carried the other two, and together they walked outside and poured the uneaten soup in the ditch.

"I'm scared," Chloe whimpered when they returned to the darkened room. "My daddy's dead."

"I know. You go climb into bed with Mama. It'll be better tomorrow when you not so tired."

Chloe looked terrified, so Hazel said, "Come on. I'll help you get ready for bed. You're safe. I promise." Her sister acquiesced and followed Hazel to the bathroom. "Pull off those stiff jeans," Hazel said after Chloe used the toilet. "You'll sleep better in just that sweatshirt and your underwear." Chloe left her jeans crumpled on the bathroom floor. Hazel folded her sister's pants and laid them on top of the toilet tank.

Lying in the other bed with her thoughts spinning, Hazel saw her phone light up—she'd put the sound on silent. She nearly picked up, thinking it was the funeral home, until she saw it was Sterling's number. She ignored the call. She didn't know how to tell him her father was dead, probably driving drunk, and other people had died, too, because of him.

***

Chloe woke Hazel, shaking her shoulders. "We not going to school today, Zell?" she asked.

"No, baby, we're staying home today," Hazel answered, half asleep. She'd been awake much of the night, dropping off finally when the dial on the clock radio beside the bed showed 3:00 am.

Slowly, she sat up, gathered her bearings. "I'm waiting to hear from the funeral home. Is Mama still asleep?"

"No, she's awake, but she's not moving," Chloe answered. "What we gonna do?"

"It'll be okay, that's what. Why don't you take a shower real quick while I get going? The warm water will feel good."

"Okay, Zell," Chloe answered and padded toward the bathroom.

It was nearly 9:00 am. when Hazel pulled her phone from under her pillow and saw the funeral home had called.

"Mama," she called after she listened to the soft voice on the message. Etta groaned. "Wainwright Funeral Home will pick up Daddy from the hospital. The Indigent Care Services will pay for a cremation."

Etta sprang up straight. "Burl's got to be buried in a coffin. Nobody should be burned up," she wailed.

"You got to listen, Mama. And understand. Indigent Care Services will only pay for a cremation, not a casket in the ground." Hazel covered her eyes with her hands and gouged her forehead with her fingernails. She didn't want to break down.

"He's got to be buried," Etta exclaimed, pulling at the tight coils of her hair springing out.

"Where you gonna get the money, Mama? Only other thing I know is you could call Uncle Huck, ask him for the money for a coffin." She didn't mean to yell. Her mother turned silent.

"Want me to call him?" Hazel asked, forcing her voice softer, looking over from her bed to her mother's. She could do this. She had to hold up for her mother's sake.

"No," her mother cried. "That bastard is the reason Burl is dead. After all the work Burl did for him…. Not unless hell freezes over."

"Then there's no other choice," Hazel said. She sat beside her mother on the bed. Etta put her head on Hazel's shoulder.

Once Etta was up and stirring, she seemed more nervous than comatose like the day before. She paced the room like she was waiting for something. What?

"I want some cigarettes," Etta declared.

"Mama, you haven't smoked cigarettes since I was a little girl," Hazel said.

"Don't matter. I want some now."

"Okay. If they'll sell them to me." Anything to settle her mother's nerves. She gathered up Chloe to walk with her to the Mini Mart.

"I miss my Daddy," Chloe's quiet voice trembled. They were walking back to the motel, a pack of Marlboros swinging in a plastic grocery bag on Hazel's arm.

"Let's try to pretend like he's still on the road today until we can take it all in." Hazel grasped her sister's hand. The bag handle fell onto Hazel's wrist as her phone rang inside her pocket. She stopped to pull it out. Sterling again. She didn't answer, but she knew he wouldn't stop because she wasn't at school. She should text him back, but she didn't know what to say.

***

She knew it was Sterling knocking. His rat-a-tat-tat was easy to recognize, insistent and lively. When she didn't answer, he paused, then resumed the drumming.

"Zell," he called. "You there? May I come in? Zell, yoo-hoo."

Unable to endure his persistence, coupled with his loud voice she knew would draw a crowd on the sidewalk, Hazel opened the door.

"Why didn't you come to school today?" He stood with his hands jammed deep in his pockets, like maybe his arms were trying to fit into them. "Seems to me you've been out a lot already."

"It's...," Hazel started, her eyes darting back into the room at her mother and Chloe.

"Our daddy died," Chloe said, coming to the door.

Sterling's hands came out of his pockets. They flailed upward. "Why in the world didn't you...how? Where...why didn't you call me?" He stepped across the threshold uninvited.

Hazel shook her head. "Was nothing you could do. It's something we have to..." She shook her head again.

"That's not true," Sterling said. "Why?"

"No," Hazel answered.

"When is the funeral?"

"No funeral," she said.

Sterling looked at her perplexed.

"We don't want a service. It's all covered."

"How can I...?" he began.

"Zell says there's no money for a service," Chloe said. Hazel turned toward her sister to shush her.

"I can get you the money," Sterling said.

Hazel waved her hand across her face to cut him off.

"Is that your fella?" Etta called. She drifted from the bathroom in sweatpants and an old plaid robe that had belonged to Hazel's daddy. "Does he know about Burl?"

"Yes, Mrs. Smalls, I know now," Sterling said, stepping across the room toward her. "I'm so sorry. Please tell me what I can do to help you all."

"Hazel says Burl's got to be burned up instead of be buried. Because of the money. It's not right."

"No, if that's not what you want," Sterling said. Etta began to cry. Sterling touched his hand to her arm. "I've got some money saved from my summer job," he said.

"No, you're not doing that," Hazel exclaimed.

"Why not?" Sterling asked. "Why won't you let me help?"

"Because it's not your responsibility," Hazel said.

"My responsibility is wanting to help people I care about." His face turned hard.

"I know Zell is right," Etta said. "But you're mighty kind to offer."

"I'll be back in a few minutes," Sterling said and was gone before Hazel could say anything, leaving the door open.

"Thank you, Mama," she said. "It wouldn't be right to take his money. We gonna be alright."

"I don't know how," Etta said. "The week's rent is due in three days. I got a piece of it—about $150—but I don't know where the other $150 is coming from. Burl, he…can't get a check now." She began to sob.

"We'll figure it out. I'll see if I can clean more rooms this weekend. Please, Mama." Her body felt like a stick of butter left out on the counter too long, all but melted. She forced herself to stand up straight.

"Zell, you're a brave, fine girl. But you can't do the impossible," her mama said.

"Nobody said anything about impossible," Hazel said.

Sterling knocked gently when he returned. He didn't seem like the Sterling she knew at all. He looked awkward and out of place, where always before in this room, he made a big show of feeling at home.

He strode over to the table and sat in one of the folding chairs. He opened his arms by his sides. Hazel sat in the chair across from him. Chloe and Etta followed and sat in the other two seats.

"May I ask how Mr. Smalls died?" he ventured.

For a moment, no one spoke. Then Etta began, wiping her eyes as she went. Hazel watched Sterling, his head rocking back and forth non-stop like the strong, steady pendulum in the big clock that had stood on her grandfather's mantel. Briefly, Hazel wondered what happened to that majestic clock after her grandfather died. When Etta stopped talking, Hazel watched Sterling put his hand to his forehead before he rested his elbows on the table.

"Life ought not be like this," he muttered. He stood and reached into his back pocket for his wallet.

"Sterling...," Hazel started.

He held up his hand. "This isn't much. It won't pay for a funeral, but it's something to help you all get through this tough time." He pulled out several bills. "Mrs. Smalls, please use this however it can help." He laid the money on the table.

Etta picked up the bills and counted. "Five hundred dollars. Good Lord. I don't know when I've held that much money."

"Sterling, no," Hazel started again.

He shook his head at her. "It's not negotiable," he said.

***

When Hazel, Chloe, and Etta arrived to retrieve Burl Smalls' ashes, the funeral home chaplain met them at the director's office. Like he somehow understood her mother's anguish about the cremation, he quoted a verse from the Bible about dust returning to dust.

They sat at a round, wooden table, the funeral director at his desk nearby. The chaplain read several other scriptures, said a prayer, and handed Etta a ceramic vase with a lid that had sat on the table the whole time.

"Burl's in here?" she asked, holding out the white urn decorated with vines of blue flowers.

The minister stood and bowed slightly. He was tall and slight, his dark hair balding across the back of his head.

"God's peace be with you all," he said and made the sign of the cross on his chest.

Hazel and Chloe stood with their mother. The chaplain grasped Etta's hands. "The Lord be with you," he said.

"And also with you," her mother answered. The refrain took Hazel back: Sundays sitting on a hard wooden pew between her parents at St.

Joseph's Catholic Church. Her father had once been a devout Catholic. A hard kernel caught in her throat. She tried to swallow, but it wouldn't budge.

"Hold Burl." Etta handed the urn to Hazel as they walked across the parking lot toward the car. Gingerly, Hazel held the rounded container with its narrow neck—the shape of something exotic from another place.

"I can hold him," Chloe said, her arms reaching out.

"I know, baby girl. But it's Hazel's turn right now," their mother said.

Terrified she might drop it, Hazel clasped the urn to her chest like a newborn baby. Her mama opened the passenger door. Hazel slipped onto the seat. With one hand she buckled the seatbelt across herself and her father. Chloe put her hand on Hazel's head as she climbed into the backseat.

"That money from Sterling gives Burl a resting place inside that fancy vase," Etta said as they pulled out. "With what's left we'll pay the rest of the rent. Maybe have enough for the battery this car needs, so I don't have to get it jumped all the time."

"Mama, that's not safe," Hazel exclaimed.

Etta glanced toward her daughter. "That and a whole lot else," she said.

The pressure hurt Hazel's chest, but she wouldn't loosen her grip. Suddenly, she recalled hugging her daddy's hard knees the same way when she was very small. In the yard at the duplex, a cocoa-colored dog—not a big dog, but it seemed so then to Hazel—had sprinted toward her from the neighbors' yard across the street. Its tongue flopped out, its tail wagged, but Hazel was scared and grabbed onto her daddy. He scooped her up, and the dog leaped up onto her father's thighs. By the time the owner arrived to call the dog, her father had convinced Hazel to stroke its head. It was a Boykin spaniel, her father said.

Without warning, Hazel began to gasp. She couldn't stop. She held on to her father's ashes as tears flowed over the ledge of her cheeks.

Chapter 20

Sterling Lovell

Sterling sat stiff-backed in Mr. Clark's calculus class and thought about Zell. What else could happen? How much was this beautiful, vulnerable girl supposed to endure? He told her he loved her, and he meant it. Yet he felt powerless. And she still wasn't back at school.

The money he gave was paltry when you considered how much more the family needed, but that $500 was pretty much the end of last summer's lifeguarding pay. He briefly imagined asking his parents for several thousand dollars to give a dead man they didn't know—a man who'd lived in his father's motel—a decent funeral, plus money to help the family. Though it would be chump change to them, he was pretty sure he knew the answer.

He felt impotent, too, because Hazel had shut him out. He'd left the motel room in a stupor two days ago. He'd been calling and texting since. So far, she'd answered his texts briefly, a phrase or two, and ignored his calls. She had pulled in to herself, and he didn't know what to do. He felt hurt.

"Sterling, I asked you a question," Mr. Clark called him out.

"Oh, sorry, my bad," Sterling said, jerking to attention. "Could you ask it again?"

"No, I could not," Mr. Clark said. "Maybe someone else can answer?" A hand shot up. His teacher turned his attention toward dipshit Franklin Johns and pointed.

"Yes sir," Franklin answered, licking Mr. Clark's behind with his toadying tone while he sneered at Sterling.

Sterling would just as soon Franklin Johns drop off the face of the earth. He was no different, really, from the Halloween carnival bully he'd been in middle school, much less all his other assaults through the years. He loved an opportunity to get at Sterling and anyone else he thought he could one-up to make himself look better.

Forget Franklin. He was a sycophantic sneak, pathetic at best. Sterling had critical things on his mind. Like how to help Zell. Like how to introduce her to his parents. So that Harriet and Hugh Lovell could see what he saw: a lovely, charming girl, full of potential in spite of her disadvantages. If she could feel comfortable in his home, secure, maybe she would let him inside.

Forgetting he was in class with twenty other people, he clamped his hands over his ears, trying to block his sister Livie's voice invading his thoughts. He didn't want to hear what she would say: their parents couldn't see outside their small, exclusive world.

Livie was living proof. They'd been pissed when she chose a field they considered inferior. "We're spending nearly $200,000 on your education"—Sterling remembered verbatim his father's angry declaration when Livie announced she was majoring in sociology during their Thanksgiving meal her sophomore year—"and you're repaying us with a slum degree."

Like a slow-motion video on replay, Sterling saw his sister push back the antique dining chair—their mother was immensely proud of her nineteenth century Hepplewhite chairs—sweep her arms into a sunburst and say, "Maybe I'll be able to help some of those poor people whose outrageous rent affords this elegance." Then she had stood and retreated to her room.

Other than his father muttering something about Livie's expensive, liberal school putting her on a high horse, their parents continued the meal as though everything was normal. Sterling had stared at the sliced turkey, dressing, sweet potatoes, and broccoli casserole uneaten on Livie's plate until he stood, too. His father had looked at him like he suddenly had three eyes. Sterling thought about his mother's pecan pie, his favorite, when he walked out of the room. A scene straight out of a melodrama.

After graduation, Livie announced she would be moving in with her lover, Elodie Teal—a woman his parents had not known existed. They screamed and demanded in vain that Livie come to her senses. When it didn't work, Harriet and Hugh Lovell made a near total break with their daughter.

Sterling was "allowed," they said—like they could have stopped him—to communicate and visit his sister, but to his knowledge, his parents had never once visited Elodie and Livie in Atlanta. Nor had Livie returned home with or without Elodie. It had been nearly two years. God, why did life have to be so hard when it didn't need to be? Why not embrace his sister as the person she was meant to be?

***

Sterling called Zell the minute he exited Ramsey High into a brisk breeze. Friday afternoon, finally. Miraculously, she answered.

"Hey, sweetie, how's it going?" he asked, amazed to hear her voice. "Have you been in all day? It's super windy. Guess March is blowing in a couple of days early." He was blathering small talk.

"Mama's leaving for work soon. I'll be here with Chloe." Her tone was flat.

"That's good? That your mom feels like returning to work?"

"I guess she doesn't have any choice," Zell answered, her voice moving toward edgy.

"Fair enough. Sorry. Hey, I'm out of my comfort zone here, Zell. I'm worried about all of you, but I don't know how to say it all right. Damn, I've only been to one funeral in my life. My grandfather—my mother's father—died of emphysema last year. It was awful. He was only seventy-four, but too many cigarettes suffocated him. He was a quiet man who loved to sit on the front stoop at his house and whittle sticks into all kinds of freeform creations. He liked jigsaw puzzles, too," Sterling continued. "I worked on a few of those crazy hard puzzles with him. We sort of understood each other, you know? I miss him."

"I'm sorry," she said. He heard a quick intake of breath. "You must have loved him a lot. I don't mean to snap."

"Hey, it's okay. My God. It's just I don't know how to show you I care."

Silence followed. Sterling cleared his throat. "Zell, you there?"

"Yes." He could tell from the tightness in her voice she was trying not to cry. Had he made it worse, talking about his grandfather?

"Is there any way I could see you tonight? I know you need to stay

149

with Chloe. Could I come over and sit with y'all?"

There was another long pause before she murmured, "Okay."

"Bring some supper?"

"Thank you," she said. The phone made its three-ding noise telling him she'd hung up.

***

Holding a cardboard box with three large cups of lemonade in one hand, Sterling maneuvered the bag of food under his other arm to knock on the motel door. Chloe answered quickly. "Chick-fil-A," she squealed.

"You got it," Sterling said, handing her the bag. "Hey kiddo, you doing okay?" He patted the top of her head.

"Yeah, but it's bad," she responded. "Our daddy is gone."

"I know, sweetheart. I'm awful sorry."

Zell appeared beside her sister. "Hey, you," she said.

"Hey, you, back. Hungry?" He pointed toward the bag in Chloe's hands.

"Thank you for doing this," Zell said.

"Are you kidding?" Sterling said.

They sat at the card table wolfing chicken nuggets, sandwiches, fries. "Jeez, we were all starving and didn't know it," Sterling exclaimed.

"I knew I was starving," Chloe declared.

"Who gets the last chicken nugget?" Sterling teased.

"I do," Chloe said, slathering it with honey mustard sauce before popping it into her mouth. "You come to stay with us tonight?" she asked. A small dollop of sauce stuck to her chin.

"If you want, you bet," Sterling said, swallowing a large bite of sandwich.

"My sister likes you," Chloe said.

"I like her, too," Sterling said, looking over at Zell, cheeks full.

"Hush, Chloe," Zell said after she swallowed.

Three sharp raps sounded at the door. Chloe leaped from her chair.

Zell rose slowly. "Wait just a minute, Chloe." Sterling didn't move, though he wanted to go to the door and investigate the caller himself.

Chloe ignored Zell's warning and ran to open the door. A young

150

girl with silky blonde curls about Chloe's age stepped inside. She pulled off her jacket to reveal a dozen or more string bracelets in myriad colors on the wrists of each arm.

"Hey, Fawn," Chloe said.

"We heard about your daddy," the girl responded. "Mama and me. She said you could come for a sleepover…if…"

"Thank you, Fawn," Zell interjected. "That's really kind. But we're doing good. Tell your mama we said thank you, though."

"But I want Chloe to sleep over," Fawn insisted. "We'll take care of her."

"Of course, but…" Zell was interrupted by Chloe tugging on the waistband of her jeans.

"Let me go, please," Chloe begged. "I'll come home early."

Sterling observed the exchange: Chloe's face alight with the possibility, Zell's full of consternation. He was on Chloe's side. Here was an opportunity for this child to get away from this godawful room and its despair for a little while. Not that her friend's motel room would be much different, but it would at least be a change, and it appeared to him—if Fawn's cheerful bracelets were an indication—she'd be with happy people. Give Zell a break, too.

Sterling touched Zell's shoulder. She twisted toward him. "Why don't you let her go?"

"I'm responsible for her," she said briskly.

"Right, so make her happy," Sterling said, "unless you have a reason to worry about her staying with Fawn and her mother."

"No," Zell acknowledged. "Fawn's mama is a widow. I don't know how her husband died. She and Fawn were alone when they moved in here."

"My daddy had a stroke," Fawn said.

"Then, I guess Fawn's mama understands," Sterling said, biting his lower lip when Zell gave him a piercing stare.

"Yay! Then can I go?" Chloe asked.

"Okay, okay. Go ahead."

Within minutes, Chloe had packed things into a plastic grocery bag.

"Hey, Chloe, just a sec, do you know Zell's phone number if you need to call?" Sterling asked.

"Yeah, but I don't have a phone to call on," Chloe said.

"We do," Fawn said.

"Good deal," Sterling said.

"That's right, dude," Fawn said. Sterling gestured two fingers to his brow then pointed his index finger at Fawn. She smiled at him.

"You be home in the morning, got it?" Zell commanded.

"Yeah, I promise," Chloe said as she and Fawn exited, hand in hand.

***

Zell cleared the table while Sterling sat watching, waiting, thinking what to say.

"Hey, you," he said finally, after watching her crunch and pitch the trash from supper. She turned toward him. "I wish I could do more."

Zell shook her head. "I don't even know what makes you be here. You got no business in this nasty place."

"Duh, meeting you in ISS was the luckiest day of my life."

She looked at him hard. "You know what I'm talking about."

Sterling walked over to Zell standing over the garbage can. He put his arms around her waist.

"Let me help," he whispered. "Let me in."

"You've done plenty. There's nothing else to do. I'm okay." Zell pushed against his chest until he released his hold. She stepped back and stood straight, her expression stoic.

Sterling's arms dangled at his sides. "Who the hell is okay after her father dies?" He stepped toward her again. But her eyes, soot black as a night without a flicker of star, stopped him.

"You want me out of here, that what you're saying? You're superhuman? Wow, glad to know it." Her cold response made him angry. He picked up his coat where he'd flung it on the back of her father's green velour chair and turned to leave. At the door, his hand on the knob, he heard something.

A squeak like an animal in pain. Instinctively, he looked back. Saw Zell's face crumpled. He raised his arms.

152

Suddenly, unexpectedly, she ran to him, collided, buried her face in his chest.

He steadied himself, letting his arms touch her back. For a moment Zell was quiet. Then, a gurgling started in her throat. He held her shoulders as she began to sob.

"Baby, you got so much on you. Crying is good. Let it go," he urged.

"I'm sorry," she said when the weeping turned to ragged breath.

"What the hell do you have to be sorry about?"

He led her toward the closer bed and pulled down the thin coverlet. She crawled in and curled into a ball. Sterling removed Zell's shoes, tossed them onto the floor. He pulled off his own shoes and climbed onto the other side of the bed. They lay face to face.

He saw she was shivering and pulled the threadbare spread over both of them. He scooted closer to her. "I can't imagine," he said.

"I'm scared," she whispered.

"Of course you are."

"I mean Mama. She's not right."

"She just lost her husband, Zell. She's not supposed to be right. Neither are you. Or Chloe." He stroked the top of one forearm protruding from the spread.

"The man you met wasn't the man he used to be. He got bitter and gave up. He used to work hard. He was a good daddy and husband most of the time back then." Zell pulled the spread tighter.

"Of course, he was."

"But Mama, now…it's scaring me. I know she's worried how she's gonna support us, even though she's mostly been the one doing it for a year. I can work more hours cleaning rooms. It's not just money. She thought Daddy would come back around like he used to be. And now, it's too late." Her voice trembled.

"Seems to me your mom is pretty tough," Sterling said. He didn't have any idea, really, about Etta Smalls, other than the strong demeanor she'd presented to him, but he wanted to encourage Zell.

Zell shook her head. "It's like all of a sudden she's used up. She acts like a zombie or something. She doesn't say much of anything unless Chloe or me asks her a question." Zell's voice was hushed.

153

"I'm sure she'll work through it," he said. "My mama had a hard time with my grandfather's death. Give her time."

"I don't know," Zell said, barely a whisper.

Sterling wrapped his arms around his girl. "You want me to stay? Or would getting you out of here feel better?"

"I know you don't want to stay here," she murmured. "But I got to watch out for Chloe."

"I want to be wherever you are," he assured her. "Right here, if that's what you want."

"What would you tell your parents?"

"If they ask, I spent the night with Alex or Kipp. Friends are glad to cover. Or hey, I can tell my old man I spent the night at his Taj Mahal and see how he reacts. It makes me sick. Your family in this place where the toilet leaks."

"How do you know the toilet leaks?" Zell sat partway up.

"I don't. Just guessing. But see, I was right."

"If your daddy didn't own it, someone else would, and it wouldn't be any different, okay?"

"You're incredible," he said. "You never complain and…"

"I'll be alright," she said. "You don't have to stay." She lay back onto the pillow.

"Let me," Sterling exhaled and snuggled closer into her. "Give me a break. I told you. I want to be wherever you are," he said. "You sleep. I'll be right here."

"I'm not sleepy," Zell said. She sat up and leaned against the wall.

"I have wine and two glasses in the car," Sterling said. "Would that relax you?"

"Glasses in your car?"

"I'm a man prepared," he said and smiled.

"I'd like some wine," she said.

He retrieved his shoes and left Zell sitting in bed.

***

"Whoever heard of such a name," Zell said, looking at the Shiraz label. They were propped up on bed pillows. Sterling said the wine came from two French grapes he couldn't pronounce.

"How do you know all this stuff? To me wine is something red or white." She held out her glass in his direction.

"Or blush or bubbly."

"Stop." She raised her hand. "You're making me feel stupid." She pulled playfully on the stem of his glass.

"Just because I know something about wine?"

"I thought guys drank only beer." She tapped her finger on his wine glass. She was getting tipsy.

"Not this guy," Sterling said, pulling his glass back and taking a sip, "but I don't turn down a beer."

"Beer I get, but—"

"Maybe it's hereditary. My parents consider themselves wine connoisseurs," he cut in. "They started pouring me a glass at dinner when I was sixteen. Now it's sort of a hobby, learning about wines. There's plenty to support my interest in my parents' cellar. A bottle here and there. They don't notice, or if they do they don't say anything."

"I can't imagine." She picked up her glass and sipped.

He shouldn't be talking about his parents' abundant wine cellar. He was such a dunce. Of course, she couldn't imagine.

"Enjoy," he said, quickly changing the subject from his family's prosperity, and clinked his glass against hers. She giggled. "Nothing like a good bottle of wine to get you feeling better."

"You're sweet to me," she said.

"Listen," he said abruptly. "What do think about—not right now, I mean, with everything you and your family are going through—but at some point coming to my house to meet Harriet and Hugh?"

"Harriet and Hugh?" Her eyebrows squinched together.

"The parents," he said.

"Oh, I don't know. I don't think so."

"Now's not the time to talk about it," he said, feeling like a double dolt. "Sorry. But hey, we're definitely going somewhere soon. Maybe Atlanta to visit Livie for a weekend. I think you'll like her."

"I already know I'd like her from what you told me," Zell said. "But Atlanta's a long way. I want to go there, but I don't see how."

"You're probably right. We'll go somewhere close where we can

155

sneak away for a night, and no one will know."

"How we gonna do that?" she asked, holding out her glass for more wine.

"You let me figure it out," he said. "The only concern I see is making arrangements for someone to take care of Chloe when your mom's working, now that—" He stopped himself, but too late. Zell licked her lips as she often did when she was uneasy, stared down into her glass.

"Sorry, baby," he said, pouring more wine, overfilling her glass. "Here you're relaxing, escaping for a few minutes until I had to go and…." What was wrong with him? He couldn't stop making an idiot of himself.

"It's okay." She patted his hand as he replaced the bottle on the table.

When the bottle was empty, he went to the car for another, this time a Cabernet. Pretty soon, he was feeling no pain. He suddenly broached the subject of his parents again. "So, Zell," he tapped her shoulder, "how about agreeing to come over?"

"Stockton Estates?" she asked. "309 Winnifree Road?"

"Uh, you been sleuthing, girl?"

She grinned at him shyly. "White Pages on the computer."

"Smartie." He reached out and tickled her ribs.

"Youch," she cried, jumping away from his probing fingers.

"Well?" he asked.

"I don't know. I'm sleepy. And I have to go to the bathroom."

"I hear you," he said. "I'll be after you." Zell threw her legs over the edge of the bed and stood. For a moment her knees bobbed before she wobbled.

In a minute Sterling heard water running. He followed barefooted into the bathroom. Zell stood at the sink, washing her face, staring in the mirror.

"What you see there?"

Zell jumped on both feet. "Aahhhh," she squealed.

"Just keeping you on your toes." He pointed to his feet, lifted his toes. She flipped the wet washcloth in her hand across his chest.

"Hey, now," he admonished her.

"You really scared me, you." Her words blended pleasantly together

156

into one long sound.

"Oh, now," he whispered, blowing air across her ear. She pushed on his chest.

"I gotta pee. You can look the other way if it makes you uncomfortable." She turned her back to him.

"What about a hot shower?" he suggested after the toilet flushed. "To warm up your whole body, not just your pretty face." She didn't object when he turned on the water and steam began to rise.

***

Stepping out of the shower ahead of her, Sterling grabbed two thin, white towels hanging on the rack. He handed one to Zell, standing naked and beautiful inside the shower stall. He watched, engrossed, as she rubbed the towel back and forth across her back, then pulled it around her body, glistening like smoky topaz. He dried himself best he could with the other threadbare towel, then wrapped it around his waist.

"How you feel?" His arousal was obvious under the towel, but what kind of jerk would he be? Tonight was not about his desire.

"I feel okay," she answered and leaned her damp head onto his shoulder.

"That's my girl. Ready for sleep?"

She nodded. "It's kinda cold out here," she murmured, hugging the towel around her as they neared the bed.

"Got any more blankets besides that flimsy thing at the end of the bed?"

"In the closet. My granddaddy's army blanket. My daddy's daddy. I don't remember him, but Daddy said he knew me. He died of cancer from Agent Orange after Vietnam."

"Oh, Jesus, sweet girl," Sterling said. "Get on into that bed." Zell dropped her wet towel on the floor, swaying—he knew—from both the wine and the warmth of the shower. He helped her climb in.

Sterling found the scratchy blanket on the shelf of the closet, spread it across the coverlet, and got in beside Zell. He wasn't surprised to find she was already asleep.

Chapter 21

Angela Wilmore

In the weeks since Zell's incident at school, Angela had tried to ramp up her courage to approach Finley. But the more time that elapsed, the harder the proposition became. If he would just call, or email, text, anything. But that was irrational, of course, because the proverbial ball lay still in her court. She feared if she lobbed it to his side, he would slam it down her throat, or worse, ignore her and let the ball drop.

Sitting at her patio table on a mild, midweek evening in March, with iridescent pink and lilac clouds blooming in front of the setting sun, she stared at the essay on top of fifth period's mostly ungraded stack. She pushed the papers aside, along with her green pen (no red ink; it made students more defensive than they already were). Her mind was on Finley. She ached to talk to him.

Angela went inside for wine in an attempt to calm—or more like distract—herself. On impulse, she also picked up her phone. Balancing the bottle and glass in one hand, phone in the other, she returned to the wrought-iron table outside.

The sun was dropping behind her hedge of tea olives. She set things down and walked back to the door, reached inside and turned on the patio light. She glanced at her watch. A little past 7:00. Daylight Savings Time had started the week before, and she was still adjusting. So it was supper time. She had leftover spaghetti in the fridge, but she wasn't hungry.

She sat sipping wine, thinking how Zell's predicament was likely only one of myriad conflicts Finley dealt with on a daily basis among students, parents, and teachers. Angela was glad to be a teacher and not a principal.

She glanced up to view the pastel streaks of clouds again, but they had gone gray in the darkening sky. She sighed. The beautiful moments of the world passed so fast. Lines in a melancholy Frost poem ran through her head: "So dawn goes down to day. / Nothing gold can stay." Time was now. Every moment was precious.

The first star of the night twinkled between the branches of the big oak tree. She picked up her phone. In an instant she had texted one phrase: *mea culpa*.

***

Dark descended and gnats began to buzz. Angela retreated inside. She pulled out a Tupperware container of spaghetti sauce. She set a saucepan of water on the stove to boil noodles. She topped off her glass of wine. Should it be red if she was having spaghetti? What did she care? The bottle of Chardonnay was already open. She glanced at her phone. No response. Even reproach would be preferable to silence.

She drained the noodles and served her plate. She stared at it. Grow up, she told herself. Eat your supper. Wishes on stars are only wishes. Move on.

Angela carried her supper on a tray into the den. She turned on *Jeopardy!*. Her phone dinged just as the $200 clue for "Double-letter, Eight-letter Words" emerged: "The adjective for a stain that doesn't come out or people who won't change their mind."

"What is stubborn? So easy," she said aloud as she peered at her phone. Finley! She sat up straight and took a deep breath. The opening words read, "I've hoped you would…." Angela pressed her fingers against her temples, felt her pulse throbbing. She was afraid to open the full message.

She glanced back at the television. Alex Trebek was interviewing his guests. The champion had met his fiancé in a Tai Chi class and was jabbering about total harmony of the self. "Alrighty then, each to his own," Angela shouted.

She muted the television and set her tray on the coffee table. She took another deep breath. She tapped her thumb on Finley's message: "I've hoped you would reach out after the episode with Hazel Smalls. I understand your affection for her. But you must understand my position, too. Your and Sterling's comments, along with Hazel's permanent record—several instances of discipline re detention hall and ISS notwithstanding—established her respectability under difficult circumstances. That said, my job requires me to look at all sides. The girls accused had no significant blemishes either."

Angela cringed at the formal tone, but squared her shoulders, took a long drink of wine, and continued.

"Apology accepted. I hope we can come to an understanding."

She stopped reading. Yes, he'd forgiven her but his message also suggested she keep her distance. She placed her phone back on the coffee table. Move on, she said to herself for the second time tonight. You've dealt with far worse. But her throat clenched in disappointment and her eyes stung. She strained for composure. Stared at the muted television, the clues in the blue boxes and the contestants mouthing their answers. The self-confident champion with his Tai Chi inner peace was losing. She was glad. He was a jerk.

"Dammit," she yelled and stood, tightening her hands into fists to make them stop trembling. She was anything but composed. Her face felt flaming hot. It was her own stupid fault for allowing the relationship. Or maybe it was Finley's? Or was it Hazel's fault because otherwise she and Finley.... Angela grabbed her phone, intending to fling it to the floor, but as she did, she noticed another line of text after a wide white space on the screen. She'd stopped reading before the end.

"I've missed you terribly, especially your spectacular smile. I'm convinced your smile could bring the saddest person joy. Yours truly, Finley."

Angela hugged her phone. She lifted the screen to her lips and kissed it.

***

Carrying her half-eaten plate of spaghetti to the sink, Angela considered her options. She could do nothing tonight and see him at school tomorrow. She could text him back now. Or she could call. Should she? What were the rules? She didn't know. Hell, she was fifty-three years old and hadn't been in this circumstance since, well, since she was a girl. Her mother once reprimanded her for calling a boy. She could hear her now:

"Never call a boy first, Angela Maryl; you wait for him to call you."

"It's a new day, Mama," she said out loud.

She went back to the den, turned off the television, sat with her phone in her lap. The bottle of Chardonnay was half gone. But maybe she wasn't gone enough to get up her nerve to call Finley.

What to say if she did? "Thank you for texting me. I know my personality can be overbearing; it's just that Hazel is the sweetest...." No, no, she didn't need to keep apologizing. So, what then? If she said what she really wanted, that she'd like him to drive to her house, and.... She felt her cheeks flush.

Don't overthink it, she told herself. Wing it. But as her finger hovered over Finley's name in her contacts, her phone rang. Like a hot sparkler too close to her fingers, she dropped it.

"Oh, no," she exclaimed. She retrieved the ringing phone from the rug, managing, somehow, in the mayhem of the moment, to touch the green circle and connect.

"Hello. Finley?" She inhaled deeply.

"Hey there. Is it an okay time to call? You sound like you've just run a 5K."

"I've been dashing around the house a bit, cleaning up from supper." She covered the mouthpiece on the phone and puffed for a moment in percussive breaths.

"Thank you for your words," he said.

"I've wanted to...but I didn't know if...," she stammered.

"It's not easy navigating our circumstances." He sounded so calm and articulate.

"I know. But I overstepped. I'm sorry. I was wrong to make assumptions. It's just that Hazel is a very special young woman, and I wanted to help." She was apologizing again in spite of herself.

"It all turned out," he said.

"Yes," she agreed. "Thank you for all you did for Hazel. I know it's got to be difficult. And Lord, that father of Courtney's...."

"I'd as soon not talk about Donovan Powell, his daughter, their transgressions, or any other school issues. Do we have a deal?" Finley asked.

Angela paused, flustered for foolishly bringing up the very topics that should be laid to rest. "Of course." If they were face to face, she could talk better. But asking him over might sound too needy, especially on a school night.

"I'm standing here jangling my car keys in my pocket," Finley said then.

Angela jumped. "What? Oh? I was going to ask if you might want to, but didn't know…this late." He said nothing for a minute. She didn't know what to do, so she stayed quiet, too.

"You think it's too late?" he finally asked.

"No, no. Not for me," Angela cleared her throat. "It's only a little past 8:00. But you have to be at school earlier than I do. Plus, I'm a night owl. I can make up for lost sleep with a nap." Oh God, she was jabbering like a birdbrain schoolgirl.

"So?"

"So I'd love to see you," she said.

***

They lay in Angela's bed, her head snuggled into Finley's naked chest. There had been no mention of Hazel and the misunderstanding. It seemed unnecessary once they were together.

"You know what's nice about being my age?" Angela asked, fingering the curly hair along Finley's forearm.

"Well, I can think of a lot of things," he said, leaning down to kiss her cheek. "But you tell me."

"I don't have to worry about birth control anymore. It's all spontaneous. Menopause isn't all bad."

"I'm all about spontaneous," he said.

Impulsively, she tickled his ribs.

"Hey now, watch out," he said and grasped her hand.

"You're not that sensitive, are you?"

"No more than you," he said, and grabbed her leg just above the knee and squeezed.

"Ooh, that tickles too much," she squealed.

"What's good for the goose…," he responded.

"Truce," she said, gasping. "I can't take it."

"Alrighty, then. Truce."

Later, dressing to leave, his pants pulled midway up, Finley said out of nowhere, "What would you think about meeting my son, Scott? He's coming this weekend."

Angela pulled the sash of her pink terrycloth robe tightly around her waist. "Are you sure?"

"I wouldn't have asked otherwise."

"I would love to. But do you think it might get out that we are...?"

"Scott lives more than three hours away near the coast. He's thirteen years old. Who's he going to tell? And if he did, what difference would it make?"

She clasped her hands and smiled. Finley smiled back.

***

Angela was up early (not easy for a teacher who relished sleeping in on Saturday mornings), waiting on Finley to finalize plans.

He called at 8:00 to say with the forecast a day full of sun and nearly 70 degrees in the mountains, he wanted to take Scott to the DuPont State Forest near Hendersonville, not much more than an hour's drive, to see a couple of waterfalls within walking distance of each other.

Angela loved any kind of waterfall. "What about I make a picnic lunch?" she asked.

"Nope. Done. I called 'Get-it-to-Go.' We're set. Chicken, potato salad, pimento cheese sandwiches. Is this good?"

"Yum," Angela said. "But what may I contribute?"

"Okay, how about water, and maybe some dessert?" She'd made chocolate chip cookies last night in anticipation. She had bottles of water galore in the pantry. Angela pumped her fist.

Within the hour, Finley arrived at her door with Scott, an adorable sandy-haired boy with a thin, lanky body he'd soon enough—Angela knew—grow into.

"Hi there, young man," she said at Finley's introduction. "Are we like ready for a mountain adventure?"

"Yes ma'am," Scott answered, and Angela threw up her hand for a high five. She felt a happy, tingling sensation when he slapped her palm.

"Uh, this is just for a few hours," Finley said as Angela handed him a blanket and a wicker basket filled with cookies, plates, napkins, eating utensils, and a half dozen water bottles.

"Might as well be prepared." Angela winked at Scott.

He nodded in return. Angela was sure she detected a slight grin.

"You're outnumbered, Finn." Angela shrugged.

Finley shook his head in mock revolt. "You'll understand soon enough, son. Women leave no stone unturned. Not this woman anyway."

"You can always eat off the ground and thirst to death." Angela stamped her foot.

"Let's get going," Finley said, grinning.

***

At Triple Falls, they watched the cascade spill heavily from three blocky rock ledges. "This is magnificent," Angela exclaimed. She remembered suddenly how she'd squeezed her sister Joanie's hand at Niagara Falls. How she'd thought her heart might pop out of her chest at the sight of all that foaming water billowing gigantic clouds of white mist, its deafening tumble over the cliff.

They wore blue plastic ponchos over their clothes, and still they'd gotten soaked. Her daddy hadn't pulled over his hood. Fat clear droplets slid down his stubbly face—unshaven on vacation—his dark hair plastered to his scalp. Cold spray slapped her own cheeks, even with the hood of her poncho pulled low. She'd been an awestruck ten-year-old in another realm of being.

Now, Finley offered his son such a moment. He must love the transcendence of waterfalls, too. Did he know of Whitewater Falls in the North Carolina Mountains, the tallest in the Eastern United States? She'd hiked there twice with Randal—summer and fall—down the steep spur trail where the falls dropped into the Whitewater River. A rainbow spread across the falls on the summer trip. She'd love to make that trek with Finley.

"Definitely wow," Scott said, bringing Angela back to the moment.

"I guess they call it Triple Falls for a reason," Finley declared. His gaze quickly returned to the water tumbling down the glistening, layered rock face.

"No kidding, Dad." Scott cut his eyes at his father, but Angela could see his mockery was good-natured.

They stood, absorbing. Until Finley pulled out his phone. "Photo op," he called. Scott rolled his eyes.

"Grand idea," Angela said, jumping to attention. "Let me take a picture of you handsome fellas." Finley handed over his phone.

"No pictures," Scott said.

"Oh, please indulge us old folk. We're all about making memories," Angela said, knowing intuitively Finley wouldn't beg.

Scott threw back his head and squinched his eyes shut.

"Won't take a minute," Angela promised. "The two of you step sideways, okay, so I can get both you and the waterfall in the background." She talked while she snapped, hoping Scott didn't know how many shots she was taking.

"That wasn't so painful, was it?" she asked, handing Finley's phone back.

"Jeez," Scott said, raking his long, dark blond bangs away from his forehead. A moment later, they flopped back down.

Finley glanced at his watch. "It's going on noon. I don't see a good picnic landing here. What say we move on to Hooker Falls? The picture online showed a lot of space at the base."

"Suits me," Angela said. Scott nodded.

Finley pulled the map from his breast pocket and studied it. "Got it," he said after a couple of minutes. "Not far. Follow me."

Angela and Scott trekked single file behind on the narrow path.

"What'd I tell you." Finley held out his hand. Hooker Falls spilled into a calm pool edged with abundant flat rocks.

"Most definitely," she agreed. "And now I'm starving. You *are* still toting our lunch?"

"You think?" He grinned and pulled the gear off his shoulders.

***

"As my great aunt Kathleen would say, I've had a great sufficiency," Angela announced. She'd devoured two pieces of chicken, a whopping portion of potato salad, and half of a pimento cheese sandwich.

"How about Scott needs to finish off the potato salad?" Finley held the final scoop aloft. Scott shook his head and held his stomach.

Angela reached into the basket. "But there's always room for cookies."

Scott stood and said something quiet into his father's ear, then walked away.

"Everything okay?" Angela held a cookie aloft.

"He just needs to, you know, find a spot."

"Oh. Sorry for being nosy," she said.

Finley flipped his hand upward in nonchalance. "I could go myself," he said and stood.

He walked behind some trees. Angela decided to do the same in the opposite direction. What a relief.

Ten minutes later, Scott had not returned.

"He's okay, right?" Angela asked.

"Well, yeah," Finley said, but Angela could sense uneasiness in his tone.

"You want to go check on him?"

"Maybe so," Finley said. "If you would stay here, so when he comes back, you know…. I'll just wander around a bit."

"I'll be right here," Angela said. More than a half hour later, Finley and Scott appeared out of the woods. Scott's head tilted down in a self-conscious posture.

"It's all good," Finley said. "Just a little expedition."

"Sorry," Scott mumbled, dropping onto their picnic blanket.

"Sorry for what?" Angela asked.

"After I…I walked a little ways down…didn't know which path I took."

"Hey, you went exploring, right?" Finley interrupted his son.

"Exactly. It's all good," Angela concurred. After being so full of life earlier, Scott's demeanor had gone leaden.

"Are we leaving soon?" he mumbled.

Though he was thirteen, Scott's voice hadn't begun to change. His body was that in-between gawky stage. She wondered if he were teased

166

at school for being a late bloomer.

Soon enough, it would all change—he had his father's strong jaw and dark, penetrating eyes. He would gain confidence. But it didn't help now when the boy was embarrassed over getting lost.

Angela suddenly unlaced her shoes, pulled them off, and removed her socks. Father and son glanced at her bare feet. "What's up?" Finley asked.

She wiggled her toes, nails hastily painted in a coat of coral before Finley's arrival earlier in the week. The bright color because it made her feel like spring coming. "What's up is I double dare Scott to wade into the pool," she announced, pointing at the bowl of water that collected beneath the falls. "After you climb over those rocks to get there, of course."

Finley shot her a confused look, but Scott looked up at her expectantly.

"What do you say?" Angela looked at Scott. "If you can do it, then maybe I'll try it, too."

"Snow is still melting in the higher elevations. That's got to be some freezing water," Finley said.

Scott began untying his shoes.

Angela whooped.

"Y'all are outrageous," Finley said.

Scott rolled his jeans to his calves and walked toward the edge of the water. He tested one long, skinny foot on a flat, wet rock, and instinctively pulled back.

"Yep, frigid," Angela called to him.

Yet he stepped back onto the rock with both feet and journeyed across the crooked path of stones. Angela held her breath. She didn't look at Finley. Once again, she'd probably overstepped her bounds, but she couldn't stand seeing Scott feel disgraced.

At the last rock—where the water lapped up and across the surface—Scott collapsed onto his butt. He sat briefly, then slowly slid both feet into the moving pool.

"Yow," he hollered when he stood, jeans wet to the knees.

"I accept the challenge," Angela called and stood. Cautiously—she wasn't a young woman any longer—she stepped across the same slippery rocks. They felt like blocks of ice. She marveled at Scott's fortitude. No way could she turn back.

Angela lowered herself onto the same rock where Scott had sat. She slipped in one leg and then the other.

"Yeah, buddy, we got this," she said, standing beside him. His lips were blue, and she knew she wasn't far behind. The water seemed barely above freezing.

"Hey, Dad, get a picture," Scott called. Finley scrambled down to the bank with his phone. Scott put his arm around Angela's waist. She could feel him shivering.

"Beat you back," she exclaimed.

"Not if I can help it," Scott yelled. Yet he deferred to her, allowing Angela to climb on her hands and knees onto the rock before he followed.

"You're tough." She applauded Scott as they walked barefooted back to Finley propped on his elbows, warm and comfortable on the picnic blanket.

"Try it, Dad. Very invigorating," Scott said, standing over his father.

"I got better sense," Finley answered.

"Wimp," Scott said, folding onto the blanket where he picked up an edge of the material to rub his feet.

"Ya think?" Angela laughed, and Scott—eyes bright—laughed too.

Hiking back on the single-file path, Scott in front and Angela in the middle, Finley caught up behind her. "You're an amazing woman," he whispered against her ear.

"He's a great kid," she whispered back.

Chapter 22

Hazel Smalls

Hazel returned from cleaning rooms at the motel Saturday afternoon to find her mama in the same excited mood she'd been in last Saturday and Sunday, and recently some of the afternoons when Hazel arrived home before Etta left for work. Maybe excited wasn't exactly right because she seemed oddly calm at the same time. Whatever way to describe it, you'd never know her husband had died barely three weeks before.

But Hazel didn't question Etta's good mood because her mama was going forward instead of that wretched state when she cried all the time.

"Baby, I bet you tired after cleaning all those rooms. I'm sorry you got to do that. It's gonna get better. We'll save up our money and get out of this dump. Wait and see," Etta said as Hazel leaned down to pull off her sneakers and set her tired feet free.

"Where's Chloe?" she asked.

"Over at Fawn's. Her mama's been so good to have Chloe over there. And gave us that ham to eat after Burl died."

Hazel nodded in agreement.

"Whoo, I feel like going somewhere. Get out of here. Where can we go?"

"I don't know, Mama. Where you wanna go?" Hazel sat and wiggled her toes up and down to loosen the cramping in her feet.

"Shopping. Buy something new for you and Chloe to wear now that warm weather's coming."

"Last I knew, we don't have money for something new." Hazel looked questioningly at her mother, who was scratching frantically at the underside of her upper arms.

"Yes, we do. Look here." Etta yanked her pocketbook from the chair and pulled out a twenty-dollar bill.

"Mama, you need that for groceries," Hazel said.

Etta pointed toward the counter they called a kitchen. "I see plenty 'a cans over there. Not to mention cereal boxes and pastries. We not going to starve. Let's get your sister and go."

"Whatever you say, Mama," Hazel said and exhaled happily. She would love something new to wear for spring, something feminine that Sterling would like.

They drove to Goodwill where Hazel picked out a floral shift with a flouncing hem that stopped at her knees. Chloe chose a unicorn t-shirt she matched with lavender shorts.

"We still got five dollars on the table," Etta announced. "What else y'all want?"

"You get something, Mama," Chloe said.

"Well now, I b'lieve I will," Etta exlaimed. "If y'all pick it out for me."

"I will, Mama," Chloe said, delighted, and ran over to the rack of women's medium-size blouses. "They're coordinated by color. What color do you like?"

"I'm in the mood for yellow," Etta said.

Chloe held out a bright yellow peasant blouse with blue smocking around the scooped neck. "Soft like a marshmallow."

"Well, I never heard of material that's soft like a marshmallow, but if you say so, I got to have it. I think it's beautiful."

They stopped on the way home at Glen River Park where they had a contest to see who could lift the highest on the swings. "Up in the air we go flying," Etta sang out as she pumped her feet. Hazel swung between her mother and her sister, propelling her body as far as she could toward a cornflower blue sky, not a wisp of cloud anywhere. She felt happy and free.

"It's a three-way tie," Etta declared, out of breath, and jumped out of her swing. She landed hard on her butt and laughed.

***

Mornings had become the hard time since Burl's death. As elevated as Etta was on weekends or in the afternoons before work, at daybreak she was the opposite, irritable. She'd mostly stopped eating breakfast with them or helping Chloe get ready for school. Often, she stayed in bed.

Hazel didn't know what to make of her mother's erratic mood swings. She wondered if everything was okay at the nursing home since Etta was generally in an excellent mood before she left for work but not the next day when she woke up. Hazel didn't dwell on it. There was too much happening in her own life with Sterling. She was sad about her father and worried about her family's future, but at the same time another part of her was joyful. Her emotions were a narrow mountain trail of highs and lows with little flat ground between.

Sometimes Sterling took her to Franks after school during the thirty minutes before she got home to Chloe. Or they wandered behind the school along the Hardwood Trail where budding bright lime-colored leaves shone out everywhere. Occasionally, they just drove around. At Franks, some of Sterling's friends would join them in a booth. They were nice to her, but they called him Sters and talked about people and things and places mostly foreign to her. If someone made a point to include her, she mostly smiled and nodded.

And now, it was suddenly tennis season. Sterling wanted her to come to the next home match against Maynor—their archrival across town. She protested. She knew nothing about the game. She wouldn't be able to follow. Her tactic didn't work. It would take no time, he insisted, to explain the rules and what he called the "etiquette" of the game. She told him she had to stay with Chloe. Bring her, he said. She was stuck.

He said a tennis competition wasn't like a football game where fans cheered at the tops of their lungs. Everyone stayed quiet while the opponents played. It sounded absurd. "What's the point of going to a game if you can't pull for the player?" she asked on the phone the night before the match.

"Of course you can pull for Ramsey, for me, but the crowd doesn't talk or anything during a point so that players aren't distracted. You cheer after the point."

She would have to listen for the players to call out the points during the game because the scoreboard reported only the final result. She also learned there were no referees. Tennis was a game of honor. Players called each other's shots in or out. Hazel thought that sounded impossible.

"I get it," she said when he'd finished telling it all. But she didn't. Plus, she was worried about his parents. Would they be there? She was afraid to ask. She was so nervous after she hung up that she briefly left Chloe on her own—busy with math homework—to walk over to Rhona's to beg her friend to go to the match with her.

"Oh, girl, yeah, what you talking about? Sure, I'll watch the tennis match with you. I like that game." Rhona barely glanced up from painting her fingernails.

"You know how to play tennis?" Hazel asked in disbelief.

"Well, I never ever tried it myself," she said, running a Q-tip around the cuticle of her thumb to soak up a drip of blood-red polish running off her nail, "but I've watched it on TV. You know who Serena Williams is, right? She won a gold medal last summer."

Hazel shook her head.

"You been living under a rock or somethin'?" Rhona flapped the fingers of her right hand in a drying motion. "What time does the match start?"

"It starts at 4:00. We can walk over to the courts after school. Sterling'll drive us home," Hazel explained.

"What about Chloe?" Rhona asked.

"Going to Fawn's."

"Go Rams," Rhona said, raising her scarlet nails high. "See you after school."

"Thank you," Hazel said and hurried back to Chloe.

***

They were at the courts in time to see Sterling before he warmed up. He strolled over to the stands and high-fived them. "My fans," he said.

"You know it!" Rhona pumped her fist.

"Hey, listen, my folks are walking down," Sterling said and pointed up the hill. "Good a time as any to meet them."

Hazel sucked her lower lip against her bottom teeth and stepped back, feeling her heart flutter. He hadn't prepared her. But she wasn't shocked. She'd somehow known he would do it casual this way.

172

"Parents, over here," Sterling called, raising a hand in their direction.

Two perfect-looking white people approached, the man in a navy, long-sleeve sport shirt tucked into khaki pants and the woman nearly matching in a khaki skirt under a navy blouse with a pink sweater across her shoulders.

"Guys, meet Hazel Smalls and Rhona Williams, two of my biggest fans," Sterling said, bouncing on the balls of his feet.

Mrs. Lovell nodded and pursed her lips. "Your name sounds familiar, Hazel. Wonder why…oh…you're…the girls' trouble in the school cafeteria…." She drew in a shallow breath.

Mr. Lovell shot his wife a warning look. Hazel froze. Though she'd never met them, the Lovells knew about her, about the knife. Of course they would have been informed by their friends, if not the school, since Sterling had testified.

"That was a hard time for Zell." Sterling touched her back. "Hey, it's all good now."

"It was a hard time for my friends' daughters," Mrs. Lovell started again until Mr. Lovell put a hand on his wife's sleeve.

"Pleased to meet you both, Hazel and Rhona," Mr. Lovell said cheerfully, but he didn't extend his hand.

"Likewise, I'm sure," Rhona responded and cut her eyes at Hazel.

"How great is it to have all my favorite people to cheer me on," Sterling said, twirling his racquet. "Hey, so, I got to warm up. See you guys after." He saluted before dashing off.

"Of course, sweetheart," Mrs. Lovell called after him and glanced back quizzically at Hazel and Rhona.

Hazel saw Mrs. Lovell look at her husband and say something. She couldn't be sure, but it sounded like "other side of the tracks." Mr. Lovell returned his wife's look with a slight movement of his head.

"You're school friends?" Mr. Lovell asked Hazel as he unfolded two cushioned seats onto the bottom bleacher.

"Yes sir. I'm looking forward to see him win." The air was crisp, but her palms were sweating. She rubbed them down the sides of her Goodwill-new, floral shift. The image of her mother swinging with her and Chloe in Glen River Park, not many days before, flashed through her mind. Oh, how she'd like to be there now.

"Should be a competitive match," Mr. Lovell said, looking off to the side at people approaching.

"Go, Ramsey," Rhona said to Sterling's parents, but she might as well have been speaking to the air, for the Lovells were now gesturing enthusiastically to another set of parents headed in their direction. Rhona grasped Hazel's elbow. "Assholes," she whispered. "Let's go." Hazel turned quickly, and they climbed upward into the bleachers, settling several rows above the Lovells, who were perched forward like they might take off on a footrace.

Hazel and Rhona clasped pinky fingers when Sterling, serving, won the first game hands down. The second game was closer. It went to deuce—a new word for Hazel—twice before Sterling finally won. He lost the third game.

"Don't worry, this is just gettin' good," Rhona said. "He'll recover and win the next one." But the fourth game was difficult, too. With the score 40-30, the Maynor opponent serving, Hazel yearned to scream out her encouragement.

Instead, she whispered, "I think Sterling might lose this one, too."

"Don't worry," Rhona whispered back.

The opponent's first serve landed in the net. "What'd I tell you," Rhona said energetically. The man beside them turned and frowned.

"Must be a Maynor fan," Rhona said in a lowered voice.

The second serve went long outside the box. Instinctively, Hazel clapped. Rhona hooted. Scowling faces turned toward them. Hazel froze, her palms together. It was okay to cheer after a point was won. Wasn't it? Sterling said so.

But something was obviously wrong. And whatever it was got worse because Mrs. Lovell turned too and stared up at her, a long, horizontal line cutting her brow into halves.

Hazel looked down. We did something wrong, she thought, but she didn't know what.

"What the hell," Rhona said, but quiet because she saw the people frowning, too.

For the rest of the match, Hazel sat still and quiet like a possum playing dead. She kept her head mostly down, glancing at Sterling's game only by lifting her eyes. Rhona, amazingly, stayed quiet, too.

Sterling won in a tie-breaking third set. While the Ramsey fans, including the Lovells, roared in excitement, Hazel breathed a sigh of relief. She'd thought it would never end. The sky was long since dark, the lights coming on during the second set. She was worried about Chloe staying too long at Fawn's.

Rhona leaned over and kissed her cheek. "You got this." Hazel looked gratefully at her friend as they descended the bleachers. Sterling ran up from the courts, stopping to speak to his parents who stepped out onto the sidewalk. Mr. Lovell clapped his son around the shoulders, and Mrs. Lovell looked at him in adoration. Anyone could see he was her everything.

"I did something wrong," Hazel said instead of praising Sterling when they met at the bottom of the bleachers, only feet from his parents.

"Nothing's wrong. Way to go, Sterling." Rhona punched his arm.

"That guy about beat me."

"No way," Rhona said. "We knew you had him."

Sterling looked expectantly at Hazel. "We knew you'd win," she assured him.

"Let's celebrate," Sterling said, hugging an arm around each girl's shoulders.

"I can't," Hazel said. "Chloe."

"Oh, yeah, that's right. Let me get my gear, quick, and I'll be right back to drive y'all home. Wait right here," he said, turning in the other direction.

Hazel and Rhona waited on the sidewalk. The other spectators had left, except for Sterling's parents. What were they waiting for? They'd see him soon enough at home; couldn't they leave?

Hazel shivered. The temperature had dropped dramatically once the sun went down. She wished she had her hoodie. Suddenly Rhona poked her in the side and Hazel jumped to see the Lovells approaching.

"Awfully nice of you girls to support Sterling," Mr. Lovell said. Hazel nodded, hugging herself for warmth.

Mrs. Lovell pressed her lips together, making Hazel think about her idiocy during the match.

"You young ladies need a lift somewhere?" Mr. Lovell asked.

"Thank you, but we have a ride coming in a few minutes."

"So long to those jerks," Rhona said behind the Lovells' backs after they turned to leave.

***

Chloe answered at Fawn's room when Hazel knocked. "Where you been?" she yelped.

"I told you I was going to the tennis match 'cause Sterling wanted me to."

"But you're so late."

"I know. I'm sorry. It took him a long time to win."

Chloe put her hands on her hips.

"Sterling won a set, then the Maynor player won a set, so they had to break the tie with a third set."

"What does that mean?" Chloe asked.

"Doesn't matter," Hazel said. "You had some supper?"

"Yeah, Fawn's mama made me a lunchmeat sandwich, but I been waiting and waiting to tell you about the lady who came this afternoon."

"Oh?" Hazel asked, just as Fawn and her nice mama, Ms. Tinsley, joined Chloe at the door.

"You can tell me at home," Hazel said and turned toward Fawn and her mama to thank them. "We want Fawn to come stay with us soon," she added. Fawn nodded enthusiastically, a collection of beaded necklaces bobbing on her chest.

"Bye Fawn, I'll see you on the bus," Chloe called to her friend as they started the short trek back to Room 103.

***

"This lady I want to tell you 'bout," Chloe said as Hazel opened their small refrigerator and pulled out a container of yogurt. "Her name is Bobbi and she brought us a Crock-Pot."

"What in the world?" Hazel exclaimed.

"She said it's called 'Caring with Crock-Pots.' She gave us a brand new Crock-Pot still in the box." Chloe pointed to the cardboard box under the kitchen counter. "And some recipes and ingredients like beans

176

and stuff. Because she says we don't have a real oven, but we can have a real meal. She was nice."

"Well that does seem nice. Maybe we'll cook something in it tomorrow," Hazel said, pulling out the box and bending over to open the top.

"She kept asking Mama questions," Chloe said.

"What kind of questions?" Hazel asked.

"Like did Mama feel okay because she was slurring her words."

Hazel stopped still. She thrust a full spoon of strawberry yogurt back into the carton.

"She thought Mama was sleepy," Chloe continued. Deep down, Hazel knew something was wrong with their mother, but she'd ignored it. Thinking whatever it was would resolve itself in time because her mama was in grief.

Now here came a stranger noticing, and Hazel knew what it could mean. That a woman named Bobbi might call the Child Protective Services to check on them. Thank goodness, at least, Chloe wasn't alone when the lady came to do her good deed. Her mama hadn't done anything wrong. It would be okay.

***

Two nights later, Hazel woke to a pounding noise. At first the sound was part of a dream. She was hammering boards onto the outside of a house—her own house—that she would move into. But then the noise grew louder and she shook herself awake. The bedside clock said 11:10. Her mama was still at work. She realized it was heavy knocking on the door. Chloe was awake, too.

"What's that?" her sister asked, scrabbling into the bed with Hazel, grabbing her waist.

"I don't know," Hazel said. She pried Chloe loose and slid out of bed, tugging down the t-shirt she was sleeping in and reaching for her jeans on the floor.

"Don't answer it," Chloe urged.

"Somebody might be in trouble and need something," Hazel answered, zipping her jeans. She approached the door and pulled the curtain back a sliver. A solemn police officer stood beside a middle-aged, white lady with thin white hair sprouting off her head. Hazel dropped the curtain quickly and stepped back.

"Who is it?" Chloe called.

"A cop and a lady," Hazel answered.

They must have heard them speaking to each other because the cop called from the other side of the door. "Hello, hello. Open the door, please. Hazel Smalls? We need to come in and talk to you. I'm a police officer. Open the curtain so I can show you my badge."

Hazel's shoulders jerked inward, up against her ears. She stood perfectly still. Whatever he wanted to say, it wasn't good. Cops didn't come to your door in the middle of the night with a round, middle-aged woman to tell you anything good. And he knew her name. Without being told, Hazel knew the lady was from the Department of Social Services and the Crock-Pot lady named Bobbi had called them.

But that wasn't the reason the policeman had knocked on their door in the middle of the night.

"We're here to help," he said, "I'm Sergeant Laney"—when Hazel gave in and opened the door, standing anxiously over the threshold. Chloe stood huddled behind, gripping her stuffed bear Snugs to her chest.

"I'm sorry to startle you," he said apologetically. He was a young cop, not many years older than Hazel. He removed his hat when he entered. "This is Ms. Neal. She's here to help us," he said, nodding to his companion.

"Your mama," the lady chimed in, "has been taken into custody. We're here to take care of you." She looked tired.

"What kind of custody?" Hazel asked. She reached around and took Chloe's hand, pulled her sister to her side. "I turned seventeen in September. I'm old enough to know."

"Okay, then. Your mother has been arrested for stealing drugs from her workplace. She's in jail. The judge will set bail soon," the cop said.

Hazel's body went ice cold stiff. "What kind of drugs? My mother is a certified nursing assistant," she said. "She handles drugs all the time, to give them to old people."

"I'm sorry. I don't...," he started, twisting his hat in his hand.

"You can tell me," Hazel commanded. "That's my mama." The cop's eyes shot back at her. She could see he didn't know whether to reprimand her or tell her what she wanted to know.

"They found opiates, different ones—Lortab, Percocet, Codeine—on her person."

Hazel's face flushed hot with adrenaline. She licked her dry lips. "My mama gives those drugs to her patients. They're prescribed," she declared. The tips of her fingers had begun to tingle.

Sergeant Laney shook his head. Ms. Neal tapped him on the arm. He leaned down to hear something Hazel couldn't make out.

"I want to know why my mama's in jail, when she's just doing her job," Hazel said, loud. Her mama pushed around a cart full of drugs, giving them to the patients to take away their pain, to help them sleep. So what were they saying?

"Calm down, Hazel," Ms. Neal said, stepping toward her. Hazel stepped back. "I told you that we are here to help."

"You can help by leaving and letting my sister and me be," Hazel answered. Chloe clung to her arm.

"That's not possible. You're minors. We can't let you stay alone."

Sergeant Laney said they had to pack a few things and leave, be taken into custody themselves because there was no adult in the house.

"I can take care of Chloe and me," Hazel declared.

"That's not what the law says," he responded. His eyes were soft and kind, pitying her. The last thing she wanted was a policeman's pity.

"I've talked to your mother. She says there's no suitable relative, so you'll be at the Child Center for a couple of nights. Until a hearing," Ms. Neal explained.

"That's not so. My uncle and his family...," Hazel started. Her head was swimming. They didn't have to go with them, did they? If she refused, would they handcuff her and Chloe? Or leave them alone? What about Uncle Huck? She had no idea how to find him.

"I want to talk to my mother," Hazel said. Tears fell down her face, collecting on the front of her shirt.

"Of course," Sergeant Laney said, "but not tonight. You got to come with us tonight." He reached a hand toward her arm. For a moment Hazel felt sorry for the policeman's predicament, having to take them somewhere they didn't want to go.

"My daddy will be home soon," Chloe announced. "We're okay."

Ms. Neal cocked her head to the side. "Your daddy is dead," she said bluntly. A gasp hiccupped in Hazel's throat. Chloe began to whimper.

Sergeant Laney stamped from one booted foot to the other.

Hazel wiped her eyes with her sleeve, trying to think. She could dash out the door with Chloe and go to Rhona's. But Sergeant Laney would quickly catch them. Or she could call Sterling, maybe, but what could he do? Nothing.

If only she and Chloe could crawl back into bed and sleep until the alarm went off, get dressed, eat breakfast, brush their teeth, and board their buses for school like any other day. All she wanted was to collapse.

Chapter 23

Sterling Lovell

Sterling woke thinking about Zell in scared rabbit mode after the tennis match last night. She'd hardly said a word on the drive back to the motel. He'd no idea why until Rhona started carrying on about people staring at them after they cheered at his opponent's double fault. Of course, Zell would be humiliated about a gaffe. That was her way.

You'd think with all the difficulties she'd endured, she'd have thicker skin. So what if a few people turned and stared? It wasn't a big deal. Probably, it was mostly Maynor fans. And his fault anyway for forgetting to tell her about subtleties. He'd wanted her to enjoy the match, and instead she'd come away embarrassed. Now, it would take considerable effort for him to downplay it all.

Sometimes, truth be told, Sterling got exhausted. He loved Zell. God, yes. But whenever she felt uncomfortable with things not familiar, she retreated into her rabbit burrow. And it was up to him to pull her out.

Sterling stepped into the shower, willed the piercing spray to shake these thoughts. And by the time he was out the door for school, he was thinking about Zell's beautiful deep eyes, not to mention her gorgeous body. He couldn't wait to see her. Only she wasn't at school. Again.

"Hey, Ms. W," he said, sticking his head in Ms. Wilmore's first period class a second time to look for Zell. Several students glanced his way, then turned back to yacking. "You know if Zell's bus came in?" It was only minutes until the start bell.

"Yes." She gestured him into the classroom. "Others who ride her bus are here. Is everything okay?" She inhaled quickly.

"I don't know," Sterling said. "This is starting to piss me off."

"What?"

"How so much has happened to her. Every time she's absent, it's something else."

"It's difficult on her, and you, too, but you know her circumstances, Sterling. Remember, what we talked about…kids in her circumstances often have far more erratic attendance than Zell. She's tough."

"Yeah, I know. I know," he said angrily. She cocked an eyebrow at him.

"My bad. Sorry." He swiped his hands down the thighs of his jeans. Ms. Wilmore nodded kindly. She was an amazing teacher, not just because her lessons kept him awake. He'd never known another teacher who cared this much. But then, he'd not gotten to know other teachers like he knew Ms. Wilmore, and it was largely because of Zell. "But at some point it's got to level out, right?" he said.

"I don't know what you mean by level out," she responded, leaning forward, crossing her right hand over her left on her desk. "Let me just say, there's a lot of world between you. Zell is a victim of poverty, and you…are…a fortunate young man who uses his resources well. I'm awfully impressed with how you and Zell navigate the expanse. Don't give up." Ms. Wilmore was looking at him intently.

"Who said I'm giving up? I just want to see Zell and don't know why she's not at school today." Sterling sighed, shifting his backpack, glancing away from his teacher's gaze.

Ms. Wilmore gave him a thumbs up. He retreated toward his own first period, ducking into the bathroom along the way to call Zell. No answer. Where was she?

***

Sterling called and texted Zell whenever he could chance it at school, without response. He skipped tennis practice and drove to his father's sorry motel, but no one answered the door at Room 103. What the hell? Where was she? Where was Chloe? It wasn't yet 4:00. Mrs. Smalls should still be there, but her car wasn't in the lot. He tried to peer through the window, but the curtains were drawn. The room was deserted. He could feel it.

At home he dialed Zell again. He paced his bedroom. Nothing. Finally, after supper—his mother's lasagna he loved but hardly touched, making her complain—he called Elysian Fields where Mrs. Smalls worked.

The woman at the switchboard informed him Mrs. Smalls was no longer employed there.

"What? Why?" he asked sharply.

"I can't give out personal information," the receptionist said like a robot.

"I'm a friend of the family. I think someone might be in trouble," he said, pulling in his tone, trying to soften the woman on the other end.

"I'm sorry, sir. But I have to follow policy." Her voice was flat in a way that said she knew something but wouldn't say.

Sterling sat in his room, his head in his hands. What now? Where were they? No secret that he could be dramatic, but this was getting to be too much. The emotional overload was exhausting.

Obsessively, he kept calling, to no avail. Frustrated, he pitched his phone across the room. He turned on his television, surfed channels. A few minutes here, a few minutes there, but nothing held his attention.

After a while, he changed into a t-shirt and pajama bottoms, retrieved his phone from the rug, set it on his bedside table, and got into bed. He lay staring at the ceiling. Then, around midnight, his phone dinged with a text: "Mama is in jail. Chloe and I are in something called protective custody. I'm sorry."

Adrenaline shooting upstream into his head, he immediately texted back: "Where?"

"Ramsey," came her response a minute later.

"I mean the name of the place," he texted again. Minutes went by. He felt cold sweat at the base of his spine. "Zell?" he texted again.

Finally, she responded, "Sure Place. I asked the address: 790 Oakwood Road, but you can't come."

"Why the hell not? You and Chloe don't need to stay in some halfway house. You can come here," he texted frantically, though he had no idea what he'd say to his parents.

"A policeman and social worker brought us. We can't leave. People are nice."

"Can you call me?"

"No, lights out. I'm sneaking." That was the last he heard, though he texted back, pleading for more information. What could he do? If he had Ms. Wilmore's number, he'd call her, no matter how late it was. She cared about Zell. And maybe she knew what Sure Place was. He Googled it, but all that came up was the name of the place, the address, and the fact that it was a temporary shelter for children in need.

If he slept, he wasn't aware. Mostly he lay awake thinking, wondering. Why was Mrs. Smalls in jail? What kind of place were Zell and Chloe in and for how long? How could he get them out? Where would they go? Yet he must have slept because his alarm jolted him. Remembering, he stepped fast out of bed and into the shower. Dressed, he took the stairs two at a time, grabbed a pastry and orange juice as he rushed through the kitchen. "Where are you going this early?" his mother called.

"Stuff to do," he called back.

He used his Garmin to find 790 Oakwood Road, a towering clapboard home surrounded by a wrought-iron fence and overgrown shrubbery. Like the haunted house in an old movie—*The Ghost and Mr. Chicken*—he watched with Livie when they were kids. Two green rocking chairs sat on the wide front porch that could have held a dozen more and not been crowded. It wasn't far from the center of town, but he'd never come down this side street near Main. He'd had no reason. It wasn't a cut-through to anywhere.

He parked out front and turned off his car engine. The house sat between a ratty office suite and a Quick Credit loan business. He could see it had once been a grand home, likely one of many—long torn down—along this street. Who knew why this one survived. The historic home of some philanthropic bigwig's ancestors maybe? Who'd donated it to the city for a good cause?

Sterling locked the car, pocketed his keys, and walked up the front steps. He told himself he wasn't nervous. He rang the brass bell beside the front door. Soon enough, he heard rumbling footsteps, and then the door opened, barely.

"May I help you," inquired a middle-aged woman—frilled, blue apron tied around her ample waist, hair pinned tight to her head.

"I, uh, yeah, good morning. I'm Sterling Lovell. I'm here to see Hazel and Chloe Smalls."

The woman looked at him sternly. She put a hand on each plump hip protruding from the apron.

"Have I come to the right place?" Sterling asked politely.

"What business you got? Folks can't come barging in unannounced." Her voice was firm, but there was a softness in her round-cheeked, bronze face. She knew he wasn't a hood come to kidnap any of the residents.

"I want to check on my friends. They came in last night."

"Well, now, I'll tell you. I can't invite you in, but you can write a note, and if those friends you mention are here, I'll pass it along."

"Please?" he implored her. "I'll stay on the porch, if Hazel could just come to the door."

"No, sir, not going to happen. You can sit there in that rocking chair," she said, pointing a thick, stubby index finger, "and write something, or go on and leave. Your choice. You need paper and pen?" She tapped her foot as she spoke.

"I got a notebook in my backpack in the car," he said, because he saw he wasn't getting by the sergeant at arms. Not without a scene, and that wouldn't help anything.

"Good enough," she said. "You slip it through this slot in the door"—she pointed at a brass mail slot cut into the heavy wooden door—"and I'll take care of it from there."

"Thank you," he said, nice as he could, even if he was gritting his teeth.

Despite suspecting the woman would read his note, he asked Zell how to see her and when. Then he drove fast to school to catch Ms. Wilmore before the bell. She was sitting behind her desk, green pen behind her ear, reading from a stack of papers. Their recent AP essays on the novel they'd just finished, *Member of the Wedding*, probably.

He thought he'd hate a novel about a twelve-year-old girl trying to find her identity, connect to the people around her, but he didn't. The more they discussed Frankie in class, the more she reminded him of Zell, how they both struggled to feel at ease in their own skin.

"Sterling?" Ms. W summoned him with an arm wave. He walked up to her desk, cleared his throat. "Zell isn't here again. Do you know anything?" She looked at him expectantly.

He spoke in a hushed, confiding tone. "Zell and Chloe are in protective custody—whatever that means—because their mother went to jail. I don't know why. But whatever it is, I think it happened where Mrs. Smalls works, or used to work, at Elysian Fields. I called. You know how you can hear things underneath that people won't say? The woman I talked to, I could tell she knew something."

"Dear God, that poor girl just lost her father," Ms. Wilmore cried. She pulled her hands through her hair, causing the pen behind her ear to clatter onto the desk. She jumped at the sound. Sterling startled, too.

The din of students sitting at their desks stopped immediately. Sterling glanced behind him to see every kid staring their way.

"Hey guys, it's cool. Ms. W and I are going over my essay, and I stunned her with my wisdom. We're chillin' now," he announced.

"You're full of it, bro." It was the brawny kid who was always mouthing off. "You done something." He started laughing and it caught on.

"That's enough, Stokes," Ms. Wilmore called out. "It's almost time for the bell. Get settled."

"Do you know where Zell and her sister are?" Ms. Wilmore asked quietly.

"Yeah, it's called Sure Place. Not far off Main Street. A big old mansion that's seen better days. You heard of it?"

Ms. Wilmore's face brightened. "I have. It provides a safe place for children who've been neglected or abused. I have a friend on the board. I make annual donations. Hazel and her sister must have been placed there while their mother is…absent."

"Well, that sweet lady at the door is like Fort Knox. She wouldn't let me see Zell," Sterling said.

"I'll do some checking," his teacher promised.

***

Sterling wasn't able to see Zell the seventy-two hours she stayed at Sure Place. But he talked to her on the phone, thanks to Ms. W's influence with someone somewhere. Zell, being Zell, talked brave, but he heard the catch in her voice from time to time. She was terrified.

Her mama had been arrested for stealing opiates from her patients. Instead of administering all their nightly pain relievers, she'd pocketed pills, a lot of pills, according to the charge. The night she was discovered, a stash of several opiates was zipped inside a pouch in her parka. Enough that she could have been charged with dealing.

"Mama's no drug addict," Zell exclaimed on the phone. They were hashing over the circumstances for the umpteenth time since she'd been sequestered at Sure Place. "She's grieving for Daddy and didn't know how else to escape the pain."

"I know, Zell, but she was pilfering pills on her shift. You know this. Serious pills. A lot of pills. They were watching her," Sterling said.

"My mama's no thief. She's just sad," she countered. Sterling didn't argue. What difference would it make? The judge had set bail at $4000, and Mrs. Smalls couldn't pay her way out to await trial.

"Can't you pay a percentage or something?" Sterling asked, the realization suddenly dawning on him. He didn't have $4000 at his disposal, but he could surely scrounge up a portion.

"Yeah, you can pay 10 percent to a bail bondsman, but then you got to give him collateral for the rest," Zell explained. "Mama could put up her car, but where's she gonna go if she gets out? She can't go back to the motel because she's got no job. We can't pay the rent."

Zell might not know about etiquette concerning an unforced error in a tennis match, but she knew things about the real world he had no clue about. He shook his head at his ignorance. He thought about what Ms. W had said, about "a lot of world" between them.

After talking with Zell the last night she and Chloe were together at Sure Place—though he didn't know it then—Sterling decided to approach his father. There wasn't any reason Hugh Lovell couldn't let Zell and her family live free at the Red Rose Motel for a while. What was one room's rent to him when it could get a woman out of jail? A woman who was probably guilty, but not in her right mind because of all she had to endure.

He walked downstairs to find his father resting in his leather recliner watching a news show and his mother curled up on the sofa, reading a magazine.

"Guys," he started, standing at the doorway into the den. His parents swiveled their gaze toward him. "You remember meeting my friend Zell at the tennis match a few days ago?"

"Sure," his father said, lowering the volume on the TV. "What's up?"

"I haven't told you, but Zell, she's my girl. Has been for a while."

"What do you mean?" his mother jabbed at him. "Is this a rebound from Courtney? That adorable, charming girl." She jerked off her glasses.

"I just told you, Mom." Sterling shuffled his feet. "Zell is my girlfriend. I want to talk to Dad about helping her out with something."

"That girl at the tennis match. The one who caused your friends to get in trouble over a knife that was under *her* seat? People still haven't stopped talking about it. Have you lost your mind?" his mother said, abruptly standing.

"She's the sweetest girl you could ever know," Sterling said. "I would have brought her home before now to meet you. But I knew you'd be like this."

"Be like what?" his mother moaned.

"Slow down, slow down," his father said, turning the television to mute. "Are you talking about that knockout at the tennis match?"

Sterling's mother shot his father a look.

"Where'd you meet her?" his father asked.

Sterling decided not to mention ISS. "In school," he said.

"Where in school?" his mother demanded. "Surely not in one of *your* classes."

"Aren't you being a bit judgmental, Mom? You think people without advantages aren't in smart classes? Zell and I have the same English teacher. At Ramsey everybody sees everybody around."

His mother looked at the ceiling then toward his father. "I warned you after Livie went away. Sterling shouldn't go to the public high school. But, oh no, Halstead Preparatory—minutes from the house—was out of the question because it didn't have good enough sports offerings," she hissed.

"Can you let up for a minute, Harriet?" his father snapped, shoving his palms toward her in a shut-the-hell-up motion.

"Listen, Dad, Zell and her family have been living at the Red Rose Motel," Sterling appealed to his father. His mother gasped.

"Why the shock, Mom?" Sterling's head jerked toward her. "Zell's rent helps you live in this nice house."

"Your nice house, too," she shot back.

Sterling looked back toward his father. "Zell's mama has fallen on harder times and I want to ask if you could let them live rent free for a while."

His father frowned at him. "What kind of harder times? Can't the parents work?"

"Her father recently died, and her mother lost her job."

"I'm sorry for that. I tell you what; I'll help this woman get a job so that she can pay her rent," his father offered.

"That won't be possible for a little while," Sterling responded.

"Why not?" His father frowned again.

"She's in jail," Sterling said.

"Dear God." His mother dropped deep into the sofa cushions. His father rolled his eyes. "Our second child, too? Where have we gone wrong?"

"Harriet, don't you think you're being a wee bit dramatic?" His father smacked his hand on the arm of the chair. "He's not marrying the girl. I'm sure she's perfectly nice. She certainly is a looker." His mother scissored one leg over the other and glared at his father.

His father winked at him, and Sterling bristled. He knew what his father figured.

Forget it, he thought. His parents were so wrapped up in themselves. "Sorry I disturbed you," he said, sharp.

"Wait, Sterling. I shouldn't have compared you to your sister. You surprised me. I got overwrought is all. Maybe you can explain more why you want to help this girl," his mother said.

"I told you she's a fantastic person. I'm in love with her, and you think she's pitiful, like I'm consorting with the devil. Dad thinks I'm having a good ol' time with a slut. You couldn't be more wrong. Maybe both of you should try looking outside of your stained-glass tower window."

Sterling turned abruptly and crossed over the doorway, out of the

189

den.

"Come back," his father demanded. "Let's discuss this civilly."

"No thanks," Sterling called back, halfway up the stairs to his bedroom.

***

Ms. Wilmore, standing at the door, touched his arm as he strode out of class fifth period. "Can you drop by after school?" she whispered.

"About Hazel?" He stopped quickly. She nodded. "I can stay now if you'll write me a pass." He kept his voice quiet, too.

"No. It's not an emergency," she assured him.

Still, he showed up quick as he could after the dismissal bell. "You're prompt," Ms. Wilmore said from behind her desk and smiled.

"I aim to please," he said, trying to match her apparent sunny mood. "You have good news?"

"Not good or bad, just news." Sterling looked at her confused. "Mrs. Smalls can't afford to post bail. She's been charged with a felony. That means Zell and her sister Chloe will be wards of the state until their mother's trial. I don't know what that means in terms of how long before she goes to trial."

"A felony? This isn't bad news?" Sterling threw up his hands dramatically. "I don't think Zell's mother has ever committed a crime. Doesn't she get a break for that?"

"She was stealing from vulnerable people who needed their medication, and she was stealing Schedule II drugs." Ms. W's face turned serious. Her former smile, he realized, was for his benefit. It didn't work.

"No disrespect, Ms. W, but how do you know all this is really true?" He was trying, for his teacher's sake—not succeeding—to keep the agitation out of his voice.

"I can't tell you that, and I'm trusting you here, Sterling. You shouldn't talk to anyone about any of the specifics concerning Zell, Chloe, or her mother, okay?"

"Okay." He lowered his arms.

"Sure?" she asked.

"Yes, deal, I promise."

"Okay. It's likely Mrs. Smalls's legal counsel can negotiate the charge down to a misdemeanor. The courts don't have the time or resources to try too many cases, especially drug cases."

"You teach English. How do you know all this?" Sterling asked. He was balancing back and forth on the balls of his feet.

"Maybe because I *am* a teacher? And didn't just fall off the turnip truck?" Her voice bordered on sharp.

"Sorry. I'm overwhelmed. And I know Mrs. Smalls can't afford a lawyer."

"She'll be assigned a public defender. She doesn't have a record. She's not a long-term user, and her husband just died."

Sterling shook his head. "Let's say I go with your theory that the public defender can make a case."

"Right now, she's not homeless on the streets, and she gets three meals a day," Ms. Wilmore interjected.

"Okay, I get it. But what the hell, sorry, heck, does that mean happens to Zell and Chloe?" He was trying to stay calm but feeling like he might hyperventilate.

"That's one reason I asked you to stop by. I want to run an idea by you," she said. Sterling's feet were cramping. He hunched over and went into a deep-knee bend. "Sit." Ms. Wilmore motioned him to a desk.

"I know you don't think so right now, but it could be a lot worse," she said. He stared at her incredulously. "A foster family has agreed to take Chloe. She should be in good hands. The parents have two biological children in the house, one a little older and one a little younger than Chloe. This family are veterans at fostering. It's harder to find a foster family to take in older teenagers. So for now, Zell will be at Bridge House. It's under the umbrella of Sure Place."

"What is that? Bridge House?"

"A place for girls age twelve to eighteen who've been abused or neglected or—"

"Zell isn't abused or neglected. She doesn't need to be with people who have all those issues." He laced his fingers—zig-zag—one hand into the other.

"If you'll let me finish," Ms. Wilmore said, closing one eye and looking at him like he was the bullseye on a target, "or girls who don't have another suitable home."

"Like a friggin' orphan?"

"No, Sterling, listen." Ms. Wilmore was getting exasperated. He shut his mouth. "She will be at Bridge House for now. There are visiting hours when you can see her. I don't know the rules about her leaving campus, but I'm sure you'll find out. What I want to ask is your opinion on my putting in to be Zell's foster parent. I've not made up my mind, nor do I yet know if it's even allowed since I'm her teacher. At this point I'm asking hypothetically. You know her on a much more personal basis than I do."

"Holy shit, I mean holy cow. Yes, yes, yes. Zell wouldn't be any trouble."

"I'm not worried about her being trouble. I teach her and know what a sweetheart she is. I'm asking if you think she'd be receptive or think me intrusive."

"Here's the truth, Ms. W." Sterling clapped his hands and held them to his chest. "Hazel respects you. She thinks of you as someone she can confide in. I know she does from how she's talked about you."

"Well, then. I'll give the idea some serious consideration," Ms. Wilmore said. "Thank you. Now get on to tennis practice or wherever it is I'm keeping you from being."

Sterling thanked his teacher, gave a little jump, and ran out of the building.

Chapter 24

Angela Wilmore

Angela rarely left school immediately after the last bell, but today she was eager to get home and make calls. She'd assumed a family would foster both Zell and her sister, but when only Chloe was placed, her heart took over. Certainly Zell would be safe, well cared for, at Bridge House, but it wasn't like.... She wanted to offer Zell a real home. Likely, on a first offense, Mrs. Smalls' charge would be lessened to a misdemeanor. Still, it would surely be the end of the school year and maybe beyond before anything was determined.

She would call Lewis Heath. He was a family court judge and one of the every-other-Thursday-night poker guys Randal played with for years. Whenever it had been Randal's turn to host, Lewis brought her flowers. It was a running joke. "My bribe?" she'd say when Lewis proffered the bundle. He always answered with a salute as he headed to the basement.

Angela hadn't told Sterling, but she'd already researched the school district's policy. Unless she was missing something, she found no rule against teachers being foster parents for their students. She slung her book satchel over her arm, dug her purse from her desk drawer, then remembered she hadn't checked her email since lunch.

No earthshaking subject lines that couldn't wait until morning, except, at the bottom of the unread list, an email from Finley. Angela clicked open the message: "You got time to drop by my office after school? I could use an English teacher's help with a letter. And something else."

Angela hiked her way through the long maze of mostly empty halls to the office, thinking about the ominous "something else." Beverly Bagley gave her the eye when Angela swung open the little gate and stood in front of the secretary. Her thin eyebrows arched. Did she suspect? It wouldn't surprise Angela. She was a frequent visitor now, and Beverly, nosy by nature—it was in her job description, wasn't it, to shield the principal from interruption?—was attuned to everything.

"He's expecting me," Angela said. Beverly pointed her thumb toward her principal's open door. Finley beckoned her inside, stood, and closed the door behind her.

"Um, what's Ms. Bagley going to think if you close your door with a female teacher inside?"

Finley waved his hand. "I have a sensitive letter to write and need an English teacher's help."

"Okay, then." Angela sat and crossed her legs comfortably.

"Pull your chair up closer, and I'll turn my screen toward you," he said. Angela scooted her chair forward. "This can't get out yet, okay? But it'd be great to have my *t*'s crossed and my *i*'s dotted to impress the district office because they'll get a copy." Angela straightened.

"Coach Dimsley, the basketball coach…," he began.

"He got terrible press in the teachers' lounge during the season," Angela interjected. "Hasn't had a winning season since he started four years ago?"

"True," Finley said. "The district has decided not to renew his contract, and I'm the lucky SOB who gets to tell him. It's tricky, too. Unlike the football coach, the basketball position carries a half-teaching load. The district decided to offer Tommy a full-time PE job if he wants it."

"So who becomes the coach?" Angela asked.

"Don't know. If we need to hire someone from the outside instead of promoting within, it means an added position. Which means finding money for the salary. But Tommy won't stay if he doesn't have to. I hope he finds a teaching post elsewhere for the sake of his ego."

"You couldn't pay me enough to have your job," Angela said.

Finley tipped his head sardonically. "Yep, lucky me, so could you read through this letter?" He swiveled his computer screen toward her.

"Good tone, but it needs a few edits. Mind moving so I can get to your keyboard?"

"Done," he said, standing, changing places with her. "You know, I'm basically a coach myself at heart. I really miss it."

"You've never told me you were a coach," she said, her eyes on the screen.

"Seems like a long-ago life now. I was head football coach at Bullock Creek High School, downstate."

Angela heard a bright, yearning edge in Finley's voice and glanced up. "Tell me more," she asked, "when we are together…?"

A few minutes later, she stopped typing and sat back. "Nice chair," she said. "Maybe I spoke too soon about not wanting your job."

"There are days I'd gladly give it to you. Thank you for your expertise," he said.

"I think you're good to go."

"What would I do without you?"

"Why, I can't imagine, kind sir," she said demurely and laughed.

"So there's something else I need to tell you," he said.

For an instant, she smiled brightly until the stiff expression elongating Finley's face changed her own. Angela slid forward in the smooth leather chair.

"Not good or bad, but cautionary," he responded. "Remember my thinking it was safe for you to meet Scott? And you weren't sure?" Angela nodded. "You were right. Scott told his mom that his father has a fantastic girlfriend, and, well, Rita might have a couple of her old friends in Ramsey snooping around."

"But no one knows about us," Angela exclaimed. "What could they possibly tell her?"

"Exactly nothing," Finley said. "Unless…"

"No. Why does she care if…does this mean we…?" Angela cried.

"Over my dead body," Finley said. "But we're going to have to be extra careful. After this meeting, keep our distance at school. For now, see each other only at home."

"I don't want to jeopardize your job," Angela said.

"You're not." Finley reached across his desk for her hand. Angela locked her fingers into his. "It's the wrong setting to be saying it"—Finley looked down at their hands wound together—"because we should be somewhere with candlelight and wine, but I want to say it now." He looked at her. "I'm in love with you."

Angela looked at his wide-set, lion eyes. A hitch caught in her throat. She took a deep breath. "Who could have imagined this?" She paused. "That we would fall in love."

"God, that makes me happy," he exhaled, gripping her hand tighter. "We'll figure it out."

Angela closed her eyes. How would Finley react when he learned she wanted to be Zell's foster mother? Now was not the time to tell him.

Angela tossed her book bag onto the passenger seat and folded in behind the wheel of her Volkswagen. A yellow gerbera daisy she bought the day before shimmied in its dashboard vase as her Bug bounced across the rutted faculty lot. Finley, the possibility of Zell living with her—it all made her nearly dizzy.

***

Angela learned from her friend Tessa on the board of Sure Place it normally took four to six months to become a foster parent. There was preparatory training, inspections, home visits, and forms, many forms, including a criminal background check.

"Jeez," Angela exclaimed to Tessa on the phone, remembering how her high school boyfriend—a long-haired, hippie football kicker who once nailed a 48-yard field goal in a playoff game—moved in with the head coach and his family midway senior year. Gary's father, his only parent, was transferred to be an Army recruiter two states away, and Gary didn't want to uproot before graduation. All it took was a phone call between Coach Freeman and Sergeant Newcomb. "Why so much hassle when all Hazel needs is a good home?" she implored Tessa.

"You're a teacher. Some of the credentials you need are already on record. It might not take as long," Tessa offered.

"So at least I'm clear to apply, even though I'm Hazel's teacher? Not a conflict of interest?"

"It's commendable, Angela. I know a couple of other teachers who have done it. Thank God for them and for you."

"I was thinking of calling Lewis Heath. A friend. Family court judge. Do you know him?" Angela asked.

"Bingo," Tessa said. "You might have just shortened your path."

Angela changed into capris and a long-sleeved t-shirt, laced up her

Nikes. She needed to take a walk to think her argument through. Heading out her side door, she set a brisk pace.

An hour later, her head felt clear. What did she have to fear? She was certainly no stranger to teenagers, and she had plenty of space to spare.

She thought she'd have to leave Lewis a message because who answered a landline anymore. It was usually a scam or a telemarketer. But he answered right away. He sounded glad to hear from her. It was a good time to call, he assured her. His wife's night to cook, so he was relaxing in his recliner with a tumbler of bourbon.

Angela asked about his family; he asked about her teaching. Then Angela poured out her story. When she finished, there was silence on the other end for a moment until Lewis cleared his throat.

"First, Angie, sweetheart, take a breath. Think," Lewis said. "You're all day with teenagers and you want one 24/7?"

"I have thought, and I do," she said.

"Whew, there's no accounting for some people's generosity. Okay then. You can speed it up, probably have her in your home within a couple of weeks, through kinship care."

"Kinship?" Angela asked. "I'm not kin to Zell."

"It doesn't have to be a relative. It can be a family friend or a child's teacher. Anyone who has a relationship with the child or a family member can be considered a kinship placement."

"Oh, wonderful," Angela exclaimed.

"There are still hoops to jump through," Lewis cautioned. "Tell me again. You're sure about all this?"

"I am," Angela assured him.

"You'll need to take a class, get fingerprints, and submit to a home study to get a provisional license."

"Doesn't sound too taxing."

"In time, you'll need to complete other stuff like a fire inspection and medical form to be fully licensed," Lewis continued.

"I can do it," Angela answered.

"I always knew you were too good, Angie," he said. "I'll get the ball rolling."

"I can't thank you enough, Lewis."

"Hope you still think that in a few months," he chuckled. "I advise you to get a stash of bourbon in the house."

"Cheers," Angela said.

Sitting on her sofa after her conversation with Lewis, cellphone lying in her palm, Angela considered the one thing that gave her pause. Finley. She hoped he'd approve. Plus, this afternoon he'd said they had to be more careful than ever, and she'd just eliminated one of their only safe places. With Zell under her roof, Finley wouldn't be able to come to the house. But Finley had a house too. And an enclosed garage to hide her car. She had only an open carport visible to the world. Solutions were possible if you didn't panic and thought them through.

Chapter 25

Hazel Smalls

Ms. Wilmore was so amazing. Hazel could never have imagined such generosity. She'd taken only clothes and her father's urn. There really wasn't anything else worth saving from the motel. Except her Mama's car. Hazel had the extra key, but she didn't know how to drive. So Ms. Wilmore arranged for her friend Mrs. Steward, who taught eleventh grade English, to ride with her to drive Etta's old Honda Accord—Chloe named it the Smokin' Possum because it sometimes played dead—to Ms. Wilmore's house. Thankfully, it started and was parked now at the top of the driveway.

On the first morning, a Saturday, waking from an antique white iron bed covered in a silky pink comforter and tons of pillows in her own bedroom, Hazel ventured into the large, bright kitchen to see Ms. Wilmore drinking coffee. Her teacher pointed out where things were. Hazel made a piece of cheese toast and poured a glass of orange juice. It felt strange and comfortable at the same time to sit and eat with her teacher.

After breakfast, Hazel asked what she could do. She was determined to show her gratitude. Ms. Wilmore directed her outside with a pair of work gloves to a long bed of daffodils under the kitchen windows. Dozens of flowers bloomed—white, cream, dark and light yellow releasing a light, sweet smell like vanilla ice cream everywhere—but the weeds were everywhere, too. Ms. W said they were chickweed and purple deadnettle. Whatever chick and dead they were, it was super hard getting that mess out of the hard dirt. Ms. W thanked her plenty, though, when she saw the mound of wilting green weeds piled up at the top corner of the flowerbed.

It was a lot better than cleaning rooms at the motel, but she needed the money she made there. It made her nervous to be dependent like this. She was beyond grateful for Ms. Wilmore's kindness. But she couldn't help her fear underneath, that she might find herself alone and destitute at any moment.

Part of her longed to be back at the Red Rose Motel because it meant being with Chloe and her mama. The motel was a miserable place, but they were together there. Free and independent. Hazel hadn't seen her sister since being transferred to Bridge House, where teenage girls without a home were sent under lock and key. She didn't even know where Chloe was, only that she was supposedly "safe" with a foster family, but Hazel knew her sister. Chloe was scared.

On Saturday afternoon, Ms. Wilmore took Hazel to visit Etta at the county jail. During the ride, Ms. Wilmore talked about every manner of thing. Hazel knew it was to distract her. Ms. W even said she'd teach Hazel how to drive. And that until new tires were put on her mother's car, Hazel could borrow Ms. Wilmore's car and drive to see her mother by herself. Hazel couldn't imagine such a feat, but it did distract her for a little bit.

It was as awful as she dreaded at the jail, her mother dressed like a spectacle in an orange top and pants with "SCDC"—South Carolina Department of Corrections—stamped on her back. The guard directed Hazel to a stool enclosed by concrete block partitions on either side, a thick pane of glass smudged with fingerprints in front separating her from her mother. To hear each other, they had to talk on old-time telephone receivers, one hooked on Hazel's side and the other on the table in front of her mother.

Hazel tried to sound positive. She told Etta—and it was true—she was glad to be staying with her favorite teacher. Her mother shouldn't worry about her, or Chloe either, because Chloe was with a good family, too. They would be fine until they were all together again.

"I'm sorry," her mother's voice rattled through the phone wire. "I wasn't in my right mind."

"It's okay, Mama," Hazel said. "You're not a criminal. You shouldn't be in jail. You were just sad."

"Look what I've gone and done," her mother's voice choked. "I lost my children."

"You know you haven't lost us. Don't say that. Stop that kind of talk."

Etta pressed her forehead and nose to the glass and Hazel brought her face up close, too. "Y'all are my life," her mother cried, the phone receiver in her hand shaking.

"Don't worry," Hazel promised. "Ms. Wilmore says they're giving you a lawyer."

"He's been to see me. He's a young man." Her mama pulled her face back. Hazel saw drops of moisture on the glass.

"Mama, don't you cry, it's gonna be okay," Hazel said, sucking in air, looking down, determined for Etta's sake not to let her own tears fall.

"You tell your teacher thank you for taking you in while I'm here, bringing you to see me. She's an angel from God."

"She is," Hazel said and lifted her eyes. "And you know what? Her first name is 'angel,' Angela."

"What'd I tell you?" Etta said and smiled thinly.

***

Sterling was parked in Ms. Wilmore's driveway, music blasting from the open door of his Audi—a popular song called "Try"—when they returned from the jail. "Just because it burns / Doesn't mean you're gonna die / You've gotta get up and try, and try, and try...," the lyrics blared at Hazel. Sterling meant to encourage her—playing this song—but the message overwhelmed her. She was already trying as hard as she could.

"Yo, my favorite ladies," he called, striding toward Ms. Wilmore's Bug after Hazel and Ms. Wilmore opened their doors.

"Sterling, cut that music way down," Ms. Wilmore hollered. "You're going to disturb the neighbors."

"They don't like a motivational tune?" Sterling called, closing in. "About trying when the world gets tough?"

"Sterling," their teacher's voice rose higher, warning him.

"Okay, okay, Ms. W. Don't get yourself riled." He trotted back to the Audi.

The music stopped altogether, and when he returned, Ms. Wilmore cocked one eyebrow at him. "We might need to set a few ground rules."

"Ah, now, come on. Y'all are back from Zell's first visit, and she survived. Let's be glad."

Ms. Wilmore tapped her foot decisively on the pavement.

Hazel laughed, surprising herself—a quick, hard laugh in her belly—at Sterling messing with Ms. W and her giving him the business.

"Hey, go ahead and laugh at me. Oh, yeah, it's just fine to laugh at my expense." Sterling stuck his hands on his hips. "When all I'm doing is *trying*." He pointed toward his now soundless car. "But God, I'm glad to hear you laugh," he shouted and stepped toward Hazel, scooping her into the air.

"Oh, for goodness' sake, Sterling, let's get inside before a crowd gathers," Ms. Wilmore said, holding out her house key.

If there was one thing Hazel knew about Sterling—he loved to push limits. So she wasn't shocked when he turned to their teacher in the kitchen and said, "Listen, I got a bottle of wine in the car. Okay if I go get it for us? To chill out after Zell's visit?"

"What do you honestly think, Sterling?" Ms. Wilmore answered. "No. You're underage and so is Zell. Or is this some of your clowning?"

"Nah, I wasn't clowning. I just know you're cool. I've been drinking wine at dinner with my parents since I was sixteen. But I get it. If a neighbor walked over and did a Peeping Tom through the window at us, you could get busted."

Hazel thought he was going too far with the mocking, so she jabbed him in the arm. "Ow." He pulled back. "That's a mean slug."

"Thank you," Ms. Wilmore said. "I'd like for the courts to allow Hazel to stay and not take her away. Not to mention that I'd be fired from teaching and maybe lose my license," she added.

"Are you serious? You could really get fired? Wow, sorry. How about you got some tasty lemonade?"

"How about I have ginger ale and a chocolate cake I made?"

"Let me at it," he exclaimed.

At Ms. Wilmore's table, Sterling started asking questions about Hazel's visit to her mama. She didn't want to talk about it, but she knew Sterling wouldn't leave her alone until she did.

"This is an extraordinary girl, Sterling," Ms. Wilmore said and scooted over, putting her arm around Hazel's shoulders.

"Hey, you're preaching to the choir," Sterling said. "Seriously, thank you, Ms. W, for everything you've done. You know I give you a hard time because I like you so much."

"Who knew that was the reason. Glad you informed me," she said, cutting Sterling a second piece of cake.

Forking up the last crumbs on his plate, Sterling announced, "Whew. Good. Didn't know you could cook, too, Ms. W."

"I'm full of surprises." She rose from the table to clear plates.

"That was just enough to build my appetite for supper. I'm not breaking any rules to take Zell for a pizza, am I?" he asked.

"No, I like that idea. I've seen you long enough for one day." Ms. Wilmore cocked her head back.

"What say, Zell? Want to grab a pizza?"

She didn't. What she wanted was to go to her pretty room with the ornate iron bed, crawl into the covers that smelled of clean clothes just ironed, and close her eyes from the day. But what she said was, "Sure." Because he'd done so much for her. Because they hadn't been alone for a long time, and she knew he wanted that. Because she loved him.

***

He suggested Marelli's, at least, not Tiffany's where Sterling's friends would be and she'd have to smile and act like she belonged.

"Ah, the beautiful young people," Mr. Marelli said when he brought a bottle of Chianti and poured a taste in Sterling's glass. "But the young lady," he said looking toward her, "she looks a little weary?"

"Oh, no, I'm good, Mr. Marelli," Hazel responded and sat up straighter.

"Hey, baby, you okay? I didn't realize…," Sterling said, raising his glass.

"I'm okay," she said.

"A toast to the bravest, strongest girl I know." He clinked his glass against hers and they drank.

"A glass or two of wine will revive you," he suggested. "Take your mind off things today."

"Nothing will take my mind off my mama sitting in jail," she said.

"I know you're trying to make it better, but what've I really got to make better?"

"What you've got? You're living with Ms. Wilmore. Chloe is in a good home. Your mama has a lawyer."

"I don't mean to seem ungrateful. I don't know where I'd be without you and Ms. Wilmore. But I don't see how they'll let Mama go and how she's going to get a job after this."

"You're thinking too far ahead. One day at a time, okay?"

Hazel nodded slowly and took another drink of wine, thankful for the melting sensation in her gut.

"Don't ask me how I know, but I do. When all's said and done, everything's going to work out. It will. Trust me." Sterling reached his hand across the table. She stared at his fingers. Then the pizza arrived. Sterling pulled back his arm, and the waitress set the steaming dish between them, cheese still bubbling on the top.

Sterling served a big slice onto her plate. "Got to keep up your energy," he said.

Hazel should be hungry—she'd eaten almost none of the lunch Ms. Wilmore offered before they drove to the jail—but she had no appetite for the triangle of crust covered in her favorite toppings: mushrooms, onions, beef, and pepperoni. She told Sterling the chocolate cake had taken her appetite.

"Bull crap," he said. "You ate like three bites of cake. Eat." And because he wouldn't stop pestering her, eventually she did.

Sterling watched her intently.

Damn her for looking tired and Mr. Marelli for saying so. She felt like her mama, trapped in a cell. Like the world was closing in and she couldn't break out. Sterling was trying so hard to make her feel better, but his fussing over her made it worse. It made her feel guilty for being here when her mama was in jail. If only she could fill her lungs with deep, deep breath.

Chapter 26

Sterling Lovell

Sterling played that song—"Try" by Pink—for Zell in hopes of boosting her. She had endured so much. Now, lying on his bed, he realized the lyrics were maybe even more for him, words about taking risks with love, no matter the consequences. That's what he'd done, wasn't it? Ventured into a realm he knew nothing about, far from the life he'd been given.

Money to reshape his ears. Money to pay the fat farm to get rid of his fleshy child self. Money for private tennis lessons to ensure a spot on the Ramsey tennis team. A good car that took him anywhere he wanted to go. A circle of friends like him. The list was endless. While Zell had been given almost nothing.

Who would Sterling be, born into Zell's circumstances? A fat, bitter loser because of the crap cards he'd been dealt? A combatant defending himself from all manner of trouble? A drug addict trying to escape a living hell? But not Zell. She was a survivor with an indomitable spirit. Sort of like Dorothy in the *Wizard of Oz,* he thought suddenly. Zell's ruby red slippers were her natural beauty and brains—but with so much against her, she didn't know how to click her heels. He wanted to be like the wizard from the Emerald City and set her aloft in a big balloon of promise. Tonight he'd failed.

He'd been so hung up on lifting Zell's spirits after she visited her mama that he'd not seen the lightning for the thick, gray cloud in his head. He'd wanted her to feel good about the accomplishment. He was too dense to realize that the visit was not the challenge as much, maybe, as the aftermath. Not until Mr. Marelli said Zell looked tired.

Sterling kept urging her to eat. What an idiot. A stomach bunched in knots from sadness does not want to eat.

After dinner, thinking the still and quiet would soothe her, he'd suggested they go to the cabin. Okay, and the truth was he hoped she'd want to make love. It had been a long time. "I'm tired. I'm sorry," she'd said and stared at him with an eerie, empty look. He'd felt selfishly as sorry for himself as he was for her.

They pulled in at Ms. Wilmore's house to find the VW Beetle gone and the carport light on. "Where's our teacher after ten o'clock on Saturday night?" he wondered aloud.

Zell's eyebrows pinched together.

"Hey, you never know. Teachers have lives, too," he said. "She might have a boyfriend."

"You think so?" Zell actually brightened.

"I hope so," Sterling said, grateful for Zell's interest in Ms. Wilmore's social life instead of worrying about her mama.

"I have a key." She pulled a single silver key dangling on a leather loop from her purse.

"Hold on, I'm coming around to get you." At the passenger door, he reached for her hand.

"Are you mad?" she said, sliding out.

"About what?"

"About, not, you know…"

He leaned in and kissed her goodnight.

***

At the knock on his bedroom door, Sterling glanced at his phone. It was past 10:00. What did a parent want with him at this hour?

"Yo," he called, rising from his bed.

His mother entered and handed him two letters. One from the Stanford Admissions Office and one from Vanderbilt. He'd heard from Davidson a while back. He was in. But he'd especially been waiting on Vanderbilt. Nashville was one cool town, and he thought the school was right for him.

His mother tapped him on the arm. "Well, darling, let's open them," she said, standing way too close.

"Yeah, okay," he said, stepping back. He ripped his finger under the sealed flap of the Stanford envelope. He shook out the page and read, his heart jumping a beat at the word "accepted."

"I'm in," he said, tamping down his elation in front of his mother.

"Oh, darling, of course you are," she exclaimed. "Now read the other."

Not only had Vanderbilt accepted him, they'd offered him a decent scholarship. His heart beat harder.

"Oooh," his mother exclaimed again. "Come downstairs, sweetheart. Let's tell your daddy."

They found his father snoozing in the den, *The State* newspaper spread across his lap, an empty bourbon glass on the table beside him.

"Wake up, Hugh." His mother shook his father's arm. "Sterling has received two more college acceptances."

His father lurched forward.

"Stanford wants our boy, and Vanderbilt has offered a fine scholarship," his mother squealed.

"Of course they want you," his father said, pulling his recliner upright. "Congratulations, son."

"Thank you," Sterling said, keeping his voice cool though he was jacked, especially about Vanderbilt. The school's English major was in the top 5 percent in the country. His parents would think an English major was frivolous and probably urge him to go to the more elite school. Still, surely they would appreciate the scholarship Vanderbilt offered.

"The world is your oyster," his father said.

"We're so proud of you," his mother added.

***

Back in his room, Sterling leaped toward the ceiling, tagging the overhead light fixture. Regardless of what he heard from the other applications—Yale, Brown, and Duke—he'd gotten into one school where he'd really like to go. He wanted to call Zell and shout the news. He didn't though, because…it might make her feel lacking, which was stupid, that's what.

Zell was every bit capable; she just hadn't taken advanced classes, hadn't had the push from home, hadn't taken a private prep course for the SAT, like he had. Her scores weren't abysmal, considering. And she had another year. If she kept up her pace, she could get a free ride or a good part of one to a state school. True, Vanderbilt was a long drive from Ramsey, but he'd get home—maybe fly sometimes—to see her.

He'd tell her soon. They'd be fine. Right now, they needed out of the Ramsey bubble for a break. As soon as the damn debutante ball was over—looming on the first Saturday in April—he could think about it. Weeks ago he tried to renege when there was still plenty of time for Courtney to ask someone else, but his parents had a dying duck fit. It would be the epitome of rudeness, his mother said. Like he really cared what people thought, but he acquiesced. Believing if he stayed on his *p's* and *q's*, he'd bring his parents around to accepting Zell.

He'd hoped Courtney would release him on her own. But such was not Sterling's luck. Though God knows she was busy going out with other guys. Even his friends. She'd called Kipp a few weeks ago, asking him to take her to a basketball game. Sterling skipped the event. Ramsey was losing most of its games anyway. Lousy coach.

Afterward, Kipp reported that Courtney acted like one cold fish as soon as she realized Sterling wasn't at the game.

"Nothing about her surprises," Sterling said.

"It cost me dinner at Tiffany's before the game. All to make *you* jealous, and *you* weren't there. She dissed you the whole time, by the way." Kipp shook his head and wiped his hand across his mouth. They were eating hotdogs at Franks after school.

"Hey, you got a little mustard there on your lip," Sterling said.

"Screw you," Kipp said.

"Hey, don't be so touchy. Not my fault my ex is heartless."

Kipp flicked a hot French fry across the table. It popped Sterling in the eye and plopped to the floor.

"Tell me how you really feel," Sterling said, rubbing his eye.

"For real, man. This thing you've got for Zell. She's a sweet girl and all, gorgeous, but what gives? All these problems this girl has…they're not going away. She's like…," Kipp started.

"Like what, Kipp?" Sterling's voice turned razor sharp.

"Look, I'm not trying to piss you off. We just don't get it. You trying to be Henry Higgins to Eliza Doolittle?" Kipp threw up his hands.

"Hell, no. You have no idea. You've been around her a few times, but you don't know her. Talk about having backbone." He jerked up from the booth.

"Calm down, man," Kipp mumbled. Sterling looked around to see other kids glancing their way. He stepped back into the booth and sat.

"I'm your friend," Kipp said. "Okay?"

"Yeah, whatever." Sterling slumped against the backboard of the booth.

"Sorry I stuck my nose in your business. I'm sure Zell is amazing."

"Amazing is an understatement," Sterling said.

Kipp had tipped his fingers to his brow.

***

Leading up to the ball, Sterling had to attend waltz lessons for several Wednesday nights with Courtney. To use his mother's expression, sugar wouldn't melt in Courtney's mouth. "We're going to make a statement," she said on the last night. "You are the best dancer."

"I just move and count like the instructors tell us to do," he said, uncomfortable at her gushy tone.

"You'll lead me perfectly." Her eyes flashed clear, pale blue. The color could stop your breath if you let it.

The night of the ball, his parents stood waiting at the bottom of the stairs when Sterling descended in his tuxedo.

"Such a handsome son," his mother cooed.

"You do us proud," his father added.

Sterling just shook his head. "Enough, guys. Listen, I'll see ya there."

His mother tugged on his arm. Harriett was dressed in a strapless, fitted turquoise gown, a sheer wrap the same color around her shoulders. She'd had her hair done—swept up and piled in a bun to one side of her head. Some of the pieces were falling out. Sterling figured it was on purpose. She wore the pearls his father had brought her from Japan—and still bragged about—when he'd traveled there on a real-estate development venture years ago. The pearls did look beautiful on his mother's slim neck. Heck, she was a beautiful woman. "We are thrilled to see you back in Courtney's company," she said and smiled.

"I'm not back in her company. I'm fulfilling an obligation," Sterling said.

His mother reached up and played nervously at a loose strand of hair.

***

Sterling stood bunched with the other escorts in the guys' waiting room, Alex and Richard among them.

"How'd we get ourselves into this mess?" Rich asked.

"You love it," Alex said. "Cavorting yourself around the ballroom floor in a penguin suit for everyone to see."

"Happy birthday to you," Rich said and threw up his middle finger.

"It's your nerves," Alex said.

Richard held up both middle fingers.

"Nobody's looking at us," Sterling broke in. "It's all about these big white dresses and long white gloves. Not to mention the low necklines with bulging breasts."

"You said it, brother," Richard said. "Let's get this ball rolling."

At that moment Donovan Powell paraded into the room, his ample stomach leading the way. All eyes turned in his direction. "A gang of handsome fellas," he declared and winked. Guys shuffled their feet, nodded politely. Then he pointed to Sterling and rotated his thumb toward the bathroom. "May I have a word?" Sterling followed.

In the bathroom, Reverend Powell dropped the courteous tone. "Courtney wanted you to be her escort. I didn't, not after what you did," he said. "I'm watching you. It's her night, you hear? You do right by her."

"Of course, sir," Sterling said, nodding politely, wanting to punch Reverend Powell in the large, starched-white expanse above his black cummerbund.

"That's all. Enjoy the evening," Reverend Powell said, extending his hand. Sterling had no choice but to shake it.

The girls entered alphabetically, putting Sterling and Courtney toward the end of the lineup. The wait seemed interminable. But finally,

210

Courtney made her bow, and he walked her around the wide circle, stopping for her to curtsy to her mother. After the last girl made her promenade, the waltz began, each couple in sync like something out of an old-time movie.

Sterling did his best not to step on the hem of Courtney's dress as they danced, though with such an enormous circumference, he caught the edge once. She smiled sweetly and stepped closer so he could remove his foot. The bodice of her dress was tight, pushing her breasts out in two big scoops under delicate, see-through lace. Yeah, he looked, and she saw him looking. "You're welcome," she mouthed. He flinched.

After the waltz, he retreated to the table where he and Courtney would eat dinner with friends and their dates she'd invited. He sat back and watched Reverend Powell—along with the other fathers—now dancing with their daughters. The Reverend smiled beatifically at Courtney, whose nose was tipped toward the ceiling.

Then, there was mingling—cocktails only to those who were of age, meaning the parents, their guests, and grandparents. Sterling was making chitchat with Courtney and a couple of girlfriends when Rich and Alex approached. Rich jerked his thumb toward the back entrance of the ballroom and nodded. Sterling lifted his thumb in agreement.

"Excuse me, girls," he said, interrupting Courtney and her friends. "I'll be back. I won't be late for dinner." Courtney screwed up her forehead, but he went anyway.

"Hallelujah," Sterling exclaimed when they were outside.

"Double hallelujah," Rich said and pulled a flask from inside his tuxedo jacket.

"My man," Sterling said.

"Our man," Alex corrected, taking the container after Rich took a pull.

"You steal this bourbon from your parents' cabinet?" Sterling took the flask from Alex.

"Yep," Rich answered, taking it back for another slug.

"Okay, you got to admit, we've never seen these girls more beautiful," Alex said.

"I'm trying to imagine Zell in one of those white dresses with the long, white gloves. She'd be beyond gorgeous, showing off her amber skin," Sterling said.

"Can't argue with that," Alex admitted.

"But not in one of those antebellum numbers like Courtney has on," Sterling continued. "Something clinging to her figure." Suddenly, the image of a slim and graceful Audrey Hepburn waltzing in a silky dress with Henry Higgins flashed in his mind. He'd seen the film last year in English class when they studied *Pygmalion*. Zell would be as lovely as Hepburn. But he was not Henry Higgins. He'd made that clear to Kipp. No way. He loved Zell for who she was. He just wanted her to have a fighting chance.

"Like the dress Madison's wearing? Fits her like a second skin," Rich interrupted his thoughts. "How lucky is her cousin to be her escort?"

"Yeah, but he can't sleep with her," Sterling said.

"You never know. Drink up." Rich held out the flask. "They'll probably send out a search party if we don't get back soon."

***

Sterling did everything he was supposed to do. Pulled out Courtney's chair. Fanned out her skirt so she could sit. Made polite conversation. Stayed attentive. And felt damn glad when the waiter came at last to pour coffee with dessert.

"Before you leave again, because I know that's what you're dying to do with the other guys," Courtney whispered, leaning toward him and taking a tiny bite of key lime pie, "did you hear about Mr. Copeland and Ms. Wilmore?"

"What are you talking about?" Sterling swallowed a mouthful of hot coffee and gasped at the burn.

"They're an item," she said and blinked, her eyes, glassy ice blue.

"What you been smokin'?" Sterling set down the delicate china cup.

Courtney tilted her head and smiled. "It's out. Daddy told me. And he's going to make sure the superintendent knows."

"What's out?" It was hard to keep his voice low.

"They're having an affair," Courtney announced loud enough for the table to hear, but no one was paying attention.

"Says who?" he asked.

"A church member told Daddy. He's upset there's an illicit relationship going on in front of innocent young people."

"Your father is a crock," Sterling said. "Who started this?"

"A friend of Mr. Copeland's ex-wife is all I know." Courtney tittered and took another small bite of pie. He was sure she'd measured out in her head exactly how much of it she would eat. Enough to be polite but not enough to add many calories. "Daddy still feels humiliated about what Ms. Wilmore did to him."

"Did to him? Are you kidding? You've got that backward," Sterling sputtered. "I got to go."

"You're coming back in soon, right? There's dancing for everyone. Then go to the after-party?" He could see anxious all over her face.

"As a matter of fact, I'm not," he said. "Ask your father to take you. Maybe he would enjoy the party. Find some more to gossip about."

But instead of going out back again with the guys, he strode through the front door, not thinking until he got to his car that he hadn't told his parents he was leaving. Didn't matter. They'd figure it out. He was headed for Ms. Wilmore's house.

"Damn," he said out loud when he saw the carport empty. He had to tell her. Or maybe it wasn't a rumor after all, because where was she, gone again on a Saturday night?

He rang the bell, dreading for Zell to see him in his tuxedo, to remind her, but this was serious. Only Zell didn't answer the door. Ms. Wilmore did.

Chapter 27

Angela Wilmore

"Hey, it's me," a too-familiar voice greeted Angela from outside her side door. She opened it to see Sterling at the top of the stoop. "I was expecting Zell," he said, backing down a step.

"Aren't you supposed to be at the debutante ball tonight?" She stared at him in the pale glow of the carport light. She pulled the sash of her pink terry robe tight around her waist. She glanced down at her worn-out plaid bedroom shoes, self-conscious.

"Yeah, but I cut out a little early." He stepped back up to the door, obviously waiting to be invited in.

"Zell isn't here," she explained. "Doesn't seem particularly sensitive of you to visit her in that attire, anyway."

"I know. I'm sorry. I was in a hurry. Because I need to talk about something. Actually, not to Zell. I mainly came to see you. But where is she anyway, and where's your car?" He shifted from one foot to the other.

"I let her drive my car."

"Whoa, you let her have your car?"

"Why not? She got her license last week." Ms. Wilmore pointed past him to Etta's old Honda. "She can't take her mama's car. The tires are slick as glass and no telling what else might be wrong."

"That was pretty cool of you," Sterling said as he trailed his teacher into the kitchen.

"She's visiting her friend Rhona at the motel. I allowed it because Zell…well…looked awfully glum this afternoon. I didn't want her thinking too much this evening about girls dancing in white dresses with boys at a storybook ball." Angela glanced at her watch. "She'll be home by 11:00." Angela thought Sterling looked unusually antsy standing in her kitchen.

"Would you like to sit?" she asked.

"Yeah, sure, thanks." He pulled out a chair from the kitchen table.

"Want a Coke or something?" She turned toward the refrigerator.

"Nah, I'm okay." Angela turned back. Sterling had begun drumming his fingers on the table. She pulled out a chair and sat, too.

"Everything go okay tonight?" she asked. "You seem jittery or something, more than usual, that is."

Sterling cleared his throat. "Oh, God, I don't know how to ask this," he moaned.

"Ask what?" Angela sat up at attention, placed both hands on the table.

"I heard a stupid rumor tonight...about..." Sterling stopped drumming and pulled at his bowtie.

"About?" Angela said. "Go ahead."

"This ain't easy."

"I have great confidence in you, Sterling," she sighed. "I've never known you to hold back." It was too late at night to deal with his antics.

"First of all, it's none of my business, but if it happens to be true, I think you ought to know."

Angela stood. "You're starting to make me nervous, Sterling. Let's don't do drama tonight, okay?"

"Okay, I know. Right, here goes." He looked straight ahead, avoiding her face. "Tonight Courtney said her old man told her you and Mr. Copeland are seeing each other. I mean, you know like *seeing* each other, and he's going to tell the big people in the district office."

Involuntarily, Angela gasped. Sterling stood, too. "I'm sorry if I said something totally disrespectful, but, you know, I wanted you to know about this rumor."

She looked hard at her student. "What else did Courtney say?"

"Nothing really, except I asked where her father heard it, and she said from a friend of Mr. Copeland's ex-wife."

Forgetting entirely in the moment she stood face to face with her student, Angela sat heavily into the chair, laid her head into her hand and muttered, "Oh, shit."

Sterling coughed nervously then said, "Hey, what's wrong with you having a love interest? You're a free agent. So is he, right?"

Angela looked up at this young man she'd sent not long ago to in-school suspension for taking over her class. A student she'd come to admire very much and who now knew of her private life. "You'll keep this to yourself?" she asked, willing her voice not to quiver. He was, after all, a teenage boy.

"You know I will, Ms. Wilmore. But what about Zell? Her, too?"

"I'll tell Zell myself," Angela said, breathing consciously, slowly, because she could feel her hands trembling.

"Reverend Powell is still pissed because you ruled that day in the hall—bruised his sanctified ego by keeping him out of our class—but what's the big deal? He's a jackass. So what if he tells the world you and Mr. Copeland are...you know? It's the twenty-first century."

"Do you know the word 'nepotism'? Showing favoritism to relations in business?" She stood again and they looked awkwardly at each other. "Nepotism isn't exactly the right word, but it's close enough. With Mr. Copeland being my superior, it will appear—though it's not true—he's preferential to me."

"Of course not," Sterling said. "That wouldn't be your style."

"Thank you for being brave and telling me," she said, "but I think right now it's best I sort out this news on my own, and you leave before Zell gets home."

"Got ya," he said, sliding his chair back under the table. "You know, I'm here for whatever." He held his thumb to his ear like he was holding his phone, turned, and was gone.

Angela lay on her bed with the door closed. She didn't move when she heard Zell turn the lock a little while later. Ordinarily, she would have come out, asked Zell about her evening. But she was too anxious. Zell would sense something. She was incredibly intuitive. So Angela lay still, wishing she'd turned off her bedside lamp so Zell wouldn't see the light under the door. She listened to her foster daughter run the tap in the kitchen, then pad through the den to her room.

Should she call Finley or wait until tomorrow? He wouldn't sleep if she told him tonight. Nothing would change between now and tomorrow. No point in both of them having a restless night.

***

Angela texted Finley she wanted to drop by his house early. She had to be on her way before Zell emerged from her room. Angela left her charge a note: "Gone to run a few errands. Fresh bagels in the pantry."

"To what do I owe this pleasure so early on a Sunday morning?" Finley asked, holding aloft a wooden spoon caked with batter, when she walked in. He wore gym pants and an orange Clemson t-shirt, his alma mater. Maybe he'd been for a run already?

"I'm making pancakes." Disheveled, handsome, Finley pushed hair off his forehead with his free hand and smiled. "How many pieces of bacon can you eat?" He walked to the stove.

"Just one," Angela said. Her heart felt like a balloon about to burst.

"Pour yourself some coffee. You know where the cups are. Breakfast soon."

They sat side by side at his kitchen bar. Angela mostly pushed her food across the plate, dragging pieces of pancake through a puddle of syrup.

"You no like my pancakes?" Finley asked. "I make excellent pancakes."

"You do," Angela assured him and ate a bite, determined to wait until Finley's plate was clean.

"I should put your plate outside and let the raccoons have at it," Finley said, clearing the bar, shaking his head.

"It's not your pancakes. They're delicious." She slid off the barstool and walked over to the sink where Finley stood. She put her hand in his.

"What? What's up? What's happened? Is it Hazel?" Finley lifted her hand to his face and rubbed her palm across his stubbled cheek. It made her arm tingle. "You know I never thought this was a good idea, your taking her in. I know how much you care about her, and the enormity of Hazel's needs are undeniable, but there were other channels.... Never mind. Sorry. I promised myself I wouldn't butt in. I just can't help worrying you've taken on too much."

Angela pulled her hand from Finley's and circled her arms around his strong, broad back. She pressed her face into his chest, into the clean soap smell of his soft t-shirt.

"Baby," he murmured. "Talk to me."

"Can we go sit in your den?"

"Sure," he said. They moved to his sofa.

"I've got something to talk to you about. It isn't good." Then she told Finley what Sterling had reported the night before.

For a long moment, he did not speak. Then he drew in a heavy, audible breath.

"I know what this means," she said. "But how will I stand it? Being without you?"

"It's my fault," he said. "I wanted you to meet Scott."

"There was no way to know this would happen. It's not your fault that Donovan Powell wants me fired," she said.

"And maybe me, too," he added. "He's an egotistical man accustomed to having his way, and he got burned. He hammered you in that meeting, and you showed him you wouldn't buckle, no thanks to me. And then, when Aubrey escorted him to the office that day he wanted to invade your classroom, I sent him on his way. It was bound to come back at us somehow or the other, no thanks to my ex-wife." Finley put his arm around her shoulders and pulled her to him.

"How can he...get away with...?" Angela choked.

"He won't," Finley said. "Not as long as I'm principal. We'll have to stay apart for now so that he has no fuel to feed the fire. Thanks to Sterling—Lord, who would've thought that errant boy would be a savior—anyone who wants to spy on us will find no evidence. But I promise you, this is temporary."

"How can you know that?" Angela pressed her fingers into the corners of her eyes to stop the tears from collecting.

"Look at me, sweetheart." Angela turned her face toward Finley's. "Where there's a will.... Trust me?"

"I'll try."

Chapter 28

Hazel Smalls

Hazel loved driving Ms. Wilmore's Beetle to the Red Rose to see Rhona. It distracted her from thinking about Sterling and Courtney at the debutante ball. Ms. W was so good to her.

She and Rhona played cards and gossiped about kids at Ramsey. Rhona was jacked because Malcolm Cureton, the football player she'd had the hots for all semester, had moved over from the back corner to sit by her in study hall yesterday. Hazel witnessed the action, or more like inaction, because after flirting with Malcolm for so long, Rhona played all cool when he actually plopped down his books on the desk beside hers.

So why had she changed her game once he came close? Hazel hadn't a notion, really, to this day how she'd caught Sterling's interest. She was just glad she did. Maybe they could all go on a double date. That would be something, she told her friend.

"I'm all for that," Rhona pronounced. "But first Malcolm's got to ask me out to somewhere. Hey, how's your mama doing, anyway?"

"She's not so sad as she was. Ms. Wilmore dropped me off at the jail while she went to the grocery this morning. Mama's reading and knitting. They give her yarn and needles, but they're some kind of special needles without a sharp point. I take her books Ms. Wilmore picks out from the library. It won't be forever. The hearing's got to come."

"Yeah, it will," Rhona said. "They'll let her off on probation. She doesn't have a record."

"Gotta be."

***

Hazel put Ms. Wilmore's car key on the counter. The house was as quiet as Mr. Monty's study hall. She walked through the den and saw the light on under her teacher's door. Hazel raised her hand to knock and then pulled back. If Ms. Wilmore was awake but not out in the den or kitchen like usual, she must want to be alone.

It worried Hazel. She knew things about Ms. Wilmore's personal life she shouldn't know. Or at least she had suspicions. She wasn't snooping on purpose when she read some curious words on her teacher's phone. Ms. Wilmore had been in the kitchen, her phone on the end table near Hazel—doing homework—when it dinged. Without thinking, Hazel looked at the screen and saw the name Finley, along with the few words you could see without the password: "Thinking we ought to…"

Mr. Copeland's first name was Finley, so Hazel assumed the message was from her principal about something important at school. She carried the phone to Ms. W, mentioning she saw the name. Ms. Wilmore glanced at the phone, and, nonchalant, thanked her.

A few days later, it happened again. Ms. Wilmore's phone beeped from the same den table near Hazel where she sat struggling with algebra homework. Her teacher was in the yard talking to a neighbor. This time the words were, "Missing you." Hazel dropped the phone back on the table and let it lie.

So now she wondered. Ms. Wilmore usually waited up or at least left her bedroom door ajar and never failed to check in—no matter how quiet Hazel tried to be. Not tonight. Was she upset about something? Was Mr. Copeland really her secret boyfriend and they'd had a fight? Maybe it had nothing to do with Mr. Copeland, and she was creating drama in her head. Possibly Ms. Wilmore was sick and Hazel should do something to help her. But if so, surely Ms. W would have left her a note. Hazel decided to tend to her own business. She headed toward her bathroom to soak.

One of the many luxuries at Ms. Wilmore's house was taking baths. She turned on the faucets and poured in bubble bath. The bottle—pink roses on the label—had been waiting on the side of the tub the first night she arrived.

Dropping her clothes in a pile on the floor, she lowered herself into hot water, into bubbles that rose to her chin, and sighed. It felt so good. She leaned back and closed her eyes, but instead of thinking about her night with Rhona, scenes of Sterling dancing with Courtney crept into her head.

She sat up to shake the thoughts away, white foam scattering across her breasts and stomach. At the same time, her phone dinged. Hazel stepped out of the tub and retrieved it from the counter.

It was Sterling. She set her phone on the edge of the tub, sank back into the bubbles, and took a deep breath. She hadn't expected to hear from him tonight. He said he'd be out late, another party after the ball. Had he had such a good time with Courtney that he was rethinking his relationship with Hazel? Was Courtney so gorgeous in her princess gown that he couldn't resist?

She didn't want to read his text yet, but she was too anxious. She had to get it over with. She grasped her phone—the screen dark again from waiting—and tapped in her password: 78377, numbers that created the name Sters.

"Hey baby, thinking about my beautiful girl tonight. Whatcha doing?"

Hazel felt her smile stretch the corners of her mouth. She pressed the phone to her cheek.

"Taking a bath in Rosewater bubble bath," she texted.

"God, you're killing me. Oh, to be in that tub with you."

Hazel giggled out loud. "Ms. Wilmore would croak," she responded.

"I'm not thinking about Ms. Wilmore."

"Something's not right with her tonight," Hazel texted back.

"What kind of something?" While Hazel was starting a response, he sent another message: "Why don't I just call you?"

"Give me five minutes to get out of the bathtub?" she typed.

The symbol for thumbs-up appeared. Sterling loved emoticons. It drove her crazy trying to memorize them.

Hazel's room was on the other side of the house from Ms. Wilmore's, but she closed her bedroom door anyway. Ms. Wilmore tuned in to the slightest noise, probably because she was a teacher. Hazel's phone rang as she was climbing into bed. She caught it quick.

"How was the ball?" she asked.

"'Bout like I expected, except for Reverend Powell's lecture in the bathroom. That was unexpected."

"Why?" Hazel adjusted both pillows against the headboard and leaned back.

"Not worth talking about. Sorry I mentioned it," Sterling said. "Mostly, I thought about you dressed up in an elegant gown. You'll be gorgeous at the prom next month. When are you and Ms. W going shopping for *the* dress?"

"Cinderella Day is this coming week." Ms. Wilmore had told her that local lawyers organized a day for high school girls to purchase donated prom dresses for cheap. The showroom was in a law office. Ms. Wilmore had offered to buy Hazel's dress, plus shoes, and Rhona's too.

"Oh yeah, that's right," Sterling said. "Can't wait to see what you choose."

"Long as Ms. Wilmore still wants to go."

"Why wouldn't she?"

"Things were funny tonight. When I got home, she was in her room with the door shut. That's never happened." Hazel looked down at her fingers, crossing and uncrossing them. "I don't think she's feeling good." There was a long silence on the other end. "Sterling?"

"I'm here. Just thinking about something."

"I'm thinking 'bout something too. But I don't know if I should talk about it." She pulled the baggy t-shirt she'd sleep in over her bent knees.

"Talk about it," he urged. "You know I won't say anything to anyone. It might have to do with something I know."

"It's not my business."

"Tell me," Sterling pressed, so she did.

"Yep, what you think is right," he confirmed.

"Mr. Copeland is really Ms. Wilmore's boyfriend?"

"Was," he answered. Sterling explained how Reverend Powell knew and how he was going to rat on Ms. Wilmore and try to get her fired. "Wouldn't surprise me if he tried to get Mr. Copeland in trouble, too."

"What will they do?"

"Not see each other anymore, I guess. If Reverend Powell can't produce any evidence, if the VIPs in the district office or school board members or whoever come up with nothing, that jerk won't have much of a case. People will gossip like the devil once it gets out, but so what? It'll only last until something else comes along. It won't take long. When you have no fuel, you have no fire."

"Ms. Wilmore must be in her room so sad because she and Mr. Copeland had to break up. I want to go in and hug her 'round the neck."

"But you can't, babe. Or she'll know you know and think I betrayed her trust. Act like everything is normal. Ms. Wilmore is tough. Take it from someone who's tangled with her. She'll tell you on her own."

"Okay," Hazel said. "Reverend Powell seems like a person who's got everything he could want. Why does he want to hurt people?"

"Because, Zell, some people can't get enough of power. They think they're God."

"Don't sound much like God," she muttered. She reached for the jar of Vaseline that stayed by her bed at night and smoothed it across her dry lips.

They were quiet for a few moments. Hazel adjusted the covers, pulled them up to her chest. She could hear her own breathing.

"Let's talk about something happy," Sterling said, breaking the silence. "Let's talk about going away for the night when school is out on Friday for Teacher Workday in a couple of weeks. I told you soon as I got this damn debutante ball behind me, we'd go somewhere. I've been working on it. Finally found a nice hotel in Asheville that will rent to an eighteen-year-old."

"For real? Asheville? It's so pretty in pictures. I've never been to the mountains up close. I'd love to go. And maybe see that mansion that's bigger than a castle?" She paused. "But I don't know if Ms. Wilmore would let me."

"We're not going to tell her."

"How?"

"Talk to Rhona. She'll cover for you. Tell Ms. W that Rhona's going through a tough time and wants you to sleep over at the Red Rose to keep her company."

"But what if she finds out? I don't ever want to upset her."

"She won't," Sterling said.

***

Sterling picked up Hazel on the ruse of taking her to an early lunch before dropping her off at Rhona's. They drove into downtown Asheville a little over an hour later. Hazel took in the sights, the elegant hotels—one of them where they'd be staying—dwarfed by the mountains all around, cloaked in purplish blue haze, while Sterling searched for a parking place.

"Asheville is all about earth food. Want that? Not me, but you get to decide."

"I don't know if I'd like it, but I'm willing to try."

"Let's go for it, then," Sterling said, maneuvering the car into a tight parking spot. He stopped to examine menus posted outside restaurant doors surrounded by luscious, blooming plants while Hazel paused at boutique windows with bright, bohemian blouses. At the third restaurant Sterling read aloud: "Zucchini noodles, sunflower seed spinach pesto, seasonal roasted veggies in ginger sauce. Oh, and a mushroom bowl. This is it. Classic Asheville."

Hazel squinched her nose. "Am I sure I want this?"

"Come on. When in Asheville, live like a hippie. Plus, it doesn't look too crowded. I got tickets for Biltmore at 3:30."

"You did?" Hazel squealed.

Chapter 29

Sterling Lovell

Had he done the right thing taking Zell to Biltmore? She said she'd enjoyed it, but still. What she'd talked about most was not the football-field-size banquet room with a table set for several dozen people, or the tiled cavern with its outrageous indoor swimming pool and underwater lights—built at a time hardly anyone had electricity. Nope, she was most interested in the servants' quarters. How the bathrooms had indoor plumbing, "a luxury back then," she said. How the bedrooms with "colorful quilts on the beds" and "peaceful pictures on the walls" made her want to sleep there. Even the servants' dining hall made her exclaim in wonder.

Sometimes he didn't have the sense he was born with. That house was an absurdity of riches, and George Vanderbilt basically went broke showing off, but did it make Zell feel…like…damn, forget it. Tomorrow they would change gears. Hike in the mountains before heading back into the Ramsey bubble.

Zell was in the shower. He stripped his shoes and socks, tugged off his shirt. He stuck his head under his arm and sniffed. Not good. He'd take his turn when she came out. At least he'd been able to rent a decent hotel room with a king-size bed.

God, was she beautiful padding back into the bedroom—wearing a soft, green t-shirt that hit above her knees, corkscrews of dark hair pouring over her shoulders. She wasn't near as timid now as she'd been early in their relationship. "Sweetheart," he exhaled. Zell cocked her head to the side and raised one shoulder. She looked sure and unsure at the same time.

"Don't go anywhere. I'll be fast," he beseeched her. She rewarded him with a coy smile. He showered in less than three minutes, pulled on clean boxers. Brushing his teeth, he thought again about the puzzlement on Zell's face. He thought he understood. She was in a different place here, out of her element. He had to make sure she felt so good that she'd be totally relaxed.

He looked around for assistance. There was a sample-size bottle of lotion beside the sink. Not slick enough. He glanced in Zell's cosmetic bag, spotted a jar of Vaseline. It was her lip addiction, but she'd forgotten to take it to bed. "Lubricant," he said out loud.

***

"Hey beautiful," Sterling said, pulling back his side of the covers, crawling in beside Zell, who sat with her back against the headboard, covers up to her chest. He set the Vaseline on the bedside table, then leaned over and kissed the side of her neck. His arms wrapped around her slender shoulders. He felt her suck in breath. "Baby, I love you," he whispered.

"I never thought I'd be somewhere like here," she whispered back.

"Why not?"

Hazel shifted and he eased her down on her back. He propped on his elbows over her and looked at her brown doe eyes, alert.

"I don't ever want to be without you," he said and lowered himself onto her. Her body felt full in a way he couldn't articulate.

"I love you, too," she said, her eyes softening.

Sterling reached his hand under Zell's t-shirt. She moaned when he touched her breasts. He pulled her shirt over her chest.

She wrapped her hands around his back and kneaded the muscles of his shoulders. He eased his hand down and massaged between her legs.

"Oh, God," she murmured.

"Let's make sure. I want it to feel good." He sat up, reached for the Vaseline and smeared a glob along the condom after he rolled it on.

The rhythm of their bodies was strong, perfect. But he let go too quick. He couldn't help himself. Not when Zell tightened her thighs around him.

Afterward, he yanked off the mess of a condom—a fine mess, he thought as he wrapped it in toilet paper and pitched it in the trash before coming back to lie next to Zell, breathing deeply, her arms above her head.

In the morning, they made love again. But slower, easier, with golden sun pouring around the curtains of the double window. How could life be this good?

Sterling didn't want to get out of bed. He wanted to stare at Zell forever. Eventually, though, she started twisting around. She wanted to experience the mountains. Of course she did.

***

Last thing Sterling wanted when they left Asheville late Saturday afternoon was to go back home. He felt suffocated in Ramsey. Same old, same old all the time. People gossiping about each other's business. Unending expectations. Walking a fine line between his parents with Zell.

When he'd told his mother Zell would be his prom date, she snorted loud up her nose. His father merely shook his head. It wasn't their business. He could choose his own company.

Would he take Zell home for photos like he'd done with Courtney last year? Not bringing her to the house long before now was nothing but cowardice. When she was tough enough to cope with her mother in jail, her sister away from her in another home, and no security for the future. Hell, he could stand up to his parents.

He couldn't wait to leave for college. He could smell the freedom. The only glitch was he dreaded leaving Zell. When she graduated in another year, she wouldn't be able to go to Vanderbilt. Or any of the schools he was considering. But Zell would get a ride to a state school and hightail it out of Ramsey, too. Things would work out.

"Let's run away to a deserted island with blue skies and constant sunshine where we wear t-shirts and cut-offs all day long and sleep in our skin," he said when they crossed the state line back into South Carolina.

Zell shook her head and looked at him sideways.

"Think guys can't be romantics?" He rubbed her thigh. "So, okay, since we're on the subject...," he started.

"What subject?" She stroked the back of his hand while he steered.

"Life after Ramsey," he said. "I'm not completely decided, but I'm pretty sure I'm going to Vanderbilt, in Nashville."

"I've always known you would leave." Her fingers stopped moving.

"I don't like that word *leave*. I'm going to college, but I'm not leaving you."

"How far is Nashville from Ramsey?" Her tone became swiftly disheartened.

"Five hours or so by car, but there's this thing called an airplane," he said.

Hazel dropped her hand. "You're so smart."

"No smarter than you, Zell. I was born lucky, that's all."

"That's not all."

"My point is I'll find a way for us to be together next year." He glanced over to see her staring straight ahead, hands folded in her lap.

Chapter 30

Angela Wilmore

Late in the night after the prom, sliding doors cracked open to let in the fresh air of a warm May night—trying not to think about her encounter with Finley, Angela sat on her sofa, feet curled under her thighs. She was trying to concentrate on a novel her friend Dianne asked her to read. She wanted Angela's opinion for her eleventh grade honors reading list. Who was she kidding? Clearly, Dianne had ulterior motives.

Angela was grateful that Dianne and Judson, too, had taken an active interest in Zell's well-being. But sometimes their continuing questions and advice made her second-guess herself. Beyond instinct—and what she'd gleaned from the classroom—she knew next to nothing about parenting a teenager.

The young protagonist, Rachel, in *The Girl Who Fell from the Sky* had obvious connections to Hazel. Not just physical similarity—both being biracial—but Rachel's fictional life paralleled Hazel's real one with themes of alcoholism, death, domestic abuse, and most importantly, identity. As hard as the trauma of Zell's life had been in the last few months—and maybe partly *because* of the difficulties—Angela could see a more confident young woman emerging. The way she handled her visits to the jail. The way she'd bounced back after nearly being expelled.

A particular line in the novel made her think not only of Zell but of herself: "I'm a story. One with a past and a future unwritten." Angela hoped she was making the right decisions to guide her foster daughter.

She glanced at her watch. Those two should be back from the after-prom festivities any minute. Yes, Sterling was cocky about his smarts and full of himself, but he was genuine and well meaning, too, and Angela had decided to trust him. He cared deeply for Zell, of that Angela had no doubt. But he was also a world away from her. Sterling was a stellar student with his future mapped out. He'd told Angela his intention to attend Vanderbilt with a scholarship.

She would do her best to make sure Zell went to college. Zell would retake the SAT in June. Angela was helping her prepare. Zell's scores were okay—890 total—but she needed another 150 points or so to boost her eligibility for in-state grant money and perhaps a scholarship. Still, Zell's prospects were not in the same universe as Sterling's. Angela closed the novel and set it on the coffee table. She glanced at her watch again. Okay, time to text one of them. Sterling, she decided.

"Hello out there. Zell's curfew was 1:00. Are you safe to drive?"

A few seconds later: "On the way, now, Ms. W. Keep calm."

Angela grabbed two fistfuls of hair. "He's going to undo me yet," she said aloud.

She walked out onto her deck. Against the deep black sky, if she could touch, like heavy velvet, she regarded the uncountable stars, their myriad unexplainable patterns. She gazed at Ursa Major, the big bear. Everything, everywhere was one large, unexplainable but—she believed—purposeful design. A breeze stirred. Angela stuffed her hands into the pockets of her worn terry robe. She'd changed out of her prom attire—a loose peasant dress printed in tiny blue and white flowers with smocking across the bodice, ruffled hem at her ankles. A vintage dress she'd worn to her own prom a hundred years ago.

She hadn't wanted to chaperone tonight. It wasn't because she wouldn't enjoy seeing the kids enjoying themselves. It was Finley. She missed him terribly, constantly. Seeing him at the dance would make it worse, if worse were possible.

"Come on, please, Ms. W," that crazy Kipp, heading up the prom committee on student council, had begged her. "We need cool teachers." The irony didn't escape her, and she caved.

She'd spent much of the evening stealing looks at Finley, garbed in a traditional tuxedo except for a loud red paisley cummerbund. A rebel underneath. Her rebel, she'd thought, then pinched herself hard on her arm for thinking it. She told herself every day to accept the inevitable. He could not be her boss and her lover, both. It was not part of the design.

She'd considered looking for another teaching position, even if—assuming the academic grapevine was correct, and it usually was—no other high school in the county treated teachers as professionally as Ramsey did. Other schools told you precisely what to teach and how to teach it. Other schools made you write out detailed lesson plans according to prescribed directives every day. As though writing down words on a whiteboard would prove kids met objectives. How would that even begin to work in AP English?

Angela was accustomed to independence in the classroom, and she appreciated the autonomy given her at Ramsey. But, maybe, she could accommodate. She would still teach English to high school students, right? Could it really be that different elsewhere? She and Finley would be free. She loved her job but she loved Finley, too.

At first, after Donovan Powell spread the word she and Finley were engaging in a "forbidden" relationship, they'd still talked on the phone, but it made the missing worse and they stopped. Angela hadn't seen or talked to him for what seemed an eternity until tonight.

If she thought she'd steeled herself, she was wrong. Every time he went onto the dance floor with a student—like precious Bonnie Henderson who would be their valedictorian—Angela felt like a jealous teenager.

As soon as the band stopped, Angela had headed out, her duty done. Approaching the double glass doors of the hotel ballroom, she saw Finley with a clique of coaches crowding the area. She circled behind them to slip away, but a foot jutted out and connected with her ankle. She stumbled, barely catching herself from a fall.

She looked down to see the foot belonged to Finley. His strained expression told her it was no accident.

"Are you okay, Ms. Wilmore?" He reached over to help her regain balance.

"Yes, fine, thank you, Mr. Copeland." She bent over to rub her ankle.

"Are you sure?" he asked again. "Were you on your way out? Uneven pavement out there. May I escort you?" His voice went lower.

"I'm parked not far from the door," she responded, straightening the skirt of her dress. "I'll be fine."

"Doesn't hurt to make sure." He stepped along beside her. "Sorry, pathetic way to get your attention, but what was I to do?" he said once they were outside. "I have to tell you how beautiful you look. Your dress reminds me of my own prom. If I didn't know better, I'd think you were one of the kids."

"You look pretty fetching yourself," she said and paused. "This isn't doing us any good, you know."

"To hell it isn't," he said. "Speak for yourself. I've been watching you all night. And I'm telling you something. This, this…is no way to live, missing you like I do."

They reached her car. She opened the driver's door.

"You didn't lock it? Parked over here in this dark corner?"

"I don't lock my car. Someone wants in, it will happen regardless."

"Glad to see that stubborn independence intact."

She slid behind the wheel and removed her beaded evening bag from her shoulder to search for the key. Finley's face tipped into the car, unbearably close. She glanced around, but there were only the two of them.

"Finn," she pleaded. "This is too hard. I've got to go." She inserted the key in the ignition, then felt a tug at her left shoulder.

When he kissed her, she felt nothing like a middle-aged woman in a bygone dress. She felt like a teenage girl again, full of desire. He held her face in his hands. "One life, get it? That's what we got. I'm done with this. I can be independent, too."

***

Sterling and Zell waltzed into Angela's den in a blaze of splendor, the smell of their youth filling the room. She'd seen them at the prom, of course, but up close at home…Zell's beautiful bronze shoulders highlighted by the cream chiffon dress dipped with a sweetheart neckline, the first dress she'd tried on. And Sterling the handsome counterpart in a dark blue tux.

"Tell me about it." She gestured for them to sit.

"Memory for the rest of our lives," Sterling said, plopping onto her sofa, pulling Zell down beside him. "Like you, Ms. W, rocking that seventies dress."

Angela shook her head. Sterling never missed a beat.

"Just you wait. You'll see how fast time passes."

"Ah, Ms. W, I'm just getting at you. You looked terrific. You'd never know you're like, however old you are."

"Enough," Angela said, motioning with her hand. "Stop while you might still be ahead. Tell me about it later. Time you were on your way."

Zell giggled.

After at least ten goodbyes at the door with long pauses between, Zell wandered back into the den. She sat in the club chair and rested her feet on the ottoman.

"Your feet have got to be killing you," Angela said, looking at the skin puckering over the straps of Zell's evening sandals.

"I can't even feel my toes." Zell unbuckled the strappy shoes with absurdly tall heels.

"I warned you. For me, beauty has never been worth pain."

"It *was* worth it. Sterling said I looked sexy."

"I'm quite sure he did," Angela said, nodding.

"I don't want him to graduate," Zell said abruptly.

"Why wouldn't you want him to graduate?" Angela asked, knowing full well what Zell meant. "Sweetie, I'm not your mom. In fact, I'm not a mom at all, but maybe I'll say it anyway: you've got to consider the inevitable."

"Sterling loves me, Ms. Wilmore," she whispered. "I love him, too."

"Of course, he does, and you do, but he's also going off to college, and you'll be here in Ramsey."

"He says he'll drive from Nashville to see me on weekends." Zell kicked both shoes from the ottoman to the floor.

"Nashville is a long way."

Zell frowned and picked at a fingernail. She looked up. "He says he can fly home. His family has a lot of money."

"Yes and yes. Of course, he will come home to see you. But college life, the new independence, how can I explain? You evolve a great deal between high school and your first year of college away from home."

Zell hugged her arms around her chest and pulled in her knees. "You think he'll forget about me?"

"No, I don't think that. Sterling is smitten. But I want you to be prepared for the changes that college brings. He comes from a family that, well, has been planning for his departure to a prestigious university probably since he was in kindergarten."

"He hates his parents trying to control him," Zell said, still hugging her knees, red-painted toenails poking out from under the hem of her dress.

"He's a gifted young man, self-determined. Still, he is dependent on his parents to pay for his education."

"He's got a scholarship to Vanderbilt," Zell said.

"That's quite a feather in his cap, but it isn't a full ride," Angela explained. "From what he told me, about half his fees would be paid. A school like Vanderbilt, if you add up tuition, dorm, food, and everything, would come to probably $60,000 a year."

Zell leaned forward, straightened her legs. "I never heard of that much money in my life. No way."

"I'm afraid so." Angela stood. "College expenses are out of control and getting worse. But fortunately for Sterling, he's in a small population whose family can afford whatever a scholarship doesn't cover at an elite school. He won't have student loans to pay back for half of his adult life." She walked over and put her arm around Zell's shoulder.

The girl stared up at Angela, her lovely brown eyes huge and alarmed. "Will I ever be able to go to college?"

"Of course, you will. Don't talk like that. You can get a fine education by starting in community college and transferring to a state school here in South Carolina."

"Not for $60,000," Zell exclaimed.

"Oh, no, the cost will be nothing like that," Angela assured her. "My guess is, smart as you are, you'll get enough grant money to see you through. There's time to figure it all out. But as far as Sterling…"

234

Chapter 31

Hazel Smalls

Hazel did not, did not, did not want to attend graduation because it meant sitting with Sterling's parents in the Ramsey High gym. Every family received five tickets, and Sterling wanted her to use his fifth one. His paternal grandparents would attend, but his maternal grandmother, a widow, lived five states away and had heart trouble. It wouldn't be safe for her to fly, Sterling explained.

Hazel said politely she would see him afterward with his friends. That he should give the ticket to someone else. Couldn't Livie attend? But she knew as soon as she uttered the idea, it was a stupid thing to say. Livie wouldn't come near her parents. Sterling's face crumpled at Hazel's refusal. And the cajoling began.

"It's high time Hugh and Harriet got to know you," he proclaimed. "Here's what we do. You come to dinner, get to know them, and you'll be fine around them at graduation."

The only thing worse than the thought of sitting with his parents at graduation was the prospect of sitting at their dinner table. "They don't like me," Hazel pleaded.

"Let's give it a chance," he countered.

That Friday night, dressed in a short-sleeved lilac dress purchased for the occasion and brown leather sandals borrowed from Ms. Wilmore, Hazel walked beside Sterling into the dim, cool entryway with a ceiling two stories tall in the Lovells' enormous house. A rug—red with a diamond-shaped center and a border of dark blue and pink flowers—covered most of the wood floor. It struck Hazel that the rug looked worn out. If the Lovells were rich, why did the rug everyone would see coming into the house have threadbare places?

Sterling's father suddenly appeared, beckoning them into a living room filled with white upholstered furniture, gleaming dark tables, and a massive mirror over the fireplace, the frame so brilliant she wondered if it was made of real gold. Another rug, similar to the one in the entry, only larger, but looking equally old and worn, covered most of the floor. Later, Sterling would tell her these were Persian rugs, more valuable because they were old. It made no sense to Hazel.

She sat beside Sterling on the sofa. Mr. Lovell poured himself a liquor drink and dropped in two ice cubes from a silver bucket on the bar. He poured a glass of pink wine for the rest of them—Mrs. Lovell called it rosé. Sterling started talking about final exams, how in one more week he'd be finished with calculus forever.

"What is your favorite subject, Hazel?" Mrs. Lovell asked.

"English," she answered.

"Because you're living with your English teacher?"

Hazel stiffened. "No ma'am. I like studying stories and poems."

"Like me," Sterling interjected.

In a few minutes, Mrs. Lovell stood and waved them into the dining room. They sat while she brought in roast beef, potatoes covered in cheese, and very thin green beans she called haricots verts.

Hazel couldn't eat because Mrs. Lovell wouldn't stop asking personal questions. About Hazel's parents, their livelihood, even though Sterling had told them her father was dead. She did not, thank God, ask if Hazel's mother was still in jail. She asked instead if her mother had found a job.

Hazel balled up the cloth napkin in her lap into a tight wad. Mrs. Lovell put the fingers of her right hand to her neck and cleared her throat.

"Let's talk about the big night," Sterling declared, steering his parents away, mercifully, from her.

Finally, Mr. Lovell had something to say. "Moment we've looked forward to." He swiped his napkin across his shiny lips. "You've got the world by the tail, son."

"Yes," Mrs. Lovell concurred. "Though I wish you'd given more consideration to Ivy League schools. So high on the wait list at Brown. You would have gotten in. You didn't *have* to have any scholarship money." She looked at Hazel, and if looks could speak, Hazel knew the woman's words would be something like, "What do you think about

236

that, poor girl?"

"How are plans for the graduation trip to Panama City Beach?" his father interrupted. "Back in my day, it was just a long weekend at Myrtle Beach. But it was some kind of a good time." He winked at Sterling and stirred his finger in his drink.

Mrs. Lovell scowled at her husband. "I don't like the idea of you boys ganged up together in a house alone for several days," she complained. Sterling rolled his eyes.

"What do you say, Zell?" Mr. Lovell asked. "Think those boys will behave themselves?" He slurped his drink. Unless Hazel had missed one, this was his third, nearly empty.

Hazel sat up poker straight. She'd not known about this trip. She stared at a large portrait on the wall across from her, a couple from another century. Under the table, Sterling touched his feet to hers. She shoved them away. She didn't care if he went off and lived it up with his friends after graduation. In fact, she'd expected it. But he hadn't told her, and she'd been blindsided in front of his parents, his tanked-up father making fun of her.

"Hope so," she managed. She had to get away. "Excuse me, would you tell me where the bathroom is?" she asked Mrs. Lovell.

"This way," Sterling said, jumping up to pull out her chair. "Sorry, sorry, sorry," he said once they were out of the dining room. "Don't be mad. I was going to tell you. Just so much going on."

"I don't care if you go off with your friends to celebrate, but it'd be nice to know." She pushed past Sterling into a bathroom with another old rug covering the tile floor. She turned the shiny brass lock and sat on the closed toilet lid. Sterling going off to college filled her head. She looked down at her feet nervously jiggling. She was a plain, tan fish swimming upstream against a school of brilliant-colored fish dazzling in the sea. That's what his parents saw. She took deep breaths. She had to calm down.

"Zell, hello, Zell, are you okay?" Sterling whispered from the other side of the door. "Let me in? Please?" She stood and cracked the door. He wedged in an arm, then squeezed through. "I'm sorry. It's my fault. Can I blame it on being an insensitive clod who can't wait to graduate?" Hazel peered at him. She was exhausted. "Really, don't pay so much mind to my parents. They're this way all the time. They like you. I promise."

"Who do you think you kidding?" Hazel half smiled.

"F... it," he said. "Why do we care?"

"So do I have to sit with them at graduation?"

"That's the only seat."

***

She'd made up her mind to skip graduation, even with Ms. Wilmore criticizing the decision. "You'd want him to be there for you," she advised.

"He wouldn't have to sit with parents from hell," Hazel countered.

"Touché," Ms. Wilmore admitted. "I'll shut my mouth."

And then Mrs. Lovell called. Not recognizing the number, Hazel answered.

"Hello there, Hazel," she said, her voice all bright. Hazel startled. What did his mother want with her?

"We have an extra ticket for graduation, I believe Sterling told you, and he would...we would, like for you to join us." Hazel didn't think his mother meant it. Sterling had put her up to the call. She imagined Mrs. Lovell touching her index finger to her skinny lips—smeared with dark red lipstick, probably to make them look fuller—like she'd done several times at dinner just before she said something badmouth in a roundabout way.

"Thank you, Mrs. Lovell. I think that...," but before she could come up with an excuse, something in her head made her say yes. It was remembering how Sterling had come to the motel room when they barely knew each other and gotten between her fighting parents. He'd been brave on her account. She could do the same for him.

***

As much as Hazel loved being with Sterling, he could be exhausting. His world was exhausting, too. Always trying to say and do the right things around his friends, not to mention his parents. She felt almost relieved when he took off the second week of June with friends packed in two cars bound for Panama City Beach.

Her period was late by more than a month. It had to be nerves. She thought about her first blood, the long, brownish smear on the crotch of her panties. She was thirteen. She'd run to her mama, who patted her back and gave her a pad to wear. The flow had stopped only a day later.

"That blood'll come once a month, mostly, for about a week. But sometimes it won't be so regular." Her mama then explained how she skipped her own period for seven months just out of high school. "I was nerve jagged," Etta said. "I didn't know where I was going or what I was about. I was eighteen and out of foster care. Even after I got a job and met Burl, it took a while for my body to get settled."

Hazel thought about her mama's words. Her cycle was messed up because her own life was unsettled. Sterling going off to school. Chloe living with a foster family, people Hazel hardly knew. Worrying about Etta's trial—not happening until fall, the lawyer said. Then wondering what her mama would do if she did go free.

Sterling always used a raincoat—what he called a condom. She sat cross-legged on the pink bed coverlet in the late afternoon, thinking what to do. Maybe if she bought one of those pregnancy tests and got the results, she'd calm down and her period would start. How much did one cost? Ms. Wilmore gave her an allowance—$40 a week—out of the $16 a day the state paid for Hazel's upkeep. Unless the test cost more than $70—Hazel's current balance—she had it covered.

Hazel wandered into the den where Ms. Wilmore sat curled up reading. Her teacher looked up, and Hazel asked if she could borrow the car for a little while. Ms. Wilmore set down her pen. She always looked sad these days. Zell hadn't seen her teacher smile like herself since when?

"Well, it *is* Friday night." Ms. Wilmore glanced at her watch. "You want to visit Rhona?"

"No, just want to run to the drugstore for some things."

"Sure, hand me my bag, and I'll dig out the keys." She stretched out her legs. "Would you get me some toothpaste while you're there? I've squeezed to the end of the tube and just now remembered."

"What brand?"

"Whatever is on sale. You need some money?"

Hazel shook her head. She was so lucky to be where she was. She needed to get over this uptight feeling. Just get to the drugstore, get the test, and get it over with. Then she could relax.

***

Hazel peed on the stick, inserted it into the plastic case, and sat on the ledge of the tub in her underwear, eyes closed to wait the long three minutes. When she looked down at the test, a bright neon plus sign had appeared clear blue as a cloudless sky. She dropped it like acid was burning her fingers. It couldn't be right. Immobile, she stared at the bathroom floor. She couldn't be pregnant. Sterling used a condom. This couldn't have happened. She could try another test. It hadn't cost but $8.

She began to shiver. She wrapped her arms around herself. She was so cold. She opened the faucets to fill the tub. Soon, she lay sweating in too-hot water, her future dissolving. How had she thought she could actually go to college? Maybe to be a teacher. Not a high school teacher like Ms. Wilmore, but little kids. First grade. Teach them to read.

She sank to her forehead, held her breath. What about Sterling? What would he do? Forego Vanderbilt to have a baby with her? Would he? If he loved her? Hazel raised her head, a turtle on its back. When the water cooled, she let some drain, then filled the tub with scalding water to the brim again. She did this over and over.

She tried to think of a positive outcome. A baby would solidify her future with Sterling, wouldn't it? They would be together. But his plans would crumble. He'd resent her forever. His parents would be humiliated. They would turn him away like they had Livie.

Maybe Sterling would go off to school anyway. Leave her. How would she ever finish high school with a baby to take care of? How could she put another worry on her mother, who'd borne more than any woman should? Hazel would be lucky to end up back at the Red Rose Motel, in the kind of poverty where she'd lived too much of her life.

The knock on the bathroom door made her whole body jump.

"Zell, you okay? You've been in there a long time. I keep hearing the water come on."

"I'm fine," Hazel whimpered.

"Why don't you sound fine?" Hazel did not respond. "May I come in?" When Hazel didn't answer, Ms. Wilmore tapped again.

"Okay," Hazel said.

Ms. Wilmore stood in the doorway in her gown and slippers, her hair brushed back off her face in a headband, her face scrubbed of makeup. "I got ready for bed, then realized you were still in the bathroom, so I...." She took a small step into the room. Hazel moaned loudly, and Ms. Wilmore rushed forward.

"What's wrong?" She glanced down at the object littering the floor. She picked it up. She saw for herself.

They stared at each other, Hazel oblivious to her shriveled, naked body in the gray water.

"Let the water out," Ms. Wilmore directed. Hazel leaned forward and opened the drain. Ms. Wilmore handed her the soft lilac towel from the rack. Hazel stood and wrapped it around herself.

"Where are your night clothes?" Ms. Wilmore asked. Her voice wasn't mean, but it was sharp. Hazel pointed toward the bedroom. "I'll be waiting in the den."

Hazel wanted to run away. But where? And what good would it do? The baby growing inside her would be with her no matter where she ran.

"How?" Ms. Wilmore asked when Hazel slunk into the room. She sat across from the woman who'd been so good to her. "What I mean is didn't you and Sterling have enough sense to take precautions?" Hazel nodded yes.

"May I ask what kind of precaution?"

Hazel lowered her head. "He uses condoms," she mumbled.

"Did one come off?" Ms. Wilmore asked. "Was there, I'm sorry, but..."

"No ma'am, nothing came off. But one time he did something different," Hazel said low.

"What kind of different?" Ms. Wilmore paused. "Never mind, it's not my business, and that's not the problem now, anyway."

But Hazel had already formed the words in her head to explain. "He put some Vaseline on it to, well..." Hazel watched Ms. Wilmore roll her neck like she was in pain.

Ms. Wilmore put up her hand to stop Hazel from speaking. "I shouldn't have let you be with Sterling so much."

"It isn't your fault. We were still going to…. But I don't know how…"

"*How* is the fact that Vaseline can break down latex, the product condoms are made of. You're supposed to use water based…not petroleum jelly." Ms. Wilmore sighed heavily. "Don't they teach you these things?"

"Who?" Hazel asked.

"Oh, honey," Ms. Wilmore said, standing. She walked over to Hazel's chair and pulled her to her feet. She wrapped her arms around Hazel's back.

Chapter 32

Sterling Lovell

Did it ever feel good to be out of Ramsey, Sterling thought from the backseat of Kipp's Land Rover—his father's, that is—as they pulled in at the coral cottage that would be home for the next few days at Panama City Beach. The car CD was cranking "Panama," Eddie Van Halen's guitar soaring into the cloudless blue.

"Paradise," Bennett said, punching Sterling on the shoulder when the car stopped. "Let me at it."

"And the chicks are only four houses down," Rich said, turning from the front seat to grin at the two in the back.

"Old man Sters. He's a married man who can't partake," Bennett tutted loudly.

"Says who?" Kipp said, opening the driver's door, stretching his arms to the sky. "What happens in Panama stays in Panama, duh. And who says it has to be a Ramsey girl, Rich?" he added. "I'm *up* for new explorations."

"You're full of shit is what you are," Rich snorted.

"Where are the others?" Sterling changed the subject, stepping onto the gravel drive into a perfect Florida afternoon.

"With Walker at the wheel, who knows? They either went over the shoulder or stopped to throw up," Kipp suggested.

A few minutes later, hauling in gear, Bennett called out, "Here they are," waving as Walker rolled his mama's Tahoe into the drive.

"Ahoy, maties." Walker exited the car. "Long drive. We've burned some rubber."

"That's a mixed metaphor," Sterling said, but no one laughed.

"You still got Jake, Alex, and Lucas?" Kipp asked when no one else stepped out.

"We're car sick," Jake hollered from the passenger window. "You know Walker drives like a crazy man."

"Yeah, yeah, suck it up. Get your stuff in the house and let's get this party started. First come first serve, room and roommate," Kipp hollered.

"Who made you boss?" Alex tossed up his palms.

"I made the reservation, dickhead," Kipp said.

"Excuse the hell out of me, oh Great One."

"No f…ing way am I sleeping in the room with Jake," Rich announced. "His feet smell like the underside of a dead skunk."

"Hey, not nice," Jake yelled, punching the air. "I can't help it if my feet have a chemical problem. I keep my socks on."

"Chemical, my ass," Lucas said and scratched the crack between his cheeks. "It's called take a bath, buddy."

Jake ignored him, threw his duffel over his shoulder.

"Enough, you guys," Sterling said. "I'll sleep in the room with sweet feet." He caught up with Jake and threw an arm around his shoulder.

***

They'd hardly unpacked before the girls appeared.

"Come into the castle, ladies," Rich said, beckoning Courtney, Jill, Madison, and Olivia through the door.

Olivia was a nice girl, Sterling thought. How had she gotten tangled up with the likes of Courtney and her two cronies? She used to hang out with the quiet, brainy girls.

"This place is a slum," Madison announced.

"Beg pardon, madam, this place is paradise," Lucas said, grinning back at the room. "You don't have to stay."

"Move over," Madison said, coming through the door with the other three in tow.

"Our place is much nicer, and bigger," Jill said. "And up off the ground."

"We prefer quaint. Besides, we'd rather spend our money on other things." Rich rubbed his fingers together.

"Whatever," Jill said.

"You girls like a beer?" Bennett asked, opening a cooler.

"Sure," Courtney said, plopping down on the faded sofa. She wore white short shorts, her legs even longer in platform wedges. She caught Sterling's eye before he could look away.

A case of beer later, Alex said, "What you girls fixing for supper? I'm hungry."

"We aren't cooking," Courtney said. "We're going to Schooners. Unlike you, we made plans."

"But it's past sunset and we missed the old cannon that we read about going off," Madison whined, setting down her can of beer with a thud.

"If the food's good, we'll go back," Courtney promised.

"Schooners sounds good," Bennett said. He exaggerated a wink at Olivia. Sterling laughed, and Courtney gave him a stare.

"I'm for the hotdog place we passed up the road," Alex said. "Anybody else?"

Everyone but Rich, Bennett, and Lucas raised their hands.

"Divide, conquer, and peace out," Jake said. "See you cowboys back at the ranch."

"Talk about mixed metaphor." Sterling bumped a hand to his head.

"Will you give it up with the school talk?" Kipp said.

"Mirror, mirror on the wall, we all know Sterling is the smartest of us all," Walker sang out.

"Don't you forget it." Sterling slapped his friend on the back, and Walker lurched forward.

"Guys' night out," Alex said, leaving Jill to eat with the other group. He crossed his eyes at the girls bunching at the door, the guys horny for Ramsey girls behind them.

No one could find where Kipp set down the key to "Lost Shaker of Salt"—the name a reason they'd rented this lame place. They locked the front door and left out the back.

***

Sterling had tanned a deep-red brown skin. He'd been in the ocean or on the sand most hours of the day, even with Courtney on the beach unnerving him, sitting in her black string bikini watching them play volleyball, whatever. He took long runs in the mornings—so much better on the beach than at home. Maybe he wouldn't have been a fat kid if he'd lived at the beach. He missed Zell, he did, but he had no one to answer to but himself.

The house was packed the last night, Sterling and Courtney the only ones unattached. Lucas and Jake brought babes they picked up walking on the beach the first day. A bleached blonde duet from Georgia, too tan and too skinny. Sterling couldn't keep them straight. Rich had hooked up with Madison—there was no accounting for idiocy—and Bennett with Olivia. Alex, of course, was with his girl Jill. Kipp and Walker—good for them—had tried out a new girl each night, until this evening when they each brought a rerun.

"There's like too many of us to go out to eat," Sterling said, mostly to himself because no one could hear him with the music blasting from Lucas's iPod and the hubbub in the small den. He pressed through the kitchen, grabbing a Miller Lite on the way, and onto the deck for air. He found Walker there. "Man with a car," Sterling shouted. "Let's go get pizza."

"I'm starving," he shouted back. "But we got to collect money. I'm not paying for all these jokers." Walker leaned toward his girl and kissed her, boobs so big his hands wouldn't have met around her back in a slow dance.

"You get ten bucks from the guys out here. I'll do what I can inside," Sterling said.

"You make me sad," Walker said on the drive to Dominos.

"What the hell?" Sterling said. "Just because I'm not getting into a girl's pants?"

"You could put it like that. All that gorgeous ass on the beach and you spend your time running like you're training for a marathon." Walker shook his head. "Zell's not here. What happens in Panama…"

"I'm good," Sterling said.

***

The last night is always the drunkest, Sterling thought, reclining in a fake leather chair, enjoying the show. Rich and Bennett had disappeared

246

with Madison and Olivia, probably to the girls' house. Alex, hammered as Sterling had ever seen him, was pointing out a front window, his arm around Jill. "Look a' there, sweetheart," he yelled over the music and noise. "A full moon just for us. You think?" He squeezed her butt.

"Fool, that's a streetlight," she said and slapped him.

Sterling shook his head with glee and stood to get another beer. "Whoo, a little dizzy," he said aloud, grabbing onto the chair arm. "I might be wasted."

Courtney stood with the skinny Georgia blondes near the fridge. She blended right in, though she was better endowed.

"Hello, Sters," she said. "Can I get you a beer?"

"Sure," he agreed, not particularly wanting to thread his way through all the long blonde hair. Where had Lucas and Jake gotten to, leaving these Georgia girls on their own?

Courtney popped the top and handed him the beer. "I'm guessing you still like Miller?"

He nodded.

Back in the recliner, he realized the place had gotten quiet except for music coming from the iPod. The Temptations. The old stuff was the best. Sterling wondered vaguely if his bedroom was occupied. Probably so. With Jake and his girl. He'd lean back and sleep here.

A tap on his arm roused him. He opened his eyes to see Courtney, blue eyes blazing. "Hey," she said. He nodded. "We're all alone."

He looked around. "So we are," he said, the room spinning and mellow.

"I messed up bad, Sters. I thought you were just rebelling, getting back at...and...I didn't behave well. I'm sorry. Will you accept my apology?"

"Accepted," he mumbled and held up a hand.

"Move over," she murmured. He felt a body slip into the chair beside him. A hand rubbed his chest. His t-shirt rose over his ribs. It felt good. He closed his eyes.

"I can make you feel fantastic," came a voice low inside his ear. "Right here." A soft hand massaged his crotch. It floated under the waistband of his shorts, then his briefs until it reached him, gripping tight. He was hard.

247

"I knew you missed me, too," the voice whispered. "Let me…"

The hand eased up and down his length. Sterling groaned. He wanted it bad. The release. He kept his eyes closed. The music had stopped. Everything was quiet. He was in a dream. A fantastic wet dream.

The front door flew open, jolting him. Sterling pulled up. The hand went away. "Oops, sorry to disturb," Bennett said. "We're out of refreshment, so I came back." Sterling looked side-eyed at his friend weaving drunkenly toward the kitchen.

Courtney's breath crossed his cheek. It wasn't a dream at all. He looked at her. "Go back to your place," he said.

"You don't mean that," she said.

"I do." For a moment there was only quiet. And then an explosion.

"You…what the hell? When is this game going to be over? What are you trying to prove?"

He covered his ears with his hands. "I'm sorry," he said. "A few too many."

"You're ruining your life," she said, her voice suddenly controlled. He felt a breeze, a quick rising from the chair. She was gone—he sensed—for good.

Chapter 33

Angela Wilmore

Angela thought the condom covered in Vaseline was surely how the pregnancy happened. But how were Sterling and Zell supposed to know petroleum jelly weakened condoms? Zell said she'd missed two periods and waited a couple more weeks before she took the test. Meaning she might be close to ten weeks pregnant. The way Angela saw it—though it was legal to have an abortion up to twenty weeks—after twelve weeks of gestation, the fetus was too far along. The decision and its repercussions could be horrific.

She knew from her own sister's experience. Joanie had gotten pregnant her junior year in college and put her head in the sand until she was sixteen weeks along. The abortion at seventeen weeks had been a two-day procedure with devastating consequences.

Worried about Joanie's denial, her roommate Christine had called Angela. Joanie was on edge from the start, already furious with Christine for informing Angela. During that terrible conversation, Angela discouraged her sister from having an abortion so late.

"I'm having the goddamned abortion, and I'll decide when and who knows. If not for Christine, you'd never have known. Mom and Dad are never to find out. Got it?"

Angela could still feel the anger and fear in her sister's voice.

"Then you have to make the appointment now," she had advised.

"You're so with it, so on top of my life, why don't you make the appointment?" Joanie had howled into the phone.

"Maybe abortion isn't the right choice," Angela suggested. "Maybe you need to talk to someone professional. You're too upset."

"It's the only choice. I know that. Make the call." And so Angela did. The abortion took place at the Columbia Clinic, not at the Garrett Clinic near home, because Joanie was a student at the university.

From the moment she entered the waiting room, Joanie had been afraid and unsure. Angela told her sister she didn't have to go through with it. There were other choices. She would take her back to school.

"There are no other choices for me," Joanie had said, clinging to Angela until her name was called. Afterward, they spent the night in a hotel room nearby, Joanie huddled in a ball on the other side of the king-size bed, except when she went to the bathroom to change her pad, weeping quietly all the time.

To this day, Angela believed much of the estrangement between her and her sister—she saw Joanie and her husband rarely—was the abortion. At first her sister had seemed okay, even relieved, but as time went by she suffered with her decision to abort so late, and Angela became the scapegoat. Joanie was like the speaker in Gwendolyn Brooks's poem, "The Mother" that Angela often taught: "Abortions will not let you forget. / You remember the children you got that you did not get…." Joanie would make the same decision again, but it didn't mean it wasn't without great pain. Joanie chose never to have children. While Angela desperately wanted to but couldn't.

***

Angela stayed out of Zell's way the day after Zell learned she was pregnant. She went outside early to tend her small garden of hybrid tea roses. A lot of work, but worth the beauty it produced. She snipped off the spent flowers to prevent them from sucking nutrients and stood back to admire the luscious blooms in the morning sun.

Zell was like those beautiful, fragile petals. Angela loved her like her own. For years, she and Randal tried everything possible to conceive. In between the fertility drugs, the surgery to repair her uterus, and finally the expensive in vitro fertilization—Randal producing sperm in a bathroom with the aid of an erotic magazine—there were four miscarriages. After the last one, her doctor advised no more.

She came inside through the den late morning to find Zell cleaning. From the start, she'd been helpful without Angela having to ask, but today Angela knew Zell was replacing her anxiety with activity. She waved but her charge didn't wave back—furiously pushing the vacuum across the rug.

Angela walked into the kitchen for a glass of water. The room was spotless. Hearing the vacuum stop, she walked quickly back into the den to find Zell dragging it toward the hall closet. She put a hand on Zell's arm. "Take it easy. I'll put it away. Why don't you call Chloe's foster mother, see if you can drive over for a visit this afternoon." Maybe seeing her sister would give Zell some perspective.

Angela offered her car—the condition of Etta's car scared her—but Zell refused, so she let it go, a car in disrepair seeming suddenly inconsequential. As soon as Zell pulled out in the old Honda, Angela called Dianne. Her younger friend's knowledge of motherhood might guide Angela into some kind of insight. But Dianne didn't answer. Nor did she text back when Angela tried that route. Probably off at the swimming pool with her precious little girl, Florence. She could think of no one else but Finley to consult. He had a child. Maybe he could offer guidance.

He answered immediately. "Angela, hey. Hello there. How are you?"

"I've been better," she said.

"What's wrong? What can I do?"

"It's not me."

She heard him exhale heavily. "Thank God you're okay."

"I called to talk about Zell," she said.

"Why?"

"Because she's pregnant."

For a long moment Finley said nothing. Then, "Are you sure?"

"I saw the proof myself, a drugstore test."

"What the hell?" Finley exclaimed. "They didn't have enough sense to take precaution?"

"They did, but Sterling was using condoms and didn't know certain...lubricating substances might destroy a thin layer of latex," Angela said.

"Good God, don't tell me anymore. You know how I worried about you taking Hazel in. This is out of your hands. Has she told Sterling?" Finn was angry, and that wasn't what Angela needed.

"No, and I'm not positive she's going to." She crossed and uncrossed her ankles.

"Why not?"

"She doesn't say, but I know she worries he'll resent her. That she'd be taking away his future."

"What about *her* future? Listen, Zell needs to talk to her mother. She's not eighteen yet, is she? So she'd have to get her mother's permission anyway if she decides…"

"I care about her deeply, Finn. I want to help her. In South Carolina, a girl doesn't need permission over age seventeen. I looked it up. The last thing her mother needs is another burden, and Zell knows it."

Another long silence. Angela looked down at her feet, still moving.

"I hope to hell Scott is never in this predicament."

"So are you suggesting abortion?" Angela pinched her lips together. It was hard saying the word when she and Randal had wanted a baby so badly. When it had changed Joanie's life.

"It's an option. Children raising children is fraught with difficulty: financial, emotional, social, just to get started. A girl Zell's age, not even graduated, isn't equipped or ready to raise a child. And with her mother's circumstances—I don't mean jail; I mean poverty—it would likely be, well, calamitous for everyone involved."

Would it? Not for her, she thought. A baby, finally, to adore, to care for. She imagined an infant—its sleeping cherubic face—in the never-used white wicker bassinet, still stored in the attic after all these years. Why not? And then she caught herself. This was her own selfish longing. She was not the mother, and she wasn't a young woman. The decision wasn't hers to make.

"You're right," Angela said quietly. "Zell deserves a fighting chance. And I can't see Sterling settled into fatherhood. He's a good kid, but he has a lot of growing up to do."

"That's an understatement. Plus, he's brilliant, Angela. He's got a lot to give to the world if he follows through with his education." Finley's tone was brusque.

"Zell can go to college, probably on a free ride. Maybe an ROTC scholarship. Or need-based grants and scholarships. The only way I know children like her pull out of poverty is through education."

"You said it," Finley remarked. "And how would she get that education with a child to take care of?"

"I hear you, but who knows how Zell will respond when I present these ideas?"

"I don't envy you." Finley's voice softened. "Keep me informed? Let me know if there is something I can do? Baby, I miss you."

Angela sighed. "I will. I miss you, too."

She sighed after she hung up the phone. If she and Finley were a couple, they could talk to Zell together. A united front would be so much easier. Instead, it was up to her alone to discuss options with her foster daughter, a girl who had spent much of her life in the unpredictable world of poverty. A world where getting from one day to the next was an accomplishment.

Angela had been required to take a training workshop on poverty when she arrived at Ramsey. She learned people in poverty thought only of survival. No long-term goals. And though Angela herself couldn't fully grasp the psychology of it, she understood that short-sightedness was one way the cycle self-perpetuated.

But Zell didn't fully fit that mindset. She did look toward the future. She paid attention to how the world operated. And there was no doubt she wanted to go to college. A single teenager with a child would be lucky to afford a room at the Red Rose Motel, much less have money for daycare she'd need to go to school. Hell, Zell might not even graduate high school.

And if she and Sterling decided to raise the baby together? Angela couldn't imagine Sterling's parents assisting; they'd be too outraged. The young people would be left to work minimum wage jobs, scraping and scrambling. A sure fiasco. Sterling was a boy with a good and genuine heart, but he was also accustomed to a privileged life and looked forward to his college days at an elite institution. Days, Angela knew, where he could grow into manhood.

Her best strategy was to appeal to that strong part of Zell that wanted out of poverty.

She braced herself when she heard gravel crunching in the driveway. She met Zell at the door. Neither spoke. Zell looked away. She started to leave the kitchen, but Angela called her back.

"Tell me, how was Chloe?"

253

"She's good. She wants me to take her to see Mama soon. The people she stays with are nice, but she's homesick." Zell hovered at the threshold between the kitchen and the den.

"I'm thankful she has you. Children need support." Angela paused. "I'm going to be frank. It would be easy not to face reality until you start to show, but if you don't, time will slip by and you'll have less control than you do right now. The longer you wait to make a decision, the harder it is." She patted the chair beside her.

Zell walked to the table and sat. "Want a ginger ale?" Angela asked. Zell shook her head. "Look, I've never been a mother, though I wanted to be, but I've seen a lot of life, and it appears I'm what you've got." Zell offered a dim smile.

"Let's consider the options I'm sure you know: keep the baby, adoption, or…abortion." Angela held up three fingers. "Before long, the third option will be gone." She lowered one of her fingers.

"I know," Zell muttered.

"This is not something to be ashamed about." Angela touched her fingers to Zell's chin, lifting it. "You're a normal young woman. Sterling is a normal young man. You're in difficult circumstances, but not because you weren't trying to be careful."

"I'm not telling Sterling. I made up my mind about that." Zell looked Angela in the eye.

"Why not, honey? It's his responsibility, too. He needs to know."

"No, he doesn't. He's at Panama City Beach having fun with his friends. I tell him I'm pregnant, and everything gets pulled out from under him. He'd be wanting to do right by me, but it would bind him up like a mummy."

"You're saying you want Sterling to be free and live his life normally while you're burdened with the decision?"

"It's not like that. It's just he…his parents would cut him off. That scholarship to Vanderbilt won't pay it all. He's going to be somebody important. I don't want to stop that from happening."

"He can still be someone important—as you say—and help with this decision. You're going to be somebody important, too." Angela reached for Zell's hand.

"I wasn't ever going to be somebody important," she whispered.

"Especially not now. No way with a baby to care for." Her hand lay limp inside Angela's.

"To hell with that kind of talk," Angela exclaimed, squeezing Zell's hand too hard, then quickly letting go.

"How'd I think I was ever going to college anyway?" Zell pulled her hand to her chest.

"You know good and well you're smart and can go to college. Try another excuse, Zell." Angela was getting worked up.

"I got to keep the baby," Zell said. "And I got to leave so Sterling doesn't know."

"You think he's going to let you disappear from his life?" Angela demanded.

"It's my duty," Zell said.

"That's not your only choice. Can we talk about it?" Angela forced her voice back into the normal range. Barely, Zell nodded.

Angela pointed out Ramsey was not a big city where Zell could hide. If she kept the baby, Sterling would eventually find out. Zell said she'd leave town. Angela asked just where she planned to go and how she planned to finance herself and the baby.

"The government will help," Zell said.

"The government might pay for some groceries. Maybe other things. I don't know how it all works. But I know it's not enough to live on and go to school and so do you. Did the government ever get you and your family out of poverty?"

Zell shook her head. "But I'm not bringing this to Mama. She's already got two children to worry about."

"So how do you imagine leaving town without your mother knowing and wondering why, not to mention her alarm when you drop out of high school?"

Zell shrugged.

"Hazel Smalls, you're too good for your own good. You want to do right by everybody but yourself. You think you can handle it all, and God knows you've gotten strong. You've dealt with more in your young life than most people could. But think hard for a minute. Even if you're willing to dismiss your own welfare, is it fair to bring a child into the kind of poverty you'd likely be facing?"

"I don't know what to do," she cried, her eyes brimming. Angela could also see Zell was shaking.

"Honey, I'm sorry. I didn't mean to sound so harsh. But you need to consider all possibilities." It was her responsibility, wasn't it, to help this dear girl think as clearly as possible, not just about next week or next month, but next year and the years beyond?

Zell left the table abruptly. Not knowing what else to do, Angela busied herself in the kitchen. She chopped vegetables for a salad and microwaved leftover chicken casserole. Zell came back with Angela's laptop. When Angela set their plates on the table, Zell was looking intently at the screen.

"There's three clinics in South Carolina. One is close in Garrett."

Angela nodded, pouring water into glasses.

"It costs $600 at the least. I don't have that kind of money." Zell looked up.

"The money is the least concern. I can loan you the money." Zell stared at Angela incredulously. "Really, honey. It's okay." Tears ran quiet along the bridge of Zell's nose.

"I got to be there for Chloe. And mama, when she comes out. What am I gonna do?" Zell swiped at her eyes.

"From all I know, you are a logical and level-headed young woman. Whatever your decision, I'll support you."

"How much time do I have, you know, if I decide to go to the clinic?" Zell held up a forkful of casserole then set it back on her plate.

"Soon, within two weeks is best," Angela said, glancing at the mixed-up food on her plate.

A little while later, Zell retreated to her room. Angela scraped the mostly uneaten food from their plates.

Chapter 34

Hazel Smalls

Hazel woke, waiting for the clinic in Garrett to open. She'd read everything on the website before she went to bed. Tossing back and forth, unable to sleep, way into the night she recalled something her daddy—still a mostly sober man—had said to her mother when she wanted to cuss out Uncle Huck for not making Daddy an equal partner in Smalls Brothers Deliver Trucking: "If no good can come from something, Etta, don't do it."

"It would make me feel better," her mama had said.

"Not for long." Her mama had hung her head in defeat.

Lying on her back in the dark in the white iron bed, she didn't see how any good could come from a seventeen-year-old girl—poor and without resources—bringing a child into the world. It wasn't about love, or maybe, in a strange way it was. She couldn't bear to bring a child into grim circumstances, without a future. It made her heart hurt too much.

What chance would either of them have? Ms. Wilmore kept saying Sterling should know, that the two of them should decide together, but Hazel didn't agree. Sterling might be able to lessen the burdens if they had a child together, instead of her alone, but he would feel trapped, his future transformed, and resent her forever. Even if it was his mistake, it was just that—a mistake. As much as she tried to talk herself into it, she couldn't rationalize telling him. For her sake, too.

Hazel watched the room fill bit by bit with light. The minute the clinic opened at 8:30, she called. The woman who answered was kind. She told Hazel to come that afternoon for an ultrasound to see how far along she was and for counseling.

"Counseling?" Hazel inquired.

"Yes, we need to make sure you know all the options," the lady said.

"I know them. I've made my decision," Hazel said courteously.

"You have to wait at least twenty-four hours after you meet with the counselor before the procedure. It's the law."

"Well, of course you *can* go alone, Zell. There's not much you can't do," Ms. Wilmore said, steam rising from her coffee cup, after Hazel said she wanted to go to the clinic by herself.

She didn't want to load more on her teacher—who'd never bargained for a pregnant foster daughter—than she had to.

Ms. Wilmore set her cup on the counter and threw up her hands. "Very well, but you're not driving that 'Smokin' Possum' out of town. You're taking my car."

"Okay," Hazel said. "Thank you."

"When is Sterling coming home from Panama City?" Ms. Wilmore asked then. "Are you trying to...before he...?"

"Yes," Hazel said.

***

Hazel gaped at picketers gathered in front of the clinic. Maybe a dozen people—the men mostly wearing overalls and women in long dresses, plus some children. The lady on the phone had warned her that protesters might be there. Still, seeing them gave her a queasy feeling, especially the man in the red bandana who stood apart from the others. He shoved his sign at her. His eyes were wild. "Don't kill your child," it read. But it's not a child, Hazel wanted to say. It's an embryo. She parked Ms. Wilmore's car, clicked the lock, and hurried toward the building.

She checked in at the window and sat in a wooden chair with arms and an upholstered seat, like any other doctor's office. There were magazines on the table and pictures of flowers on the walls, like any other doctor's office. But, of course, it wasn't an ordinary doctor's office. Across from her a woman patted the arm of a young teenage girl—fourteen at the most—surely her daughter. The girl stared at the wall above Hazel's head. In a corner a couple held hands, whispering. All there for the same reason as Hazel.

A pretty blonde lady with glasses, dressed in black pants and a loose pink sweater, called her name. "I'm Marsha Till, one of the counselors," the lady said, leading Hazel through the door and down a long hallway painted bright yellow. "You're going to get an ultrasound first; then we'll talk." Hazel merely nodded.

A little while later, Hazel sat across a beat-up metal desk from Ms. Till in her office, papers spread in front of her. She thought a woman who seemed as important as Ms. Till deserved better furniture.

"The good news is you're within the first trimester, at about nine weeks." Ms. Till's fingers fluttered onto the table. "We can proceed with counseling."

"I already made up my mind," Hazel said as she had to the receptionist that morning.

"It's my job to make sure you understand the options."

"I do," Hazel said. The counselor launched into a discussion anyway. Hazel didn't want to listen, but she sat quietly nodding with her hands in her lap.

Then, Ms. Till explained about the abortion itself, if Hazel decided to return. She held up an instrument called a speculum and pointed out body parts on a plastic reproductive system to show how Hazel's cervix would be dilated and the pregnancy "terminated." The word sounded like something you'd hear in a sci-fi movie. Harsh and mechanical.

"Will it hurt?" Hazel's knees pulled together involuntarily.

"It shouldn't. The nurse will put a sedative in your IV called Versed. You'll be in what's called conscious sedation. You'll feel very drowsy. You'll probably fall asleep and won't even be aware of anything."

"That's good," Hazel said, trying to sound confident, even though she felt scared.

Ms. Till stood and walked around her desk. She reached into Hazel's lap and held both her hands. "If you want, I can go back into the operating room with you."

Hazel looked into the woman's kind eyes. "My teacher's going to bring me."

"But she has to stay in the waiting room. Let's decide tomorrow." Ms. Till let go of Hazel's hands. "All you need to do now before you go is sign a lot of papers. Remember though, if you change your mind, you can call me before your appointment. We have an opening in two days."

That night, Ms. Wilmore turned on the local news, like she always did when they were preparing dinner.

"A man wielding a gun stormed the Garrett Women's Clinic this afternoon, injuring three people during a procedure." The news anchor's stern voice pierced the room. Hazel swiveled from setting silverware on the table toward the television. Ms. Wilmore clanged a lid onto a pot.

"The man identified as Leo Jones was arrested at the scene," the newsman continued. A picture flashed onto the screen. Hazel gulped. She'd seen this man only hours before.

"Don't these people have their own lives to tend to instead of hurting others? The irony is incredible. Don't look at it, Zell," Ms. Wilmore muttered, picking up the remote.

"Don't turn it off," Hazel said.

"You don't need to hear…"

"I saw that man today. I know from the red bandana."

"Attending physician Dr. Anthony Irwin suffered a gunshot wound to his thigh, barely missing his femoral artery. Eloise Turner, RN, suffered a broken arm when the attacker assaulted her as she attempted to crawl from the room for help. Both were treated and released from Garrett General Hospital. A patient undergoing a procedure at the time of the incident remains hospitalized in serious condition after falling from the table under sedation," the report concluded.

"It could have been me," Hazel said quietly.

"Oh, honey." Ms. Wilmore silenced the television and pulled Hazel to her.

***

The same pleasant receptionist called Hazel to say her procedure would have to be postponed and offered her an appointment early the next week.

"I saw what happened on the news," Hazel said.

"Oh…" The woman briefly paused. "Yes, we're sort of shaken up around here. But we'll be back to normal soon. Should I put you on the schedule?"

"I don't know. Can I call you back?"

"Of course, sweetheart. But don't wait too long."

Hazel hung up and stared at her phone. Sterling would be home before next week. They rarely went a day without seeing each other. He came by Ms. Wilmore's house all the time. She logged on to her teacher's laptop, desperate. She read about abortion pills, but how would she get them, and by the time she did, it'd be too late. You couldn't take the pills after ten weeks. She read about herbs—mugwort and pennyroyal. She could even drink turpentine, but any of these might kill her. There seemed only one option left, the one her mother had told her about not long after Hazel's period first started, meant as a warning against having sex.

She had to do it. Quickly, before she could think about it too much. Ms. Wilmore was outside watering plants, but there was nowhere inside. The house didn't have stairs. The carport was the only place. She paced, waiting for her foster mother to come back in. Minutes went by. Hazel sat again, pulled up Facebook in an attempt to calm herself with distraction. But it was only kids bragging about themselves and other inane, stupid stuff. Perspiration rolled under her arms. She turned off the computer. Nearly a half-hour passed before the sliding glass door opened from the deck and Ms. Wilmore walked in where Hazel perched on the sofa.

"You feeling okay?" her teacher asked.

"Yeah."

Ms. Wilmore nodded at her laptop. "Don't read any more about what happened. No good can come from it. Maybe you should call the clinic to see if your appointment is still on schedule, you know..."

"I will," Hazel said abruptly.

"Let's go somewhere happy this afternoon. I was thinking a walk around the lake at Hampton Park? But right now I'm starving. Can I fix you a sandwich, too?"

Hazel nodded. As soon as she heard Ms. Wilmore making noises in the kitchen, she slipped out the den door. Conscious of every step, she moved around the house to the carport where she quietly mounted the brick steps to the stoop. She surveyed the concrete floor below. It should be enough.

She stood at the edge and folded forward. Not right. Her head should be up to land on her belly. She looked toward the ceiling. Her heart rolled over and over like Silly Putty in her chest. She had to focus. She took deep breaths and closed her eyes. She lifted her arms. She counted in her head and dove. The toe of one shoe caught the edge of the stoop and she lost control.

***

Hazel's ears rang and her head hurt badly.

The young doctor's voice was crisp. "Let's get this nasty gash under control. Then, we'll send you for a CAT scan."

"Then I can go home?"

"You'll stay in the hospital overnight for observation," the doctor instructed. "With your headache and vomiting in the ambulance, you've likely had a concussion."

"What does that mean?"

"It means you need to rest and stay quiet." She held a threaded needle between her thumb and index finger. "This shouldn't hurt after the lidocaine I injected."

Hazel tensed when the doctor began to stitch.

"Ten sutures and done," she announced a little while later. "You rest. Radiology will come for you shortly."

Hazel's head hurt worse than ever, not from the stitches but from contracting her forehead muscles.

***

Ms. Wilmore jumped up from a red recliner when the attendant wheeled Hazel into the hospital room. "Oh, sweetheart. When I heard the sound—I thought that huge bag of potting soil had fallen off the shelf—and opened the door...all that blood, I was...I'm sorry. Let's get you situated."

The man lifted Hazel onto the bed. "Y'all need anything, just push the button above the bed," he said, backing out the gurney.

262

"Thank you." Ms. Wilmore turned to Hazel. "You're going to be okay. That's all that matters."

Hazel blinked and touched the long bandage across her forehead.

"Do you want to sit up or lie flat?"

"I don't know," Hazel murmured.

"Let's try in between." The top half of the bed began to rise. "Good there?"

Hazel nodded. "My baby…is still here. They sent me for an ultrasound. I saw the heartbeat."

"Yes." Ms. Wilmore nodded.

"I can't go back there. I might get killed," Hazel said.

"Don't think about that right now. You've been through an awful trauma."

Hazel felt dizzy.

"Rest, Zell. It's going to work out. It doesn't seem like it, but it will."

The room was spinning. Hazel gripped the rails of the hospital bed. Ms. Wilmore bent over and kissed her cheek. "I've never known anyone so young with so much courage."

"What about you? I've made it awful hard on you."

Ms. Wilmore smoothed Hazel's hair back from the bandage covering her forehead. "It's okay. Yes, I'm worried about you, and that makes it hard. But I wouldn't change my decision for one second. I love you."

Chapter 35

Sterling Lovell

The conversation on the way home was all about sexual healing—thank you, Marvin Gaye—followed by beach, booze, and food, respectively. Sterling got tired of the guys ragging him for not finding a beach babe, especially Kipp who'd tried out a smorgasbord.

"Too much work," Sterling said at one point to get them off his back.

"Uh, you just want us to think you've got the cream of the crop," Rich complained, turning toward Sterling in the back seat of the Land Rover.

"I do, so what's the point of f...ing it up." Sterling grabbed Rich's shoulders and shook them good-naturedly.

"Get out of here, Commodore. You know you ain't staying with a high school girl back home from the Red Rose Motel when you get off to Vandy," Rich continued. Sterling squeezed his friend's shoulders hard then, to bring pain. "God a'mighty, lay off," Rich said, flipping double birds toward the back seat.

"Pansy," Sterling sneered. Kipp turned up the music and Alex started to sing along. The moment passed.

But a little bit of Rich was right. Sterling wanted Zell, but he also wanted to experience the social life at school. He'd take it as it came, one day at a time. Big picture though, he couldn't see himself without Zell.

It was late when he got dropped at the house. Hauling in his gear, Sterling thought about calling Zell, but he was beat. He'd call her tomorrow. They'd talked a few times during the trip anyway, though he hadn't been able to reach her this morning before they left Panama City Beach.

***

"Would you like to tell me what you boys did that has you so knocked out?" His mother's voice. Sterling opened his eyes.

"It was a long ride. What time is it?"

"It's nearly noon," his mother said, tapping an imaginary watch on her arm. "I came to check on you, make sure you're alive."

"Yeah, okay. Give me a few minutes, Mom, and I'll be down."

She left and Sterling shook his head clear. Like who in the hell would spend a lot of time sleeping when you were celebrating at Panama Beach? You can sleep at home. Jeez.

He took a shower, donned a t-shirt and gym shorts, thought about unpacking his bag, changed his mind, and took his phone off the charger to dial Zell. She didn't answer. Yesterday and now today? What was that all about? Maybe she was in the yard helping Ms. W with one of her flower gardens.

Downstairs, his mother was puttering around in the kitchen. "Much too late for breakfast," she said. "You want a sandwich?"

"That'd be great."

"When do you start back lifeguarding at the club?" she asked, sticking a knife in the mayo.

"Tomorrow," he responded as his mother set a plate with a giant sandwich in front of him. He picked up the top piece of bread to inspect the filling.

"I saved some of last night's meatloaf for you," she said and smiled like a schoolgirl.

"Way to a guy's heart." He looked at his phone. No word. He devoured the sandwich and called again on his way to the sink to refill his water glass. He stood and downed a glass, filled it again. Still no answer.

"Goodness, why are you so thirsty?" His mother was unloading the dishwasher now.

"I might be a wee bit dehydrated. I'm restoring myself." His mother shook her head.

"I'm heading out for a little while," he said, handing her his empty plate and glass. "I'll unpack when I get back."

"I hope you aren't going to see that girl, Hazel, are you? Sterling, you're going off to school soon. Isn't it time to...?"

"Nope, it isn't, and as a matter of fact, you're right. I'm off to see

265

her." His mother let out an exaggerated sigh.

He pulled into Ms. Wilmore's drive, expecting to see them both in the yard. But no one was outside. He walked into the carport and tapped on the side door. No answer, but both the Bug and the Smokin' Possum were here. Had they gone for a walk or something? Maybe. It was a beautiful day.

He knocked again, harder this time. He was about to give up when Ms. Wilmore cracked open the door.

"Well, hey there. I was trying to figure out if you and Zell had taken off on foot somewhere," he offered.

"No, no, we're here." Ms. W sounded a little edgy.

"Hello there Sterling, glad to see you're back," Sterling mused, putting his fist up to his chin like the sculpture of "The Thinker."

"I'm glad to see you're back in one piece. You haven't changed a bit." Ms. Wilmore made her voice jovial, but he could tell something was off.

"May I come in? Where's Zell? Everything good?"

"She's resting in her room. She had a little accident yesterday, got some stitches in her forehead. The doctor thought she might have a concussion, so she stayed in the hospital overnight. I brought her home about an hour ago."

"Holy shit, I mean holy something else. What happened?"

"I'll let her tell you about it. Come on in. I'll see if she's awake."

"Can't you just tell me?" he asked.

"She'll tell you." Ms. Wilmore opened the door wider. "Sit in the den."

Ms. W returned a couple of minutes later saying Zell was asleep. That it would be better if he came back later in the afternoon.

"How much later?"

"A couple of hours."

No wonder Zell didn't answer her phone. No wonder his teacher seemed weird. Good God. What had happened? Sterling went home, unpacked, then headed back out, stopping at the Fresh Market to buy yellow roses.

Ms. Wilmore was at the door before he could knock. "She's propped up in the den," she said, waving him in.

266

"Zell, baby, what in the world," Sterling exclaimed, pointing at the long bandage across her forehead. "Got you and Ms. W some flowers to look at while you're stuck inside." He handed Zell the roses wrapped in cellophane.

Zell stuck her nose into the bouquet and breathed in. "Beautiful." She handed them back, putting a hand to her brow.

"You still hurting, girl?"

She nodded.

"Here, I'll put those in a vase. What a nice gesture, Sterling." Ms. W took the flowers and left for the kitchen.

Gingerly, Sterling sat on the sofa beside Zell. Her bare feet were tucked up beside her hip, and she was wearing a robe. Her head rested against a bed pillow.

"What happened?" He picked up the limp hand that lay in her lap. It was bruised. The other one was still attached to her forehead.

Zell spoke so quietly he almost couldn't hear. She'd been on the phone with her mother, she said. The lawyer had told Etta they'd have a date soon, probably mid-October. She got disconcerted by the conversation and tripped on the top step going down into the carport. She landed face down on the concrete floor.

"Damn. That's not like you. You got excellent balance. And I thought you already told me the lawyer said the trial would be in October," Sterling said.

"Well, yes, but this was more specific."

"How?"

"I can't explain it all right now, but it was." Zell twisted, pulled her hand free from his, lowered her feet to the floor, and put both hands to her head.

"Main thing is get you to feel better," he said. "You need a pain pill or something?"

"I can have another one in about an hour," she said. "I have ten stitches."

"Whoa, that was quite a tear. Was Ms. W here to take care of you?"

"Yes, she's amazing. She took me straight to the emergency room. I had to stay in the hospital last night. She brought me home today."

"Your ears must be burning," Sterling said when Ms. Wilmore

walked back into the den with the roses arranged in a crystal vase. "Zell says you're a hero. Must have been blood everywhere."

"Oh, plenty of blood," Ms. W concurred. "But that's all behind us now."

"What can I do? Hey, I'm hungry. Must be getting close to dinnertime. Want me to get some takeout? I'm good at takeout."

"That's a capital idea," Ms. W said. "Zell, what would you like?"

"Mama says chicken soup always makes you get well faster."

"Done. Chick-fil-A has good chicken noodle soup, unless you know of somewhere else. Ms. W?"

"A Chick-fil-A sandwich would hit the spot. Thank you."

Zell's phone rang from the other room, and Ms. Wilmore dashed off for it. "It's Rhona," she said, handing the phone to Zell. "She's out of breath."

Sterling could hear Rhona hollering through the phone from where he sat next to Zell. He caught a few phrases. "Really won't believe…got to tell it in person."

"I can't come get you," Zell explained. "I busted my head open and can't drive for a few days."

Sterling gestured toward Zell to hand him the phone. "We can all hear you," Sterling said after hello. "Slow down and lower the volume. You've got something to tell us that we won't believe, right?"

A couple minutes later, Sterling hung up and announced, "I'm driving over to the motel to pick up Rhona and bring her back if that's okay. The girl is out of her mind with excitement. Something about a gas leak, and evacuating the motel, and we won't believe who was there. She wants to tell it in person. I swear; a guy goes off for a few days and comes back to a world in chaos." Zell shrugged. "I won't forget to stop for food," he added.

***

"I told this girl I've had about enough suspense for one day, but she still wouldn't spill the beans on the way," Sterling announced, following Rhona into the house, handing the Chic-fil-A bags to Ms. Wilmore. "So we're here. Let's get on it." Sterling plopped onto the sofa beside Zell, who winced. "Oh, sorry, baby, so sorry. You okay?" She nodded. "I'm hyper from being in the car with a life-size Mexican Jumping Bean about to explode," he added.

"You're always hyper, Sterling," Ms. Wilmore said and rolled her eyes. "Nice to have you here again, Rhona. Have a seat." She gestured to the chair with the ottoman.

"No, I got to stand to tell this. Y'all ready?" Rhona was pretty much hollering. Ms. W sat by Sterling on the sofa, and the three of them looked expectantly at Rhona.

"So, early this afternoon, this ancient pickup rolled down the hill behind the motel and hit a gas meter sticking out the ground. Some fool must have left it in neutral, or maybe the truck just gave way. Who knows. My Grandma Lolly and I could smell gas inside our room. She said we needed to get out fast, so I grabbed up her walker, and we were out the door. People were scurrying like roaches out of rooms. We walked over to the lobby to see what was going on."

Rhona took a breath and Sterling broke in. "I bet you saw my old man. Hugh would be there in a flash."

Rhona shook her head. "I didn't see him, but I sure did see some-body."

"More interesting than Hugh?" Sterling chuckled.

"Oh yeah, just wait." Rhona nodded vigorously. "Pretty soon, here comes every firetruck in town screeching up the street to the motel. Firemen ran up to doors, knocking, yelling, making everybody get out. I'm thinking about where Lolly and I can go until this thing is over and who do you think I see come out of Room 135?" Rhona looked at each of them in turn.

Ms. Wilmore raised her shoulders. "The suspense is killing us, Rhona. Tell it."

"Okay, here goes. Room 135 is Meridian's room. Everybody knows about Meridian. She's the highest price whore at the motel." Rhona paused for effect. Sterling drew in a breath, impressed.

"She comes busting out, wearing this slinky purple robe tied around her waist, and who do you think is trailing her?" She paused again. Rho-na was good.

"Who?" Sterling yelled dramatically.

"Reverend Donovan Powell, that's who! Stuffing his shirt into his pants. I saw it with my own two eyes. Anybody out there could see him scuttling across the front parking lot to his car. If your daddy *was* there near the office, he saw that fool, too."

Ms. Wilmore gasped. Sterling whooped.

"In a way, it doesn't really surprise me," Rhona said, dancing from one foot to the other. "I knew the way that man acted toward Ms. Wilmore at school that he's got no respect for women."

Zell opened her mouth but didn't speak. "Well, what you got to say?" Rhona asked. She looked at Zell as though she was just now noticing the bandage. "Girlfriend, Sterling told me what happened to your head. What the hell? Whoops, sorry, Ms. Wilmore. You gonna be alright? That looks serious."

"I'll be alright," Zell said, shifting. "What I have to say is you never know what people are inside. I already thought that man was a creep, but now he's worse than a snake. I feel sorry for his wife."

"Hey, don't be dissing the poor old snake by comparing him to Reverend Powell. All those church members he's duping. What a fraud," Sterling said. He thought about Courtney, and for a moment he felt really bad for her. Then, he thought how she tried to get Zell expelled from school and changed his thoughts. "Wait till this gets out. That asshole hypocrite is history," he said.

"Whoa, whoa, whoa, Sterling," Ms. Wilmore said.

"What?" he yelled. "You don't want that jerk to get what's coming to him? Look how he treated you. What gives?"

"Donovan Powell was awful to me, and Courtney was cruel to our Zell. That sticks deeply in all of us. But do you really want to be part of destroying his family's life, Sterling? Can you live with that?"

"Well, maybe Mrs. Powell is a victim, but as far as I'm concerned, I have no love lost for Courtney or especially her father. The guy is a scumbag. Taking money from his church members while he pretends to care about their welfare. He only cares about himself and his ego."

"We don't need to be the ones to spread this story."

"You know what, Ms. W? You got to stop being a saint. The radiance from your halo is burning us. Come on," Sterling said.

"I got news for you. I've got plenty of my own demons, Sterling."

"Could have fooled me," he said.

"Me, too." Rhona scrunched up her face. "But Lord, we don't need to argue about spreading the news on Mr. Preacher. Plenty of people saw what I saw. We all had to leave the property for a couple of hours, so Grandma Lolly and me took a bus to the mall and hung around. My grandma loves to do some people watching. Anyway, that's why I couldn't call sooner. You know that after this much time, the word about Preacher Man is out."

***

Rhona was right. News of Reverend Donovan Powell shacking up with a prostitute at the Red Rose Motel spread all over town like the smell of that leaking gas. Sterling's father had indeed been in the office with his manager Rudie before they had to evacuate. When Sterling asked, his father said he'd spotted Donovan Powell trotting across the parking lot. "He'll be out of Ramsey quicker than you can blink," he said calmly. Neither of them mentioned Courtney.

It wasn't quite as quick as his father predicted, but within a couple of weeks, the deacons at Grace Church met and decided Reverend Powell was not fit to serve the congregation.

"So much for forgiveness of sins. What goes around comes around," Sterling snorted when he told Ms. Wilmore and Zell that Reverend Powell had lost his job. Though by then Sterling's exuberance regarding Reverend Powell's fate had subsided a little. A corner of his heart felt sorry about the damage the son of a bitch had done to his family.

The summer wore on. He went to the pool, slathered up with sunscreen, and sat in the lifeguard chair to make sure little kids didn't sink or dive in and hit their heads on the bottom.

He invited Zell to the pool on a regular basis, but she visited only a few times in late June after her stitches came out. After that, she had one excuse or another. She felt out of place among the country club girls in their string bikinis, all chattering with each other while they basked in the sun, girls who barely spoke to Zell. They were probably jealous, he thought, because Zell looked sexier in her low-back one-piece than all the nearly naked socialites put together. He didn't blame her, really.

Still, ever since he'd returned from Panama Beach, since Zell's accident, something was off. He didn't know how to describe it. On one hand, when they were together, she cleaved to him, almost desperately. During a double date with Rhona and her boyfriend Malcolm in early July to see the *Titanic* movie released in 3D, Zell held on to his arm nearly the whole film. At the end, as Jack dies of hypothermia and sinks into the ocean, Sterling had to pry her loose from his torso, her arms clinging around him like a drowning person herself.

At other times, though, it seemed Zell did her best to avoid him. He'd ask to hang out with her at Ms. Wilmore's house, and Zell would say she was tired. Or he'd ask if she wanted to get dinner out, and she'd say her stomach was queasy.

When they could be alone together, usually at the cabin, and made love, it felt like Zell was holding back. Yet afterward, she wrapped herself around him like a honeysuckle vine curling around a pine tree. It had to be she was worried about him leaving for Vanderbilt. Of course, she was. They'd been inseparable all these months, and now he was disappearing. It would just take time. Once she knew he was coming home to visit often enough, she'd be herself again.

Chapter 36

Angela Wilmore

The mostly calm routine she'd settled into after Randal's death—teaching, seeing girlfriends on weekends for movies or lunch, gardening, reading—was gone. Her second semester at Ramsey High had turned Angela's life sideways. She'd had no notion whatsoever of falling in love again. Now she was in love with her principal, who was unavailable for as long as she taught at Ramsey High.

Then there was Hazel. Not to mention Sterling. For her entire teaching career, Angela had followed a self-directed policy not to get overly involved in students' lives. It could lead to all kinds of problems, not the least of which was getting fired for student partiality. She'd seen that happen to a history teacher at Bonds Cross Community College. Now, she'd somehow broken her own rule in a 180-degree turn.

In about three weeks, Sterling would leave for Vanderbilt—freshmen arrived a week earlier for orientation, he explained. Hazel remained determined not to tell him about the baby. Angela wanted to make everything turn out right for her. But she couldn't. Nor could she confess the longing in her own heart for a baby to love. Such was an impossible fantasy. She could only be a support. She felt the way water looked in a pot starting to boil, just before it spilled over.

Lately, Zell spent a lot of time in her room on Angela's laptop, and though she shouldn't, Angela checked the computer's history—snooping to learn her foster daughter was researching expensive boarding schools for pregnant teens.

Angela studied the websites. What was Zell thinking? She couldn't go to one of these schools that cost as much as $2500 a month. She, too, was indulging in fantasy. It broke Angela's heart. Zell would have to stay in Ramsey where everyone knew everything. The rise on her belly that Angela saw would soon be apparent to everyone. Word would travel quickly to Sterling in Nashville.

Maybe there was a government-sponsored maternity home where Zell could go. It was worth considering, even if she suspected that spots would be hard to come by. She would do the research. It would at least make her feel useful.

***

Zell had gone to the grocery for ingredients to make tacos—Angela didn't think spicy food was a good idea, but that's what Zell craved for dinner. Angela stood at the kitchen sink tearing lettuce for a tossed salad when her phone rang from the den. She ignored the call. A few minutes later as she was chopping celery, the phone rang again. It might be Zell. Angela quickly rinsed her hands, dried them on the towel over her shoulder, but didn't make it before the ringing stopped.

The number on the screen was Finley's! They'd not talked since she'd called back in June about Zell's pregnancy. Their only communication had been texts, mostly about Zell. She'd wanted to tell him about Donovan Powell. Had he heard about the man who'd given them such a difficult time, tried to jeopardize both their jobs?

Hurriedly, she finished slicing and chopping, put the salad bowl in the refrigerator. She retreated to her room, closing the door to stay out of Zell's earshot when she returned.

Finley answered quickly, like he was holding the phone in his hand, waiting for her call. His voice was upbeat, "May I come over? I've got something important to talk about."

"Zell will be home in a minute. She would see you. But you sound so happy. Has something wonderful happened with Scott or what?"

"Nothing at the moment I know of. This is about me."

"You?"

"Yep. How about you come over here, then?" His tone grew more excited.

"Someone might see me."

"I don't care," he said.

"What? Okay, soon as Zell and I have supper, I'll tell her I'm going out for a little while. I should be there by eight."

"I'll use the time to grab a bite and go to the grocery for champagne."

"Bubbly? You sound like you're about to burst. Can you give me a hint?" Angela pleaded.

"Not on the phone," he said.

***

Finley pulled her into his arms at the door.

"What are you doing? It's still daylight. Neighbors gossip. Your job," she cried.

"Loving on you," he exclaimed. "Come in the house."

"What are you smoking?" she asked, half serious. His arms still circling her, she stumbled inside.

"What kind of question is that to ask a man about to make a serious career change?"

Angela pulled away. "Did something happen with your job? But we haven't been together…"

"Nothing happened to my job, but I've gotten another, outside the confines of Ramsey High."

"No, Finley. I didn't tell you, but I've applied to Maynor High. No opening yet, but there are always teachers who decide not to start the school year back last minute."

"Didn't you come to Ramsey because it was $10,000 more a year than your salary at the community college and you needed the income to keep your house? Didn't you think about Maynor but dismissed it because of the administration's micro-control, as you put it?"

"Yes, but, if Maynor has an opening and will hire me, I can make it work. You're not leaving. You've worked hard to be where you are."

"Let it rest, sweetheart. I'm the new offensive line coach at Garrett University, Division II. I'll teach some PE classes as well, in the spring." Finley popped the cork on a sweating bottle of champagne. Foam rolled over the lip. "Oops," he said, licking the side of the bottle.

"But you'll have almost an hour's commute," Angela said, thinking about driving Zell to Garrett Clinic such a short time ago. "You won't make as much money," she added. Garrett University was a small, coed

275

liberal arts college with an enrollment of maybe 2500 students. No way could they match his current salary.

"Correct on both counts. But it's a relaxing, four-lane drive. Give me time to chill." He lifted his shoulders. "And yeah, my salary will be a little less. So what? I'll work my way along. Be excited, honey." He poured two flutes full and handed one to Angela. "Here's to the future." Finley clinked her glass and drank.

Angela took a sip. Bubbles tickled her nose. "All these months after the prom, you've been looking for a football job?"

"Pretty much. My good buddy, Gill Parker—we played together at Clemson—is offensive coordinator at Garrett. He lobbied for me. Who knows? Parker and Copeland might be the good luck charm for a winning season. Something they haven't seen in a couple of years."

"But you're the principal here."

Finley reached over and patted the top of her head. "Worry, worry, worry. Stop. Be happy. I miss coaching. Going back for a degree in Education Leadership, becoming assistant principal, then principal more quickly than I expected—it all seemed like the right path. But the stresses are plentiful and constant. I want to be back out on the field."

"Isn't coaching stressful?" Angela asked. She was starting to feel elated in spite of herself.

"A whole different kind of stress, baby doll," he said. "Cheers." He clinked her glass again and took a deep swallow.

Angela set her glass on the counter and threw herself into Finley's chest. Champagne from his glass sloshed down her neck. She didn't care.

He pulled an arm around her waist and leaned down. She tilted up her chin. His kiss was long and deep. She sighed when he released her.

He picked up the bottle of champagne, balancing it and his glass in one hand, the other still holding Angela's waist. "Grab your glass and let's take this celebration elsewhere, what do you say?" He leaned his head toward the bedroom.

"I say lead the way, Coach."

***

Angela had wanted a baby so badly during her childbearing years. Now, she sat at her kitchen table early morning with Zell to discuss a baby Angela would likely never see. Finley arrived with coffee from Starbucks. It felt surreal.

None of the maternity group homes she'd called within a couple hundred-mile radius had an open spot. Most housed only six to ten girls at a time. One home would have an opening in early November, far too late for a baby due in mid-January.

"Perhaps we could register you for the fall semester at a high school in Garrett," Finley suggested. "I'll be traveling there every weekday and could take you to school. Without establishing residence, it'll be tricky. But I can talk to some people." He picked up his coffee cup.

"I never thought my principal would do something like this. I don't know how to thank you, Mr. Copeland. But I got my own plan," Zell insisted. "Like you say, where there's a will, there's a way."

"What kind of plan, Zell? There are only so many choices." Angela exhaled in exasperation.

"Ms. Wilmore, I keep telling you. Don't worry. I got a plan." Zell covered her mouth and burped loudly. "Excuse me," she said and rushed off to the bathroom.

"I don't know what to do. She's in la-la land," Angela said after Zell bolted. "She's become a mature, resilient young woman, but she's still a child, too. The reality hasn't fully dawned on her."

"I wouldn't be so sure," Finley said. "She's been through a lot of hard knocks for a girl her age."

"You're right. I'm going to stop harassing her. When school starts in August, she'll probably go to Ramsey. Soon, her pregnancy will become obvious. I know she wants to continue school. I wish she could go to a government or religious-sponsored group home, but it's like you have to apply from the moment of conception. There's a lot that needs doing to assist pregnant teenage girls."

"Apparently there is. But let's don't count out her going to high school in Garrett if she wants to keep the pregnancy a secret. I'll work on it. And, hopefully, after the baby comes, if adoption arrangements are in place, she can return to Ramsey and graduate on time."

"Thank you for supporting us." Angela grasped Finley's hand and squeezed tight.

Chapter 37

Hazel Smalls

Hazel lay awake waiting on the sun to brighten the bedroom. When it did, her plan would begin. Being with Sterling these months had been the most joyous in her life; they had also been the hardest. Unable to keep her secret of living in a motel, in poverty, from him; nearly being expelled; the shame of her father; his death; her mother jailed. Yet nothing was any heavier on her heart than what she was about to do. When she was older, maybe married with children, she'd look back and know there had never been a day any more difficult than the one ahead.

She could change her mind. She could. It would be several days before Sterling left. What would he do? Be angry and go off on her? Not so much about the pregnancy but for not telling him when she first knew. He wouldn't blame her for the pregnancy. How could he? He wasn't like that anyway. He was the kindest, noblest person she might ever know. Still, she didn't want to put him to the test.

He might try to forfeit Vanderbilt. Say he'd go to community college in Ramsey and work second shift somewhere for minimum wage while she started her senior year, until she dropped out to take care of the baby. His parents would disown him like they had Livie. Hazel didn't think Sterling could grow accustomed to living without luxuries, even so many little things he took for granted.

They'd be no better off than Hazel had been for much of her life, living in poverty. Only now, Sterling would be dragged into it with her. He would grow tired of drudgery with no way out, especially after the baby came. He had a lot of life to live before he settled down. So did she. Hazel wanted to go to college, too. Wanted out of the life her mama had endured.

She had weighed it all carefully. Bringing a child into poverty was no life at all. She'd been prepared—body, mind, and spirit—for the abortion. But after the protestor with the gun…Hazel was so afraid. She couldn't go back to the clinic.

The embryo was growing. Her breasts were sore. She vomited every day. She could tell Sterling or put the baby up for adoption without his knowledge. She'd chosen the latter, and the only way to keep him from knowing was to leave town. Hazel pinched the skin on her forearm between her thumb and forefinger, hard. To feel the burning pain, make her aware of the present. She could not change her mind. She had to be strong.

Spots of sunlight sprinkled onto the pink bedspread. Hazel took a deep breath, threw off the covers and stood quickly. Too quickly. Her stomach roiled, and she rushed to the toilet.

***

Hazel sat at the kitchen table eating dry toast and sipping orange juice. The house was quiet, Ms. Wilmore still asleep. She wished she could live in this moment forever. The moment before she texted Sterling to come over and everything changed.

He arrived not long before noon, his mood buoyant.

"Girl, three days. I'm gonna miss you like crazy." He bounced into Ms. Wilmore's kitchen like he was dancing on coals. "It'll be alright. You know that? I'm not going to another planet. Just to Nashville."

"I do. That's what I want to talk about." He shot her a peculiar look. "Let's go out on the patio," Hazel said, walking through the den toward the back door. She was working hard to be composed.

"Don't sound so serious. Where's Ms. W?"

"Gone to meet her friend Dianne—you know, Mrs. Steward—for lunch," Hazel said.

"What do you think English teachers talk about when they're together?" Sterling asked.

"Probably not students and English," Hazel said offhandedly. She couldn't let herself get distracted.

Sterling nodded. "Not if they want to stay sane."

Outside, Hazel sat stiffly on a wrought-iron chair. Sterling plopped into the chair across from her at the round table. "This is awful hard," she said. Sterling frowned at her.

"I want you to go to college and do all the things you want to do," she continued. She wanted to sound neutral, but she could hear the gravity in her voice.

Sterling straightened abruptly. "What's this about? Are you..." He looked at her sternly, his eyes suddenly drained of their exuberance.

"This is about you living your life in Nashville," she broke in.

"Whoa, whoa, what's going on here? You're not about to break up with me, are you?" His voice joked and jumped at the same time.

Hazel swallowed hard. "I don't like that word 'breakup.' How about be apart for a while?"

"Are you serious? God. No, Zell. Not happening. We've been over this. I'll come home often, as much as I can. I promise. You're not doing this to us." His mouth twisted.

"I'm doing this *for* us," she said and got up from her chair. She looked across at the boy she loved with all her heart. "I want you to go to college, be free. Later, if it's meant..."

"You can stop the cliché and heroic horseshit. I thought you loved me." He stared at her, dark eyes blazing.

"I do. That's just it. I do." She looked briefly away from his glare.

"You got a mighty funny way of showing it," he said angrily and stood. He jammed his fists into his pockets.

"Sterling, please. It doesn't have to be forever. Just for now. Okay? Give yourself some time to see what..."

"You got another guy? Is that what this is about? You're waiting on me to leave so you can take up with him?" He continued to glare at her.

"No, no," her voice caught. "There's nobody else." There won't ever be anyone I love like you, she thought. The baby was the reason. But at that moment she knew in her heart she would have broken off with him anyway before he left for school. Because deep down, she still wondered if Sterling only thought he loved her when what he really felt was lust and pity. There was no way to know until he left her, experienced a life she could hardly imagine, and time passed. No way for her to know either. She pressed her fingers into her eyelids, trying to stop the tears before they started. It didn't work. They flowed anyway.

"Why are you doing this if it makes you cry?" His voice was suddenly comforting. "Are you afraid I'll get to school and you'll never hear from me again? Is that it? You're trying to head me off at the pass?"

"Don't either one of us know what will happen once we're apart," she said, wiping her nose with her hand.

Sterling pulled up the tail of his t-shirt and dried her face. "You're my girl," he said. "Okay?"

"Okay, but we're not going to see each other for now."

"Fine, fine." His voice rose again. "Just remember, Zell. This is not my idea." He paused.

"We've always known you'd be leaving," she said quietly.

"That's a lot different from breaking up. How about this? A compromise. We'll talk regularly, okay? We'll be friends, or something like that. Whatever you want to call it."

"Okay." He held her shoulders and she leaned into him.

"But I'm not gone yet." He lifted her face. "We have three more days."

She shook her head. "I can't go through this again." He pulled her tight against him, and she breathed deeply into his chest, into the scent of his boy skin beneath his t-shirt. To remember when he was gone.

***

Hazel put her head down on the hard patio table and cried. She wept until the heaves were dry and she felt a strange, empty relief. Then, she stood. She smoothed her hands over the small protrusion of her stomach, noticeable, she prayed, only to her. She didn't have time to feel sorry for herself. She had to follow her plan.

She had to tell Rhona next. Or what would her friend think when Hazel disappeared? Rhona would keep her secret. She would.

"I been knowing it," Rhona said after Hazel blurted it all fast as she could on the phone a little while later. "You've been acting funny. I mean, I know you been upset about the end of the summer coming and Sterling leaving, but I'm not stupid. I've seen you be hot and cold with him. Plus, obviously, you haven't been drinking when we all go out, not that you ever drink too much anyway, but when you don't have nothing? Sterling doesn't have a clue, though. That's a guy for you."

"Why didn't you tell me?"

"I figured you'd tell me when you wanted me to know."

Hazel nodded into the phone, let out a short humming sound.

"You some kind of gutsy, Zell," Rhona continued. "You used to be kind of scared of your shadow, but you're sure not that way anymore. I hope it works. I'll be right here being your friend the whole time."

"Thank you," Hazel said softly, "for being my best friend."

***

Hazel had saved every dime of her allowance to pay the enrollment deposit. She'd talked them down from $500 to $300 by explaining she wouldn't be staying after the birth for the classes that taught you about being a mother because she'd made up her mind already on adoption. She signed a paper she printed off the computer for proof and mailed it.

The day Sterling left, Hazel told Ms. Wilmore her proposal. Her teacher was shocked, skeptical—fussing at her for paying a deposit when there was no guarantee her strategy would work.

"It's going to work," she said. "You don't know Sterling's parents. I do. What people think means everything to them."

"I understand what you mean. It's just that people, even rich people who care greatly about appearances, have their limits. I don't want you to get your hopes up and have everything fall down around you. You need a Plan B."

Hazel shook her head. "Soon as they get back from taking Sterling to school, I'm going to tell them. You'll see."

***

Mrs. Lovell answered Hazel's call quickly, without a hello. "If you're looking for Sterling, he's already at Vanderbilt. We are on our way home from helping him get settled," she said, her tone imposing.

"Yes ma'am, I know that. I'm calling because I want to talk to you and Mr. Lovell, not Sterling." Hazel held the phone with her shoulder to her ear, balled up her fingers, expecting the long pause that followed.

"Goodness, whatever for?" Mrs. Lovell let out the kind of sigh that lets you know a person thinks you're dog shit.

Hazel continued undeterred. "I don't know if Sterling told you, but we decided to break off our…"

"Why no, he didn't mention it, so it must have slipped his mind," Mrs. Lovell cut her off. Hazel cringed. "The two of you are wise to realize the impossibility of the circumstances," she continued.

"Actually, that's not my reason, Mrs. Lovell. Like I said, I need to talk to you and Mr. Lovell. It needs to be soon. How about tomorrow?"

"Whatever for?"

"I'd like to talk in person."

"Alright then," Mrs. Lovell said.

***

Ms. Wilmore wanted to go with her, but Hazel refused the offer. She didn't know how to explain it. She just knew confronting the Lovells was her responsibility. If she didn't, she was no more than the scared rabbit Sterling said she was when they first met.

She rang the doorbell. A slim African American lady—an older woman, perhaps in her late sixties, with huge wide-set eyes and prominent cheekbones—answered the door.

"So you're Hazel," she said and put her hands on her hips. "Come in the house. I'm Beatrice."

"Sterling has told me about you." Hazel smiled in spite of her nerves.

"And I know all about you from Sterling. That boy is like my own—since he was in diapers—nearly grown up now and crazy about you. He went through so much when he was a little boy and now my strong, smart boy's gone off to school."

"What you mean he's been through so much? You mean his parents?" Hazel asked.

Beatrice paused. Waved her hand toward Hazel. "That's all gone now. Sterling told me what a sweet girl you are."

"I love him," Hazel said. "Please tell me."

Beatrice looked hard at Hazel, then nodded. "Okay. Before he had surgery, Mr. Sterling had the biggest ears you ever saw. Ears that made his face look like a clown to other children. They made jokes and laughed at him. It hurt him something dreadful. The more they mocked him, the more he ate, until his little body grew twice as big as it should be. I'd make his bed after he left for school, and sometimes his pillow would be wet."

"That's awful." Hazel couldn't imagine Sterling crying into his pillow. Not the handsome, self-assured boy she knew.

"I'm so proud of him," Beatrice said.

"Me, too," Hazel murmured. The understanding hit her suddenly. It had never been pity Sterling felt for her. He'd wanted to hide from embarrassment, too. He'd felt what she felt.

"You watched after him?" Hazel asked softly.

"Child, yes. And always loved on him best I could."

"Lucky for Sterling," Hazel said. "No wonder he's so kind." Beatrice smiled at her.

"And here you come all by yourself to this house. You something else. I'm proud of *you,* too." Beatrice pointed at her and winked.

Hazel wished she felt as self-assured as Beatrice thought she was. Instead, she stood trembling on the worn Persian rug in the foyer.

"Come on." Beatrice put her hand on Hazel's shoulder. At her touch, Hazel calmed. This beautiful lady Sterling had described as his second mother was an unexpected gift. She worked barely part-time now, and Hazel was fortunate to have come on a day when Bea—as Sterling referred to her—was at his house.

Beatrice gave a little push at the small of Hazel's back and then, like Cinderella's fairy godmother, she disappeared as Hazel entered the den. Mr. Lovell stood.

"Nice to see you," Mr. Lovell said. "Please, sit."

She sat in a green-striped, upholstered chair where he directed her. "I've got something to discuss," she began.

Mrs. Lovell shifted forward in a twin chair a few feet away.

"Well, then," Mr. Lovell said. "Would you like a glass of water or anything?" Hazel shook her head. At least he acted pleasant, even if he didn't mean it.

"I'm pregnant with Sterling's baby." Hazel had decided it would be best to tell it straight up. Mrs. Lovell gasped and looked in disbelief at her husband.

"I see," Mr. Lovell said composed, like it wasn't all that big a shock to him. "Does Sterling know?"

"No. I don't want him to know," Hazel said.

"I'd think there's nothing you want more." Mrs. Lovell's voice was thin and crisp as winter air.

"I never gave you cause to act ugly to me," Hazel said, a fire inside her, pushing her. "You want your son to end up with a rich woman, just like you, looking down your nose at people without the advantages you've had," she continued. "Sterling's got his own mind, and so does Livie, and when her way didn't suit your way, you cut her off like pie-crust. You'd probably do the same to Sterling if he married me one day. But that's not what I came to talk about."

"Oh dear God, Sterling isn't thinking about marrying you. And my daughter's life is none of your business," Mrs. Lovell cried.

"*Neither* of us is thinking about marriage. Sterling's got to go to school. I do, too."

"So what do you want, young lady?" Mr. Lovell cleared his throat.

"I want to go to a boarding school for pregnant teens in Virginia. Near the mountains. A quiet, pretty place. When the baby is born, the school will arrange for an adoption."

"Oh, thank God," Mrs. Lovell exclaimed.

"It costs a lot of money. I need you to pay for the school and some other things, too."

"I see." Mrs. Lovell's voice was eerily cool, even as she frantically rubbed her hands together. Hazel forced her own hands to stay still in her lap.

"How much?" Mr. Lovell asked.

"Tuition, room and board is $2500 a month. The baby is due in about five months, in the middle of January. After that, I might stay at the school through my senior year or come back to Ramsey to finish. I don't know. Either way, I want your guarantee you'll pay until I gradu-ate if I decide to stay in Virginia."

"Hugh, you cannot let this girl...," Mrs. Lovell started.

"Hush, Harriet, and let Hazel finish," Mr. Lovell said. Mrs. Lovell let out an anguished huff.

"The other things I want concern my mother," Hazel said. "Like you know, she's sitting in jail because she's got no money for bail. She shouldn't be there. She was grieving my father's death and made a mistake of taking some pills to escape from her pain."

"What kinds of things?" Mr. Lovell asked.

"This is blackmail," Mrs. Lovell interrupted. Mr. Lovell lifted his hand toward her to be quiet again.

"I want you to pay my mama's way out of jail. I want you to give her a place to live till she can get back on her feet. Somewhere better than your nasty motel where we lived. You own a lot of apartments. I want Mama and my sister to be in a decent apartment," Hazel said. Mr. Lovell nodded.

"And I want you to give Mama a good job. She's a hard worker, and she can learn anything. The last thing is money to fix up her car. It needs new tires and probably a lot more. If you say yes, you can pay my bus fare to Richmond, and I'll be on my way."

"What's the name of this school and what guarantee do we have that you'll keep your word and not tell Sterling?" Mr. Lovell stood with his fingers tented together at his chest.

"It's St. Gerard for Girls, and I guess you have no guarantee other than I'll do what I say."

"It's a lot of money."

"But not to a rich man like you." Hazel swallowed, her mouth dry.

"This is awful," Mrs. Lovell whimpered. She pulled her knees up into the chair, arms wrapped around her body. Hazel couldn't help it. She liked seeing the woman withdraw.

"We'll get back to you very soon," Mr. Lovell said. "Tomorrow."

"Tomorrow will be good." Hazel stood.

"I'll walk you to the door," Mr. Lovell said.

"I know the way." Mr. Lovell continued to stand as she exited the abundant den. Beatrice—leaning against the gleaming round table in the foyer, maybe waiting for her—winked at Hazel on her way out.

***

"Have we thought of everything?" Ms. Wilmore asked. Her teacher tossed new bedroom shoes into the giant suitcase she'd bought for Hazel's trip. Not to mention all the maternity clothes and toiletries already loaded in.

"You have been the best foster mother who ever was," Hazel said. "Look at all these things you've given me, Ms. Wilmore."

"If even a fraction of the young people coming along have your stamina and character, the next generation is going to be amazing," she said. "I'm going to check in on Chloe until your mama gets settled." Ms. Wilmore gave one of her characteristic, authoritative classroom looks.

"Thank you."

Mrs. Wilmore pointed at Hazel's ankle. "The way I see it, you've become that beautiful butterfly."

Hazel glanced down at her butterfly tattoo, its wings of indigo poised to fly.

She had been to the jail, told her mama what she could, and now her mama was in an apartment on Weaver Street. In a matter of days, Chloe would move in with her. Etta's new job was desk clerk at The Winslow, a real motel that didn't rent rooms by the week.

The public defender believed Etta would get off on probation. If so, her mama would be free to go back to nursing, maybe go to school to be an LPN or even an RN, if that's what she wanted to do.

"I wish you'd change your mind and let Finley and me take you to St. Gerard tomorrow," Ms. Wilmore said, her voice gone from firm to pleading.

Hazel shook her head. "Mr. Copeland already started at the college, and Ramsey High starts Monday. No."

"Finley wants to take the day off to drive us. He offered. We'd like to see the campus and how enjoyable to ride through the Blue Ridge Mountains."

Hazel wavered. It would be a lot more comfortable to ride in Mr. Copeland's Tundra truck than on the Greyhound bus. But no, she'd come this far. She'd get there on her own. The truth was, she looked forward to the long ride by herself, to get hold in her head of all that lay behind and before her.

"What I'd like is for you to take me to the bus station," Hazel said.

"Done. But why, with everything else, didn't you insist the Lovells

287

buy you a plane ticket to get you to Richmond quicker?" Ms. Wilmore's eyes lifted in curiosity.

"No way." Hazel sucked in breath. "I'm not ready to get on an airplane. Maybe someday. But not now. I know about riding a bus."

"I get it," Ms. Wilmore said with a laugh. "I'm not too crazy about flying myself. But you're sure someone will be in Richmond at the station to drive you to the school? It's about an hour. I mapped the distance online." She cocked an eyebrow, questioning, as she often did.

"Yes." Hazel paused before she said very softly, "You've taught me so much. About who I am."

"Whatever I've taught you, you've taught me more." Ms. Wilmore reached out her arms. Hazel walked in, their embrace so close she felt her teacher's heartbeat inside her own chest. She didn't have words to describe it, the steady rhythm merging with her own, but words didn't matter. The feeling said it all.

Acknowledgments

While writing a novel is a largely solitary process, it is also one that would never reach completion without the assistance and encouragement of many people to whom I am exceedingly grateful. Most significantly, I thank all of my former students (I estimate around 7,000). I could never have written this book without teaching and knowing them.

I especially thank my agent Marly Rusoff, who in spite of her incredibly busy life always makes time to offer invaluable guidance and believes in this book.

I thank my team at Mercer University Press: Director Marc Jolley, Publishing Assistant Marsha Luttrell, and Marketing Director Mary Beth Kosowski. They are amazing. Many thanks, also, to Kathie Bennett, president of Magic Time Literary Publicity, who is a phenomenal author advocate for me and many others.

A number of thoughtful readers offered helpful and honest feedback: author Cassandra King Conroy, Anna Page, Camilla Cantrell, Erin Hubbell, author Carolyn Hooker, and Catherine Ayers. Most of these readers were or are career public school teachers, as I was, and understand firsthand the classroom circumstances in this novel. I am especially grateful to poet and professor Peter Schmitt for his keen insights and willingness to be my primary reader.

From Charlotte Taylor, honored as Teacher of the Year in Greenville County, South Carolina, I learned how a dedicated teacher can push beyond her very full life in the classroom to foster parent a student in need. When no one at an abortion clinic in South Carolina could talk to me, my gynecologist and obstetrician Dr. Aaron Toler (though he does not perform the procedure) kindly helped me understand the medical process of surgical abortion. My friend Edward Jennings, a regional truck driver, patiently explained the trucking industry to me.

I thank Dr. Gloria Close, founder of CAST (Care, Accept, Share, Teach), a nonprofit organization in Spartanburg County that assists homeless families living in motels, for her compassion and information, and for inviting me to serve motel residents at a Christmas dinner hosted by First Presbyterian Church, Spartanburg, South Carolina. CAST has been a mission focus at First Presbyterian for nine years. I am also appreciative of understanding more about motel living from Bobbi Duncan, who initiated "Caring with Crock-Pots," a community mission supported by Saint Paul United Methodist Church in Spartanburg to deliver Crock-Pots, recipes, and food staples to families who must survive without kitchens.

Finally, I thank my daughters Kassie and Susanne and my husband Wayne, who helped cheer me to the finish line.